CHURCHILL'S
SECRET
MESSENGER

Books by Alan Hlad

THE LONG FLIGHT HOME

CHURCHILL'S SECRET MESSENGER

Published by Kensington Publishing Corp.

CHURCHILL'S
SECRET
MESSENGER

Alan Hlad

JOHN SCOGNAMIGLIO BOOKS
Kensington Publishing Corp.
www.kensingtonbooks.com

JOHN SCOGNAMIGLIO BOOKS are published by

Kensington Publishing Corp.
119 West 40th Street
New York, NY 10018

All Kensington titles, imprints, and distributed lines are available at special quantity discounts for bulk purchases for sales promotion, premiums, fund-raising, educational, or institutional use.

Special book excerpts or customized printings can also be created to fit specific needs. For details, write or phone the office of the Kensington Sales Manager: Kensington Publishing Corp., 119 West 40th Street, New York, NY 10018. Attn. Sales Department. Phone: 1-800-221-2647.

ISBN-13: 978-1-4967-2843-2 (ebook)
ISBN-10: 1-4967-2843-2 (ebook)

ISBN-13: 978-1-4967-2841-8
ISBN-10: 1-4967-2841-6
First Kensington Trade Paperback Printing: May 2021

10 9 8 7 6 5 4 3 2 1

Printed in the United States of America

For the courageous women and men of the SOE
and French Resistance

Part 1

Le Recrutement

CHAPTER 1

LONDON, ENGLAND—FEBRUARY 12, 1941

On the one hundred fifty-ninth day of Hitler's bombing of Britain, Rose Teasdale was typing correspondence in Room 60 of Winston Churchill's underground Cabinet War Rooms. A soft patter of keys, striking the inked-cloth ribbon, emanated from her Remington Noiseless typewriter. As typists pressed their carriage return levers, their eyes remained steadfast on their handwritten notes. The secretarial staff—crammed inside the masonry bunker with several switchboard operators—was drafting documents generated by a frenzied afternoon of cabinet meetings.

"One of your reports will help lead us to victory," Rose whispered to Lucy, a young bespectacled typist sitting next to her.

Lucy, her shoulders slumped from fatigue, smiled and increased her words-per-minute pace.

Room 60, a twenty-by-twenty-foot bunker deep beneath the Treasury building in Westminster, was one of several chambers in Churchill's Cabinet War Rooms. Instead of containing military officials, Room 60 was comprised of civilian women. Seven switchboard operators, wearing headsets and poking corded plugs into a wall of communication circuitry, sat on swiveling bar-like stools with their backs to the typists. The rest of the space was comprised of several typists sitting at small wooden desks. It was a tight space for the women, but Rose, a petite five-foot-tall twenty-two-year-old woman, didn't mind the cramped quarters. Unlike the other women, who were much taller, Rose had short legs that fit splendidly under her desk.

Some of the typists, including Rose, were products of Mrs. Hoster's Secretarial Training College in London, which had a brilliant reputation for turning out dependable assistants. And Rose believed that this schooling likely had something to do with her accelerated path to Room 60. She had not set out to work in the heart of the British military command. But when Hitler began his aerial bombing campaign on London back in September, Rose—working as a secretary in the Treasury building—was provided security clearance, led by a military guard to the basement of the building, and given a new assignment: typist for the Cabinet War Rooms.

The initial days of working in the war rooms were unnerving for Rose. The close proximity of the prime minister and senior officers gave her a bout of the jitters, causing her to type mistakes and, on one occasion, spill a tepid cup of tea on a document she had drafted. The burnt scent of Churchill's cigar, which lingered in the stagnant basement air, had turned her stomach sour. To compound matters, the Luftwaffe air raids, which occurred on an almost nightly basis, had forced many Londoners to spend nights in shelters. And when she wasn't sleeping between shifts in the sub-basement below the war rooms, often referred to as the "dock," Rose had spent nights—as the city was bombarded—with her parents in the Bethnal Green tube station.

As days passed, Rose grew accustomed to the gruff demeanor of Churchill and his staff. *Their fortitude will help us survive*, Rose told herself, typing a confidential report on potential locations where Hitler would commence a land invasion of Britain. The thought of Nazis marching through London sent chills up her spine. Rose, like most Londoners, forced herself to carry on, despite the horrid destruction and loss of life. But the source of Rose's resilience wasn't entirely self-motivated. It was fueled, Rose believed, by the death of her brother, Charlie.

Charlie, Rose's only sibling, had been killed in August when his RAF Spitfire was shot down over the Channel. His body was never recovered, and she prayed that he died fast and didn't suffer. Rose and her parents, Emilienne and Herbert, were heartbroken. Family photographs were forbidden to be displayed on desks, so Rose kept a childhood picture of Charlie, a curly-haired boy with dimpled cheeks and an infectious smile, tucked inside the top drawer of her desk. The photo was taken at their grandparents' home in France, where Rose and Charlie spent summer holidays. When Rose was doleful or exhausted, which occurred far more often than she liked to admit, she opened her drawer to see Charlie. *I miss you terribly*, she would often say to herself. After closing her drawer, she would return to typing, more determined than ever to do her duty to help Britain survive.

As Rose was placing a fresh sheet of stationery into her typewriter, the approaching sound of a woman's shoes clicked in the hallway.

"Gwyneth has contracted tonsillitis," a middle-aged woman announced, entering the room. "We need a typist to work a twenty-four-hour shift."

Rose looked up. The secretarial supervisor, Gladys Goswick, wearing an olive wool skirt and matching jacket, stood near the doorway.

The women paused, resting their hands beside their typewriters. Some of the switchboard operators, their ears covered by headsets, were unaware of Goswick's presence and continued to plug their cords into circuitry.

"Lucy?" Goswick locked her eyes on the typist.

Lucy nodded and then lowered her head.

The typists had little, if any, say in the schedules. When overtime was needed, or when someone called out due to illness, they were randomly drafted to work double shifts. Goswick was viewed as a fair supervisor, but she seldom conversed with the staff about personal matters, unlike Rose, who thought one should strive to know a little something about coworkers. And Rose knew, from joining the women on breaks at the canteen in the Treasury building, that Lucy had plans to spend the evening with her boyfriend, Jonathan, a firefighter who was receiving his first night off in over two weeks.

As the supervisor turned to leave, Rose interrupted. "Miss Goswick."

Goswick paused, placing her hands on her hips.

"Would it be all right if I worked this evening instead of Lucy?"

Lucy's eyes widened.

"I have some reports I'd like to finish," Rose said, pointing to a stack of papers. "I'm not tired, and I'm thinking that I could accomplish a fair amount of work," she added, hoping her supervisor didn't notice the dark circles under eyes.

Goswick nodded, and then left.

"Thank you, Rose," Lucy said, leaning in. "I promise to make it up to you."

"No need," Rose said. "Enjoy your evening with Jonathan."

Lucy and Jonathan, a man who risked his life to save Londoners from fires and collapsed buildings, had been dating for over a year. Rose suspected that they would eventually be married. She hoped that someday she'd meet someone that she fancied spending time with, but with the war, she'd placed her personal endeavors on hold. And since the death of her brother, she'd preferred to bury herself in her work.

At her break, Rose went to a public phone box, located outside of the Treasury building. Typists were not permitted to use the telephones in the Cabinet War Rooms, which were limited to official government business, so she climbed the stairs, cleared security, and then walked to the end of the street. Stepping inside a telephone box, she picked up the receiver, inserted a coin, and rang her parents.

"Teasdale Grocery," her father said, rather abruptly.

"Hello, Dad."

"Rose," he said, his voice turning bright. "Everything all right?"

"I'm going to work an extra shift," she said. "I'll be home in the morning."

"Chin up," he said. "Churchill needs you, and I'm sure you're doing a brilliant job, otherwise he wouldn't require you to work so much."

I volunteered. "Churchill has his own personal assistants," Rose said. "I'm merely a staff typist."

"You're helping us win this bloody war."

Rose's chest swelled with confidence. *You always have a way of making me feel rather plucky.*

"Those oranges are for children!" Herbert blurted.

Rose pulled the receiver away from her ear. She envisioned the sign that her mother had made to place beside a small basket of oranges, a rare shipment that came from America. The consumption of oranges was restricted to children only. Her parents loathed rationing, but strictly followed the government's protocol for grocers.

"Sorry," Herbert said. "Bloody customers keep overlooking the sign for the oranges."

"It's okay."

"How about I make you and your mum eggs and fried bread for breakfast."

"That'd be splendid," Rose said.

"Would you like to talk to your mum?"

"If she's nearby."

"Emilienne!" Herbert called. "It's Rose!"

As Rose waited for her mother to come to the phone, she thought of her parents. During the Great War, Herbert had been in the British infantry, stationed on the western front. Emilienne, a seamstress from Paris, had volunteered as a French nurse. They'd met, fallen in love, and then moved to London after the war. Despite how bad things were in London, she felt fortunate that her parents had chosen to reside in Britain, rather than France, otherwise they'd now be living under Nazi occupation.

"*Bonjour, ma chérie,*" Emilienne said, answering the phone.

"*Bonjour,* Mum."

"Working late again?" Emilienne asked.

"Yes," Rose said, feeling a bit disappointed that her mother did not continue the conversation in French.

"You work too much."

You too, Rose thought. When Mum wasn't working in the grocery, she was earning extra money by taking on seamstress work, which she completed at night in an air raid shelter. "How's your back?"

"Stiff," Emilienne said.

"The concrete floor in the tube station is bad for your spine," Rose said. "Take some extra blankets to the shelter. And use the pillow from my bed. It's soft. You can place it under your back."

"All right," Emilienne said, sounding grateful for her daughter's concern.

Rose spoke with her mother for a few minutes, avoiding topics that would remind them of Charlie's death. It'd been several months since the funeral, but there was a lingering sadness embedded in the timbre of her mother's voice. And Rose wondered if their heartache would ever go away.

"Try to get some rest tonight," Emilienne said.

"You too," Rose said.

Rose left the phone box. The sun had disappeared behind a building, casting the street in an inky shadow. The falling temperature caused her to stuff her hands into her coat pockets. Shops were closing, and the sidewalks were beginning to fill with people on their way to shelters. *Will the Luftwaffe ever stop?* As she descended the military-guarded stairs leading thirty feet below the Treasury building, she wondered if the war room bunker could sustain a direct bomb strike. She shivered, and then shook the thought from her mind.

She returned to Room 60, where the majority of the women had gone home for the evening. Tonight's crew consisted of two typists, including Rose, and three switchboard operators. Two hours into the shift, the lights on the switchboards flickered. The operators jammed their plugs into jacks, connecting communications. *The Luftwaffe have been spotted over the Channel.* Rose typed faster. The air raid sirens sounded, producing a muffled, horrid howl—even deep below the building—causing goose bumps to crop up on her arms. Fifteen minutes later, the sirens stopped. Under the patter of her key strokes, Rose heard the muted rumble of bombs erupting over the city. She pulled the carriage return lever on her typewriter. *God help us.*

Movement in the corridor caused Rose to look up. Two military officers, whom she recognized as General Ismay and Commander Thompson, passed by the doorway on their way to the Map Room.

Footsteps echoed in the corridor. A door slammed against its frame. The switchboard operators increased their pace of answering calls and plugging their cords into a maze of circuitry. Her breath quickened. She pulled a finished paper from her typewriter and stapled together a report.

The Luftwaffe raid lasted well past midnight. At 1:34 a.m. the all-clear signal sounded. The women in Room 60, except for Rose and a thirty-one-year-old switchboard operator named Margaret, went to the dock to get a few minutes of rest. Margaret handled periodic calls to the switchboard, while Rose finished drafting a report. Struggling to remain alert, she ceased typing and opened her desk drawer.

"We made it through another air raid, Charlie," Rose said, staring into the drawer.

"To whom are you speaking?" a low voice asked.

Rose looked up. Standing in the doorway was Prime Minister Winston Churchill, wearing a charcoal wool coat and felt hat with a curved brim. A half-smoked cigar was clamped between his molars, making his left jowl appear swollen. Her heart rate accelerated. She glanced to Margaret, who was taking an incoming call. Tired and unable to think of an excuse for talking to herself, Rose stood—her chair scraping the floor—and said, "A picture of my brother, sir."

Churchill drew on his cigar, causing the tip to glow, and then stepped into the room.

Rose's knees quivered. She gripped her desk with her hands. Churchill had never entered Room 60 while Rose was working, and his advisors rarely, if ever, paid a visit. Although the typists produced loads of documents for his staff, their work—both assignments and finished documents—went through the supervisor, Gladys Goswick. Direct interactions between the civilian women and Churchill's advisors were, by protocol, extremely limited.

"May I," Churchill said, stepping to her and gesturing to the open drawer.

She nodded.

Churchill looked at the photograph.

"It's my brother, Charlie, when he was a child. We're not per-

mitted to display pictures on our desks, so I keep it in my drawer."
Rose drew a jagged breath, taking in the scent of burnt tobacco.
"He was killed in August when his plane was shot down over the
Channel."

Churchill raised his head. "What is your name?"

"Rose Teasdale, sir." Her heart hammered against her rib cage.

"Miss Teasdale," Churchill said. "I'm deeply sorry for the death
of your brother. His valor to protect this island from Nazi tyranny
will forever live in the hearts of our people." He paused, removing
the cigar from his mouth. "Britain will not forget Charlie's sacrifice. Nor will I."

"Thank you, Prime Minister," Rose said, struggling to hold
back tears.

Churchill turned to leave but stopped. "Miss Teasdale."

"Yes, sir."

"Please relay a message to our switchboard operator." He gestured with his cigar to Margaret, who was transferring a call. "If
Mrs. Churchill should inquire as to my whereabouts, please inform her that I am resting in my room."

"Yes, Prime Minister."

Churchill tipped his hat and left.

Rose, stunned and standing by her desk, listened to the clack
of Churchill's footsteps on the stairway. *He's not going to his private
bedroom.* She'd heard rumors of Churchill observing Luftwaffe
bombing raids from the roof of the Treasury building. *What would
he see tonight? Which sections of the city are destroyed? How many people have been killed?*

Despite Churchill having a staunch, brash reputation, she believed that he wholeheartedly cared about the people of Britain.
And that he was the right leader to help the world to survive Nazi
aggression. Inspired by her encounter with the prime minister,
she took out a sheet of paper and placed it in her typewriter. Instead of taking a break, she worked until dawn.

Finishing her shift, Rose left the underground war rooms. Outside, resilient Londoners were going about their daily routines,
despite the roar of fire brigade engines. Smoke rose from various
sections of the city, but most of the fires appeared to be in the

vicinity of the East End docks. She boarded the train at Westminster tube station. In her carriage, she leaned back in her seat and tried to rest, but her belly ached with hunger. She'd foolishly skipped dinner and hadn't taken a meal break during her shift. She looked forward to having breakfast with her parents and, even more, telling them about her brief conversation with the prime minister, which she didn't think would breach any war room confidentiality.

Arriving at the Bethnal Green tube station, she exited her carriage to the underground platform and was relieved to find the shelter intact. She scaled the steps. Outside, a stench of burning wood and petrol filled her lungs. The proximity of blaring fire brigade sirens caused the hair to stand up on the back of her neck. She quickened her pace along Bethnal Green Road, but with each step the intensity of the sirens grew. Ahead, she saw a crowd near her home on Pott Street. A lump formed in her stomach. She ran, pushed her way through dozens of people congregating on the corner, and found the area blocked by a fire brigade. Firemen, their faces covered in a mixture of sweat and soot, sprayed water onto the remains of several buildings.

"No!" She pushed her way through the crowd on the sidewalk. "Let me through!"

The Teasdale Grocery, including the upper floor, where Rose and her parents lived, had been transformed—by what appeared to be a direct bomb strike—to a smoldering mound of brick and charred timber.

"Mum!" Rose screamed. "Dad!"

As she neared the rubble, a hand grabbed her arm.

"You can't go in there," a policeman said.

"It's my home," Rose cried. "Was there anyone inside?"

"They're working to find out," the policeman said, releasing Rose's arm. "Stay clear."

Rose maneuvered through the crowd, calling her parents' names until her throat turned raw. She encountered several neighbors, most of whom had spent the night at the tube station, but none had seen her parents. After several minutes, the hoses were turned off. A fireman wearing a harness with an attached rope was lowered into a cavity that led to the basement of the Teasdale Grocery. Minutes later, he was hoisted to the surface, holding an ash-covered body. Limp limbs hung toward the ground. A medic rushed forward, examined the body, and then sadly shook his head.

Rose, using all her strength, broke past the policeman protecting the perimeter. She darted to the medic and fell to her knees. Despite the thick layer of soot covering the body, she immediately recognized the woman by the nightgown and length of her hair.

"No!" she screamed. A wave of nausea rose from her stomach, producing the urge to vomit. Using her finger, she gently dusted ash from her mother's eyelids. She placed her head on her mother's silent chest and wailed. When she gathered the strength to open her eyes, she saw two firemen removing her father's lifeless body from the rubble.

CHAPTER 2

PARIS, FRANCE—FEBRUARY 13, 1941

Lazare Aron, twenty-three, with a square chin and thoughtful chestnut eyes, slipped on a hand-carved wooden prosthetic—covering the three remaining appendages of his right hand—and stepped into the kitchen. He found his father, Gervais, pouring coffee into ceramic cups, and his mother, Magda, placing slices of gray toasted bread onto the table.

"Bonjour," Lazare said, taking a seat at the table.

Magda, a slender woman with exquisite posture and high, pronounced cheekbones, sat next to him. "Sleep well?"

"Oui, Maman," Lazare said, despite having had two hours of sleep. A pang of guilt curbed his appetite. He hoped, for his parents' safety, that they would remain unaware of his illicit activity. Not only was he breaking strict German curfew by venturing outside between nine in the evening and five in the morning, he was posting Resistance propaganda throughout Paris, a Nazi offense that would, if he were caught, result in his execution.

Their home on rue Cler in the seventh arrondissement, the neighborhood that contained the Eiffel Tower and Champ de Mars, was a two-bedroom apartment on the third floor of a Lutetian limestone building. Oak parquet flooring spanned the residence, with the exception of a woven area rug, brought by his parents when they immigrated to Paris from Warsaw, that lay in the living room. His mother's paintings, which had once been on consignment at a Montparnasse gallery, covered the walls. A large bookcase displayed books, magazines, and stacks of newspaper articles, some of which had been written by his father. The apartment's décor, Lazare believed, was created by the strokes of Maman's paintbrush and Papa's typewriter.

Lazare, who dreamed of becoming a journalist like his father, had not expected to be living at home at this stage of his life. But shortly after he'd graduated from the University of Paris in 1939, France and Britain declared war on Germany, following the Nazi invasion of Poland. Committed to fighting for his country, he attempted to join the French army and was rejected due to the limited use of his hand. Dispirited, he watched all of the able-bodied Frenchmen—cheered by Parisians waving miniature flags—march through the streets on their way to defend France.

The following summer, the Nazis invaded France. Thousands of Parisians fled the city, seeking sanctuary in the south, but the Aron family chose to stay. "I will not let the Nazis drive us from our home," his father had said. Within forty-six days, Germany conquered France. The country's young men, including all of Lazare's friends who went off to fight, were killed or captured and taken to German prison camps. Lazare, with ire burning in his chest, witnessed a Wehrmacht infantry division—their polished jackboots clacking on pavement—march along Avenue Foch. And he vowed to do everything he could to liberate his homeland.

But his first priority was to help his family survive. Obtaining food and money was a constant struggle. The prospect of finding work at one of the newspapers, which were under collaborationist control, was not an option. After months of struggling to find employment, he landed a job as a janitor, after displaying to a supervisor how the handle of a mop fit perfectly in his wooden hand, to clean the floors and toilets at the Gare du Nord train station.

"How does it taste?" Gervais said, sliding a cup of coffee to Lazare.

He sipped, tasting a bland, broth-like liquid. "It's good."

Gervais grinned, causing his salt-and-pepper mustache to rise on his face. "It's roasted barley, mixed with used coffee grounds."

Their kitchen had once contained fine coffees, cheeses, breads, and meats. But now, the cupboard was bare, except for two tins of sardines—which they were saving for a special occasion—wilted carrots, moldy cheese, a sprouted potato, and three ugly turnips. Parisians were required to use rationing cards, classified according to a person's age and food needs. In addition to the lack of food, the temperature in the apartment was horribly low. Coal was almost nonexistent, only to be found on the black market. Struggling to stay warm during the winter months, they often wore their coats indoors and slept under layers of blankets.

Lazare bit into his bread, hardened with wheat husk. "Provisions are getting worse. Train cars, loaded with France's food, leave each day from the Gare du Nord station for Germany. Our people are starving. You'd have a better chance of gaining access to food if you left for Vichy France."

"This is our home," his mother said, dipping a bit of her bread into her coffee.

"Your *maman* is right," Gervais said. "We mustn't give in to the Nazis. In time, de Gaulle, with the aid of Churchill's military, will regain control of France."

What if Britain falls to Germany? "It'd be safer for you in the south," Lazare insisted.

"Papers, which we don't have, are needed to cross the demarcation line," Gervais said.

"I'll find a way to get you and Maman papers," Lazare said.

"Assuming you can obtain fake identifications, do you plan to join us in Vichy France?" Gervais asked.

Lazare shook his head. *I plan to fight for our freedom.*

"Things will get better," Magda said.

Gervais, with ink-stained fingers, gently touched his wife's hand.

Prior to the invasion, Lazare's father had been a successful and well-respected journalist at *La Chronique* newspaper. With collaborationists in control of the media, the journalists were relieved of their duties, with the exception of Gervais, who had mechanical expertise with printing presses. The typesetter, who was responsible for keeping an unreliable fifty-year-old printing press running, fled the city when the Germans broke through the Maginot Line. Demoted from a journalist to a typesetter, Gervais now spent his days inking plates with Nazi propaganda on the same machine that had, many years before, stolen his son's fingers.

Lazare had been eight years old on the day of the tragedy. He was on summer vacation and, rather than play kick ball at a park near their apartment, he'd asked to join his father at *La Chronique.* He loved everything about the newspaper business. The ringing telephones. The tapping typewriters. The enthusiastic journalists and editors who worked to keep Parisians informed of local and world events. But most of all, Lazare loved to watch the large printing press, located in the rear of the building. It was where everyone's work came together, pressed through large steel rollers to form printed newspapers, which were packed into bundles, loaded onto trucks, and delivered to newsstands throughout Paris.

"Don't get close to the press," Gervais had said to Lazare in the printing room. But when Gervais was summoned to take a telephone call, Lazare found himself alone, with the exception of two laborers—one feeding paper to the press, the other stacking finished newspapers. To Lazare, the spin of the rollers was mesmerizing. The scent of turpentine and oil were intoxicating. As minutes passed, he stepped closer to the press. And when the laborers turned away, Lazare inched his hand toward the paper that was moving at lightning speed through the steel rollers. He'd only intended to touch the paper, simply to feel how fast it was traveling. But as his finger touched the paper, a laborer dropped a large bundle of newspapers, causing a loud crack. Lazare jerked. His hand was sucked forward. A sharp pain shot through his arm, and he collapsed to the floor. The laborer screamed, and then scrambled to shut off power to the press. As the steel rollers slowed to a stop, Lazare shrieked and clasped his crushed hand to his chest.

Gervais had wrapped his son, pale and shivering with shock, in his suit jacket and rushed him to the hospital. Emergency surgery was performed, but the doctor was unable to save his right thumb and forefinger. When Lazare awoke—nauseous with anesthesia—his mother and father told him the news. Lazare looked up to his father, his white, starched shirt stained with blood, and whispered, "I'm sorry, Papa. It's all my fault." Gervais hugged him and wept, his tears raining into his son's hair.

Lazare, an angst building in his chest, placed his wooden hand on the kitchen table. He took a sip of coffee, and then looked at his parents, tired and hungry. "Paris is no longer safe for Jews."

"This isn't Germany," his father said.

"No, it's not. But the Nazis are in control, and there are many rumors about what they are doing to Jews in Germany."

"We have French citizenship, and we have our police," Magda said.

"I served in the French army during the Great War," his father added. "They won't let anything happen to us."

The safety of Jews was a frequently discussed topic, usually initiated by Lazare. While he admired his parents' grit and wisdom, they were, however, not exposed to the daily behavior of the Nazis at the train station. On many occasions, he had heard German soldiers hiss the word *Jude* when stopping citizens to inspect papers. Rumors were rampant about Jews being removed from government positions. The police, Lazare believed, were collaborating with the Germans. *How long will it take before we can't differentiate our police from Nazis? A month? A year?*

"I need to get to work," Lazare said, deciding he had said enough, for the moment, to influence his parents to leave Paris. "Thanks for breakfast."

"I'll walk partway with you," his father said, standing from the table.

Lazare stepped to his mother and kissed her on the cheek. "If you barter more of your artwork today, please keep the *Arc de Triomphe*." He pointed to a painting in a gilt frame that hung in the hallway. "It's too beautiful to trade for vegetables."

Magda smiled. "I'll save that one for last."

Outside, cold air bit at Lazare's exposed skin. He buttoned his jacket and walked with his father, who was bundled in a black, knee-length wool coat. Few people were on rue Cler, which was eerily absent of exhaust fumes and the rumble of vehicles. It was apparent, to Lazare, that Parisians preferred to venture outside only when necessary, such as going to work—if they were lucky enough to still have a job—or standing in line for bread. Last year, the streets were a buzz of cars, buses, and taxis, and the sidewalks were filled with mingling pedestrians headed to markets and cafés. Now, the roads contained few automobiles, which were reserved for permitted drivers who were Nazi collaborators. The public bus service was greatly reduced, causing people, including Lazare, to forgo fighting for a seat and choose to walk. This meant that Lazare's journey to work would take nearly an hour.

"I'll walk with you to the other side of the river," Gervais said, his hands stuffed into his coat.

"That's out of your way," Lazare said.

"I need the exercise."

You need food and rest, Lazare thought as he glanced to his father, who'd lost far too much weight. Instead of creating another debate with Gervais, Lazare simply nodded.

As they approached a street corner, Lazare saw one of his signs, a thin piece of white paper with the words *La France Libre* in large black letters, that he had taped to a street pole during the night. The propaganda would no doubt be torn down by a German soldier during street patrols, but for now, at least some Parisians would see the sign and know that resistance to Nazi rule was alive and well. Reaching the pole, Lazare's pulse rate accelerated. Papa's eyes locked on the sign, but he continued walking. And Lazare wondered if his father had recognized the slanted handwriting, considering Gervais had taught him, a child with maimed fingers, how to write left-handed.

Nearing the Pont de la Concorde, an arched stone bridge across the River Seine, Lazare noticed an old man and a woman carrying an empty cloth bag. *Getting an early start to avoid the long ration lines*, Lazare thought. But the couple stopped at the mouth of the bridge. The old man pointed to a wall. And Lazare knew, from where he had posted propaganda, exactly what had caught the couple's attention. A mixture of excitement and patriotism swelled within Lazare.

A black car, bearing a red swastika flag on each of the front fenders, appeared on the bridge. Lazare's breath stalled in his chest. The old man, with his back turned and seemingly unaware of the approaching vehicle, continued to gesture to the wall as he spoke with the woman, who appeared to be his wife. Nearing the couple, the vehicle stopped. The old man turned and lowered his arm.

A Waffen-SS officer wearing a field-gray uniform stepped out of the vehicle.

The old man motioned to his wife to leave.

"*Halt!*" the officer shouted.

"Head down. Keep walking," Gervais whispered.

A knot formed in Lazare's gut. They continued on their path toward the bridge, twenty meters away.

The officer stepped past the old man and ripped the piece of paper from the wall. "Do you know who did this?" he asked in French.

The old man shook his head.

In a swift, fluid motion, the officer pulled out his pistol and raised his arm.

"*Non!*" the woman screamed.

A wave of shock jolted Lazare. He attempted to run to their aid, but Gervais, wrapping his arms around his son, pushed him to the side of a building.

The crack of the bullet, discharging from the weapon, caused Lazare and Gervais to flinch.

Lazare struggled to break his father's grip.

The old man, like a marionette with its strings severed, crumpled to the ground.

Wailing, the woman fell to her husband's side.

The officer slipped his weapon back into its holster and returned to his vehicle.

As the Nazi vehicle sped away, Lazare slipped from his father's grasp and ran to the bridge. He found the woman weeping at her husband's side. Lazare dropped to his knees. With trembling hands, he removed his scarf and placed it over a hole, the diameter of a hazelnut, in the man's head. Near a pool of blood was a crumpled paper with Lazare's handwriting. His heart wrenched with despair. "I'm so sorry," he said, his voice dropping to a whisper.

The woman howled and clutched the man's lifeless chest.

Feeling his father's hand touch his shoulder, Lazare looked up with tear-filled eyes. *What have I done?*

CHAPTER 3

LONDON, ENGLAND—FEBRUARY 17, 1941

Rose's parents were buried during a frigid rain in Manor Park Cemetery. Despite the inclement weather, there was a large attendance for the graveside service. Emilienne and Herbert had developed innumerable friendships with the people of Bethnal Green. Under a canopy of umbrellas, there were dock workers, teachers, lorry drivers, police officers, nurses, laborers, hairdressers, firefighters, children—who'd purchased sweets at the grocery before the days of rationing—and two vicars from parish churches, which the Teasdales had never attended. The Teasdale Grocery had been a cornerstone of the community, and it was evident to Rose that her parents had accomplished far more with their lives than canceling coupons in ration books.

Most of Rose's coworkers were present, including Gladys Goswick, who rarely, if ever, joined the typists outside of the Cabinet War Rooms, even for tea at the Treasury canteen. Rose was moved by the overwhelming support of her fellow workers, as well as the community of Bethnal Green. But the hugs and condolences, as well as the minister's eulogy—promising that her parents were in a better place—did little to alleviate her heartbreak.

Rose, unable to rid herself of the horrid images of her parents encased in ash, had barely eaten since the tragedy. Lucy, Rose's best friend, had insisted that Rose move into her Spitalfields flat that she shared with two women. Lucy helped with the burial arrangements and worked double shifts to allow Rose extra time off from work. Rose, grateful for Lucy's support, had used the time away from the war rooms to seek answers for why her parents had not found shelter in the tube station.

Speaking with neighbors, she'd learned that her parents had, on occasion, skipped sleeping in the Bethnal Green tube station—when Rose worked a night shift—to allow Emilienne's sore back a temporary reprieve from the hard masonry floor. And according to a baker who worked two streets away from Teasdale Grocery, her mother had insisted that Herbert go alone to the tube shelter on the occasions that her back needed rest. But Herbert never left her side. Her parents, along with seven other people on her street who had not sought underground shelter, were killed that dreadful night.

As the caskets were lowered into the ground, whimpers came from the crowd. Rain pattered Rose's umbrella. Tears fell to her cheeks; she made no effort to wipe them away. Next to her parents' graves was a headstone bearing the name Charlie Teasdale. An image of her brother's empty casket, save for a few of his personal belongings that her mother had selected, sent a wretched pang through her gut. Her heart and head reeled with regret. *Why did I insist on volunteering for the night shift? How did I not know that Mum and Dad were skipping the tube shelter?*

After the thirty-minute service, the crowd slowly departed. Lucy, accompanied by her boyfriend, Jonathan, was the last to leave, despite the rain worsening and creating large puddles over the cemetery grounds.

"I'm so sorry," Lucy cried, her umbrella quivering in her hand. "If I hadn't had plans with Jonathan, you'd never have volunteered to work that night. And . . ."

"Don't," Rose said, dropping her umbrella and hugging Lucy. "Don't you think that. Not for one second."

Lucy dropped her umbrella and squeezed Rose.

"It wouldn't have made a difference," Rose said. Raindrops saturated her hair. "I'd have volunteered to work that night, regardless of your plans."

Lucy sobbed.

"It's not your fault," Rose cried. "You must believe that. There's no one to blame but Hitler and his bloody war." Rose lowered her arms and stepped back. "Your glasses are wet."

"Don't care," Lucy said, making no effort to wipe rain droplets from her lenses.

Jonathan picked up the umbrellas and held them over their heads. "If there is anything you need, Rose, please let me know."

"Thank you." Rose turned to Jonathan and, having to stand on her toes, kissed him on the cheek. He smelled of smoke, which reminded her of Emilienne's ash-covered body. She buried the thought and realized that he was wearing his fire brigade clothes under his raincoat. "You've come directly from work."

"Sorry," Jonathan said. "I would have been late if I had taken time to change."

"I'm glad you're here." Rose hooked arms with Lucy and Jonathan. Maneuvering around swaths of puddles, they left the cemetery.

The following day, Rose returned to work on the evening shift. The women of Room 60, many of whom were preparing to leave for the day, warmly greeted her as she hung up her coat.

"How are you?" Margaret asked, standing in front of her switchboard.

"I'm okay," Rose said, doing her best to hide the despair in her voice.

"It's good to have you back," Goswick said, extending her hand with a file folder that contained typing assignments.

"Thank you, Miss Goswick." Rose took the file to her desk.

"There's a letter for you," Lucy said, pointing to an envelope on Rose's desk.

Rose nodded. "Perhaps I'll read it later, during a break." She placed the letter—her name typed on the front—into her desk drawer.

Lucy stood and put on her coat. "I'm going to my mum's for supper. She made a cottage pie. I'll save a piece for you."

"That'd be lovely," Rose said, despite the fact that she had no desire for food.

Within minutes, only the evening shift remained in the room—
Rose, two other typists, and three switchboard operators. She
sorted her assignments and went to work. The soft patter of keys
on her Remington Noiseless typewriter was strangely reassuring,
like the voice of an old friend. She typed several reports, feeling—
for the first time in days—her mind stray from crestfallen thoughts.
A few hours into her shift, a few of the women left to take a break,
leaving Rose and a switchboard operator. With a bit of privacy, she
retrieved the envelope from her drawer and opened it, revealing
the prime minister's letterhead. A knot formed in her stomach.
She gripped the paper.

```
Dear Miss Teasdale,        13th February 1941
Pray accept my deep sympathy in your most
sorrowful loss.
Winston Churchill
```

Her eyes watered. Although the letter was brief and did not
contain a handwritten signature, she was grateful that the prime
minister had taken the time to dictate a message, which would
have been typed by one of his four personal assistants, to express
his condolences. She rubbed away tears, and then placed the letter back in the envelope. Opening her drawer, she stared at the
picture of her brother and vowed to do everything she could to re-
quite Hitler's Luftwaffe. With every fiber of her body, she wished
she could do something to honor her family and help Britain survive the heinous aerial onslaught.

As Rose slid Churchill's letter under Charlie's picture, the
switchboard lit up. The clamor of footsteps grew in the hallway.
The women who'd taken a break returned to their posts. A moment later, the air raid siren sounded. Rose, her fear replaced with
an intense hatred of Hitler, returned to typing a report. And she
swore to herself that she'd find a way, no matter what the cost, to
avenge the killing of her family.

CHAPTER 4

PARIS, FRANCE—FEBRUARY 27, 1941

The image of the old man, who'd been executed for merely viewing Resistance propaganda, filled Lazare's head. Wails of the woman resonated in his ears, as if her shrieking voice had cut phonographic grooves into his brain. The passing of weeks had done little to diminish a cancerous guilt that spread through his heart. *If I hadn't posted the paper on the bridge, he'd be alive.* Unwilling to confide in his parents, he carried the burden alone. Lazare had no intentions of revealing his clandestine activities to his parents; he feared they'd be implicated if he was arrested. But things changed when Lazare came home from work and found his parents rummaging through their painting and writing supplies, searching for items they could barter for food.

"Have you seen my paper?" Gervais asked, going through his desk drawers.

Hairs stood up on the back of Lazare's neck. He stalled by hanging up his coat.

"*Non,*" Magda said, kneeling with her head poked inside a cabinet. "Some of my paint supplies are gone."

Lazare's skin turned cold. He stepped into the living room, struggling to think of an explanation for the missing paint and paper, but it was only the three of them and clearly no one had broken into the apartment. Since his parents were no longer painting or writing, he'd assumed that there would be plenty of time to restock supplies. However, he hadn't accounted for the dwindling rations forcing hungry Parisians to part with nonessential items in exchange for something to eat.

"Lazare," Gervais said, turning to his son. "Have you seen . . . ?"

"I took them," Lazare interrupted.

Magda stood. Her eyebrows rose with confusion. "Why?"

A wave of shame jolted Lazare. "I used the paper and paint to make Resistance propaganda."

Magda's eyes widened.

Lazare looked at his father, a mixture of fear and sadness in his eyes. "I was the one who posted the sign on the Pont de la Concorde bridge."

"*Oh, bon Dieu.*" Gervais's shoulders slumped.

Magda gasped.

"A man was killed because of me," Lazare said, feeling compelled to reveal his sin.

"*Non!*" Gervais stepped to Lazare. "A Nazi killed him."

An acidic bile rose in Lazare's throat. "If I had not posted the sign, that man would not have stopped at the bridge. He would have avoided the German officer and would be alive today."

Tears formed in Magda's eyes.

"The posting of signs must stop," Gervais said, as if he were trying to protect his family. "The Nazis have no tolerance for those who publish Resistance propaganda."

Lazare knew that his father's comments were true. While mopping the floor of a public restroom at the train station, he overheard two police officers talking about the recent arrests of several intellectuals who were publishing an underground newspaper, urging Parisians to resist the German occupation. "They'll be executed," an officer said, standing next to his comrade at the urinals. "*Les imbéciles,*" his comrade responded while zipping up his trousers. Anger boiled in Lazare's belly as he dipped a mop into a bucket of dirty water.

"We must continue to fight," Lazare said. "I hate what I've done. And I'll have to live with the fact that a man is dead because of my actions. But how am I, or any Frenchman, for that matter, to do nothing? Should we allow Hitler to control our homeland? Are we to behave as sheep and allow the Nazis, and our police, to lead us to slaughter?"

"It's too dangerous," his mother said.

"We're all at risk," Lazare said. "Anti-Semitic comments are being made by collaborators. The Nazi infection is spreading through Paris. You should escape to *zone libre*, before it's too late."

"Your mother and I are not leaving," Gervais said. "In time, France will be liberated."

"I have no plans to leave, either," Lazare said. "But I fear things will get much worse before Allied forces can attempt to free France."

Magda clasped Lazare's hands. "Promise me that you'll stop."

Lazare hadn't posted Resistance propaganda since the man was shot on the bridge. The ensuing guilt had caused him to temporarily pause and reflect on his actions. While he believed that the dissemination of anti-Nazi posters was important, he was convinced that it would take far more than inspirational words to free France.

"I have no plans of posting further propaganda," Lazare said, squeezing his mother's fingers.

Although his words were true, a foreboding swelled in his chest. For his parents' safety, he had no intentions of informing them of his plans against the Nazis, which were far more perilous than hanging patriotic signs.

Chapter 5

London, England—January 5, 1942

R ose pulled a finished document from her typewriter, and then stapled together a report. She rubbed her eyes, attempting to thwart her need for sleep.

"Good morning, Rose," Lucy said, entering the room. She hung up her wool coat and scarf, and then sat at her desk. "Did you get any rest in the dock?"

"A little," Rose said, recalling the thirty-minute nap she'd taken in a sub-basement bunk.

"Your shift is over," Lucy said, pointing to a clock on the wall. "Go home and sleep."

"I've one more assignment I'd like to finish before . . ."

"Off with you," Lucy insisted.

Rose nodded, and then tidied her desk to leave.

Much had changed over the past several months. In May, the Luftwaffe ceased their nightly bombing of London, although frequent raids and ensuing civilian deaths continued across Britain. In June, Hitler betrayed Stalin and invaded the Soviet Union, temporarily reducing Londoners' fears of an inevitable German invasion of Britain. *Will that maniacal Führer ever stop?* Rose had thought as she listened to Churchill's radio broadcast declaring Britain's full support of the Soviet Union. And last month, the

United States joined the war when the Japanese bombed Pearl Harbor. Britain was no longer alone. For the first time in over a year, there appeared to be hope, although small, that the Allies could prevent Hitler from conquering Europe.

The landscape of the war had altered, but little changed for Rose. Her heartache remained raw. The passing of time did little to diminish her sorrow. She visited Mum, Dad, and Charlie's graves often, leaving bluebells and tulips, her mother's favorite flowers. "I miss you terribly," she often whispered to their headstones. *Are you in a better place? Did I make you proud?* Other than an occasional glass of scotch, provided by Lucy, who believed a wee dram could deaden the pain of an awful day, Rose preferred to administer labor as a medicine for her misery. But no matter how many reports she typed, and no matter how many hours she worked, the pain in her heart never went away. *There must be more that I can do.*

As Rose was retrieving her coat to leave, Miss Goswick stepped into the room.

"Can anyone speak French?" Goswick asked.

"I can," Rose said.

Goswick turned to Rose. "Fluently?"

"Yes," Rose said. "*Je parle français couramment,*" she added, hoping to instill confidence in her supervisor.

"Good," Goswick said, sounding satisfied. "Come with me."

Rose glanced at Lucy, left her coat, and followed Goswick.

"An interpreter called off ill," Goswick said, walking at a brisk pace.

Rose nodded, struggling to keep up.

"You'll be interpreting for Commandant Martel. Sit to his right, away from the others, and simply tell him in French what is being said."

"Okay."

"Only repeat. Do not engage in the conversation."

"Of course," Rose said.

Goswick stopped in front of a closed door to the Cabinet War Rooms.

Here? Rose's heart rate accelerated.

"And for goodness' sake," Goswick said, placing her hand on the doorknob, "speak softly and do not interrupt."

Rose nodded.

Goswick knocked and opened the door. "Prime Minister, we have an interpreter for Commandant Martel."

Prime Minister! Rose's breath caught in her chest.

At the head of a U-shaped table sat Winston Churchill. Behind him was a large map of the world. Sitting across the table from Churchill were two men, one of whom Rose recognized, from the newspapers and his visits to the war rooms, as General Charles de Gaulle, a tall, mustached man with hooded eyes. Rose knew, from de Gaulle's BBC broadcasts, that he'd fled France during the Nazi invasion and moved to London to lead the Free French Forces. Sitting to the right of de Gaulle was a gray-haired military officer whom Rose did not recognize and assumed to be Commandant Martel.

Goswick motioned with her eyes for Rose to enter.

Rose gathered her courage and stepped into the room. The door closed behind her. With unsteady legs, she took a seat to the right of Commandant Martel, all the while wishing she had never spoken up to Goswick about her ability to speak French. *Where are Churchill's aides? Why a private meeting?* Her drowsiness from working through the night was gone. Her heartbeat, fueled by adrenaline, thudded under her ribs.

Commandant Martel glanced at Rose, and then turned his attention to Churchill and de Gaulle.

Rose regretted that she hadn't brought a pad of paper and pencil. Feeling completely unprepared, she clasped her hands to keep from fidgeting.

General de Gaulle leaned over Churchill's desk and removed a cigar from a box, leaving the lid open. "Roosevelt is sympathetic of Vichy and Marshal Pétain," he said with a French accent.

His English is good, Rose thought. *Is this going to be about the president of the United States? Or the Vichy leader, who collaborates with the Nazis? Don't think. Only interpret.* She turned to Commandant Martel and translated de Gaulle's comment in French.

Martel nodded, his eyes remaining on de Gaulle.

"You should not have ordered the landing without consulting Roosevelt and me," Churchill said, his voice filled with irritation. "If I had not been in Washington following the attack on Pearl Harbor, this international incident you've created would have been far worse."

Good God! Her mouth turned dry. Using a soft voice, she interpreted Churchill's comments for Martel.

General de Gaulle lit his cigar, puffed on it, and then expelled a lungful of smoke.

The scent of burnt tobacco irritated Rose's nose. She fought the urge to cough.

"Canada does not want Vichy forces close to Quebec, and neither do you," de Gaulle said. "If Free French forces hadn't invaded Saint Pierre and Miquelon, Canada would eventually capture the islands for themselves."

"You've gone too far," Churchill said, closing the lid to his cigar box.

"You feel the same way," de Gaulle said, tapping ash into Churchill's ashtray. "I have complete confidence that you can explain matters in a proper way to US President Roosevelt and Canadian Prime Minister King."

For an hour, Rose interpreted a debate between Churchill and de Gaulle. She learned—despite trying to focus on her translation duties—that on Christmas Eve, Free French naval forces, with 360 sailors, on the orders of de Gaulle, captured two small islands under Vichy control near the Canadian coast of Newfoundland. The invasion took less than thirty minutes and no shots were fired. But with the United States joining the war and still adamantly opposed to any change in control of the islands by force, de Gaulle's rogue action had caused a major international incident. It was clear to Rose that Churchill was mitigating the aftermath with Allied leaders.

"Do you desire to be a permanent guest of Britain?" Churchill asked.

"I plan to reclaim France from Germany, *and* I will lead my country," de Gaulle said, as if he were speaking as a man who believed he had a destiny. "My people think of me as a rebirth of Joan of Arc."

"Perhaps you should be reminded," Churchill said, rubbing his jowl, "the English burned the last one."

Oh, Lord! Rose gripped her chair.

General de Gaulle, his face turned stoic, stroked his mustache with his fingers.

Rose interpreted for the commandant.

Martel's eyebrows rose.

Rose expected the meeting to abruptly end, either with de Gaulle and Martel storming out of the room, or by Churchill calling military guards to escort them from the building. To her surprise, de Gaulle and Churchill carried on their adversarial banter for twenty minutes, as if they had grown accustomed to each other's behavior.

"If we are to stop Hitler and his lust for blood and destruction," Churchill said, "we will need the full support of the United States and Canada." He clasped his pocket watch, which was attached by a chain to his vest. "I trust that you will consult with me and our Allied leaders prior to future missions."

General de Gaulle snubbed out the remains of his cigar in the ashtray, and then stood. "I will keep you informed. And I will expect the same in return."

Rose interpreted the exchange for Martel.

Martel stood, and then spoke to de Gaulle in French.

Rose took a deep, but quiet breath, relieved that the tense meeting was coming to a close.

"Commandant Martel thanks you for your support," de Gaulle said to Churchill. He gestured with his hand to Rose. "The commandant is also curious as to how you managed to hire a Frenchwoman to work in your war rooms. He said that the last woman, with a Cockney accent, was quite difficult to understand."

Churchill looked at Rose.

A knot tightened in her abdomen.

"Miss Teasdale is English," Churchill said, standing from his chair.

The general leaned to Martel and told him what Churchill had said.

Martel glanced at Rose, and then turned to de Gaulle. "*Je pense toujours qu'elle est Française.*"

"Perhaps you should more thoroughly examine the backgrounds of your staff," de Gaulle said to Churchill. "Martel is convinced that she's French."

Churchill slid his hands into his trouser pockets. "That will be all, Miss Teasdale."

"Yes, Prime Minister." Rose left the Cabinet War Room, closing the door behind her. She went to Room 60 and stealthily retrieved her coat. She didn't want the typists, nor the switchboard operators, to see her frazzled. Her mind and body exhausted, she scaled the steps of the underground bunker, hoping she'd never be asked to be a French interpreter again.

Churchill woke from his afternoon nap in his private bunker bedroom. He crossed the small room and sat at his desk, and then poured a glass of Johnnie Walker scotch whisky from a crystal decanter and diluted it with water. Lighting a cigar, he took a deep lungful of smoke, and then lifted the receiver on his telephone.

"Connect me to Hugh Dalton," he said to the operator.

He sipped his scotch, the peaty taste of the alcohol reviving his senses, and thought of Dalton, the minister of Economic Warfare, whom he'd appointed to take responsibility for his secret organization. *Set Europe ablaze*, he'd told Dalton.

"Prime Minister," Dalton said, answering the telephone. "To what do I owe the honor?"

Churchill swirled a bit of scotch in the bottom of his glass. "I have someone your recruiters should meet."

CHAPTER 6

LONDON, ENGLAND—JANUARY 13, 1942

Rose and Lucy ate breakfast, cooked oats with bits of dried gooseberries, and then left the flat for work. Today, for the first time in nearly a week, their work schedules aligned, which occurred with less frequency, considering Rose volunteered at every opportunity to work extra shifts.

"Perhaps we could make you a second home in the dock," Lucy jested as they waited at the tube station. "We can make curtains for imaginary windows."

Rose forced a smile.

"With the aid of a few lamps, maybe we could make an indoor garden. We could acquire you a pet, although we'd have to settle for something that lives underground."

"Like a shrew," Rose said, doing her best to play along.

"Precisely!"

"I get your point," Rose said. "I'm working far too much, and you're worried about me."

"You're clever," Lucy said, looping her arm around Rose's elbow.

"All right," Rose said. "If Goswick needs someone to work tonight, I promise to be the last person to volunteer."

Lucy lowered her glasses and stared at Rose.

"You have my word," Rose said.

They boarded the train and chatted during their commute to work. Rose was appreciative that Lucy had not brought up last week's impromptu interpreting assignment, and neither did her coworkers during lunch breaks at the Treasury building canteen. The women of Room 60, it seemed to Rose, understood the critical importance of war room confidentiality. She tried not to think about last week's meeting, but the adversarial relationship she'd witnessed between Churchill and de Gaulle had remained on her mind.

Arriving at the Treasury building, they cleared security and made their way down the stairs into the bunker. They found Miss Goswick waiting in the doorway.

"Hello," Lucy said, unbuttoning her coat.

"Good morning," Goswick said, dryly. She stepped to Rose and handed her an envelope. "I've been informed by my superior that you have been summoned to attend a meeting."

Rose looked at the sealed envelope, her name typed on the front. "Interpreting duty?"

"I don't know, but you can keep your coat on. Your meeting is in Marylebone." Goswick turned and walked away, the click of her heels echoing in the basement corridor.

Rose looked at Lucy and shrugged. "I guess I'll see you later."

Lucy nodded, and then took her seat behind her typewriter.

Rose opened the envelope and read the letter, which resembled a telegram.

        Rose Teasdale is hereby summoned to
        attend an interview with Captain Selwyn
        Jepson at 9:00 a.m. on 13th January 1942.
        Location: 64 Baker Street, London

Interview? Goswick likely knew nothing about the interview, Rose believed, otherwise her supervisor, a blunt and honest woman, would have told her more. Rose glanced to the clock and realized that she'd need to leave immediately if she were to make her appointment on time. She slipped the letter inside her coat pocket and left the Treasury building. Taking a bus headed toward the West End, she soon arrived at 64 Baker Street and entered a six-story stone building with no signage, which didn't seem out of the ordinary for Rose, considering she worked in secrecy in the Treasury basement.

"Hello," Rose said, greeting a male receptionist, who wore a charcoal-colored suit and smelled strongly of aftershave. "Captain Jepson, please."

The receptionist scanned his papers. "Miss Teasdale?"

"Yes."

"Room twenty-four," he said. "Second floor."

"Thank you."

She climbed the stairs. Turning in the wrong direction in the hallway, she had to backtrack to find the room. She took a deep breath and knocked on the door.

"Come in," said a low voice.

She opened the door and saw a middle-aged man wearing an olive military tunic.

"Good morning," the man said, standing from his desk to greet her. He shook her hand, firm but gentle. "Captain Jepson."

"Rose Teasdale."

He took her coat and hung it on a rack. "Have a seat," Jepson said, motioning on a wooden chair beside his desk.

Rose sat.

Jepson took his seat and opened a small box on his desk. "Cigarette?"

"No, thank you."

Jepson closed the box. "I suppose you're wondering what this is all about."

"Yes," Rose said.

"Consider this an interview," Jepson said.

"For what position?" Rose placed her hands under her legs.

"After the interview, I'll tell you all about it, assuming you meet the qualifications." Jepson retrieved a file and pencil from his desk.

Rose thought this to be a rather odd way to conduct an interview. But she'd been conditioned, from following orders in the war rooms, to simply perform as instructed. Jepson seemed pleasant, aside from keeping the role a mystery, and this certainly looked to be a far more pleasant meeting than the one she attended with Churchill and de Gaulle. "Very well," she said.

The interview started with standard questions. Education. Work experience. Language skills. But Jepson's inquiries soon became uncomfortably personal.

"I understand that you often spent summers in France while growing up."

How does he know this? What's in that file? "Yes, my grandparents lived there."

"Are your grandparents deceased?"

A knot formed in her stomach. "Yes."

"What was your grandparents' political party affiliation?"

"I don't know. I was young, and they never spoke of politics."

Jepson scribbled on his pad. "How well do you know Paris?"

"Well, I suppose. My grandparents' home was in Puteaux."

He turned to a fresh piece of paper. "Are you afraid of heights?"

What kind of question is that? Hairs stood up on the back of her neck. "A little."

"What's 'a little'?"

"I'm perfectly fine in high office buildings, but prefer not to be seated near a window."

"Have you ever been in a scuffle, Miss Teasdale?"

"No," she said, feeling offended.

"If confronted by a Nazi," Jepson said, abruptly, "could you kill them?"

Rose gripped her seat. "Why are you asking me this?"

"Simply answer the question, Miss Teasdale."

A flash of her parents' broken bodies, covered in ash. Charlie's empty casket. "Yes."

"What makes you think you could fight the Nazis?"

"Because," she said, looking into Jepson's eyes, "I hate them."

"Good," Jepson said. He scribbled on his paper.

"Captain, this interview is rather unconventional. What are you trying to accomplish with these questions?" Rose asked, a mixture of curiosity and nervousness stirring within her.

"I'm attempting to assess if I can risk your life," he said, rolling a pencil between his fingers. "And if you have the fortitude to risk it."

Rose's mouth turned dry.

"Shall we carry on?" Jepson asked, calmly.

Rose nodded.

For the remainder of the morning, Rose answered Jepson's probing questions. Finishing the interview, Jepson informed her that he'd be in touch with his decision. They shook hands, and she left the building on Baker Street. A foreboding ache grew in her gut. If she were to be selected for the undisclosed job, Rose believed, with great certainty, that her life would be changed forever.

CHAPTER 7

PARIS, FRANCE—FEBRUARY 21, 1942

Lazare eased the window open, and frigid air poured into his bedroom. The bit of old soap he'd used to lubricate the frame worked well to prevent the window from squeaking. The street, lit by a crescent moon, was void of movement. The unmistakable grinding of a German car engine faded in the distance. It was a Wehrmacht patrol, Lazare believed, considering the strict curfew imposed by the Nazis. Maman and Papa had gone to bed hours ago. Certain that his parents, as well as the neighbors, were asleep, Lazare stepped onto the fire escape landing and slipped on a black cap and a pair of gloves, which included an oversized mitt to conceal his wooden prosthetic hand. He gently closed the window. As he descended the metal steps, bottles—filled with accelerant—jostled in his coat pockets. Adrenaline surged through his veins.

He made his way toward the fourteenth arrondissement, maneuvering through alleys and less traveled streets. His destination was near Montparnasse, a once-vibrant artist community that had, before Nazi occupation, attracted people from all over the world. Nina Hamnett. Pablo Picasso. Chaim Soutine. Diego Rivera. Marie Vassilieff. Salvador Dalí. As a child, Lazare and his mother—a humble woman who chronically felt undeserving of having her artwork displayed in the company of such accomplished artists—had often visited the galleries. "I like your pieces better, Maman," he'd once said on their walk home. "You're a good boy," she'd said, smiling and tussling his hair with her fingers. "Always be sweet."

Lazare's walks with his *maman* in Montparnasse seemed like a lifetime ago, the German occupation driving a wedge between the past and the present. His reason for risking his life by breaking curfew and venturing into the fourteenth arrondissement had nothing to do with paintings or sculptures. It was about disrupting the Nazis. In the washroom at the train station, he'd overheard a Wehrmacht officer providing his comrade with the address of a Frenchwoman who supposedly serviced German officers. In addition to knowing their planned rendezvous, it provided Lazare with a precise location of where German vehicles would be parked.

His path to becoming a saboteur had started months ago, with a paring knife he removed from the kitchen. With the blade wrapped in a rag and tucked into his leather boot, he'd left for work. Along the route, he'd stopped beside a parked Wehrmacht *Kübelwagen*, a light military vehicle with a convertible canvas top and an antenna protruding from the rear. *Radio vehicle?* He'd scanned the area. With the driver nowhere to be seen and the sidewalk free of pedestrians, he kneeled. Pretending to tie his bootlace, he removed the knife and stabbed the blade into the rear tire. Air hissed. His pulse raced. As he was about to flee, he'd noticed a spare tire mounted on the hood of the vehicle, and quickly punctured it. He'd slipped the knife into his boot, and then strolled away to work, all the while wondering if he would someday be required to use his crude weapon, once used by Maman to peel potatoes, to kill a Nazi.

With each German tire Lazare slashed on his various routes to and from work, his confidence grew. But ruined tires were mere inconveniences to the Nazi occupiers, and the vehicles were repaired and on the road within days, if not hours. Desiring to do something more meaningful, he'd begun siphoning petrol into empty wine bottles, using a piece of garden hose. Inserting rags for fuses, he used his homemade petrol bombs to torch several Wehrmacht vehicles, a train car—filled with requisitioned French commodities headed to Germany—and a small hotel, billeted solely by German soldiers. To help with his cover, he randomly selected locations in various areas of Paris, and he spaced the dates of his attacks. At times, Lazare viewed his acts as futile. The Nazis replaced their equipment, took possession of more Parisian hotels, and stole more food from the starving French. Despite the risk of being caught and executed, he was compelled to continue his vigilante vandalism to free France from German occupation.

Ahead, Lazare spotted his targets near a three-story apartment building. Parked along the sidewalk were four German automobiles with swastika flags raised from the front fenders. He hid in a doorway and scanned the area. In a second-floor window, a smidge of light seeped through the corner of a blackout drape. With strict blackout rules, most Parisians wouldn't risk having lights on, even with blackout shades, unless they were collaborating with the enemy. *This might be the apartment of the woman the Nazis had spoken about.*

As he pulled a petrol bottle from his pocket, a phosphorous flash caused his heart rate to spike. He pressed his back to the doorway. A Nazi officer—whom Lazare hadn't noticed sitting on the apartment steps, due to the cars blocking his view—stood and inhaled his cigarette. The German tossed his match, still burning, into the gutter.

Damn it. Lazare wedged his body farther into the doorway.

Laughter radiated from the second-floor room. The German officer glanced up to the window. He smoked half of the cigarette, and then flicked the butt into the street. Adjusting his cap, he climbed the steps and entered the apartment building.

Lazare exhaled and retrieved the wine bottles from his coat. He removed the corks and inserted rags for wicks. With four German cars, he wished he'd been able to carry more than two bombs. Removing the matchbook, he envisioned tossing a petrol bomb through the apartment window, from which a mixture of laughter and carnal noises emanated. He thought of the Nazi who had executed an old man for loitering near Resistance propaganda. Revenge burned in his belly, but he refused to risk killing the woman, regardless of whether she was fraternizing with the enemy. Some French befriended Nazis to gain access to better food for their families. Although he loathed collaborators, he also believed that good people had a breaking point and could resort to extreme measures to feed themselves, or their hungry family.

Lazare stepped from the doorway and placed his petrol bombs on the sidewalk. Striking a match, he lit the wicks. The glow produced murky shadows over the street. Limited by his wooden prosthetic, he picked up a bottle with his left hand, stepped to the closest German vehicle, and threw the bomb, smashing it through the driver's side window. The interior of the car erupted in flames. A wave of heat flashed near Lazare's face.

As he turned to retrieve his second bomb, a Nazi shot up in the seat of the farthest car. Lazare's blood turned cold. The officer had been sleeping, or waiting his turn to enter the apartment, and Lazare had neglected inspecting the vehicles.

Oh, God.

The Nazi flung open the car door and raised a pistol.

Lazare hurled the bomb. Missing the Nazi, the bottle shattered on the fender, sending petrol and flames over the hood of the car. Shots exploded.

Lazare ran.

"Halt!"

The window to the apartment was flung open. A bare-chested man, his skin covered in sweat, pointed a pistol and fired.

A bullet struck the pavement near Lazare's foot. He dashed onto a side street, as bullets ricocheted over a brick wall.

A car engine started. Guttural shouts. Lazare's pulse pounded in his ears. He forced his legs to move faster and searched for a place to hide. Another car engine roared. Tires squealed. *It's over.*

Near the street corner, a dark figure stepped from the shadows.

I'm surrounded. Lazare searched for a fire escape to climb. A window to break into.

"Follow me," a male voice said in French.

Lazare sprinted to the corner to find a mustached man wearing a knee-length wool coat and beret.

"Hurry," the man hissed, ducking into an alley.

Lazare followed the man, moving at a brisk pace.

German vehicles sped past the alley entrance, and then screeched to a stop.

We're spotted. He pressed on, wondering if the Nazis would run them over, or shoot them down.

The Frenchman ran into an adjoining alley, and then darted onto a main street. Ahead stood an arched gate, which led to a cemetery.

They'll find us in the open. Lazare's mind raced, contemplating if he should abandon the man for a better escape route.

Instead of running into the cemetery, the Frenchman veered to the curb and pointed to a sewer drain. "Help me lift it."

Using his good hand, Lazare grabbed the iron grate and, with the aid of the man, pried it from its place.

"Go," the man demanded.

Lazare descended into the sewer. Above him, the man stepped into the hole, and then, grunting with effort, maneuvered the iron grate back into place. Seconds later, the gleam of headlights flashed over the grate. The roar of engines grew, and then faded as the vehicles sped through the fourteenth arrondissement.

"Thank you," Lazare whispered, struggling to catch his breath.

"You're a lucky bastard," the man said, lowering himself to the bottom of the sewer.

Lazare's feet turned frigid and wet, and he realized that he was standing in ankle-deep water. He struggled to see with the absence of light.

"I spotted you, peeking from a doorway, several streets away," the man said. "You need to be more careful."

"You followed me?"

"Oui,"

"Why?"

"To see what you planned to do," he said. "And to determine if you could be trusted."

Trusted?

"Follow me," the man said, sloshing through the sewer.

"Wait." Lazare stepped forward and bumped his head on stone.

A sharp sting shot through his forehead. Hunching his back in the darkness, he followed the squelching sound of the man's boots. "Where are we going?"

"I'll tell you when we get there," the man said, his voice echoing in the masonry tunnel.

Placing his hand on the wall to guide him, Lazare followed. The man maneuvered through the darkness, taking multiple turns in the tunnel, as if he had been here many times before. A foul stench filled the air. His toes turned numb. Lazare walked near the wall, which kept his feet out of the water, but in doing so caused squeaks to resonate through the sewer. Something nibbled his pant leg. *Rats.* He pressed forward, kicking away rodents from his legs.

Several minutes into the trek, the man stopped. "Crawl through the hole on your left."

With his hands, Lazare located the hole. He followed the man, squeezing his body through a stone crevice. Once inside, Lazare found the floor to be dry, free of rats, and he was able to stand upright. He squinted at a flash of light.

Using a lighter, the man lit a lantern, which was stashed in the chamber. He turned to Lazare, providing him with a better look at his guide. The man was middle-aged with a gray mustache. Crow's-feet were etched in the corners of his brown eyes, which were rimmed by bushy eyebrows. Except for stubby sideburns, extending down from his felt beret, the man appeared to be bald.

"I'm Claudius," the man said, extending his hand.

"Lazare." He squeezed the man's hand, using three fingers.

Claudius looked at Lazare's hand.

"Prosthetic."

Claudius nodded. "It's a little farther ahead."

Lazare followed Claudius through a series of limestone tunnels. *Catacombs?* His suspicion was confirmed when Claudius turned into an adjoining chamber. Along the wall, stacked like precisely placed masonry stones, were hundreds of skulls. Areas of Paris were built upon the ancient limestone quarries, which now contained centuries of Parisian dead. But despite living his entire life in Paris, he'd never ventured into the catacombs.

Ahead, the tunnel glowed. Voices murmured.

"It's Claudius," the man called.

Following Claudius, Lazare stepped into a large room. Sitting around a small fire, made from what appeared to be broken chair legs, were several men, most of whom were middle-aged or older. On the floor was a five-foot-long metal container resembling a torpedo without fins. In the corners of the room were stacks of ancient human femurs.

An older man stood and slung a rifle over his shoulder. "Who's he?"

Lazare straightened his back. *They have weapons.*

"His name is Lazare," Claudius said. "I found him setting fire to a Nazi officer's vehicle."

The men chuckled.

A man with a rifle approached Lazare. "You acted alone?"

"*Oui,*" Lazare said.

The men, including Claudius, interrogated Lazare with questions, including where he lived, names of family members, and inquiries into his political views. *They are determining whether they should invite me to join their group. And if I'm not selected, they'll likely kill me rather than risk having an outsider with knowledge of their location.* His mind and heart raced, hoping he wouldn't fail what appeared to be a life-or-death interview.

"Why weren't you in the army?" a bearded man asked, his voice filled with suspicion.

"I was rejected." Lazare removed a glove and held up his wooden prosthetic. "I lost a thumb and forefinger as a child."

"He won't be able to shoot a weapon," one of the men muttered.

Lazare unstrapped leather bands and removed his prosthetic. He gestured for the bearded man to give him his weapon.

The bearded man looked to Claudius.

Claudius nodded.

The bearded man removed the ammunition and handed the rifle to Lazare.

Although he'd never fired a weapon, he did his best to demonstrate how he could operate the rifle left-handled. "I'd have no limitations using a pistol," he added, returning the rifle.

"He clearly has never shot a firearm," said a man holding what appeared to be a military-issued knuckle knife.

"And neither had you," Claudius said, "until you fought in the Great War."

The man spat on the floor, and then slipped his knife into a leather sheath.

It became clear to Lazare that Claudius was the leader of the group. And he hoped that he'd done enough to convince the man that he was committed to fighting for France.

"Your decision," Claudius said to the men.

Lazare's breath turned shallow. A cold sweat beaded on his forehead.

The men glanced to their comrades, and then nodded.

A rush of relief and excitement filled Lazare. But as the men approached to greet him, a memory of his parents flashed in his mind. *They'll find out sooner or later.* "There's something you must know," Lazare said.

Eyes stared. The room turned silent, except for the crackle of embers.

"I'm a Jew," Lazare said, his words echoing in the chamber.

"Religion is of little importance to the Resistance," Claudius said, staring at Lazare. He tapped a fist to his chest. "We're seeking hearts committed to liberating France."

A sense of purpose and belonging swelled within Lazare. The men greeted him with handshakes and pats on the back.

"Now," Claudius said, stepping to the metal container and opening the lid. "Let's see what our British friends have delivered."

Inside the container were packages of plastic explosives, grenades, two machine guns, three rifles, several pistols, ammunition, and a stash of food. Lazare's eyes widened.

"Welcome to the Resistance," Claudius said, handing Lazare a pistol, a tin of mutton, and a bar of chocolate.

Lazare joined the men sitting around the container, which he learned was parachuted into a remote field, northwest of Paris, by the British Royal Air Force. The men had smuggled the container to Paris by hiding it beneath a truckload of lumber, and then lugged it through another secret entrance to the catacomb. As the men feasted on canned meat and inventoried their armament, Lazare, despite his hunger, slipped his food into his coat pocket. For the rest of the night, he listened to the men discuss plans for using their plastic explosives.

The French army rejected me. The Resistance accepted me. His heart pumped with honor and vindication. Holding his pistol, he swore to himself that he'd do whatever he could to free France, even if it meant his life.

At 5:00 a.m., Lazare left the catacombs, guided through the maze of subterranean tunnels by Claudius. Before they parted ways, Claudius informed him of when and where they'd meet again. Lazare, a pistol and food hidden in his coat pockets, took a long and less-traveled route home, hoping to avoid soldiers, who often stopped pedestrians to examine their papers. With curfew over, a few Parisians, likely on their way to get a good place in the ration lines, began to venture outside. A German infantry truck sped by, blasting him with wind. He lowered his head and continued his pace.

On Rue Cler, he saw two Wehrmacht soldiers smoking cigarettes on the corner near his apartment building. Unable to use the fire escape without drawing attention to himself, he entered the front door to his building and climbed to the third floor. He gently inserted his key and turned the lock, hoping his parents were still asleep. Opening the door, he found them standing in the kitchen.

"Where were you?" his mother asked, tightening her robe.

"Out for a walk," Lazare said. He closed the door and bolted the latch.

"You didn't come home last night," Gervais said.

Hair rose on the back of Lazare's neck. *They know.* He turned and nodded.

"What were you doing?" his father asked.

"I'd rather not say," Lazare said.

"We don't keep secrets in this house," Gervais said, crossing his arms.

"It's for your safety."

Magda's shoulders slumped. "Oh, Lazare."

"I'm sorry, Maman." Lazare approached them. "I'm unwilling to stand by and watch the Nazis ravage France. I intend to fight."

"We must wait for the Allies to free France," Gervais said. "There's nothing we can do."

"There's no time," Lazare said, raising his voice. "Yesterday, a woman who was riding a bicycle in front of the train station was stopped by a German officer. He inspected her papers, pulled out a pistol, and shot her in the head."

Magda gasped.

"Her crime: *Jews* are not permitted to ride bicycles." Ire burned through Lazare's arteries. He paused, removing his cap, and decided it was best not to tell them that it was *he* who was charged with mopping up the woman's blood and disposing of bits of her cranium.

Gervais, his skin pale, stared at Lazare. "Our police will let nothing happen—"

"The police are collaborating," Lazare interrupted. "The Nazi anti-Semitic plague has spread."

"There's no doubt that some police conspire with the Germans," Magda said. "But we must have faith that, in time, the Allies will free France."

"I will fight, with or without your blessing," Lazare said.

His mother rubbed her stomach, as if she were about to become sick.

"You're wrong," Gervais said. He stepped to Lazare and clasped his maimed hand. "But I know that I cannot stop you."

Lazare wanted to pull his hand away, but, out of respect for his father, he remained still.

"Since your accident," Gervais said, "I've lived with the guilt that my son lost his fingers because I failed to protect him."

"It wasn't your fault, Papa—"

"Let me finish," Gervais said, firmly. "When you were rejected from joining the French army, I was tormented with culpability. But all of your friends, who'd gone off to fight, are now dead or in German prison camps."

A wave of wretchedness crashed through Lazare's body as their faces appeared in his memory.

"It recently struck me," Gervais said. "If I had, many years ago, protected you from injuring your hand, you would've met the same fate as your friends." He released Lazare's hand. "I'm grateful that you're alive, and I want to keep it that way."

"Nothing will happen to me," Lazare said, despite knowing that he was making a promise that he might not be able to keep.

Magda and Gervais, appearing exhausted from the exchange, sat at the table.

"I have food," Lazare said, removing a tin of mutton and bar of chocolate from his pocket.

"Where did you get it?" Magda asked.

"Resistance." Lazare opened the tin, releasing the smell of boiled mutton. He retrieved forks from a cabinet and gave them to his parents. "Eat."

"What about you?" Magda asked.

Lazare looked at his mother. Bony clavicles protruded through her robe. She'd lost weight, and her eyes were dark and sunken. From months of malnourishment, her once lustrous hair had turned dry and brittle. "I've already eaten," he lied.

CHAPTER 8

PARIS, FRANCE—MAY 29, 1942

On the day of the German decree, requiring Jews in occupied France to wear the yellow star, Lazare came home to find Maman sewing a patch onto Papa's coat.

"I'll sew yours after I finish your father's," Magda said, stitching at the kitchen table.

"That won't be necessary," Lazare said.

"You must," Gervais said, taking a seat beside Magda. "You'll be arrested if you're caught without it."

Lazare stared at the yellow star patch with *Juif* written in the center. Resentment boiled beneath his sternum. "I'm proud of my heritage, Papa. But I refuse to be branded, like cattle."

Magda put down her needle and thread. "You won't be permitted to work or receive rations."

"I'm not going back to the Gare du Nord train station," Lazare said, feeling a bit guilty for not telling his parents that he'd quit his job weeks ago.

Gervais sighed, shaking his head. "How will you live?"

Lazare thought of his fake papers and ration card, provided by the Resistance, disguising him as a non-Jew named Laurent Allard. He didn't tell them about his alias, nor any of the details of working for the Resistance. If he were to be arrested by the

Gestapo, his parents would no doubt be interrogated, and it was best to keep them uninformed about his clandestine activities.

"I'll manage," Lazare said.

"You're rarely home anymore," his mother said, a timbre of gloom in her voice. "What have you been doing?"

"I'm sorry, Maman," he said, touching her shoulder. "For your safety, I cannot tell you. Please trust that my absence is to free France." Lazare spent his days and nights with the Resistance. He rarely slept at home. Instead, he stayed in safe houses, arranged by Claudius, or, on occasion, in a secret catacomb bunker.

Gervais rubbed stubble on his chin, as if contemplating the potential repercussions of his son's rebellious behavior.

Magda lowered her eyes and picked up her needle.

"I've brought you something," Lazare said.

"More tinned meat?" Magda asked, making a stitch through the star.

You look good, Maman. The meat is keeping you from losing more weight. "Yes, I've gotten more food, but I have something else for you." Lazare reached into his coat, removed two sets of papers, and handed them to his parents.

"What's this?" Gervais opened a booklet containing his photograph. His eyes widened.

"Fake identification. Travel papers. Ration cards," Lazare said.

"How?" Magda asked.

"The Resistance has resources for creating documents," Lazare said. "I used old photographs of you and Papa."

"Why?" Gervais asked, his eyebrows lowered.

"To enable you and Maman to leave Paris."

Magda glanced at her husband.

"The papers will get you safely to Tours," Lazare said. "From there, I've arranged for a courier to guide you to *zone libre*."

"We've already discussed this," Gervais said firmly. He placed the booklet, facedown, on the table.

"This is no time to be stubborn, Papa," Lazare said. "The window to leave is nearly closed. You and Maman can come back to Paris when France is liberated. You'll return to being a journalist."

He stepped to his father and looked into his weary eyes. "And I will join you."

"Nothing would make me happier than to someday work alongside you at a newspaper publisher, free from Nazi propaganda. But we're not going to *zone libre*," Gervais said.

"But Papa—"

"Your father and I have already decided that we're not leaving," Magda said, sliding her papers across the table. "Paris is our home, and we intend to stay."

Lazare's heart sank. For twenty minutes, he pleaded with his parents to leave, but they held their ground. "Please, give it more thought," he finally said.

Gervais shook his head. He collected the papers and gave them to Lazare. "You'll need to dispose of these."

"I'll hide them," he said. "In case you change your mind."

Despite his parents' objection, he took the papers and went to the living room. He removed Maman's painting of the Arc de Triomphe—the last remaining artwork in the apartment—from the wall. All of the other paintings had been bartered for food, with the exception of two pieces that were burned in the fireplace last winter, when temperatures had plummeted and there was no coal available on the black market. Using a knife hidden in his boot, he removed the thin board backing, and then placed the papers inside the frame. He fixed the backing, tapping the metal tabs back into place with the butt of the knife. He raised the painting and, after struggling to slip the wire over the hook, fastened it to the wall.

"It's crooked," Gervais said, stepping into the living room. "Tilt it to the left."

Lazare adjusted the frame. "*Bon?*"

"*Oui,*" Magda said, joining them. "I saved that one because you loved it."

"I'm glad you did," Lazare said, turning to his mother.

Magda pointed to a glove protruding from Lazare's pocket. "Too warm to be wearing those."

Lazare's breath stalled in his chest. With his wooden thumb, he nudged the glove into his pocket, dreading to explain to his mother why he was carrying winter garments in spring.

Magda paused, staring at Lazare's wooden prosthetic, and then said, "Gervais, please collect my paints, brushes, and palette from the cabinet, and then bring them to the kitchen."

Gervais scratched his head, and then went to the cabinet.

Soon, at Magda's request, they were sitting at the kitchen table. The yellow star stitchwork was pushed aside, making room for Maman's art supplies.

"Hold out your hands," Magda said.

"Why?" Lazare asked, shifting in his seat.

"Please appease your mother," she said.

Lazare placed his hands on the table.

Magda ran a finger over the prosthetic. "The wood has turned dark. It doesn't match your skin. And the curvature of the thumb is worn."

"It's fine," Lazare said.

Magda leaned in, examining the border between the wood and his skin. "Your hands smell like motor oil."

Plastic explosives. He swallowed, burying the thought of the electric transformer that he'd sabotaged the night before. "What are you planning to do?" he asked, hoping to redirect the conversation.

"Protect my son," she said.

Gervais smiled.

Magda untied the leather straps and removed his prosthetic. She squeezed dabs of red, yellow, blue, and white paint onto her palette.

"Please don't," Lazare said, fighting the urge to retrieve his prosthetic.

Magda mixed the paints with a brush, creating a flesh color.

"Looks good," Gervais said.

Magda nodded.

Lazare's angst grew. He felt as if he'd been tricked into sitting in a dentist's chair for a surprise tooth extraction. "Maman—"

"Patience." She added more white paint, lightening the shade.

Using the tip of her paintbrush, she made a small stroke over the edge of the wooden prosthetic. She blew on the paint, expediting the drying time, and then held the prosthetic next to Lazare's skin. "Close but not perfect."

"There's no need to paint my hand," Lazare said.

"But there is," Gervais said, placing a hand on his son's shoulder. "I think what your mother is intending to do is provide you with options for your appearance. To look ordinary and blend into a crowd—wear your prosthetic. To display that you are of no threat to the Nazis—don't wear it."

"*Oui*," Magda said.

It certainly can't make my hand look worse, he thought, staring at his scar and three fingers. Without telling his parents exactly what he was doing for the Resistance, they had drawn their own conclusion. Most importantly, it seemed to please his mother, who hadn't picked up a paintbrush in nearly two years, that she was doing something to help.

"All right," he said.

For the afternoon, Magda painted the prosthetic, using Lazare's good hand as a model. After painting a flesh-colored base, she mixed more paint onto the palette, and then added subtle vein maps, wrinkles, and even micro hair follicles. To protect her work, she added a clear, flat finish. While waiting for the hand to dry, they drank a bland coffee-like mixture that Papa made from roasted wheat bran.

"It's dry," Magda said, touching a finger to the finish. "Try it on."

Lazare slipped on the prosthetic, and then attached the leather straps to his forearm. He put his shirt sleeve back into place, buttoned at the wrist. He stared at his hands. Except for a shadowy seam between the prosthetic and his skin, they were almost identical. *From a distance, my hands will look ordinary.* His heart swelled with appreciation.

"Beautiful work," Gervais said, placing an arm around his wife. Magda smiled.

"Thank you," Lazare said. He kissed his mother on the cheek.

"I'm sorry I didn't do this years ago," she said.

As Lazare admired his painted hand, it occurred to him that he'd come home to protect his parents. He'd failed to convince them to leave Paris. And now, they were trying to safeguard him. He prayed that in the end, they'd somehow be able to save one another.

CHAPTER 9

MORAR, SCOTLAND—MAY 29, 1942

Rose, tired from the early-morning train trip, exited a carriage and descended the stairs of the Arisaig station landing. A scent of sea air, mixed with steam from a coal-fueled locomotive, filled her nose. She carried a suitcase containing a few clothes and her only remaining family photograph—a picture of Charlie—wrapped inside a wool sweater.

"Miss Teasdale?" a throaty voice asked.

Rose turned.

A man with unruly gray hair and beard, save a shaven chin, removed his cap and held it politely to his chest. "I'm Murdo, your driver to take you to Garramor House."

Rose shook the man's hand.

"May I carry your bag?" he asked.

"No, thank you, Murdo. It's rather light," she said, raising her suitcase.

Rose followed him to an automobile and got in the back seat. "How far?"

"Fifteen minutes," he said, taking a seat behind the wheel. "The others arrived last night. You're the last of the lot."

"Splendid." It had been months since her first meeting with Captain Selwyn Jepson, and she was finally embarking on the first stage of training. Throughout the spring, she'd attended several interviews with Jepson, who provided no details on the role. She'd suspected the position was some type of risky, high-level intelligence work, given the questioning. And she was convinced that she'd failed when the interviews abruptly stopped. But two days ago, she was summoned into Jepson's office at 64 Baker Street.

"I want you to work in occupied France," he'd said, smoke swirling from his cigarette. "Your role will be to organize resistance, and act as a liaison with London."

France! She'd dropped her purse, spilling an empty powder compact and the key to Lucy's flat.

Jepson gave her a moment to collect her items, as well as her breath, and then revealed that he was a recruitment officer for the French Section (F Section) of the Special Operations Executive (SOE), a secret British organization that conducted espionage, sabotage, and reconnaissance in Nazi-occupied Europe. And that if she passed a series of grueling physical and instructional training programs, she would be transported to France by either sea or air. Jepson finished by giving her a few hours in which to accept or decline the offer for SOE training. But as she was leaving his office, a macabre image of the bombed Teasdale Grocery filled her head. A flash of her parents' broken bodies pulled from the rubble. Charlie's headstone.

A surge of revenge flowed through her veins. Despite Jepson's candor that her life would be at risk, she turned to him and said, "I can give you a decision now, Captain. My decision is yes."

Jepson instructed Rose to finish her afternoon shift at the war room, collect any personal items, discreetly leave, and never return. She was to take the evening train out of London. He'd take care of sending a telegram to her supervisor, providing a cover story that Rose had been reassigned to a confidential secretarial unit. Above all else, she was to tell no one about her mission or the SOE.

She'd been unable to concentrate during her last shift in the underground bunker. Jittery fingers, unable to strike the proper keys, resulted in mistakes. Her mind raced with thoughts of returning to France. Beneath her fervor to serve Britain and, more importantly, for a chance to honor the deaths of her family, she was disheartened by the fact that she'd no longer work alongside the stalwart women of Room 60. And to make matters worse, she was unable to say goodbye to Lucy, who had the day off and was visiting her mother.

Finishing her shift, she slipped her photograph of Charlie into her purse and left her desk, doing her best to hide that she'd never step foot in the war rooms again. As she climbed the stairway, she caught a whiff of burnt tobacco, causing her to pause.

"Goodbye, Miss Teasdale," a low voice said.

She turned.

Churchill, holding a cigar, stood at the base of the stairs.

Her heart rate accelerated. "Goodbye, Prime Minister."

Churchill tipped his hat, and then disappeared down the hallway.

He knows! She left the underground bunker with determination burning in her eyes.

During her last few hours in London, she purchased silk flowers from a vintage décor shop and placed them on Mum, Dad, and Charlie's graves. She preferred fresh flowers, but with not knowing when, or if, she would return, she wanted something that would last longer than bluebells or tulips. She had kneeled, under the songs of a goldfinch that was perched in an alder tree, and prayed. Within her heart, sorrow welled up. Her vision blurred with tears. Over a year had passed since their deaths, but her anguish remained raw. At sunset, when the bird's music vanished, she touched her lips and then placed her fingers on each of the headstones. She left the cemetery, vowing to make her family proud.

Rose went home and packed her suitcase. She hated leaving things this way with Lucy. She could've tried ringing Lucy at her mother's home, but she dreaded having to lie. So, she placed her key to Lucy's flat on the kitchen counter with a note.

> *Dearest Lucy,*
> *I've accepted a position outside of London. I'm sorry to leave on such short notice. I'll write when I can. I'm forever grateful*

for your kindness and friendship. I wish you and Jonathan all
the best.
  With the warmest of regards,
  Rose
  PS I have no doubt that one of your reports will help us win
the war.

At the train station, she'd purchased her ticket, as instructed by
Jepson, and then found a seat in a carriage. As the train chugged
away, and for much of her long journey—to Glasgow, and then
through the Scottish Highlands—she wondered if she would live
to see London again.

"It's up ahead, Miss Teasdale," the driver said.

Rose shook away memories of London and peered through the
automobile windows. Along the secluded road was a sandy beach.
Across a sea the color of a dark-blue peony were rocky land masses.
"Islands?"

"Aye," the driver said. "Isles of Eigg, Rùm, and Skye."

Rose squeezed the handle of her suitcase, wondering what it
would be like to cross the Channel to France, assuming she'd be
able to pass her training.

The driver turned onto a dirt and crushed-shell lane. The
car rumbled over ruts, bouncing Rose in her seat. The property
was expansive and private, without another home in sight. Oak,
birch, and rowan trees covered the grounds, unlike many areas
of the Highlands, which were covered in mountainous mixtures
of granite and grass. Soon they reached a large two-story stone
house. A pair of gabled windows, reminiscent of looming eyes,
jutted from a wing of the residence. On the peak of the house
was a weather vane, its arrow pointing the direction of the North
Sea wind.

The driver dropped her off near the entrance, and then drove
away. She took a deep breath and exhaled, fighting off the nervousness that swelled in her belly. Stepping forward, she rang a
mechanical doorbell. Footsteps approached from inside the house,
and the door swung open.

"Teasdale, I assume," a mustached man said with a Scottish accent.

"Yes, sir."

"Major Gavin Maxwell," he said, shaking her hand. "I'm your instructor for the next six weeks."

The instructor, wearing army fatigues, was tall and lean with a bony nose. His eyes were intensely confident, yet humble, as if he had acquired a secret knowledge that he was eager to share.

"Come in," Maxwell said. "The others are out back. We're about to begin fitness training. Place your bag upstairs, second room on the right. You'll be sharing a room with Brown."

Brown?

"Get changed," the major said, glancing at his watch. "Your clothes are in your room. Be outside in five minutes."

"Yes, sir." She climbed the stairs and found her room, a cozy space with two twin-size beds and a small dresser. The walls were bare and the sole window was missing curtains. *No need for privacy in a secluded home.* She located a stack of wool army clothing, changed, and then tossed her civilian items into her suitcase, which she slipped under her bed. Surprisingly, the military-issued leather boots fit comfortably. However, the pants were another matter. They were several inches too long, requiring her to roll up the legs.

Downstairs, she maneuvered through a series of rooms toward the rear of Garramor House. She passed a dining room, which contained a large oak table surrounded by a dozen chairs. The living room had a timber-beam ceiling and two sofas placed on opposite sides of a stone fireplace, which was large enough to roast wild game. There was a library covered in shelves containing leather-bound books, with an art deco liquor cabinet with several bottles of scotch. Exiting a door in the kitchen, she found Major Maxwell standing with another military officer and her soon-to-be companions for the next several weeks.

"Everyone," Maxwell announced, "this is Rose Teasdale."

Rose nodded. There were nine candidates, in addition to Rose, and two of them were women. *Thank goodness.*

"This is Lieutenant Clarke," Maxwell said, gesturing to a

barrel-chested man with thick, meaty hands. "He'll be one of your instructors."

Clarke crossed his arms, as if he was irritated that Rose had arrived later than the other candidates.

Rose swallowed.

Major Maxwell, announcing each person's name, walked down the line of candidates. There were two candidates who stood out among the others. One was Felix Renaud, a fit man with a chiseled jaw and cheekbones in his late forties, judging by his slicked-back salt-and-pepper hair. The other was Muriel Brown, an attractive, athletic-looking woman in her mid-twenties, with wavy chestnut-colored hair.

"Your six-week course will begin with physical training," Major Maxwell said, his hands clasped behind his back. "We'll then move on to weapons handling and explosives training."

Hair stood up on the back of Rose's neck.

"You'll also undergo unarmed combat and silent killing," Maxwell said. "At any stage of the training, you'll be removed if we determine you are unfit for the job. You may quit at any time. The role of an SOE agent is voluntary."

Rose bit the inside of her cheek. *I'll never quit.*

"*If* you have the physical and mental tenacity to pass training, you'll be sent to parachute instruction, and then on to extensive classroom study." Maxwell paused, adjusting the cap on his head. "Lieutenant Clarke, they're all yours."

Clarke puffed his chest. "We'll begin with the Garramor Grind." He split the candidates into three groups, with Rose partnered with Felix and Muriel. The lieutenant handed each of the groups a folded map and a small compass, and then gave a brief, but thorough, instruction on how to use them.

"Ever use a compass?" Felix whispered with a French accent.

Rose and Muriel shook their heads.

"Then I will hold it." Felix slipped the compass into his pocket, appearing a bit disappointed to be partnered with two women.

"The route is marked," Clarke said, finishing his instructions. "Use your map and compass if you get sidetracked." He glanced at his wristwatch. "Be back in under three hours. Move out!"

The candidates dispersed, running eastward on an earthen path. The other groups sprinted, leaving Rose and her companions behind.

"Pace yourself," Felix said, glancing to Rose and Muriel.

"Perhaps we should try to keep up with the others," Rose said, jogging next to Felix.

"We might be dismissed if we finish last," Muriel added, her voice distinctively Scottish.

"It's not a race," Felix said.

"How do you know?" Rose asked, between breaths. With her short legs, she struggled to keep up, despite the moderate speed.

"Because I used to be a French Grand Prix race car driver," Felix said. "And I know a race when I see one."

Muriel looked at Rose and shrugged.

"They'll burn themselves out," Felix added. "We'll catch up with them in less than an hour."

They jogged into a dense forest, falling well behind the other group. Their boots pattered on the moss-covered ground.

"What were you doing before this, Rose?" Felix asked, pointing out the path through a row of pines.

"I was a typist in London," she said, feeling that her profession was far inferior to that of a race car driver.

"Muriel?" he asked.

"I'm originally from Edinburgh," Muriel said. "I was recruited while working as a switchboard operator in the General Post Office in London."

Despite the burn in Rose's lungs, she felt comforted to know that Muriel had a similar background to her. Regaining her confidence, she glanced at Felix and said, "Where in France are you from?"

"Saintes," Felix said. "My family owned a vineyard and a cognac distillery. We escaped to England during the German invasion."

"Were you recruited?" Rose asked, feeling out of breath.

"I volunteered." He slowed, examined the map, and then folded it and slipped it into his pocket. "I'm returning to liberate my country."

I'm going to honor Mum, Dad, and Charlie.

Rose was eager to learn more about Muriel and Felix, but the terrain turned rocky, forcing them to climb over slabs of granite. Their conversation dwindled to sparse comments, pointing out loose scree and obstacles. Their pace slowed as they trekked up a mountain. Rose's leg muscles burned. She took in quick breaths, her body craving oxygen. Her desk job, compounded by taking the tube instead of walking to work, had done little to build her cardiovascular endurance. As she climbed, using feet and hands, her heart hammered against her breastbone.

Within an hour, they reached the summit. Another group, gasping for air, rested near a boulder.

"Told you," Felix breathed. He sucked in air.

Rose and Muriel, too out of breath to answer, nodded their heads.

The descent was far more challenging than the climb, although not as exhausting. The footing was tricky, the slope lined with unstable rock. Rose slipped and fell, scraping her back and sending a flare of pain through her spine. Muriel stumbled and nearly tumbled down an embankment, but was steadied when Felix clasped her elbow. At times they had to hold hands, helping each other down the mountainside. It was clear to Rose that this task was not merely an exercise for the body, it was a test of teamwork.

At the base of the mountain, they reached a stream and stopped. As Felix checked the map, there was movement through the trees. "There," Rose said, her vocal cords dry, her voice hoarse.

On the opposite side of the stream, another group disappeared into the forest.

Felix pointed. "We go through."

They waded into bone-chilling water, which was thigh high for Felix and Muriel, but for Rose, the stream was waist deep. Frigid water seeped up her shirt. She shivered. Her legs turned numb. While the air temperature hovered near fifty degrees, the stream was far colder. Goose bumps cropped up on Rose's arms.

For the remainder of the journey, they hiked through dense underbrush. Rose's feet squished inside her boots, causing blisters to rise on her skin. Her body ached. Her teeth chattered. She

forced herself to slog along a trail covered in rocks and ruts, until
reaching Garramor House. They finished the trek in two hours
and thirty-eight minutes, slightly behind the first group. The last
group finished barely within the three-hour time limit. The candidates congregated in the yard, drinking from canteens that had
been placed in the grass.

Rose gulped water, and then handed the canteen to Muriel.
"We did it." A wave of pride muted the pain from her cuts and
bruises.

"Aye," Muriel said, wiping water from her chin.

"Don't get comfortable," Felix said. "I don't think we're finished."

Considering everyone was tired, cold, and soaking wet, Rose
had expected that they'd be given food and rest, or at least a
change of clothing. But Felix was proven right when Lieutenant
Clarke, a machine gun slung over his shoulder, emerged from the
house.

Rose shivered. *What's he going to do with a weapon?*

They were led by Clarke to a nearby assault course, a series of
wooden and wire obstacles. Major Maxwell, holding a pencil and
clipboard, positioned himself on a hill to observe the exercise.

Clarke segregated the candidates into groups of men and
women. Rose, Muriel, and a young lady named Phyllis, with
blonde hair tied with ribbon, were directed to a starting line.
Rose's mouth turned dry. Her stomach felt bloated. *I shouldn't
have drunk so much water.*

Clarke pointed the barrel of his weapon to the sky. Gunfire exploded.

Rose's heart rate soared. She sprinted, along with Muriel and
Phyllis, along the course. Muriel took the lead and was the first to
scamper over a series of felled logs. Phyllis and Rose were trailing
farther behind, when they encountered the second obstacle, a ladder made from a cargo net. Two steps into the ascent, Rose's boot
became entangled. She strained to lift her leg.

"Move it!" Clarke barked.

Rose kicked her foot free from the webbing, and then went up
and over the ladder.

Reaching a ten-foot sheer wooden wall, Rose found Phyllis struggling to climb the obstacle. Muriel, who had successfully scaled the wall, sprinted ahead.

Rose climbed the obstacle's angled wooden brace, which ran halfway up the structure, to give her a good head start. She leaped, but her hands landed shy of the top, and she fell to the ground.

"I don't care if you're short, Teasdale!" Clarke shouted. "I'll send you home if you can't climb this wall!"

Rose willed herself to make three more attempts, each time resulting in failure. Phyllis did no better.

"Damn it," Clarke said, shaking his head. "Go around!"

Rose and Phyllis ran to the next obstacle, which required them to crawl on their bellies beneath a checkered weave of barbed wire. Being small, Rose was able to wriggle ahead of Phyllis.

"Keep your bloody heads down!" Clarke sprayed gunfire into the forest.

Good Lord! Rose's adrenaline surged. She pressed her chin to the earth and slithered forward.

"Ow!" Phyllis cried.

Rose stopped and turned her head, her cheek pressed against soil.

Phyllis struggled to free her hair, tangled in barbed wire.

"Move it!" Clarke shouted.

"I'm stuck," Phyllis whimpered.

Rose hesitated, a few feet from exiting the barbed wire obstacle.

Blood dripped from Phyllis's forehead.

A decision burned in Rose's gut. Before she changed her mind, she turned and crawled toward Phyllis. "Don't move."

"Leave me," Phyllis said.

Rose crawled faster, her limbs scraping over the ground.

"Teasdale!" Clarke shouted.

"Turn around," Phyllis pleaded. "You'll get in trouble."

Rose ignored Phyllis, as well as Clarke's command. Reaching Phyllis, Rose worked to free her hair, pinned and tied with ribbon, which was tangled in barbed wire. Rose tugged. A metal spike sank deeper into Phyllis's scalp.

"It hurts!" Phyllis cried. Blood seeped into her hair.

"God damn it," Clarke said. He stepped through the barbed wire maze and reached the women. "I told you to keep your bloody head down!"

Rose looked up through the wire.

Clarke slipped a knife from a sheath attached to his belt.

Rose's eyes widened.

Clarke placed the blade to Phyllis's scalp and cut away a chunk of hair.

Phyllis lowered her cheek to the ground.

Clarke glared at Rose. "If you disobey my orders again, Teasdale, I'll send your ass home."

"Yes, sir," Rose said, fear flooding her body. She rolled onto her belly and crawled away.

Rose completed the assault course ahead of Phyllis, who crossed the finish line with her hand pressed to her head. While the men took their turn on the assault course, Rose and Muriel examined Phyllis's wound, a short but deep cut that Rose believed could use a few stitches. As Rose applied pressure to Phyllis's head, using her sleeve to stop the bleeding, she saw Major Maxwell on the hillside. Their eyes met. He lowered his head and scribbled onto his clipboard. Her skin turned cold. *Please don't send me home.*

Rose, covered in bruises and scrapes, grimaced as she sat on her bed. She rubbed the ache in her thighs, wondering how she would survive physical training. The cold shower, clean clothes, and a hot meal of salmon, which Major Maxwell instructed the candidates to catch by using plastic explosives, had done little to rejuvenate her body. Even the glasses of scotch she and Muriel had drunk with the other candidates failed to numb her soreness, or her disappointment with how poorly she performed on the assault course.

"Get some rest," Muriel said, lying on her bed. "Tomorrow's another day."

"Clarke will fail me if I can't climb that wall," Rose said.

"Aye," Muriel said. "But you can do it. It simply takes practice."

And to be taller. Rose turned to Muriel. "How is Phyllis?"

"I knocked on her door, but she didn't answer."

"Me too," Rose said. "I wish she would've joined us in the library after dinner."

"A wee dram would have done her some good," Muriel said. "She barely ate her salmon and taties."

Phyllis, her bandaged scalp hidden by a scarf, had spoken little during dinner. Her eyes, filled with a mixture of defeat and embarrassment, had avoided her comrades.

I'll talk with her in the morning, Rose thought. *She needs to hear that she's done nothing to be ashamed of.*

Muriel propped a pillow behind her head. "Why did you join the SOE?"

"I was recruited, like you," Rose said.

"Aye," Muriel said. "But that's not what I'm asking."

Rose hesitated, reluctant to reopen her heartache. But with the next several weeks of arduous training, she needed someone to confide in. And that someone, she decided, would be her roommate. She retrieved the photograph from her suitcase and handed it to Muriel. "My brother, Charlie, as a young boy. He was an RAF pilot."

"Handsome," Muriel said, staring at the picture. "May I ask what happened?"

"His plane was shot down over the Channel." Rose's alcohol buzz vanished. "His body was never recovered."

Muriel sat up. "I'm so sorry."

A tide of melancholy rose in Rose's chest. "Last year, my parents were killed in a Luftwaffe bombing raid on London."

"Crivvens," Muriel whispered.

"I want to honor my family by joining the fight," Rose said.

Muriel stood, and then propped the framed photograph on the dresser. "I'm thinking we should keep Charlie's picture here, rather than in your suitcase."

"Are we permitted?" Conditioned from having to keep her war room desk clear of personal items, the thought of displaying Charlie's photo hadn't crossed Rose's mind.

"The worst thing that could happen is that the major, or the lieutenant, will tell you to put it away."

Rose nodded. "Why did you join the SOE?"

"It's a rather long story," Muriel said, crossing her arms.

Rose patted her bed. "I've got six weeks, assuming I'm able to climb that bloody wall."

Muriel sat on Rose's bed. "Before the war, I was studying foreign languages at the University of London. During my third year of school, I met James, who was in some of my classes, and we began dating." Muriel placed a hand on her belly. "I got pregnant and dropped out of college."

Rose's eyes widened.

"Rather than return home to Edinburgh, I stayed in London and landed a job at the General Post Office. I thought James and I were going to have a life together. Marriage. Family. But he left me three months before Mabel was born."

"I'm so sorry." Rose stared at Muriel. "You're a mother?"

Muriel nodded. "Mabel lives with my parents, safely away from London. When the frequency of bombing raids declined, I considered bringing her back to live with me. But I was recruited for the SOE, likely due to my ability to speak both French and German." She ran her hands over her knees. "I was surprised that they wanted me, considering I can't shed my Scottish brogue. I'll need to change how I speak, or I'll have no chance of fooling a Nazi."

"Why did you—" Rose stopped, concerned that she was being intrusive.

"Leave my daughter to join the SOE?"

"Yes."

"I guess that I don't want Mabel to grow up in a Hitler-controlled world," Muriel said. "I've seen enough death and destruction in London to make me want to do everything I can to win this war."

"Do you have a picture of Mabel?" Rose asked.

"Aye." Muriel smiled, and then produced a small photograph from her purse and gave it to Rose.

"She's beautiful," Rose said, staring at a curly-haired toddler wearing a checkered dress.

"Mabel's a wee 'un."

"She's going to be tall."

"Soon to be a skinny malinky longlegs, like her mother," Muriel said.

Rose smiled, and then stepped to the dresser. "Mabel is far too lovely to keep in your purse. Would it be all right to put her next to Charlie?"

"Aye," Muriel said.

Rose tucked Mabel's picture into the corner of the frame. *Muriel is making an enormous sacrifice to join the SOE. I cannot begin to imagine the pain she must be going through, leaving her child for a quest to fight the Nazis.*

"If you want to develop a French accent," Rose said, "I'd be glad to help."

"That'd be lovely," Muriel said. "And I'll help you practice to get over that wee wall."

Rose nodded.

The sound of an approaching car engine grew. They rushed to the window. Outside, a vehicle slowed to a stop near the front door. Headlight beams illuminated the crushed-shell rotunda. Phyllis, wearing a coat and scarf, placed her suitcase into the trunk, and then got into the back seat.

"She's not coming back," Rose said, her heart sinking.

"I'm afraid not," Muriel said.

Had Phyllis left on her own accord, or had she been deemed unfit for service? But it didn't matter. Phyllis was gone, leaving Rose and Muriel as the last remaining women at Garramor House. As the vehicle drove away, determination surged through Rose's veins. *They can dismiss me if they want, but I'll never quit.*

CHAPTER 10

MORAR, SCOTLAND—JUNE 5, 1942

Rose had never touched, let alone fired, a weapon. But this changed when Major Maxwell, who served as chief weapons instructor, issued each of the candidates an M1911 semiautomatic .45 caliber pistol. The weapon held eight rounds—seven in a magazine and one in the firing chamber. Maxwell demonstrated how to fire the pistol, using his signature "double tap" method, which was two quick shots into the torso of a densely stuffed humanoid scarecrow. The candidates took turns, maneuvering through a weapons course on which they attempted to shoot moving targets, dummies that ran along wire between trees. At first, Rose was tentative. She worried that her pistol could discharge by accident, or that she'd badly miss a target and injure a candidate. But with each day of practice, Rose's marksmanship improved. She grew accustomed to, if not fond of, the scent of discharged gunpowder, and her hand no longer quivered when she aimed her pistol. Within a week, she was recording one of the best accuracy rates in the group.

"You still need to get over that bloody wall," Lieutenant Clarke muttered, writing on Rose's firing scorecard.

Rose's confidence waned. She'd spent what little free time she had, usually in the early hours of the morning before everyone was awake, practicing the assault course. Muriel, who disregarded

Rose's insistence that her roommate continue sleeping, joined Rose to provide encouragement. In near darkness, usually compounded by a thick fog that engulfed the west coast of Scotland, Rose struggled to scale the ten-foot wall. Twice Rose had come close, her fingers grazing the top, but still, she failed to successfully climb the obstacle. And with each defeat, her fear of being rejected by the SOE grew worse.

Muriel stepped to Rose, out of earshot of the lieutenant. "You're performing well. Don't listen to Clarke. Maxwell won't let him send you home for not climbing the wall."

Rose, her skin hot with determination, nodded and reloaded her pistol.

The most unusual aspect of weapons training, Rose believed, was that the candidates were required to practice their "double tap" before brushing their teeth. Rose supposed that Major Maxwell wanted the candidates to become comfortable with their weapons, as if they were merely household utensils. A dummy was placed in each of the washrooms. Mornings and evenings were filled with gunfire exploding from the loo. As Rose prepared to brush her teeth, she fired her weapon, blasting two holes into the dummy's belly. Strangely, the prebrushing ritual reminded Rose of her childhood, when she and Charlie had conspired to fake cleaning their teeth by simply waving their brushes under running water. *If Mum and Dad had permitted us to fire bullets into a mannequin, we would never have gotten a cavity.* She grinned, spreading paste onto her toothbrush. *I wish you could see me now, Charlie.*

Additionally, the SOE candidates performed demolitions and explosives training, conducted by Major Maxwell. Being short didn't thwart Rose; she excelled in mastering the use of plastic explosives. Rose, paired with Muriel and Felix, practiced blowing up a section of an abandoned railway line. They learned precisely where to place an explosive charge on a locomotive to render it disabled for months. The agents were taught how to sabotage vehicles, factory boilers, and telephone exchanges. For Rose, the use of explosives was empowering. Fueled by revenge, she yearned to wreak havoc on the Nazis. But to get to France, she first needed to pass her SOE training. *I just need to get over that damn wall.*

But climbing the wall became the least of Rose's worries when she embarked upon silent killing and unarmed combat training. To her dismay, this particular course was led by Lieutenant Clarke, who appeared eager to display his physical strength, as well as vent his aggression, by demonstrating on the candidates. The women were expected to undergo the same level of combat training as the men, which was of no surprise to either Rose or Muriel. Clarke demonstrated lethal techniques, including throat grabs, eye gouges, arm dislocations, stomps to the knee, and neck breaks. The combat training, according to Clarke, was designed to make it feasible for a person of average brawn and expertise to encounter and win against a well-trained opponent. However, Rose was far below average size and strength. Unlike Muriel, who was tall, strong, and athletic, Rose struggled with most, if not all, of the lethal maneuvers. And matters grew worse when Lieutenant Clarke singled out Rose, ordering her to perform a choke hold on him.

"Teasdale!" Clarke shouted, pulling away Rose's arm from his neck. "You're doing it wrong."

Rose, standing behind Clarke, nodded.

"Wedge your bloody elbow around my trachea!" Clarke pointed to an area on his neck, below the larynx. "Clasp your wrist and squeeze to cut off the air."

"Yes, sir." A knot formed in her stomach.

"Try again," Clarke said, turning his back to Rose.

SOE candidates stood by and watched the demonstration. Major Maxwell scribbled onto his clipboard.

Rose stared at the back of Clarke's thick neck. Her anxiety grew. Due to the lieutenant's height or, more precisely, Rose's petite size, she had to leap and wrap her arm around his neck.

"Bloody hell," Clarke grumbled.

The lieutenant grabbed her forearm. Instantly, her arm and body were pulled away, and he tossed her to the ground.

"Is that all the strength you've got?" Clarke asked.

"No," Rose lied, rubbing a twinge in her tailbone.

"Again," he said.

Rose stood, glancing at Muriel.

"You can do it," Muriel mouthed.

Rose sucked in air and leaped onto the lieutenant. Mustering all of her strength, she squeezed his throat.

Clarke twisted. He swung an elbow, striking Rose in the face.

Her head flailed backward. Pain shot through her cheek and nasal cavity, and she fell to her knees.

Clarke shook his head. "Your headlock is weak—it's a real cock-up."

Blood dripped from her nose. She swallowed, tasting copper. She fought back tears and stood.

"Lieutenant Clarke," Felix said, stepping forward. "Would it be okay if I took a turn?"

Major Maxwell scribbled onto his clipboard.

"You'll get your chance later." Clarke motioned with his hand to Rose. "Again."

You're twice my size. Despite knowing the outcome, Rose used every ounce of her power and grappled another choke hold on the lieutenant. She was careful to keep her head away from another strike, but she failed to anticipate Clarke's elbow jab to her stomach, dropping her to the ground. She gagged. Saliva, strewn with blood from her nose, dripped from her lips. Her diaphragm felt broken.

"Ready to quit, Teasdale?" Clarke asked.

Struggling to get to her hands and knees, she took in minuscule breaths until her lungs began to work. Rose locked her eyes on the lieutenant. "No," she wheezed.

Clarke's lips formed a thin smile.

"Lieutenant Clarke," Major Maxwell said, glancing at his wristwatch. "I think that's enough for today."

"Yes, sir." Clarke ran his hands over his tunic, smoothing over the wrinkles.

The candidates and the instructors left the training area and headed back to Garramor House. Rose, battered and downtrodden, lagged behind. Embarrassed by her performance, she preferred to walk alone but was joined by Muriel and Felix.

Rose glanced at Felix. "Thanks for trying to take my place."

Felix nodded. "Have you considered going home?"

"*Haud yer wheesht*," Muriel interrupted. She pulled a handkerchief from her pocket and handed it to Rose.

Rose wiped her bloodied nose and looked at Felix. "I'm never going home."

"Why not?" he asked.

"The Luftwaffe killed my family," she said, ire smothering her pain.

"I'm sorry," Felix said. "But you must realize that you'll face much worse if you go to France. The only reason you, and I, for that matter, are getting a chance to train for the SOE is because the young male agents are being captured, tortured, and killed. France is now a country of women and old men. The agents have become easily noticed by the Germans."

"That's why we'll have better odds of survival," Rose said.

"Perhaps," Felix said, running his hand through his salt-and-pepper hair. "But going home might just save your life."

"Then why don't you go home, Felix?" Muriel asked.

"France is my home." Felix paused, slipping his hands into his pockets. "You're not the only one around here who has suffered loss. The Wehrmacht didn't just requisition my family vineyard. They took my only son."

"Oh, no," Muriel said. "I'm sorry."

"*Merci*," Felix said. "Mathieu was an officer in the army. He was captured at the Maginot Line when the Germans invaded France. I intend to fight until the Allied forces reclaim our prisoners."

"And bring Mathieu home?" Rose asked.

Felix nodded.

They spoke little during the remainder of the walk. *We all have our reason to fight*, Rose thought. Reaching the house, Rose wiped dried blood from her nostrils. Her face ached, and her two lower incisors felt loose.

Felix examined Rose's nose. "It's not broken. But you'll have two black eyes in the morning."

"Lovely," Rose said. She turned to Muriel. "Thanks for the handkerchief. I'll give it a good washing before I return it."

"Keep it," Muriel said.

"I think I'll take a little walk before going inside," Rose said.

"Would you like some company?" Muriel asked.

Rose shook her head and left her companions.

She dreaded having to face the other candidates, as well as the instructors—most of all Lieutenant Clarke. She was in no physical shape to practice on the assault course, so she walked to the shoreline, the sand littered with remnants of discharged explosives. Cupping her hands, she splashed frigid sea water on her face, hoping to reduce the swelling to her nose and eyes. Under the rhythmic sound of lapping waves, she made a solemn vow: "I will never quit, no matter how much pain and suffering I endure."

Returning to Garramor House, she passed near an open window of the instructor's office, located in a rear wing of the house. She stopped when she heard voices.

"It takes more than brawn to become an agent," Major Maxwell said. "We need candidates who are cunning, tenacious, and don't look like spies."

"Sir," Clarke said. "With all due respect, I think we should send Teasdale home."

Rose's mouth went dry. She pressed her back against the house.

"She performed well with weapons and explosives training," Maxwell said. "We should give her more time, at least until she's undergone a mock interrogation."

"Teasdale's weak," Clarke said. "She wouldn't last a month in France."

Vexed, Rose inched her ear closer to the window.

"She'd never survive an encounter with the Germans," Clarke added.

Seconds passed. Rose hoped that Maxwell would deny his request.

"I'd like your written recommendation on my desk this evening," Maxwell said. "We'll meet with Teasdale first thing in the morning."

Rose's heart sank.

"Thank you, sir," Clarke said.

Rose, reeling with dejection, quietly stepped away. She went to her room, and then showered. She did her best to pretend that she had no knowledge that she'd be expelled in the morning.

Later, she joined everyone for dinner, including an evening glass of scotch in the library, which did little to numb her dismay. Afterward, she helped Muriel practice her French dialect, but said nothing of the instructors' decision to send her home. *No need for Muriel to worry. It'll all be over soon.* She settled into her bed and prayed that Muriel would avoid being captured by the Gestapo and that she would safely return home to be with her baby, Mabel.

Hours passed. Unable to sleep, Rose thought ahead. *I wish there was something I could do to change Major Maxwell's mind.* Long after the house turned silent, Rose slipped from her bed. She crept downstairs, remembering her promise to herself, determined to risk everything to change the course of events.

CHAPTER 11

MORAR, SCOTLAND—JUNE 6, 1942

Rose raised her pistol and fired two quick rounds into the dummy propped in the corner of the washroom. She slipped her weapon into her holster, and then proceeded to brush her teeth. *That'll be the last time I fire a pistol.*

"Nice shot," Muriel said, staring at the bullet holes in the dummy's abdomen. She fired her own weapon, landing shots into the stuffed head.

Rose forced a smile, and then rinsed her mouth with water. As gunfire erupted in the washrooms at Garramor House, Rose knew that the candidates would soon be dressed and downstairs. She wondered if she'd be sent home before or after breakfast. Regardless, she dressed in her combat fatigues—all the while hoping that her instructors would somehow change their minds—and then went to the dining room. First to arrive, she prepared a cup of tea. She sipped and waited. Minutes later, the sound of Clarke and Maxwell's voices echoed in the hallway.

They're coming. She gripped her cup. Hairs rose on the back of her neck. Her anxiety grew. She briskly walked through the doorway, attempting to leave the room, and bumped into Clarke. Rose dropped her tea cup, sending tea and shards of broken ceramic over the floor.

"Bloody hell!" Clarke barked. "Watch where you're going!"

"I'm sorry, sir," Rose said, bending down to pick up the shattered remnants of her cup.

"Leave it," Clarke said, wiping droplets from his uniform.

Rose froze.

"Miss Teasdale," Maxwell said, calmly. "We'd like to have a word with you."

Rose nodded, and then followed them to the major's office.

Major Maxwell sat behind his desk. Rose and Clarke took chairs across from the major.

"How is your face?" Maxwell asked, leaning forward on his desk.

"It's fine, sir." Rose rubbed her swollen nose. Under her eyes were dark-purple bruises, giving her the appearance of a racoon.

Maxwell nodded. "You're probably wondering why you're here."

"You're worried about my physical abilities," Rose said.

Clarke folded his arms. "We have concerns that you'll be killed, or that you'll put your fellow agents at risk of death or capture."

"Have you considered resigning?" the major asked.

"No." Rose's breath turned shallow.

"We believe it's best that you leave the SOE," Clarke said.

Rose clenched her hands, her nails digging into her palms. "May I have permission to speak openly, sir?"

"Yes," Maxwell said.

"I have one of the highest weapons firing scores in the class. I'm competent with explosives—good as any male candidate."

Clarke sighed.

Rose's pulse pounded. "My French is as good or better than any of the other candidates. I've finished all of our training exercises within the target time requirements. The areas where I need improvement are one obstacle on the assault course and—"

"The wall," Clarke interrupted.

"And unarmed combat," Rose finished.

"You're simply too small and weak to be an agent," Clarke said, firmly.

Rose, gathering her courage, gripped the arms of her chair. "Have you been to France, Lieutenant Clarke?"

"That has nothing to do with it," Clarke said.

"It has everything to do with it," she said.

Maxwell leaned back in his chair.

"I've been to Paris many times. I know the culture, streets, parks, cafés, as well as the train stations. And I have yet to encounter a ten-foot wall that needed climbing."

Clarke shook his head.

"Also, it would be unwise to confront a Nazi without having a weapon, especially if he were over a hundred pounds heavier and was well aware of my presence."

"Sir," Clarke said, looking at the major and pointing to a folder on the desk. "You have my recommendation."

"Miss Teasdale," Major Maxwell said. "I commend you for your commitment to serve Britain. But Clarke has trained many agents, and his judgment has proven to be accurate with selecting candidates for the SOE."

Were any of the candidates women? Rose wanted to ask, but held her tongue.

Maxwell paused, smoothing his mustache. "Unfortunately, we're going to have to ask you to leave."

Rose took a deep breath and exhaled, realizing that she was far beyond the point of no return. With nothing left to lose, she looked at Maxwell and asked, "Would you please read to me Lieutenant Clarke's report?"

Clarke, appearing thirsty to hear his words spoken by his superior, nodded to Maxwell.

"Very well." Maxwell opened the file on his desk and retrieved a typed piece of paper. "It is clear that Rose Teasdale is committed, keen, confident, and highly capable. She's the best shot in the group, and she's full of guts."

"Sir," Clarke interrupted, eyebrows lowered. "That's not my report."

"It has your name on it." Major Maxwell slid the paper to the edge of his desk.

Clarke leaned in. His eyes widened as he scanned the report.

Rose leaned forward and pointed. "I like the part where you say that I'm plucky and ideally fit for the job."

"Bloody hell," Clarke scoffed. "You broke into the office and stole my report! Not only will you be dismissed, but I'll make sure you are charged with burglary, as well as forging a confidential government document."

"Miss Teasdale," Maxwell said. "Did you break into the office and write this report?"

"Yes, sir," Rose said. A memory of crawling through the un-locked window filled her head. A flash of slowly pressing type-writer keys to avoid noise. "I also broke into Lieutenant Clarke's room while he was sleeping."

Clarke's face turned red. "You did no such thing!"

"You're quite a heavy sleeper," Rose said, struggling not to show fear in her voice. "Check your pocket."

Clarke dug through his pockets, and then removed a small note from his tunic.

> *If I had been a Nazi, you'd be dead.*

"This is an outrage!" Clarke handed the note to Maxwell.

Maxwell read the message, glanced to both Rose and Clarke, and then placed it facedown on his desk, next to the phony report. "Leave us, Miss Teasdale."

Rose left the office and closed the door behind her. Avoiding the dining room, where the candidates were eating breakfast, she stealthily climbed the stairs. *I didn't think about being charged with burglary or forging government documents! Good Lord, what have I done!*

Through the bedroom window, she saw a parked black sedan. Seated behind the wheel was the same driver that had brought her to Garramor House. She shuddered. An overwhelming sense of defeat flowed through her veins. As she removed civilian cloth-ing from her suitcase, she recalled climbing through the unlocked window to Major Maxwell's office. *Let them think that I was smart enough to pick the lock.* She'd lied when she'd claimed to have bro-ken into Lieutenant Clarke's room while he was sleeping. She simply slipped the note into the man's pocket when she intention-ally bumped into him. The spilled tea and shattered cup served only as a distraction. And considering the lieutenant had nearly fractured her nose, as well as given her two blackened eyes, she had no intention of telling him the truth.

A knock on the door. Rose turned.

Major Maxwell entered.

Rose swallowed. *Will I be arrested?*

"Teasdale," he said, stepping to her. "What you did was a crime."

A wave of trepidation surged through her chest. She lowered her eyes.

"But it's precisely the type of skills that are needed for a brilliant SOE agent."

Rose straightened her back and stared at him. "Sir?"

"Our young men are too conspicuous. They're being caught, tortured, and executed by the enemy. We need women, who I believe will make brilliant agents."

"What about Lieutenant Clarke?"

"He's furious," Maxwell said. "But we've spoken. He's not completely convinced you'll pass your training, but he's agreed that you should carry on with the rest of the candidates."

She exhaled. Tension faded from her shoulders.

"It won't be easy, Teasdale. It's going to get a lot harder for you."

"I can do it, sir," she said.

"Clarke is going to make it even more difficult for you."

"I'll handle it," she said.

"Successfully finish your physical training, and I'll send you on to parachute and classroom training."

"Yes, sir."

"Get some breakfast," Maxwell said. "You'll need your strength if you expect to climb Clarke's wall."

"Yes, sir," Rose said, her confidence surging.

Maxwell turned and left the room.

She shoved her suitcase under her bed. Making her way to the dining room, she prepared for the wrath that Clarke would bestow upon her. *I'll endure anything you make me do. And I'll find a way to climb your damn wall.*

CHAPTER 12

PARIS, FRANCE—JULY 16, 1942

Lazare, joined by Claudius, entered the secret chamber deep inside in the catacomb. The room, dimly lit by an oil lamp, smelled faintly of charred wood and tinned meat. Four members of the French Resistance rose from their spots on the limestone floor and greeted them.

"How did it go?" a bespectacled man asked, adjusting a red bandana around his neck.

"Good," Claudius said. "Thanks to Lazare, the Germans will have difficulty making phone calls to the fifteenth arrondissement."

The men grinned.

An hour earlier, Lazare and Claudius had sabotaged a small telephone exchange near Montparnasse. Claudius served as a lookout, peeping through a window to monitor a lone Wehrmacht guard, who was taking a break to relieve himself in a washroom. Lazare, wearing a bandana to conceal his face, had pried open the rear door of the building by using a small crowbar and slipped into the switchboard room, where two women were working the late shift. Lazare, his adrenaline surging, concealed his maimed hand inside his coat pocket and instructed the switchboard operators to quietly leave and to stay clear of the building. Once the operators had left, he packed plastic explosive to the switchboard, lit a fuse, and fled. Moments later, a concussive blast quaked the building. The guard, struggling to pull up his trousers while carrying his rifle, had sprung from the toilet, only to find the telephone exchange deserted and black smoke billowing from a demolished switchboard.

Claudius removed his beret, exposing his bald head, and looked at Lazare. "You're quite a saboteur."

Lazare smiled, but apprehension churned in his gut. The Montparnasse telephone exchange had been relatively small compared to more expansive communication centers that were controlled by the Germans. This particular act of vandalism posed little risk to innocent life, considering the operators had followed his requests. Deep down, he worried that there would come a day when his actions would result in the death of innocent people, like the old man who'd merely stopped to view his homemade propaganda.

"Perhaps we should have Lazare blow up the SD headquarters," the bespectacled man jested to his comrades.

The men laughed.

The Sicherheitsdienst (SD), the counterintelligence branch of the SS, was located on Avenue Foch. It was a palatial residential boulevard in the sixteenth arrondissement. Lazare was infuriated that the Nazis had chosen to billet a building near the Arc de Triomphe, a monument which honored those who fought and died for France in the French Revolutionary and Napoleonic Wars. Also, the Arc de Triomphe happened to be his favorite—and last remaining—painting by Maman, which made the location of SD headquarters a personal matter for Lazare. Without hesitation, he looked at the bearded man and said, "I'll do it."

Laughter faded.

"I was joking," the man said.

"I wasn't." Lazare adjusted a strap on his prosthetic hand, Maman's paint beginning to fade from the thumb.

"No need for a suicide mission," Claudius intervened. He glanced at his watch. "It's 4:00 a.m. We'll get some rest, and then leave for a safe house when curfew is over."

Lazare nodded. He buried thoughts of sabotage and wondered which safe house they would be staying in. They were constantly on the move. When they weren't hiding in the catacombs, people—whom Claudius trusted—smuggled members of the Resistance into their basements and attics, and provided them with occasional meals. When outside of the city, they typically stayed in barns and root cellars, their backs resting on straw and dirty blankets. Claudius, a superstitious man who went to great lengths to never follow a routine, often flipped a coin to randomly select their destinations. *A predictable schedule will get you killed,* Lazare thought.

Lazare no longer stayed at home; the risk to Maman and Papa was too great. He did, however, visit once a week to bring them food, usually British military rations or vegetables from the countryside, which he obtained through his growing network of Resistance fighters. He longed for the day when he and his parents would be liberated from Jewish persecution. To be free to sit in a café. Free to ride a bicycle. Free to own a telephone. Free to walk the streets of Paris without the fear of being arrested or shot. Free to wear unadorned clothing—absent a yellow star. And to live in a city that was no longer stained with anti-Semitic signs, some of which depicted an old bearded Jew with distorted facial features clutching a globe as if he were aspiring to obtain world supremacy. Most of all, he longed for a joyful life, like his parents had prior to German occupation. *Someday, I'll meet someone, fall in love, and raise a family, just like Maman and Papa.*

Rather than join the men resting on the limestone floor, Lazare stepped to a metal British parachute container that was stored in the corner of the chamber. With his adrenaline still high from sabotaging the telephone exchange, he chose to expel his energy by conducting inventory of their remaining supplies. Inside the container were two grenades, three boxes of ammunition, several food tins, and two bars of chocolate. *We're out of plastic explosives.* The remaining armament would be barely enough for a few acts of vandalism. And without plastic explosives, Lazare's role as a saboteur would become far more difficult. Fortunately, Claudius worked in collaboration with a British SOE agent called Prosper, who organized a network in Paris called Physician, and more supplies were to be parachute dropped into a secluded location in two weeks.

As he closed the container, footsteps grew in the catacomb passageway. Weapons were retrieved. Within seconds, a flashlight beam sprayed over the doorway. Lazare, his pulse rate rising, pulled a pistol from his pocket.

"It's Raphael," a boy's voice called.

Lazare exhaled, and then motioned for the men to lower their weapons. Raphael, whom Lazare believed to be no more than twelve or thirteen years of age, given his size and the adolescent cracking of his voice, was a recent addition to the group. Claudius, who had a knack for recruiting loyal Resistance fighters, discovered Raphael scavenging for food in an alley behind a café that catered to Wehrmacht soldiers. Lazare had insisted that the boy was far too young to fight. Although he didn't agree, Claudius limited Raphael's role by having him serve as a scout, providing information on the movements of the Germans and police. But it was only a matter of time before the boy was carrying a weapon or, even worse, plastic explosives. *A boy should be going to school and playing with friends.* The Nazis had not only forced Raphael to prematurely become a man, they'd stolen his childhood.

"The police!" the boy shouted, running into the chamber. He struggled to catch his breath. "They're rounding up Jews!"

Lazare's skin turned cold. "Where?"

"Everywhere!" The boy, his hair wet with sweat, took in gulps of air.

Lazare looked at Claudius. "I need to go."

"No," Claudius said, blocking the stone passageway.

"I must warn my parents," Lazare said.

Claudius shook his head. "I can't risk having you captured and breaking our cover."

Lazare looked into the man's eyes. "I'm leaving."

Claudius glanced at the men.

The men raised their weapons. The click of a magazine shoved into a pistol pierced the air.

Lazare swallowed. "Either step aside or order them to shoot me."

"Damn you, Lazare." Claudius ran his hand over his bald head, and then motioned him to leave.

Lazare, without the aid of a flashlight, maneuvered through the catacomb maze. Conditioned from months of practice, he was able to navigate the underground arteries by counting his footsteps and running a hand along the stone wall to locate intersections. But in his urgency to warn his parents, his quickened pace caused him to miss a juncture. Realizing his mistake, he backtracked—losing precious time—and found the intersection in the tunnel.

Exiting the catacomb through a hidden passage in a sewer drain, he emerged from the subterranean labyrinth. The sky was dark, except for a faint glow in the east. It was before 5:00 a.m., the end of curfew, which meant he'd be arrested if he were found on the street, regardless of the fake papers that were stashed in his pocket. But he didn't care. Committed to warning his parents, he ducked into an alley, and then maneuvered through a series of side streets toward home.

With curfew, there should have been no one on the streets, except for periodic German-enforced patrols. But it was clear to Lazare that something had drastically changed, given the rumble of vehicles. And it was the distinct whirl of bus engines that caused hairs to rise on the back of his neck.

Nearing an intersection, he approached an apartment building and froze. A bus and two police cars were parked on the street. Random windows of the building glowed, giving it a chessboard appearance. Cries erupted from several apartments. Seconds later, French police officers with flat-top brimmed hats escorted a family—a man, woman, and two teenage girls, all wearing coats with sewn yellow stars—onto the bus. Wails grew from inside the building.

No! Lazare pressed his back to the wall, staying out of sight of the police. He glanced up and noticed people peeking from behind closed curtains. Seconds later, more than a dozen people carrying only coats and blankets were loaded into the bus. From his hiding spot, he helplessly watched a police officer, pointing a baton, force a woman with a baby to climb into the bus. *How can you do this?* But deep down, he knew the answer.

He retreated into the alley and then took another street toward home, only to witness more buses—packed with people—traveling toward the Eiffel Tower. *Where are they taking them?* To avoid detection, he took a longer route, avoiding residential areas, to get to his parents' apartment building on Rue Cler. The street was bare. No buses. No police. *Please, let them be inside,* he prayed.

Rather than use the entrance, he climbed the fire escape to reach his bedroom window, which his mother left unlocked for his unannounced visits. He eased open the window and stepped inside. The bed was neatly made, the pillow fluffed and propped against the headboard. Everything appeared normal. He exhaled, the tension drifting from his shoulder muscles. *I'll wake them. We'll leave before they arrive.*

Opening his bedroom door, he froze. Pieces of clothing—Maman's sweater and two of Papa's shirts—were strewn over the hallway. The kitchen cabinets and drawers were in disarray. Panic pierced his chest.

"*Non!*"

A rustle came from his parents' room.

He stepped forward and flung open the door.

A woman rummaging through his mother's wardrobe turned and shrieked.

Lazare flinched.

"Keep . . . keep away!" The woman, her eyes wide, dropped a navy dress, which Maman had worn on special occasions, including Lazare's college graduation. Around the woman's neck was a gold pendant given to Magda by Gervais as an anniversary gift.

"I won't hurt you," Lazare said, recognizing the woman. She was a widow named Victorine, who lived on the floor above them. His mother, years earlier, had cared for her during a horrid bout of influenza. "It's me, Lazare."

The woman took in shallow breaths. She ran a hand over her untamed, oily hair.

"Where are they?" he asked, his chest filled with dread.

"The police took them."

"*Oh, mon Dieu,*" he breathed. His body and mind felt gutted.

The woman glanced around the room, as if she were looking for an escape route or searching for something to defend herself.

Lazare blinked away tears. "Where did they take them?"

"Away," she said, her voice cold.

His stomach turned nauseous. Fighting an impulse to gag, he pressed his head to the doorframe.

The woman, her arms trembling, abruptly turned. She fumbled with a latch, and then threw open a window. "Police!"

Fear surged through Lazare. "Please, don't—"

"*Juif!*" the woman screamed.

Lazare shuddered. "Victorine!" he pleaded, hoping the use of her name would stifle her cries.

"*Juif!*"

Footsteps radiated from the floor above them.

He reached into his boot and produced a knife.

"*Non!*" she screamed, eyes locking on the blade. She turned and poked her head out of the window. "Help!"

Reeling with shock, he staggered into the hallway. The painting of the Arc de Triomphe, although cockeyed, still hung on the wall. He sank the blade into the corner of the frame.

"*Juif!*"

Please be gone. He made a long cut, following the edge of the frame. He hoped that the woman was mistaken, and that his parents had fled before the police arrived. But reaching the base of the frame, he found the fake identification papers that he'd made for his parents, untouched from where he'd left them months ago. Heartache ravaged his body.

"Police!" The woman slammed the bedroom door shut and bolted the lock. Furniture scraped over the wood floor.

She's moving the bed to barricade herself inside. Lazare, his eyes filled with tears, slipped the papers into his jacket.

"Up here!" the woman shouted to someone on the street.

Lazare rolled up the painting, and then placed it under his arm.

Heavy footsteps. The front door slammed open.

Lazare darted to his bedroom. He climbed onto the fire escape as two police officers sprang into the apartment. He descended the iron ladder, skipping rungs, and dropped onto the street. A sharp pang shot through his left foot. He struggled to run, his ankle ligaments burning with each stride. He buried his pain and sorrow as he desperately searched for a place to hide, all the while praying he'd find a way to free his parents before it was too late.

CHAPTER 13

VÉL' D'HIV ROUNDUP—JULY 16 AND 17, 1942

Devastated, Lazare retreated to the sanctuary of the catacombs. He found Claudius alone, refilling a lantern with oil.

"The police took them." Lazare's chest ached, as if his torso were being compressed in a vise. He placed the painting, rolled like a poster, and his parents' fake papers in a dry corner of the chamber.

"I'm sorry." Claudius removed his beret and held it to his chest.

"They're rounding up hundreds, possibly thousands, of Jews," Lazare said. "I witnessed a woman, holding the hands of her two children, leap from a third-floor window, attempting to escape the police." Images of their broken bodies, splayed on the sidewalk, filled his head. His hands trembled.

"Mon Dieu," Claudius whispered.

"There were buses, filled with Jews, headed toward the Eiffel Tower."

"They're likely being taken to the Vélodrome d'Hiver," Claudius said. "The police used it last year to contain arrested Jews."

The Vélodrome d'Hiver was an indoor cycle track. Growing up, Lazare had attended cycling events, as well as an occasional circus, at the velodrome with his parents. Years earlier, it held sporting events at the 1924 Olympics. And if Claudius was right, the civic center, where Lazare once cheered alongside his parents and thousands of Parisians, had been transformed into an internment camp.

"Where are the men?" Lazare asked.

"I sent them to a safe house, outside of the city."

"We must bring them back."

Claudius shook his head. "There's nothing you—or any of us—can do."

"We must try!"

Claudius rubbed his thick eyebrows. "The men are committed to fighting with you, Lazare. But I doubt that *all of them* would risk their lives for Jews."

Claudius's words stung Lazare. An acid bile rose in his esophagus. From his time working for Claudius, Lazare had learned that there were numerous Jews fighting for the Resistance networks across France. He would not hesitate to risk his life for any one of his compatriots. And it saddened him to think, although deep down he suspected this all along, that not everyone in the Resistance would do the same for him, simply because he was a Jew.

"Lazare," Claudius said, the timbre of his voice like a father, "the velodrome will be heavily guarded by the police. I can't risk men on a futile mission."

"Then I'll go myself." Lazare turned and rummaged through the British parachute container. Dispirited by the fact that they'd used the last of the plastic explosives, he resorted to stuffing a grenade and an ammunition clip into his jacket.

"What do you expect to accomplish?" Claudius approached Lazare and placed a hand on his shoulder. "Do you want to die? Is that what your parents would want you to do?"

"I have to try." Lazare met Claudius's gaze. "Could you talk to your British SOE contact, Prosper? Maybe agents of the Physician network could help. Or perhaps they could accelerate the date for the RAF to deliver explosives."

Claudius sighed.

"Please," Lazare pleaded.

"I can't make any promises," Claudius said. "But I'll see what they can do. In the meantime, stay underground. Don't venture outside. I'll be back by this evening." He placed his beret on his head and left the chamber.

Lazare listened to Claudius's footsteps fade from the catacomb. He waited for twenty minutes, his anxiety intensifying with each breath of stagnant air. Unable to remain idle, he added another grenade into his jacket, and then slogged his way out of the underground cemetery.

The streets were busier than normal, given the parade of buses headed in the direction of the Eiffel Tower. Non-Jews, who did not fear being arrested, ventured outside of their homes to view what was taking place.

"It was the Germans who ordered the police to round them up," Lazare overheard a woman say as he passed a bread line. A knot tightened in his abdomen. He wished there were something he could do to wake up from this nightmare. *This can't be happening!* He gripped the grenades, hidden inside his pockets, knowing that if he was stopped by the Wehrmacht or police, he'd have no choice but to pull the pins. And it would be over.

Lazare learned that Claudius was right when he neared the corner of Boulevard de Grenelle and Rue Nélaton. The area near the Vélodrome d'Hiver was congested with bystanders blocking the sidewalks. Ten buses, filled to capacity with people standing in the aisles, were lined up near the entrance to the velodrome. Scores of people, including children, with yellow stars emblazoned on their clothing were led inside by baton-wielding police officers. More buses rounded the corner and screeched to a stop. *There must be thousands of people in there.* He blinked back tears.

Lazare pushed his way through the crowd. Beads of sweat formed on his forehead. It was far too hot to be wearing a jacket, and he hoped that being overly dressed would not attract attention. He stared at the velodrome's glass roof, which had been painted dark-blue to avoid bombing raids. All of the windows had been screwed shut. *It must be excruciatingly hot for them! It's inhumane!* He maneuvered deeper into the crowd, hoping to get a better look.

For the next few hours, Lazare traveled around the block, trying to look as inconspicuous as possible. He wore his cap low, covering his brows. His hands were tucked inside his jacket pockets to hide his prosthetic, as well as conceal his small arsenal. He hoped that no one would recognize him, and that he wouldn't be stopped by either a German soldier or French policeman. Fortunately for Lazare, the police were preoccupied with the people that they'd arrested. And many of the Wehrmacht patrols stayed clear of the area, allowing their French accomplices to round up their own people. *The world has gone mad!*

By late afternoon, it became evident to Lazare, given the number of police and the manner in which they secured the building, that there was nothing he could do. Tossing a grenade would kill innocent people, or police officers who were forced to comply with German orders. He felt powerless. A deep-seated guilt filled his heart. *I should have done more. If only I could have persuaded them to leave, they'd be in* zone libre, *or safely out of France.*

A hand grabbed Lazare's shoulder. He flinched, causing a finger to tug the pin of a grenade.

"I told you to stay put," Claudius said. He pulled Lazare into a doorway, out of earshot of pedestrians.

Lazare, his pulse spiked, palmed the grenade in his pocket. He found the pin intact and exhaled.

"The Physician network is unable to help," Claudius said, lowering his voice.

Lazare's heart sank.

"But I know someone who can get inside the velodrome."

"Who?"

"Later." Claudius scanned the area. "Follow me, but keep a safe distance."

Lazare took one last look at the velodrome, hoping that his parents had escaped. As they traveled through the crowd and out of the fifteenth arrondissement, Lazare, despite his desperation to learn of the person who could help, followed a full block behind Claudius. The route, Lazare believed, was not leading to one of their safe houses. Crossing the River Seine, they traveled for nearly forty minutes to reach their destination, a small apartment complex near a hospital in the second arrondissement. The sun was beginning to set. He followed Claudius inside the building, and he found him on the third-floor landing. Before Lazare could speak, Claudius knocked on an apartment door.

Footsteps. The door opened, revealing a middle-aged woman wearing a nurse uniform.

"Quickly," she whispered.

Lazare and Claudius stepped inside.

The woman shut the door and bolted the lock. She stepped to a turntable, flipped a switch, and lowered a stylus to a record, sending the sound of a piano concerto through the room. "The music will cover our voices," she said, gesturing for them to take a seat at a table.

"Marcelline is my sister," Claudius said.

Lazare shook the woman's hand, realizing that Claudius was placing his family at risk to help him.

"A few doctors and nurses are permitted to enter the velodrome," Marcelline said. "I am one of the nurses."

"Can you find my parents?"

"I'll try," she said. "But there are thousands, and more coming in by the hour. It will be difficult to find them."

"Thank you," Lazare said. He ran a finger over a scratch in the table. "Tell me what is happening in there."

The color drained from Marcelline's face. She hesitated, shifting in her seat.

"Please," Lazare said. "I need to know."

Marcelline looked at her brother.

Claudius nodded.

"There are no lavatories," Marcelline said. "They were sealed because they had windows that could potentially offer a way out."

A lump formed in the back of Lazare's throat.

"The velodrome is covered with urine and feces," she said bluntly.

Oh, God. Lazare's shoulders slumped.

Claudius took out a cigarette. Striking a match, his quivering hand struggled to light the tip.

"The temperature is unbearable. Many suffer from heat exhaustion, and there is only one working water tap."

Lazare lowered his head. "How can they do this?"

"The police are acting on the orders of the Germans."

"Bastards." Claudius exhaled smoke.

"Is there a way to escape?" Lazare asked.

Marcelline shook her head. "All the exits and windows are sealed or guarded. People who attempt to escape are immediately shot." She grabbed Claudius's cigarette and placed it between her lips. She took a drag and exhaled smoke through her nose. "Some of them have taken their own lives."

The ache in Lazare's chest grew. "What are they going to do with them?"

Marcelline handed the cigarette to Claudius. "There are rumors that they are being sent to Germany to work. But I do not believe them."

"Why?" Claudius asked.

"A nurse saw several people in wheelchairs. There are many who are too old or too young to work. I believe that the German plans for these Jews are something much worse."

"There must be something we can do," Lazare said.

"I'm sorry," Marcelline said. "I'll do my best to find them."

A foreboding grew inside him. "Their names are Gervais and Magda. Last name is Aron."

She nodded, and then wiped her eyes.

Lazare described his parents. "Tell them that I love them," he said, his heart aching.

"I will," she said.

"And that I'm working to get them out."

She nodded.

"We must leave," Claudius said, tapping out his cigarette in a clay ashtray. "With police raids still underway, it's best that we are not outside during curfew."

Lazare thanked Marcelline for her help, and then left with Claudius. Separately, they returned to the catacombs. Unable to eat or sleep, Lazare remained awake, the tomb void of light.

Above their subterranean refuge, buses filled with more arrested Jews rumbled over Paris. He prayed that he'd discover a way to free Maman and Papa. But by morning, nothing came.

The roundup lasted two days. There were rumors that over ten thousand Jews, including their children, had been apprehended by the French police. Given the convoy of buses Lazare had witnessed at the velodrome, he had no doubt that the rumors were true, or perhaps underestimated.

He spent his time canvassing the area around the Vélodrome d'Hiver. He searched for a way to break inside, but as the population of Jews swelled inside the velodrome, so did the presence of police and Wehrmacht soldiers, making it impossible to get near the building. His heart and mind were tormented by the thought that thousands of people were suffering from unbearable heat and lack of food or water. Lazare prayed that his parents had somehow escaped, or avoided the police and fled Paris. Returning to the catacomb, he found Claudius waiting for him.

"Marcelline asked me to deliver this to you," Claudius said, giving him a folded piece of paper.

Lazare unfolded the message, revealing his father's handwriting. His mouth turned dry.

> *My dear son,*
> *Maman and I pray that this letter finds you well. We are safe and doing our best to find a way out of here, but conditions are getting worse. We've been told that we'll soon be transported to Germany.*

Lazare squeezed the paper. He sniffed, fighting back tears, and continued reading.

> *I'm sorry that I did not listen to you. You were right when you predicted that the Nazi anti-Semitic plague would spread to our beloved France. We should have left Paris months ago. It was foolish of me to believe that our government, as well as our police, would not give in to Hitler's quest to persecute Jews. If I had*

listened to you, Maman and I would not be here. None of this is your fault. My stubbornness, and my stubbornness alone, caused Maman and I to remain in Paris.

Lazare wiped tears from his eyes.

You were correct in refusing to wait for a potential Allied liberation of France. I implore you to fight, my son. Fight for France. Fight hostility toward Jews. Fight to never allow criminal acts against humanity to ever occur again.
We are proud of you, my son. Always know that we love you.
Papa and Maman

Lazare fell to his knees and wept, his sobs echoing through the limestone chamber.

PART 2

LA MISSION

CHAPTER 14

RAF TEMPSFORD, BEDFORDSHIRE, ENGLAND—MAY 20, 1943

Rose, her nerves surging like electrified wire, followed Muriel and Felix into a makeshift airplane hangar. The structure, which had once been a barn near a runway at RAF Tempsford, contained a staging area for SOE agents. Instead of planes and mechanics, the hangar contained tables filled with supplies—wireless transmitters, clothing, provisions, weapons—giving it the appearance of an elaborate quartermaster's office. After months of training, followed by months of living in a holding flat waiting for when, or if, they would be deployed, they were about to receive their final briefing before being dropped into German-occupied France.

"We're actually going," Rose whispered.

"Aye," Muriel said.

Felix smiled, exposing teeth stained by iodine drops.

You look much older, Rose thought. She was still getting accustomed to Felix's disguise to age his appearance. He now had a freshly grown mustache, which matched his hair—bleached to a dingy white—and round-rimmed glasses. *The Nazis, as well as the French, will never recognize the former Grand Prix race car driver from Saintes, France.* Fortunately, Rose and Muriel, having lived their lives in Britain, had no need for such drastic alterations to their appearance, except for Parisian-style haircuts and having their British dental fillings removed and replaced with gold, as was often used by French dentists.

During physical training, Rose never climbed Lieutenant Clarke's *bloody wall*. In fact, she barely passed the combat module of her training, given the limitations of her bantam size and strength. But she'd excelled at weapons and explosive training, as well as raid tactics, silent killing, and elementary Morse. And her French fluency was better than any other candidate, with the exception of Felix, who'd lived his entire life in France. She'd impressed Major Maxwell, Rose believed, by her pluckiness to break into the instructor's office and change Clarke's report. After Rose's six arduous weeks at Garramor House, Major Maxwell granted her permission to proceed with her SOE candidacy, and to move on to parachute school. Clarke agreed. Either the lieutenant feared further embarrassment from Rose's ability to break into his sleeping quarters, Rose thought, or his respect for her mettle had grown. Either way, she didn't care. She was carrying on with her quest to become an SOE agent, and that's all that mattered.

Parachute school at RAF Ringway in Manchester had lasted a week. When she'd arrived at RAF Ringway, the first thing Rose noticed was that she and Muriel were the only women, with the exception of ladies from the Women's Auxiliary Air Force (WAAF), who were packing the parachutes. "If it doesn't open, you can bring it back for a replacement," the women had jested as they passed out parachutes to the candidates. Rose would have found the joke funny, she believed, if she didn't have a fear of heights, which she had downplayed during her recruiting interviews.

Although the parachute course was much shorter than the physical training in Morar, she found the school to be equally intense, but far more dangerous. Initially, they trained by jumping out of a large, modified hydrogen-filled barrage balloon, which had an attached cage with a hole in the bottom. Rose's anxiety had escalated as the balloon gradually ascended into the atmosphere. Her heart pounded when she was given the order to jump, and she plummeted from the hole, all the while praying that her parachute would open. She expected that jumping out of airplanes would be far less taxing on her nerves, but that was not the case.

The airplanes had to avoid German radar detection, so the candidates had to jump from elevations of between five hundred and six hundred feet, which would provide them with less than fifteen seconds before they hit the ground. Despite her acrophobia, Rose passed her parachute training, grateful that she didn't have to take up the ladies of the WAAF on their guarantee to replace a defective parachute.

Following parachute school, they attended several weeks of finishing school, located on the estate of Lord Montagu at Beaulieu in the New Forest. The palatial manor reminded Rose of a Cistercian abbey, given the ancient arched-stone architecture. To Rose, the instructors were more like university professors than hardened military officers, considering much of the training was completed in classrooms. They learned how to recognize all ranks of the German services, how to use codes and invisible ink, how the BBC sent personal messages during the French news, and how to escape from handcuffs. Additionally, they gained expertise with personal security, burglary and picking of locks, field communication, and maintaining a cover story and proper behavior while under police surveillance. They'd gone through rounds of mock interrogations with the instructors dressed as members of the German Gestapo. The most important thing for an agent, she learned, was to successfully lead a clandestine life. But if one was caught by the enemy, they were trained to lie and stall, buying as much time as possible to protect their fellow agents and the SOE network. Although a mock interrogation was realistic, it didn't include physical torture, which would no doubt be the case if she were captured by the Nazis. She finished her training at Beaulieu, hoping that the skills she'd acquired would keep her alive. *I will not be captured*, Rose had often reassured herself. *But if I am caught, I'll never talk. I'd never sacrifice another agent.*

"Place all of your personal belongings on the table," a military officer said, pointing. "They'll be returned to you when you come home."

Rose placed her suitcase on the table. Before stepping away, she opened the case and took one last look at her photograph. *Goodbye, Charlie. I'll do my best to make you, Mum, and Dad proud.* Closing her suitcase, she turned to Muriel, who was holding the picture of her baby, Mabel. She felt horrible for Muriel, who'd been informed by SOE authorities that the enemy could potentially identify the photography paper as British. But it didn't matter. The SOE was strict on their protocol; no personal items were permitted to go with them.

"You'll see her again," Rose said, placing a hand on Muriel's shoulder.

Muriel nodded. "Goodbye for now, sweet lamb," she whispered, placing her baby's photograph on the table.

Rose and Muriel stepped away from the table, leaving any evidence of their former lives behind. The military officer examined their clothing, making sure that there were no traces of British tags or markings. SOE tailors used smuggled fabric from France, as well as repurposed clothing from secondhand shops. The clothing that was required to be fabricated was carefully modified to include French clothier tags. Buttons, a few of which contained a hidden compass, were stamped with *Élégant* or *Mode de Paris*. British zippers, which were all branded with the name Lightning on the metal pull, were carefully ground off with a dentist's drill. The SOE, Rose believed, had gone to meticulous lengths to ensure that their clothing would appear to be authentically French.

The officer handed each of them a small stack of papers. "These are identification papers, travel papers, ration cards, and French currency."

My new identity. Rose stared at her papers, realizing she was no longer Rose Teasdale, an orphaned typist who worked in Churchill's Cabinet War Rooms.

"Now," the officer said. "Let's go over your cover story one last time, shall we?"

"My code name is Conjurer," Felix said in French. "My field name is Jules Laberge. I'm a mechanic, working at the Granet Garage in Paris."

"Good," the officer said. He looked at Muriel.

"Code name, Sporran," Muriel said. "My field name is Marie Caton, and I'm a seamstress, working from my apartment."

The officer nodded, and then turned to Rose.

"My code name is Dragonfly," Rose said, the hairs sticking up on the back of her neck. "Field name, Aline Bonnet. I'm a traveling cosmetics saleswoman."

"Splendid," the officer said, seeming satisfied.

Rose, Muriel, and Felix had been assigned their SOE roles during the final phase of their training. Rose, given her mediocre—at best—performance in combat training, had expected that she'd be assigned to be a wireless operator. But due to her French fluency, familiarity with Paris, and unthreatening demeanor, her instructors had believed that she would be well suited to perform the role of a courier, delivering communications between the French Resistance and British agent networks.

Muriel, who excelled in her code training, was assigned the role of a wireless operator. With Rose's nightly tutoring, Muriel had improved her French dialect, to the point where her Scottish brogue was unnoticeable, except under the duress of a mock interrogation. And Felix, whom the SOE directors viewed as a confident and capable leader—although at times, his former race driver tendencies caused him to act decisively and sometimes take high risks—was selected as the leader of their network. Together, Rose, Muriel, and Felix formed the SOE F Section network called Conjurer, same as Felix's code name. They were to be a subcircuit of the Physician network—organized by an agent under the code name Prosper—which was already operating in Paris.

The officer gave them a dropping map, and then assisted them with sorting their belongings, supplies, and equipment, most of which would be dropped from parachute canisters. "And one last thing," he said, sounding a bit remorseful. He opened a desk drawer. "Your pills."

A knot formed in Rose's belly.

"When needed, the Benzedrine will keep you awake," he said. "The sulfa pills are for infection." He gave them small medicinal bottles, and then cleared his throat. "And this is your L-pill," he said, holding out his hand.

Lethal pill. Rose stared at the rubber-covered tablet.

"Bite down on it," the officer said, "and death will occur in under fifteen seconds."

Rose swallowed.

The officer inserted the pill into the chamber of a fountain pen, screwed on the casing, and then handed the pen to Felix. He then produced two shiny brass tubes from his desk. "Your suicide pill is hidden in the bottom of the lipstick."

Rose, fighting the urge to shudder, took the lipstick.

They slipped jumpsuits over their French clothing, put on their parachute harnesses, and then stepped outside to a moonless sky. Accompanied by the officer, they crossed the runway to an Armstrong Whitworth Whitley, a twin-engine night bomber.

"Prosper has arranged for members of the French Resistance to be your reception committee," the officer said. "They'll meet you when you land, and they'll smuggle you into Paris."

"Got it," Felix said, appearing eager to begin the mission.

"Good luck." The officer shook their hands.

Rose climbed into the airplane and took a seat on the floor of the fuselage, between Muriel and Felix. A disgusting chemical scent filled the air, which appeared to be coming from lacquer that covered the interior of the Whitley. The cramped, windowless fuselage of the bomber gave it the appearance of a flying coffin.

As soldiers loaded their supplies into the bay of the bomber, Rose looked to the cockpit, where a pilot and copilot—members of the Royal Air Force Special Duties Service—were reviewing their flight plans. She fidgeted with a pocket on her flight suit.

"We're in good hands," Felix said, nudging Rose. "The pilot will get us safely to France."

Rose nodded, but it wasn't the flight she was worried about, even though she dreaded heights. It was jumping out of the plane or, more precisely, the fear that her parachute wouldn't properly deploy.

During parachute school, a paratrooper trainee, who was not an SOE candidate, fell to his death when the silk canopy of his parachute failed to open. Instructors referred to this as a "Roman Candle," and they assured the candidates that this was quite a rare occurrence. But it didn't stop Rose's fear of her own parachute failing, or her nightmares of getting tangled in parachute cords, like a fly wrapped in spider silk.

Muriel squeezed Rose's hand. "We'll be all right."

Rose took a deep breath and exhaled, appreciating Muriel's efforts to calm her nerves.

A crew member named Sullivan, a young man with pasty skin and freckles, took a seat across from them. Another crew member, whom they didn't formally meet, examined the machine guns in the tail, and then secured himself in his turret.

The engines of the bomber turned over, and then grew to a roar. The plane vibrated.

Rose looked toward the pilots, but the dropping containers, each over five feet in length, blocked much of her view of the cockpit. Unfortunately, the only unobstructed view was to the gun turret, comprised of glass panels. The engines screamed. The plane accelerated. She gripped her legs, digging her nails into her thighs. Seconds later, the bomber lifted off, pressing her into the floor.

The pilot banked the plane toward the Channel. Once they reached their cruising altitude, the crew member crawled to them.

"Did you ever think about putting seats in this airplane?" Felix asked.

"Why?" Sullivan said, grinning. "All of our passengers jump out before we land."

Rose wiggled her feet, attempting to dispel her rising apprehension.

"Get comfortable," Sullivan said. "I'll let you know when we approach the drop zone." He stood, his back bent from the low fuselage ceiling, and then went about his duty, checking over the dropping containers.

Felix folded his arms, and then leaned back to rest. Muriel lowered her head to her knees.

Rose, her adrenaline pumping through her body, discreetly checked the hardware on her harness. *Will my parachute open? Will I remain unnoticed by the Nazis? Will I be captured? Will I make it back to London? Will I survive this war?*

Rose's assignment as a typist in Churchill's underground war rooms felt like a faded memory, and living in a prewar London seemed like a lifetime ago. To Rose, the drone of the bomber's engines was a constant reminder that Hitler's Luftwaffe had taken away the lives of thousands of Londoners, including Mum, Dad, and Charlie. She toiled to bury her doubts, committed to do her duty for Britain, and to honor her family.

An hour into the journey, the plane dipped.

Rose felt her stomach rise, and then her bottom abruptly pressed into the fuselage floor.

The plane shuddered. Muriel raised her head from her knees and clasped her harness.

Rose patted Muriel's leg. "A bit of turbulence," she said, suddenly realizing that she was also reassuring herself.

Muriel nodded.

The crewman named Sullivan, disregarding the turbulence, made his way through the fuselage like a seasoned sailor maneuvering across the bow of a bobbing ship. He retrieved an insulated flask and tin cups from an ammunition box. He stepped to them and said, "Got you something to drink."

The plane dipped sharply, sending a wave of nausea through Rose's belly. "No thank you," she said, hoping no one would notice her discomfort.

"It's tradition for us to serve SOE agents a drink," Sullivan said, opening the lid to the flask. "It's for good luck."

"Gladly," Felix said, taking a cup.

Muriel, her face pale, nodded.

Sullivan poured them each a drink. Steam rose from their cups.

Rose sniffed, noticing the scent of cloves. "Spiced tea?"

"Hot toddy," Sullivan said.

Rose sipped the tea doused with whisky. Her throat burned.

"It's good," she said, hoping the liquor would act as a medicine for her motion sickness.

Sullivan smiled. "Made it myself."

Felix gulped down his tea, and then poured another cup.

More whisky than tea. Rose slowly drank her hot toddy, but it did little to calm her nerves.

A red light went on near the door.

Muriel straightened her back, spilling a bit of her tea.

"We're approaching the drop zone," Sullivan said.

Rose's heart rate accelerated. She gulped the remains of her hot toddy, wishing it was spiked with more whisky.

The agents put down their cups and stood, their backs sharply bent, and approached the door.

Sullivan retrieved helmets, and then helped the agents with securing the straps under their chins.

The helmet, which felt to Rose like she was wearing a leaded-glass cake dome, was far too big for her head. She pushed up the brim, which fell over her eyes. Her mouth turning dry, she lined up behind Felix and Muriel.

Using metal clasps, Sullivan attached their parachute cords to a static line mounted near the door. Behind Rose, he attached the dropping containers to the same line. "Brace yourself." He opened the door.

Air blasted Rose's face. Goose bumps cropped up on her skin. The roar of the engine battered her eardrums. Her breath quickened. *All I need to do is jump; the parachute will automatically deploy.* She peeked around Felix, hoping to see the ground, but only saw a black void. She turned her eyes to the light, expecting it to turn green, signaling for them to jump.

"Good luck!" Sullivan shouted, his voice drowned by buzzing engines. "Give them hell!"

Felix nodded.

Rose checked the front clasp of her harness. The light turned green. Her breath stalled in her lungs.

"Go!" Sullivan shouted.

Felix jumped and vanished. Muriel dove forward, disappearing into the night.

Rose, her adrenaline surging, sprang toward the open door.

"Wait!" Sullivan grabbed her harness. "It's tangled!"

Rose's heart rate soared. She gripped the doorframe, her body inches from the ledge. Wind rippled her flight jacket.

Sullivan unhooked Rose's harness from the static line. She felt him adjust something on the back of her parachute, and then refastened her cord to the static line. "Okay!"

Rose hesitated, her legs turning weak. "Are you sure?"

"Yes!"

Rose swallowed. She gathered her courage and leaped. *Please open!* Her body soared through the sky. Air whistled. Her mind raced, praying that Sullivan had fixed the problem with her parachute. Seconds passed. *Oh, no!* She struggled to push up her helmet and look up, expecting to see the canopy tangled in cord, and felt a hard tug, like a giant hand lifting her toward the sky. She gasped, relieved to feel the pressure of her harness under her arms. Above her, a blossomed parachute. *Thank God.*

She scanned the horizon, searching for Felix and Muriel. In the distance, she spotted their mushroomed canopies floating onto a field. *They're a mile away!* The time it had taken Sullivan to fix her gear had created a large distance between them. She looked down and realized how severely she'd missed the landing zone when she saw what looked to be a forest rushing toward her. She pulled hard on the parachute cords, attempting to veer away from the trees, but it was too late. Her boots struck the top of a pine. She crashed through several branches, scraping her back, and came to a jarring stop.

Rose wriggled her legs, suspended in the air. Her harness pressed hard against her armpits and thighs. As her eyes adjusted to the lack of light, her predicament came into focus. Above her, cords were twisted in the tree. Below what appeared to be a twenty-foot drop was the forest floor. She felt like a marionette strung over a utility pole. *Bollocks!*

Rose attempted to swing her body toward the trunk of the tree, but she was too far away. And there were no limbs within reaching distance. She contemplated unbuckling herself from the harness, but she'd likely break a leg, given the height of the drop. So, she decided to wait, hoping that Felix and Muriel, or the reception committee, would find her before a German patrol.

Minutes passed. The harness, acting like a tourniquet because of her constant weight, cut off blood flow to her extremities. She flexed her arms and legs, fighting away numbness. As she attempted to loosen her leg straps, a branch snapped. She froze. She scanned the forest. Her heartbeat thumped inside her chest. A crunch of boots on dry leaves grew. She held her breath, hoping to see Felix and Muriel emerge from the dense undergrowth. Instead a shadowy figure, pointing what appeared to be a pistol, stepped from beneath a pine.

Rose strained her eyes, attempting to identify the intruder. *French? German?*

The stranger stopped.

A breeze flowed through the trees. The silk parachute flapped against a limb.

The intruder dropped to a knee and pointed the weapon.

Rose threw up her arms. She stifled her instinct to scream.

The figure lowered the weapon and stepped to the tree. In closer proximity, she noticed it was a man, and he wasn't wearing a German helmet or a uniform.

"Reception committee?" she asked in French, her voice quavering.

"*Oui.*"

Rose exhaled. *Thank goodness.* "I was blown a bit off course, I'm afraid. Could you help me down?"

The Frenchman slipped his pistol into his jacket, and then examined the tree. "There are no low limbs for me to climb up to free you."

"Lovely." Rose worked to loosen her harness.

The man collected brush and placed it on the ground, making a pile.

"What are you doing?" she asked.

"Getting you down." He grabbed an armful of fallen leaves.

"I'll break a leg," she said. "Find the others. They could use some rope from a dropping container to throw over a limb and lower me to the ground."

"No time," he said. He collected more brush, leaves, and pine needles, and then placed his pistol at the base of a tree. Removing his jacket, he placed it over the pile, creating a small pad. "I'll catch you," he said, stepping onto the pile.

"I'll hurt you," she said.

He raised his arms. "Hurry."

Burying her indecision, she undid the straps around her legs. *This is going to hurt.* She released the clasps on the front of the harness, expecting to slowly lower herself. But she lost her grip and plummeted into his chest, toppling them to the ground.

"Are you all right?" he asked.

"I think so," Rose said, getting to her knees. "You?"

"*Oui*." He helped her to her feet.

Rose stood on shaky legs. She struggled to see his face in the dark. "*Merci*," she said, extending her arm. As she shook his hand, she noticed a distinctive, firm but gentle, three-finger grip.

CHAPTER 15

PARIS, FRANCE—MAY 21, 1943

"**D**ragonfly," Rose said, using her code name. She glanced to their clasped hands hidden by the tenebrous forest. His thumb and forefinger felt frozen, like his hand was partially wrapped in a plaster cast.

"I'm Lazare." He released Rose's hand.

Rose rubbed her legs, attempting to dispel numbness, and then removed a miniature folded shovel that was attached to her belt. She slipped off her flight suit and began digging a hole.

Lazare retrieved his jacket and pistol. "The canisters should be nearby."

Rose looked up at the parachute stuck high in the tree. *Not much I can do about that.* She placed her helmet and flight suit into a shallow hole and covered it with soil.

"This way," Lazare said, pointing.

Rose, carrying her shovel, followed Lazare through the forest. "Did you see where the others landed?"

"*Oui,*" Lazare said, ducking under a branch. "My group should have already reached them. I came for you, when I saw the separation between parachutes."

Group? Rose wondered if the reception committee was solely made up of French Resistance, or if the group would include a British agent from the Physician network. The SOE did not provide specific names, saying only that they'd be met upon landing, and then smuggled to Paris. She trudged deeper into the murky forest, despite the sensation of needles prickling her feet.

A few minutes into the trek, they located the first canister, its parachute spread over the forest floor. The remaining canisters were dangling from limbs but were fortunately low enough to the ground to be retrieved. While Lazare lugged the containers, one by one, into a small clearing, Rose dug another hole, and then inserted the parachutes and shovel. Using her hands, she covered the evidence of their arrival with mounds of dirt.

"We'll need the others to help get these canisters out of here," Rose said, approaching Lazare.

He nodded, and then retrieved a small flashlight from his jacket. "Normally, we only use electric torches to signal the RAF where to drop supplies. But it'll be difficult for the others to find us, and if the Germans have been alerted about the sighting of an enemy airplane, we won't have much time before their patrols infest the area."

"Okay," she said.

Lazare raised his flashlight and produced two brief flashes.

Rose scanned the trees.

"There." Lazare pointed.

Rose turned. She saw a light, several hundred yards away, briefly flash, and then disappear.

"They're on their way," he said.

Hurry, Rose thought, realizing that there was little they could do but wait, and hope that the reception committee would arrive before the enemy.

Minutes later, while Rose and Lazare were arranging the canisters to be carried, several members of the French Resistance, carrying Sten submachine guns, emerged from the trees. Following closely behind them were Felix and Muriel.

"Are you all right?" Muriel asked, hugging Rose.

"Yes," Rose said.

"Trouble exiting the plane?" Felix asked.

"A little," Rose said, feeling enormously grateful to Sullivan for fixing her parachute harness. "I also got stuck in a tree." She turned and saw the man who had helped her greeting a few of his comrades.

"I'm Claudius," a middle-aged man interrupted. He removed his beret, exposing a bald head, and then shook Rose's hand.

"Dragonfly," Rose said, realizing that the Physician network had relied solely on members of the French Resistance for the reception committee.

"Welcome to France," Claudius said.

"Thank you." A wave of satisfaction flooded Rose's body. *I've made it. But our journey has just begun.* Burying her gratification, she turned her thoughts to fleeing the forest.

Claudius ordered the Resistance fighters to pick up the canisters and place them on their shoulders.

For over an hour, Rose, Muriel, and Felix trekked through the woods, each taking turns with helping the Resistance fighters carry the canisters that were heavily loaded with equipment and supplies. Rose's short height required her to lift by raising her hands over her head, rather than resting the canister on a shoulder, like the others. Driven by her sense of duty, she continued her efforts to help with the supplies, regardless of the ache in her arms. Reaching a winding, shallow creek, they followed a path to a remote farm.

"In the barn," Claudius said, giving orders to his men. He turned to Felix. "We have a network of people who are sympathetic to our fight. This farmer, who prefers to be detached from our clandestine work, permits us to use his barn."

Felix nodded.

Rose helped the Resistance fighters carry the canisters into the barn. A faded scent of manure filled her nose. As she rubbed the pang in her shoulder, the phosphorous flash of a match caused her to squint.

"We'll stay here until sunrise," Claudius said, lighting a lantern. "Then we'll smuggle you into Paris."

"Where are we?" Felix asked.

"Ableiges." Claudius adjusted the lantern, casting an amber glow. Empty of livestock or feed, the barn contained a few small piles of straw.

"Very well," Felix said, stepping to the aluminum canisters. "Let's check our supplies." He undid the latches and opened the lids.

Muriel examined her wireless radio set, which was concealed inside a leather suitcase. "It looks to be in perfect order," she said, testing the power.

Felix pointed to a dent in the bottom of the second canister, which was larger and squarish in shape as compared to the other cylindrical containers. He reached inside and produced a cracked bicycle rim.

"Lovely," Rose said, staring at the fractured rim, its spokes bent like wire pipe cleaners. The French-manufactured bicycle, which the SOE had obtained and disassembled for transport, was crucial for Rose's role as a courier, as well as her cover story as a traveling cosmetics saleswoman. "Can it be repaired?"

"I doubt it," Felix said.

"We can find you a bicycle," Lazare said.

Rose turned. The glow of the lantern provided her with a better view of the man who'd helped her down from the tree. Lazare, who looked to be in his early to mid-twenties, was over six feet in height, with dark hair, and eyes the color of chestnut. He was cleanly shaven, unlike other members of the Resistance, who were older and had mustaches, or their faces covered in gray stubble. Over his right hand, he wore a wooden prosthetic, which appeared to have been professionally painted, given the realistic replica of a thumb and forefinger. *War injury?*

"No need," Felix said. "We'll radio headquarters for a replacement."

"Perhaps it is better for one person to take the risk of stealing a bicycle," Lazare said, "than to risk the lives of many to retrieve RAF supplies."

The Resistance fighters whispered to each other.

Felix paused, retrieving a cigarette from his pocket.

"We should have little trouble acquiring a bicycle," Claudius said.

Felix lit his cigarette, and then nodded.

Rose noticed a bit of disappointment on Felix's face. *Maybe he's eager to show his authority to order British supplies.*

Lazare walked to the corner of the barn, near an empty horse stall, and sat on the floor. He leaned against the timber wall and closed his eyes.

"Claudius," Felix said, exhaling a lungful of smoke. "Let me show you the supplies the British have provided the Resistance."

Claudius grinned.

Rose and Muriel rested on a pile of straw, while Felix and Claudius, smoking cigarettes, inventoried the munitions. The Resistance fighters sat in a circle, eating British tins of mutton, while Lazare lay alone.

"What happened in the airplane?" Muriel asked, resting her head on a pile of straw.

"The crewman noticed something wrong with my parachute," Rose said.

"Crivvens," Muriel gasped.

"It took him a moment to fix it," Rose said, dreading what might have happened if the crewman hadn't noticed the tangled cord. "It's the reason why I landed so far away. And to make matters worse, I got stuck high in a tree."

"How did you get down?"

"He helped me," Rose said, motioning to Lazare. "Or more precisely, he broke my fall when I landed on top of him."

Muriel smiled. "Brilliant."

Rose nodded, feeling grateful to have Muriel as a fellow agent and, even more, a friend.

"Let's get some rest," Muriel said. "We'll want to be fresh for our arrival in Paris."

Rose rolled onto her side. Visions of nearly jumping from a plane with an impaired parachute filled her head. Her heart thudded with the anticipation of returning to Paris. Unable to sleep, she rehearsed her cover story in her head, over and over. Gradually, the voices of the Resistance fighters dwindled as they settled down to sleep. Before closing her eyes, she glanced to Lazare, resting with his maimed hand on his lap. *What happened to you? How much did you sacrifice to join the fight?* Drifting toward sleep, she wondered how much suffering she would endure before the war was over.

Rose woke from the creak of the barn door's iron hinges. Morning sun sprayed over her face. She sat up and brushed straw from her hair.

"Good morning," Felix said, standing in the open doorway with a cigarette stuck to his lips.

"*Bonjour,*" Rose said. "How long have you been awake?"

"Not long. They're retrieving a lorry." Felix inhaled and blew smoke through his nostrils. "We'll leave in twenty minutes."

Rose nodded, noticing that all the Resistance fighters were gone except for Claudius, who was standing in the yard.

Muriel stretched her arms and yawned. She stood, brushing the wrinkles from her clothes.

Rose retrieved her suitcase and cosmetics, stowed inside a canister. She had never been one to wear makeup. Even on dates, which were few and far between since the start of the war, she seldom applied creams or powders, let alone lipstick. But given her cover story, she'd become quite knowledgeable about beauty products—reading prewar French magazines supplied by the SOE—and she was determined to look and live the role of traveling cosmetics saleswoman.

Opening a round, ornate cosmetic case with a small mirror, she put on eyeliner, and then brushed powder onto her cheeks. As she applied a cherry-red lipstick, her mind wandered to the secret chamber in the bottom of the tube that contained her lethal cyanide pill. She paused, taking a few deep breaths, and then finished applying her makeup.

"You look bonnie," Muriel said.

Rose smiled. She shook away thoughts of her L-pill and closed her compact.

Minutes later, a large stake-body lorry arrived, driven by a member of the French Resistance, who appeared to be a lumberman. Rose, Felix, and Muriel gathered their belongings and met Claudius in the yard. The bed of the lorry, Rose noticed, was filled with twelve-foot-long planks of wood extending past the tailgate.

"Your apartments," Claudius said, giving each of them a key. "You're in the same building. Dragonfly and Sporran will share an apartment."

Rose nodded, feeling strange to hear her code name spoken from someone outside of the SOE.

"Conjurer," Claudius said, looking at Felix. "Your apartment is across the hall."

"Perfect." Felix slipped his key into his pocket.

"I'll deliver the supplies you're unable to carry with you." Claudius turned to Rose. "And I'll show you the locations of the dead drops and live drops."

Rose nodded, anxious to perform her role as courier, passing information between SOE networks and French Resistance by use of secret locations. During her training, she'd practiced numerous dead drops, where agents left hidden messages and didn't meet directly, to maintain security. And she'd arranged several live drops, a method for agents to meet to exchange information or munitions. But in training, she had no risk of being captured and executed. *Practice is over. This is the real thing.* A lump formed in the back of Rose's throat.

"Once you know the drop locations, you'll be able to contact Prosper," Claudius said.

Code name for the organizer of the Physician network. Rose wondered how difficult it would be for her to arrange communication between Physician and their subnetwork, Conjurer.

"Good," Felix said.

"You'll be driven to the outskirts of Paris," Claudius said, stepping to the lorry. "From there, you'll need to split up, and then separately make your way to your apartments."

Felix looked at the driver wearing ragged clothes. "There are sure to be German checkpoints. With the way we are dressed, we'll look quite out of place, hitching a ride with a lumber driver."

Claudius smiled, wrinkles forming in the corners of his eyes. He climbed onto the bed of the lorry and removed layers of boards, revealing a hidden compartment. Although the cargo appeared to be entirely comprised of twelve-foot boards, the center was cut out, creating enough space to hide three people and a bit of luggage.

"Bloody brilliant," Muriel said.

"Well done." Felix shook Claudius's hand. He climbed onto the lorry and loaded their suitcases. After helping Rose and Muriel into the hidden compartment, he lowered himself into the wooden cavity.

"When you need to communicate with the French Resistance," Claudius said, peering into the hole, "contact either me or Lazare." He adjusted his beret, and then lifted a board. "Lazare can be trusted."

A flash of the young man with the prosthetic hand filled Rose's head.

"*Au revoir.*" Claudius placed a board over the hole.

Rose's body pressed tightly between Muriel and Felix. She watched Claudius cover the hole, board by board, until everything went black. The engine started, causing the boards to vibrate, and the lorry drove away.

Inside the cramped space, Rose had little room to bend her arms or legs. Within minutes, the air turned stagnant, recycled from their breathing. Minuscule cracks between the boards were the only source of fresh air, but it was laced with the lorry's acrid petrol fumes. Rose hoped she wouldn't suffocate before they arrived.

Thirty minutes into the drive, the vehicle slowed to a stop. Rose, eager for oxygen, hoped that they had arrived. But her wish for escaping their confinement was doused when she heard a muffled, but distinct, sound of guttural German dialect.

"*Prüfen Sie das Bauholz,*" a man's voice said.

Goose bumps cropped up on Rose's arms. She struggled to control her breathing.

Boots clacked against the ground, rounding the bed of the lorry.

Rose's adrenaline surged. She felt Muriel squeeze her arm.

"*Gehen!*"

The engine revved. The grind of gears, and the lorry pulled away.

Rose exhaled.

"Good God," Muriel whispered.

"We'll be there soon," Felix said, as if he were trying to reassure his companions.

Twenty minutes later, the lorry slowed to a stop. As boards were removed, Rose prayed that they were not at another German checkpoint. Seconds later, she was relieved to see the lumber driver, his grin exposing a missing tooth.

Retrieving their bags, they climbed out of their truck and sucked in air. Rose scanned the area, which appeared to be a lumberyard, empty except for a stack of broken wood pallets.

The driver pointed. "Stay off the busy streets."

Rose turned and saw the skyline of Paris. Her heart rate accelerated.

Felix patted the driver on the shoulder.

Rose, Muriel, and Felix quietly fled the lumberyard. Reaching the street, they spread out, taking different routes toward their destination in the fifteenth arrondissement. Within minutes, Rose was walking alone, her companions out of sight. She fought away fear and insecurity. *I'm Aline Bonnet, a cosmetics saleswoman,* she repeated to herself. She squeezed the handle of her attaché case filled with samples of beauty products.

From a distance, the city looked the same as when she visited as a child. Same magnificent architecture, distinguishable from any other city in the world by the Eiffel Tower, its iron tip pointing toward the heavens. But crossing a bridge over the River Seine, Rose witnessed how much things had changed. The once bustling sidewalks were uncrowded. The Parisians, eyes sunken with protruding cheekbones, evidence of their meager rations, made their way to and from bread lines. Armed Wehrmacht soldiers wearing shell-like helmets patrolled the streets. Cafés, which had been filled with patrons drinking coffee and eating pastries, were now establishments catering to German military. And many of the luxurious hotels, which had been filled with travelers from around the globe, were now homes for Nazi officers.

As a child, Rose adored her family's summer trips to see her grandparents in Paris. They'd visit the Louvre, which contained, according to her mum, the world's finest art. They'd walk through the Latin Quarter, with Mum and Dad meandering through bookshops, newspaper stands, and florists, while she and Charlie—accompanied by their grandparents—sailed paper boats in a fountain. Charlie was particularly fond of Notre-Dame Cathedral. "I'm going to fly someday," he'd said, pointing to one of the many grotesque winged gargoyles perched high on the church.

But Rose's favorite memory was a far more modest experience than colossal churches, extravagant shops, or priceless art. Rose adored eating ice cream, usually pistachio, while walking with her family in Champ de Mars, a park near the Eiffel Tower. Rose, licking her treat, took turns holding a grandparent's hand. Charlie sat on Dad's shoulders, ice cream dripping from his cone. And Mum, using a handkerchief, wiped droplets of melted cream from her husband's hair. It had been, and always would be, one of Rose's most cherished memories.

Now, everyone she loved was gone, and Rose was the last living branch of her family tree. Her beloved Paris, and all the memories that she treasured deep within her heart, were marred by Hitler and his quest to conquer Europe. Swastika flags hung from buildings. Wehrmacht vehicles covered the streets. The gargoyles of Notre-Dame, which had been keeping evil spirits, as well as rainwater, away from the church since the thirteenth century, had done nothing to deter the German occupation. To Rose, Paris was a shell of its former grandeur. Hitler had not merely conquered France, he'd driven Parisians into a prolonged, deep state of hibernation, only venturing outside for means of survival. She bit the inside of her cheek, forcing back tears.

As she approached an intersection, two Wehrmacht soldiers turned the corner and headed toward her. Their eyes locked. Her heart pounded. *Damn it.* Too late to cross the street without drawing attention, she lowered her head and continued walking.

The soldiers stopped, blocking her path.

Her breath stalled in her lungs.

"*Papiers,*" a soldier said.

Rose stopped and put down her suitcase.

"*Na los, beeilt euch ein bisschen,*" the second solder said, his eyes glancing over Rose's body.

She handed him her papers from her purse.

The soldier glanced at the papers and gave them back to her.

As Rose placed her papers into her purse, the second soldier nudged her suitcase with his boot.

"*Offen.*"

Rose kneeled and opened her suitcase.

Using the nose of his rifle, he pushed aside her clothing to reveal the attaché case.

Rose lifted the case, hoping they wouldn't inspect the inside lining of the suitcase, which hid her pistol. She flipped open the attaché, displaying an assortment of makeup powders, lotions, oils, and lipsticks. "Would you like to buy something for your girlfriend?" Rose asked in French.

One of the soldiers, who appeared to understand a little French, laughed and said something in German to his partner, causing him to frown and shake his head. Appearing satisfied, or perhaps a little embarrassed for being solicited for women's cosmetics, the soldiers slung their rifles to their shoulders and continued their patrol.

Rose, her stomach in knots, put away her belongings and continued her journey through the city.

Reaching the address of a brick building in the fifteenth arrondissement, she entered and climbed the stairs to a fourth-floor apartment. Before she could knock, the door swung open. Muriel and Felix ushered her inside and shut the door.

"Thank goodness," Muriel said, giving Rose a hug.

She dropped her bags and squeezed her. "We made it."

"Get settled in," Felix said, smiling. "Lots of work to do."

Releasing Muriel, Rose glanced around the small two-bedroom apartment. It was sparsely furnished with a badly worn sofa, a table with four chairs, and a tiny kitchen with the cabinet doors missing. Cracks and water stains marred the plaster ceiling, and the air contained a faint, but distinct, scent of mildew.

"My apartment across the hall is smaller," Felix commented. "And it's not as nice as this place."

To Rose, the apartment was more than adequate, and it certainly fit in well with their cover story professions. But she understood how Felix, a man who'd come from wealth, might be accustomed to more elaborate accommodations.

"The place is quite fitting for what a mechanic, seamstress, or cosmetics saleswoman could afford," Rose said.

Felix nodded, and then turned to Muriel. "What do you think about informing headquarters that we've arrived?"

"My pleasure," Muriel said. She retrieved her suitcase, which weighed over thirty pounds, and carefully placed it on the table near a window. She opened the lid, exposing a radio panel of nobs and switches, and then plugged in a telegraph key and headset. She peeked outside, scanning to make certain no one was looking. Cracking open the window, she extended an antenna, which was a thin rubber-coated wire that was wrapped around a Paxolin card.

"All right," Muriel said, sitting. "What would you like me to transmit?"

Using a pencil and paper, stored in the case, Felix scribbled a message and handed it to Muriel.

As Muriel transposed the communication, using a secret cypher code, Rose stared at the message.

Conjurer, Sporran, and Dragonfly have landed.

Dragonfly. Rose's chest swelled with pride and patriotism.

Muriel flipped a switch on the wireless. The radio tubes produced a soft hum. She put on her headset and tapped out the encrypted message in Morse code, being careful to include both of her security checks.

Felix burned the message in an ashtray, using his cigarette lighter.

"Done." Muriel retracted the antenna and closed the window.

"I'll be back later to make plans to connect with Prosper," Felix said.

A soft knock on the door.

Rose flinched.

Muriel's eyes widened.

"Were you followed?" Felix whispered to Rose.

Rose shook her head. A flash of the Wehrmacht soldiers, inspecting her papers. Her breath turned shallow.

Muriel stashed her wireless transmitter behind the sofa, and then sat at the kitchen table.

Felix slipped a pistol from his jacket and stepped into a bedroom doorway. He motioned for Rose to answer the door.

Rose, her heart rate flaring, approached the door. She swung the small brass pendulum covering the peephole. As she placed her eye near the hole, she prayed it was a building resident rather than a Wehrmacht soldier. Instead, she saw the young man with the prosthetic hand. A bicycle leaned against his leg. *Lazare.*

Chapter 16

Paris, France—May 21, 1943

The door opened, revealing the woman for whom Lazare had brought the bicycle. He hadn't gotten a good look at the woman called Dragonfly, considering their nocturnal forest escape and the dull glow of a barn lantern, but he recognized her from her petite stature. She wore a gray wool skirt with a matching jacket. Her hair, the color of toasted caramel, was neatly combed and rested in soft curls on her shoulders. A bit of makeup accentuated her cheekbones and sapphire-blue eyes.

She motioned for him to come inside.

Lazare rolled the bicycle into the apartment and saw the wireless operator sitting at the kitchen table. *Sporran.*

Rose closed the door. "It's okay," she said.

Felix, placing his pistol back into his jacket, stepped from the bedroom doorway. "I guess you were right; it doesn't take the Resistance long to deliver a bicycle."

Lazare leaned the bicycle against the wall.

"*Merci*," Rose said. "Where did you get it?"

"I stole it," Lazare said, his face turning warm with shame. He detested thievery, among many other unlawful acts, but it was for a greater cause. Despite his angst, he hoped that there would never come a day when his conscience would be numb to committing a crime, regardless of its size.

Rose frowned. "If I had known you were going to steal a bicycle, I would have arranged for the SOE to deliver a replacement."

Lazare looked at her. "Any French patriot would condone having their bicycle stolen, if it were to aid our liberation from Hitler."

Muriel grinned. "Hard to argue with that."

"If I'm stopped by the enemy to have my papers examined," Rose said, "I'd rather not be on a stolen bicycle."

"I've removed the serial number tag," Lazare said, hoping to ease her concern. "And I've distressed the blue paint with a sandstone. It will be impossible to identify. There are many bicycles, similar to this one, all over France."

Rose took a deep breath, and then exhaled.

Felix examined the bicycle, even checking under the seat for markings. "It should be fine."

Rose nodded.

Lazare turned to Felix. "Claudius has been detained with another matter. I'll show your courier the locations of the dead drops, so you can communicate with Prosper." He glanced to Dragonfly, who crossed her arms.

Felix rubbed his jowl. "Very well."

"I'll have someone deliver your remaining supplies tonight," Lazare said.

"Good." Felix joined Muriel at the table. "Let's prepare a message for Prosper; we'll let him know that Conjurer is up and running."

While Muriel coded Felix's message, Rose collected her purse and cosmetics case, and then placed them into the basket of her bicycle.

Felix folded the note and gave it to Rose.

"Good luck," Muriel said.

Rose nodded, and then hid the paper inside the lining of her jacket.

Lazare stepped to the door. "May I carry your bicycle?"

"*Non*," Rose said. "I need to get accustomed to lugging it up and down the stairs."

He nodded. "Follow me, but stay a block or two behind."

"Are you walking?" she asked.

"*Oui.*"

"Tell me the location, and I'll meet you there," she said.

Lazare paused, placing his hand on the doorknob.

"I'll draw less attention if I don't have to pedal slow or frequently stop," Rose said. "I know the city well."

Lazare gave her the address, and then left the apartment. Outside, he waited on the corner until he saw Dragonfly leave the building, get on her bicycle, and pedal away. For forty-five minutes, he traveled toward his destination using streets where Wehrmacht patrols were less frequent, hoping that Dragonfly would have no trouble reuniting with him. Arriving in the fourth arrondissement, he found her gazing at the flying buttresses of Notre-Dame Cathedral.

As Lazare approached, their eyes met. He walked past her, without speaking, and then crossed the river into Le Marais. Reaching an unmarked alley, he stopped and pretended to tie his bootlaces. With his eyes, he scanned the area. Across the street, an old man was pushing a wooden cart filled with empty bottles. Glass clanged as the cart rolled over cobblestone.

Rose pedaled to him and stopped.

"I'm going to walk through the alley," he said, his eyes focused on his bootlaces. "There's a loose brick in the masonry wall, near a sealed window. It's a dead drop to reach Prosper and the Physician network."

"Okay," she whispered.

"It's difficult to find, so I'll run my hand near its precise location as I pass by. When you're certain no one is looking, remove the brick and insert your message. Be sure to replace the brick the same way it came out, otherwise it will not fit properly."

"*Oui.*"

"When you're finished, follow me to Montparnasse," Lazare said. "Along the way, I'll show you which cafés and apartments are controlled by the Resistance. These places will be safe for you to arrange live drop meetings." He adjusted his boot, and then walked into the alley.

A few seconds passed. The bicycle squeaked as Rose pedaled into the alley.

I should have taken time to oil the chain. With his prosthetic hand, he brushed a brick near a board-covered window and continued walking. Nearing the street, he glanced back to see Dragonfly insert a message, and then seal it with the brick.

For the afternoon, he pointed out safe-haven venues for clandestine meetings, as well as which streets were best to avoid checkpoints and encounters with Wehrmacht patrols. But for much of the journey, they traveled apart from one another. The idle time between scouring the area for soldiers and police allowed Lazare's mind to wander to Maman and Papa. The thought of his missing parents, as well as the thousands of other Jews that were rounded up by the French police, weighed heavy on his heart. His mind and body ached with remorse. It had been months since French authorities had removed the arrested Jews from the Vélodrome d'Hiver and shipped them in cattle cars to German work camps. But there were far more macabre rumors of what the Nazis planned for the Jews, considering many of them were far too young, old, or physically unable to work.

Regret scarred his heart. *I should have done more to convince them to leave Paris. If only I had been home on the night of the roundup, I might have been able to help them escape.* He prayed that they were alive. And he vowed to somehow find a way to bring them home, despite knowing that there was nothing he, the French Resistance, or the SOE could do. He pressed on, compelling himself to concentrate on safely leading Dragonfly to the next dead drop.

He entered the gate of the Montparnasse Cemetery, and then made his way toward the back of the grounds. The cemetery was empty, except for a gray-bearded man digging a gravesite. When the man hunched into his hole, Lazare picked up wilted flowers near a headstone and walked to a limestone burial crypt partially covered in vines. He kneeled and placed the bouquet at the base of the grave.

A moment later, Dragonfly arrived. She parked her bicycle, using its kickstand, and kneeled beside him.

"Why are we praying?" she whispered.

"I have never seen that worker," Lazare said.

Rose turned her eyes.

Twenty yards away, the man stood, his head extending above the hole, and tossed a shovelful of soil.

"Best to pretend we are here to pay our respects," Lazare said.

She clasped her hands.

"When you come here, I suggest staying for several minutes. Leaving too quickly might draw attention."

"Okay," she said.

Lazare waited for the gravedigger, covered in grime and sweat, to lower his head into the hole. Lazare touched the crypt's plaque, a weathered-green bronze family seal missing one of its screws. "This is the dead drop to contact Claudius or me." He turned the plaque, exposing a small cavity created from chiseled limestone.

"Clever," she whispered.

He swiveled the plaque, hiding the dead drop.

The gravedigger grunted, pitching dirt from his excavation.

"It's getting late," Lazare said. "I'll have your supplies delivered at midnight."

She nodded. "Showing me the dead drops would have gone much faster if you would have stolen a bicycle for yourself."

Jews are not permitted to ride bicycles, he thought. A flash of the Jewish woman who was shot at the train station, her blood covering the sidewalk. His shoulder muscles tensed. He harbored his memory and tapped his prosthetic. "Riding a bicycle will draw more attention to me."

"I'm sorry," she said. "I didn't mean to—"

"It's all right," he said, standing. "Can you find your way home?"

"*Oui,*" she said, brushing dry leaves from her skirt. "But you haven't yet shown me the dead drop for Conjurer. How will the Physician network and the French Resistance be able to contact us?"

The gravedigger grumbled, tossed his shovel, and then climbed out of his hole.

They walked to the bicycle. He leaned in and whispered the address of a building two blocks from her apartment. "There's a hidden compartment in the left side of a flower box on the first floor of the building. It's a false wall. It's the lone box on the building. You'll find it, now that you know where to look."

"Left side?"

"*Oui.*"

She sat on the bicycle, balancing tiptoed.

"I can adjust the seat for you."

"No need," she said.

He slipped his hands into his jacket pockets. "You did well."

She smiled. "*Merci.*"

Rose pedaled away, maneuvering around the maze of weathered headstones and monuments. As she disappeared from the cemetery, rue gnawed at Lazare. He wished he would have responded differently to her comments about him using a bicycle. He didn't necessarily fear the repercussion of using a bicycle, considering he carried fake papers. In fact, he'd ridden—his blood pumping with defiance—the stolen bicycle to her apartment. He was simply accustomed to walking; it gave him a clear view of his surroundings, as well as helping him blend into crowds.

How do you tell someone, especially an SOE agent who has been in German-occupied France for less than a day, about anti-Semitic atrocities? Do the British know that thousands of French Jews have been arrested and shipped away in cattle cars? Like his journalist father, Lazare felt a burning desire to inform the world about what was taking place, and he would start, he decided, with Dragonfly, assuming he'd see her again.

Also, Lazare had spent much of the day with Dragonfly, and he regretted that he hadn't had the opportunity to ask about her, regardless of the fact that an SOE agent would reveal little, if anything, about their background. Still, he wondered what would drive the woman to risk her life by joining the SOE and parachuting into German-occupied France. *What is your real name? Why do you want to fight the Nazis? How did you develop a perfect French accent?*

Lazare buried his thoughts about Dragonfly and left the cemetery. He had a few hours to arrange the delivery of SOE supplies. As he made his way to a secret entrance to the catacomb, it occurred to him that he had already been standing many feet above the ancient subterranean passageways. *If the gravedigger continues excavating, he'll eventually uncover our lair.*

CHAPTER 17

PARIS, FRANCE—JUNE 1, 1943

As a burnt orange sunset loomed over Paris, Lazare made his way to meet Conjurer at his mock automobile repair shop in the fifteenth arrondissement. Ahead on the sidewalk, he noticed a woman who was stopped by a Wehrmacht soldier to show her papers. Lazare discreetly crossed the street. A sense of foreboding churned in his gut. Although he had performed numerous acts of sabotage, this particular mission would lead him to the sixteenth arrondissement, near the headquarters of the SD. He adjusted his jacket, the inside lining packed with plastic explosives, and continued his journey.

Conjurer had wasted no time planning their first mission. Within a day of their arrival, Lazare received a dead drop message from Dragonfly requesting that he and Claudius meet with Conjurer. The following day, Lazare and Claudius met with Conjurer in the basement of a café, where they planned the destruction of an electric transformer station. If successful, the SD headquarters would be rendered without electrical power. The mission called for two saboteurs—one SOE agent and one Resistance fighter—to break into a guarded, fenced compound and destroy high-voltage transformers. "I need your best man," Conjurer had said, showing them a diagram of the property. "Lazare," Claudius had responded, placing a hand on Lazare's shoulder. "He's not only our best saboteur, he's next in rank to lead my Resistance fighters."

Lazare appreciated Claudius's confidence in him, and he was grateful that Claudius had taken him under his wing and trained him to fight. Lazare had no aspirations to succeed his comrade and friend. Because, Lazare knew, it required something dreadful to happen to Claudius. But over the past few months, it became increasingly clear to Lazare, as well as to the F Section SOE networks, that Claudius was transferring greater responsibility of the Resistance group to him.

It wasn't unusual for SOE missions to include members of the French Resistance, considering their local knowledge and, perhaps most importantly, their desire to seek vengeance upon Hitler's regime. "We are embraced because we are hiding the SOE agents and their munitions," Claudius had often jested. However, the British were clearly in charge, considering they—not the French Resistance—had the authority to contact London and order supplies to be dropped by the RAF. Lazare was cautiously optimistic that Conjurer, who appeared to be a Frenchman, given his perfect accent, could provide his Resistance group with the resources they gravely needed to fight. But at what cost? Would disrupting a day or two of electrical power to the SD be worth the risk? If Conjurer, within a week of his arrival in Paris, had the thirst to target a facility near the SD's den, what would he plan next?

Reaching the automobile repair shop, he walked around the perimeter of the building, using a rear alley. *Never go to a rendezvous without first checking for escape routes,* Claudius's words echoed in Lazare's head.

He crept along the back of the building. Passing a garage door, its windows blackened with a tar-like substance, he heard voices murmuring from inside. He approached the window and paused.

"Felix," a woman's voice said.

Dragonfly, he thought, recognizing the timbre of the woman's voice. *Who's Felix?*

"We should consider moving Muriel," she continued. "It's only a matter of time before the SD's counterintelligence unit tracks down our apartment."

Lazare leaned to the glass.

"We have time, Rose," a low voice said.

Conjurer is Felix. And Dragonfly is Rose.

"We've had only two brief wireless transmissions in the past week," Felix continued. "We'll move her later."

Lazare stood, listening to their conversation filter through the poorly insulated garage. Irritation burned in his chest. *There's no room for mistakes.* He left the alley, making a mental note of the building escape routes—two windows and a garage door—and then went to the front of the building and knocked.

Footsteps. A lock clicked. The door opened, revealing Conjurer, wearing oil-stained coveralls.

Your name is Felix, Lazare thought. He stepped inside. A scent of petrol and corroded metal filled the air.

Felix bolted the door. "Follow me."

Lazare followed him around a rusted sedan, raised on floor jacks for repairs, and into a back room. Standing near a small wooden desk covered with mechanic tools was Dragonfly. *Rose.*

"*Bonjour,*" Rose said.

"*Bonjour.*" Lazare turned to Felix and said, "You need to do something about the rear garage door."

Felix raised his eyebrows.

Lazare pointed. "It's not soundproofed. If someone is in the alley while you are speaking, they can hear what you are saying."

Felix's face reddened. "Were you eavesdropping?"

"I make it a point to walk the perimeter of an unfamiliar building before I enter," Lazare said. "If I had been eavesdropping, do you think I would bring this to your attention?"

Felix rubbed his mustache. "*Non.*"

"What did you hear?" Rose asked.

"A debate about moving your wireless operator."

Rose lowered her head.

"I assume you might have heard our names," Felix said, stepping to him.

"Yes," Lazare said.

"Do you know *who* I am?" Felix asked.

Lazare looked at him. "Only that you go by the names of Conjurer and Felix."

"Good," Felix said, appearing satisfied. "And just so we are on equal terms, perhaps you could tell us your real name?"

"It's not necessary," Rose said, crossing her arms.

"It's about trust," Felix said, turning to Rose. He retrieved a cigarette from his pocket and placed it to his lips. "I'd feel more comfortable knowing his identity."

"You already do," Lazare said. "My name is Lazare Aron. My forged paperwork lists my name as Laurent Allard."

"Quite dangerous to be using your real name," Felix said. He lit his cigarette and took a drag.

"No more perilous than being branded," Lazare said, raising his prosthetic.

Felix exhaled a lungful of smoke. "*Oui*, I suppose you are right."

"Nail blankets or old rugs over the garage door," Lazare said. "It'll block the sound."

Felix nodded.

"Also," Lazare said. "Rose is right."

Rose straightened her back.

"It doesn't take the SD long to pick up wireless transmissions," Lazare said. "You'll begin to see their black cars, equipped with antennae, circling your streets. There will be a man in the back seat wearing a headset."

Ash dropped from Felix's cigarette.

"I can arrange for Muriel to alternate transmissions from safe houses," Lazare said.

Rose glanced at Felix.

"In time, I will take you up on your offer," Felix said. "But for now, we'll stay in our apartments."

"Very well," Lazare said, deciding it would do no good to pressure Felix. "When you are ready, I'll be prepared to move Muriel."

Felix tamped out his cigarette in an ashtray. "Let's get to work. Do you have the explosives?"

Lazare unzipped his jacket and displayed the lining filled with bricks of plastic explosives.

"Fuses?"

Lazare produced a handful of fuses from his pocket.

"Good." Felix retrieved a coat from the back of a chair and slung it over his shoulder. "I'll leave you two to go over the plans."

Lazare glanced to Rose, and then Felix. "I thought you and I were—"

"*Non*," Felix said. "We planned for you and an SOE agent to perform the mission."

"I must have misunderstood," Lazare said.

"Looks like we both have made mistakes today," Felix said. "Rose will accompany you on the mission."

I should have known, Lazare thought. *SOE network organizers often lead by directing their agents, unlike Claudius, who prefers to fight alongside his men.*

"I'm well trained with explosives," Rose said, her voice sounding a bit defensive.

"Rose was tops in the class with demolition training," Felix added.

"Okay," Lazare said.

Rose placed her hands on her hips.

"Really, I'm good," Lazare said, hoping to alleviate her concern.

"I suggest that you perform the mission before curfew begins," Felix said. "It'll give you the chance to escape while pedestrians are still permitted on the streets. But if you should need a place to hide while enroute back to the apartment, use the garage." He tossed a key to Rose.

Rose caught the key, and then slipped it into her jacket.

"Good luck." Felix turned and left the garage.

Rose cleared the tools from the desk. "Let's review the plan."

"I didn't mean any disrespect," Lazare said.

"None taken," Rose said, her eyes focused on a piece of paper containing a diagram of the transformer station.

Lazare leaned over the desk. For thirty minutes, they reviewed their plans. She was clearly well prepared, Lazare realized, when she informed him that she had ridden her bicycle past the guardhouse at precisely the same hour they were planning to commit the sabotage. Lazare had also done his own inspections of the area, and he was pleased that she'd done her homework.

"The guard typically reads a newspaper," Rose said. "After sunset, he drinks from a flask and smokes cigarettes."

Lazare nodded.

"I couldn't tell if he's armed, but I think he has a guard dog."

"Why do you think that?" he asked.

"He keeps bending over, like he's petting a dog."

"I've seen the guard shack; it's the size of a phone box. I doubt it has room for both a guard and dog."

Ignoring his comment, Rose pointed to the diagram. "It's best if we cut through the wire at the southeast corner of the property."

"Agreed," he said, anxious to get started. "Do you have cutters?"

Rose opened a desk drawer and handed him a pair of wire cutters. She folded the diagram and burned it over an ashtray. "Ready?"

"*Oui.*"

They left at 8:00 p.m., an hour before curfew commenced. An indigo sky, strewn with fading pink clouds, cast dull shadows over the city. Although few people were on the streets, Lazare walked far behind Rose, who was wearing a wool skirt and jacket. Her cosmetic case, dangling from her left hand, swayed with the graceful click of her heels on the pavement. *She looks like she's headed home after a day of work. The Germans would never guess that she's on her way to blow up a transformer.*

Reaching the transformer station, an open lot surrounded by old buildings, Rose crossed the street and traveled to the rear of the property. He caught up with her, crouching beside a chain-link fence entwined with weeds and topped with razor wire.

Lazare, his eyes adjusted to the lack of light, stared through the fence. Twenty yards away were several transformers, reminiscent of giant ribbed spark plugs protruding from blocks of iron. Above the transformers was a framework of steel girders from which wires spanned over electrical poles through the arrondissement. At the front of the property was the guard shack, its windows absent of light, except for the intermittent glow of a cigarette ember.

Slow and quiet. Lazare, his pulse accelerating, kneeled and removed the wire clippers from his pocket. He placed the tool to a wire nearest the ground.

Rose raised her hand.

He paused, gripping the cutter.

Rose produced a rag from her jacket, covered the head of the tool, and then nodded.

Lazare squeezed. The wire broke, producing a muffled snap, like a pencil being broken inside a dishtowel. *She's clever.*

They worked in tandem, starting at the base of the fence. Lazare cut and Rose muted the noise with the rag. After several cuts, Lazare slipped the tool into his pocket and glanced to the guard shack. No movement.

Entwining his finger in the chain link, he pulled, creating enough space to crawl under the fence. He looked at Rose and noticed, even with the absence of light, that she appeared confident and unwavering.

She motioned for him to go first.

Lazare crawled under the fence. He turned to help Rose, but she deftly slid through the opening and stood. As they crept to the transformers, a high-voltage hum grew. Hairs stood up on the back of his neck. He unzipped his jacket and handed bricks of plastic explosives to Rose, who proceeded to maneuver to the opposite side of the transformers. *She's wasting time. We can place them here.* With no time to gain her attention, he crept around the transformers and joined her.

Rose packed a brick to the base of a transformer, then moved to set another explosive.

As Lazare pressed the charge into place, he could sense the high voltage within inches of his hands, causing his skin to prickle. He moved on and placed another explosive, hoping he wouldn't be electrocuted.

In less than a minute, they'd placed their explosives and inserted the fuses. Lazare removed a lighter from his pocket. Rose produced a book of matches. Simultaneously, they lit the fuses. Wicks sizzled. A sulfuric odor filled his nose.

Rose scurried toward the fence.

As Lazare turned to run, a fuse that he had set came undone. He pressed the fuse deep into the explosive and sprinted, taking a shortcut between two transformers. His boot struck a metal girder protruding from the base of a transformer. He stumbled, scraping gravel.

A bark pierced the air.

Lazare's heart rate soared.

The door to the guardhouse flung open. A flashlight beam pierced the air, illuminating the silhouette of a large dog.

Shit. Lazare sprinted.

The dog's bark grew closer.

"*Halt!*" The guard blew on a whistle.

Lazare forced his legs to move faster. His pulse pounded in his eardrums.

Nearing the fence, he saw that Rose had already crawled through the hole. He scrambled through the opening, and then pushed the chain link into place as the dog, growling and baring its teeth, slammed into the fence.

"Run!" Lazare shouted.

Rose hesitated, attempting to block the dog, using her cosmetics case, from crawling through a gap in the fence.

A whistle blew. "*Halt!*"

The dog bit Lazare's knuckles. Pain flared. "Go!"

Rose turned and ran.

Using his hands and feet, Lazare struggled to block the dog— a Beauceron, given its chiseled head and muscular build—from penetrating the wire and mauling him. It gnawed at his fingers, sending stings through his hand. He tightened his grip, determined to hold the fence in place a few seconds longer.

As the guard's flashlight beam passed over his chest, the first charge exploded, immediately followed by the others. The shockwave knocked Lazare to the ground. The dog yelped. The guard tumbled, dropping his flashlight. Lazare, his ears ringing, reached his bloodied hand into his pocket, and then struggled to jam the wire cutters into the chain link.

The dog, having regained its composure, growled and chomped at his hands.

"*Halt!*" the guard shouted.

Ignoring the pain, Lazare plunged the handle of the cutters into the wires, linking the two cut pieces of chain-link fence. He turned and ran, praying that his futile attempts to create a dead bolt would provide them with a little time before the dog broke through the fence.

He darted down the darkened street. A siren sounded. Then another. His lungs burned. Pain flared through his hands. He envisioned the police, SD, and Wehrmacht surrounding him, and then riddling his body with bullets. Disregarding his fatigue, he willed his legs to run faster.

Sirens grew closer. Grinding engines roared. Realizing it would be impossible to make it back to the catacombs, he dashed through an alley and onto a side street. Minutes later, he reached Felix's automobile repair garage. The door swung open and Rose pulled him inside.

Lazare sucked in air.

Rose bolted the door. Seconds later, a police car, its siren howling, sped down the street.

"That was close," she panted.

He strained to see her in the blackened room. "You were right about the dog," he said, catching his breath. "I'm sorry. I should have paid more heed to your warning."

"It's okay; we did it," she said. "They'll be searching the area. We should hide in the back of the garage in case we need to flee."

He stepped forward, bumping his knee on something hard. He extended his hand and found what appeared to be the fender of an automobile.

"I'll show the way." She clasped his hand, warm and sticky. "You're hurt."

"I'll be okay."

She loosened her grip but didn't let go of his hand. She guided him through the unlit garage. She found a doorknob and opened the door. "Water closet. Wait inside."

Lazare felt her hand slip away.

She rummaged through cabinets and drawers. Returning, she lit a candle and placed it, along with a half empty bottle of an amber liquor, on a stained sink. "Let's have a look at you."

Lazare placed his hands over the sink. Blood droplets spattered the faucet.

"Blimey," she said, pushing up his sleeves. "The dog chewed you up a bit."

"*Oui*," he said. "I think it was a Beauceron."

"I'm going to remove your—" she touched his wooden thumb.

"Prosthetic."

"Prosthetic," she repeated. "And then I'll clean the wounds to your hands."

"Okay."

She undid the straps, removed the prosthetic, and then gently placed it on the ground. She turned on the faucet, producing a rust-colored stream of water. She waited for the water to clear, and then rinsed his mauled fingers, revealing several deep gouges.

"You saved my life," Lazare said.

She looked at him. "Nonsense, I'm merely bandaging your bites. And I doubt that a guard dog would be infected with rabies."

"You chose to place the explosives on the opposite side of the transformers," he said. "I would have planted the explosives on the side nearest the fence, and the shrapnel might have killed me when I couldn't flee the property."

She carefully rinsed his fingers. "We were taught in demolition training to place explosives, if possible, out of one's escape path."

"*Merci.*"

She turned off the water. "I was thinking that I owe you a bit of gratitude."

"For what?"

"You plugged the hole in the chain-link fence, while a dog mauled your knuckles, allowing me to escape. Why didn't you run?"

"I wanted to make sure you were safe." He paused, their eyes meeting. "No need for two to be caught."

Lowering her eyes, she picked up the bottle and removed the cork. "There's no soap or antiseptic. Fortunately, Felix is quite fond of apple brandy." She dribbled the alcohol over his wounds.

A burn flared through his appendages.

Rose retrieved the rag that she'd used to muffle the wire cutters. She tore it into strips and carefully wrapped his fingers. Reaching the area of a missing thumb and forefinger, she paused and gently touched his scar. "What happened?"

His skin tingled, deadening the pain in his knuckles. "Childhood accident."

"Oh, my," she whispered.

"Papa had been a journalist at a newspaper. When I wasn't in school, I loved to join him at work. He and Maman had forbidden me to play near the printing press. But one day, when my father was called away, I stepped too close."

"I'm sorry," she said, still holding his hand.

"My parents believed the injury saved my life."

"How?"

"Most of the Frenchmen who joined the military are dead or captured. I was rejected from joining the army because of my injury."

"Do they know you're a saboteur for the Resistance?"

Lazare swallowed. "They're gone."

"I'm so sorry."

He nodded, sorrow swelling in his chest.

"My parents are dead," she said, finishing the bandage. "And my brother."

"Oh, *Dieu*," Lazare said. "I'm sorry."

She released his hand, and then sealed the bottle of brandy. "Some days, I wonder if the death will ever end."

He gently placed his hand on her shoulder.

Rose, her eyes beginning to water, looked at him.

"You're making a difference," he said. "This war will end, and you'll go on to live a long and beautiful life."

Rose smiled and blinked away tears.

The rumble of a vehicle traveling through the alley grew.

Lazare lowered his hand. *Wehrmacht patrol.*

Rose blew out the candle.

The walls vibrated, and then the vibration faded as the vehicle drove away.

"We should rest," he whispered. "It will be safer to leave in the morning."

"*Oui.*"

Fumbling through the dark, they located the disabled automobile and climbed into the back seat. Rose reached into the glove box and retrieved a pistol. She removed the magazine, checked the ammunition, and inserted it back into the weapon.

"In case we have company," she said, placing the pistol on the seat beside her. She rubbed her arms and shivered.

Lazare removed his jacket and placed it over her lap.

"You'll get cold," she said.

"I have my bandages to keep me warm."

She chuckled.

"Get some rest. I'll stay awake."

"*Merci.* But we'll take turns," she said, her voice sounding exhausted. "Wake me up in a few hours."

"Okay," he said.

She leaned back, pulling the jacket to her chin, like a blanket.

As Rose drifted to sleep, he listened to the intermittent grind of German patrols, no doubt searching the arrondissement for saboteurs. Hopefully, the guard had reported that men were responsible for the destruction, extinguishing the search for a woman.

A dull ache permeated his hands. He regretted not telling her more about his parents, and he wished he would have asked her more about her family. *What happened? What were they like? Were they French? Did you join the SOE because of them?*

He listened to her breathing gradually slow. Her muscles relaxed, and she leaned into him, resting her head on his shoulder. His skin tingled, numbing the pain in his hands. Tenderly, he rested his cheek on her hair and inhaled, taking in a subtle scent of lilac. For hours, he stayed awake, wishing that morning would never come.

CHAPTER 18

PARIS, FRANCE—JUNE 2, 1943

Rose woke with her head on Lazare's chest, his warmth radiating into her body. Minuscule streams of sunlight filtered into the garage, casting shadows over their makeshift bed in the rear seat of the automobile. She listened to the slow cadence of his breath, rising and falling. A sense of timelessness and peace encompassed her. It had been ages since she'd felt the comfort of a man. She'd had a few boyfriends, but none of the relationships were serious. And despite giving her virginity to a Royal Navy petty officer named Sidney, she had never been in love.

Sidney, a jovial young man who lived in a Bethnal Green flat and fancied playing darts at a local pub, had attended secondary school with Rose. They'd been friends for years, but in December of 1940, during the German bombing campaign on London—when Sidney was preparing to ship out for military duty—he asked her on a date at a tearoom in Whitechapel. Rose, seeking a distraction from the recent death of her brother, accepted his invitation. Thirty minutes into their meal of tinned meat sandwiches, roaring sirens compelled them to flee the tearoom and seek sanctuary in a nearby tube station. In the early hours of the morning, after the all-clear signal was given, Sidney surprised Rose by inviting her to his apartment. *If I'm going to die, why not live in the moment?* The sexual intercourse was awkward, considering they both were partially clothed, and it lasted merely a few minutes. Afterward, she felt no better than she had the day before. Her heart continued to ache from the death of her brother, and she feared that she could die in an instant from a German bomb. Declining his invitation to spend the night, she kissed Sidney on the cheek and made him promise to stay clear of German torpedoes. She walked home, wondering if she would ever experience true intimacy.

Rose nuzzled her cheek to Lazare's chest. *He's quite different from any man I've ever met.* She wondered, although briefly, what it would be like to get to know him under different circumstances. Her heart wanted to stay, but her mind, conditioned by SOE training and her sense of duty, compelled her to leave. Reluctantly, she lifted her hand from his sternum.

Lazare stirred.

Rose sat up. "Sorry," she said, feeling a bit embarrassed.

"It's okay," Lazare said.

She looked at him and noticed that she'd left a small, but obvious, drool spot on his shirt. *Lovely.*

"Did you get some rest?" he asked.

"*Oui.*" Rose placed his jacket—that she'd used as a blanket—onto his lap. She hoped that he'd put it on, hiding her slobber. "We were supposed to take turns staying awake. Why did you let me sleep?"

"I thought you could use the rest." He rubbed his eyes, using the back of his wrists.

"How are your hands?"

He flexed his fingers, the bandages seeped with blood. "Better."

"You'll want to clean your wounds to keep them from getting infected," she said. "Do you have any sulfa pills?"

Lazare shook his head.

"The SOE provided us with medicine. I'll leave the pills in your dead drop."

"*Merci,*" he said.

She looked at her watch. "I should get back to the apartment and inform Felix. I have work to do."

"Selling cosmetics?"

"It's my cover story," she said.

"You do know that most Parisians do not have the means to purchase makeup," Lazare said. "Your customers will either be wealthy or collaborating with the Germans."

"Precisely," she said.

"It's dangerous."

"No more precarious than sabotaging a transformer," she said.

He rubbed stubble on his chin. "Perhaps."

"I'm not trying to sell loads of cosmetics," she added. "It's merely a way to explain, if I'm stopped to have my papers examined, why I'm traveling around Paris." *And maybe along the way, I'll gather useful intelligence.*

Lazare nodded.

Rose leaned forward and looked in the rearview mirror. A swath of her hair, where she'd slept on his shoulder, jutted out from her head. "Speaking of cosmetics, I could use a bit of grooming. I look dreadful." She returned to her seat, combing her hair with her fingers.

"You look good," he said.

Her stomach fluttered. "Nonsense." She brushed wrinkles from her skirt.

"Impressive work last night."

She looked at him, his dark-brown eyes filled with reverence.

"If it wasn't for your decisiveness to place the explosives on the other side of the transformers, I might have been killed." He placed a bandaged hand on her arm.

Her skin tingled. *You injured your hands, attempting to give me time to escape.*

"*Merci,*" he said, softly.

She swallowed. "I should be thanking—"

A knock came from the front door.

Her heart rate accelerated. She retrieved her pistol.

Rose, followed by Lazare, quietly exited the automobile by crawling out of a side window, rather than risk the noise of a squeaky hinge.

Rose pointed her weapon at the door.

Lazare peeked through a blind covering a front window. "It's Felix."

Rose exhaled.

Lazare let Felix inside, and then shut the door and bolted the lock.

"How did it go?" Felix asked.

"Splendid." Rose put the weapon in the vehicle's glove box and approached Felix. She removed the garage key from her jacket and gave it to him. "But the explosion created quite a ruckus. The area was swarming with patrols, so we stayed here."

Felix looked at Lazare's bandaged hands and frowned. "What happened?"

"Guard dog," Lazare said.

"His tussle enabled us to escape," Rose said.

"What about the security guard?" Felix asked.

"He didn't get close enough to identify us," she said, hoping she was right.

"Are you certain?" Felix asked.

"*Oui,*" Lazare said.

Felix smiled. "Well done."

"I was about to return to the apartment," Rose said. "Why did you come?"

"It's important for me to maintain my cover story of a mechanic," Felix said, running a hand over his oil-stained coveralls. "Changing my routine could draw attention." He kneeled and removed a piece of paper from inside his boot, and then gave it to Rose. "Go to the apartment and tell Muriel that we'll send a message to London tonight, after I've had a chance to determine the extent of the power outage. Then deliver that message to Prosper."

Rose nodded. She glanced at the coded message for the leader of the Physician network, whom she'd never met, communicating solely via a dead drop.

"Muriel was worried about you," Felix said. "She'll be glad to see you."

How long can Muriel continue wireless transmissions from the same location without being detected? Rose's shoulder muscles tensed. "We should move her."

"We will," Felix said.

"When?" Rose persisted.

Felix removed a cigarette from his pocket and stuck it to his lips. He lit the end and puffed. "Soon."

"In the interim," Lazare said, "I'll arrange the safe houses. We'll be ready to accommodate her, when you are ready to make the move."

Felix nodded.

Rose looked at Lazare. *Thank you.*

Lazare stepped to the washroom, and then returned, wearing his prosthetic. He climbed into the automobile's back seat and retrieved his jacket.

Felix, his brows raised, looked at Rose.

Her skin turned warm.

Lazare slipped on his jacket. "*Au revoir.*" His eyes met Rose, and he left the garage.

Felix took a drag on his cigarette and blew smoke through his nose.

"It's not what you think," Rose said.

"We're all under a lot of stress," he said. "It's war, and I understand that things can happen."

Rose crossed her arms. "Nothing happened."

He flicked ash from his cigarette. "Be careful."

"I will," she said. "I'd never do anything to jeopardize our mission."

He nodded, and then placed his cigarette in an ashtray. "Well, we should get to work."

Rose retrieved her purse and cosmetics case, and then left the garage. She had no doubt that Felix's intentions were good. He was deeply committed to the fight and, like her, he'd suffered the loss of family—his only son, Mathieu—to the war. In his eagerness to set Nazi-controlled Paris ablaze, he'd planned their first operation in proximity to the SD headquarters, and he was taking more risk than necessary by not having Muriel conduct her wireless transmissions from alternate locations. Felix's experience as a Grand Prix race car driver, Rose believed, had curbed his sensitivity to fear. *And he's telling me to be careful!* As she made her way back to the apartment, an irritation grew in her belly.

Arriving at the apartment building, Rose quietly scaled the

stairs, hoping not to encounter one of the neighbors, who might notice that she hadn't come home last night. Fortunately, their building, which had been arranged through the French Resistance, contained occupants who rarely left their apartments, with the exception of trips to gather their rations.

Reaching her apartment, the door opened. Muriel pulled her inside and shut the door. "Thank goodness you're all right," she said, hugging her.

Rose squeezed her.

"I was worried when you didn't make it home last night," Muriel said, releasing her.

Seeing Muriel's concern caused Rose's vexation with Felix to fade.

"Did it go okay?" Muriel asked.

Rose sat with Muriel at the kitchen table, and she told her about last night's mission, including the encounter with the guard dog and hiding in the garage due to police and enemy patrols.

"You're quite a plucky courier," Muriel said.

"No," Rose said. "Lazare was the brave one. He injured his hands fending off a guard dog to allow me to escape."

"Goodness," Muriel said, her eyes wide. "Will he be okay?"

"Yes, but he's received some horrible bites. I'm going to deliver him some of our sulfa pills."

"If you get the chance," Muriel said, "please pass along my gratitude to him for looking out for you."

Rose nodded.

"What's he like?" Muriel asked.

A flash of waking next to him. Rose fought away a smile and blurted, "He's quite competent."

Muriel tilted her head. "That's it? You spent the night in the garage with him and that's all you have to say?"

Rose's face flushed. "He's nice." *He's caring and sensitive. And he lost his parents, like me.*

"Did he tell you how he came to wear a prosthetic?" Muriel asked.

The image of bandaging his fingers filled Rose's head. "Childhood accident with a printing press."

"Oh, my," Muriel said.

"He was rejected by the French army, so he joined the French Resistance."

"Anything else?" Muriel asked.

"When Lazare arrived at the garage, he overheard Felix and me discussing plans." A lump formed in Rose's stomach. "He knows our names."

Muriel took a deep breath and exhaled. "Can we trust him?"

"Yes," Rose said.

"Okay," Muriel said, without hesitation. "Out of curiosity, what did he overhear you talking about?"

"Moving you."

Muriel lowered her head.

"It'll be safer for you," Rose said.

"When?" Muriel asked.

"Soon," Rose said, hoping that Felix would follow through with his promise.

Muriel fiddled with a scratch on the table.

"Are you all right?"

Muriel produced a slim smile. "A bit of the collywobbles, I'm afraid."

"Let's get you out for a walk. You've been stuck inside far too much."

"Life of a wireless operator," Muriel said. "It's what I signed up for. But that's not what is bothering me."

"Mabel?" Rose asked, noticing the melancholy in Muriel's voice.

Muriel, her eyes filled with burden, nodded. "I miss her."

Rose pulled her chair close and squeezed her hand. She couldn't begin to imagine how heartsick Muriel must be, leaving her baby back in Britain.

"I know she's in good hands with my parents," Muriel said. "But I wonder if she thinks I abandoned her? Will she remember who I am when I come home?"

"Of course, she will," Rose said. "And when she's old enough to understand, she'll be so proud of her mum."

Muriel sniffed back tears. "I wish the SOE would have permitted us to bring photographs. I'm worried that I'll begin to forget what she looks like."

"That'll never happen," Rose said. "Ever."

"It's silly of me to worry," Muriel said.

"*Non,*" Rose said. "It's natural for a mother to miss her daughter."

Muriel stood and wiped her eyes. "Enough of my snivel. Did Felix indicate when I'm to send the next wireless transmission to London?"

"Tonight," Rose said. "First, he wants to scout out the area of the power outage."

Muriel nodded, and then pointed to the kitchen counter. "You must be famished. I saved you a bit of toasted bread."

"I owe you," Rose said.

"You might feel differently when you taste it," Muriel said. She chuckled.

Rose ate her breakfast, bland from lack of jam or butter, and washed it down with a cup of coffee made from roasted barley and hot water. She complimented Muriel on her culinary skills, and then went to the washroom, where she bathed using a washcloth and scentless soap, a concoction of fat and caustic soda. She dressed, pairing a clean, pressed white blouse with her gray wool skirt and jacket. Retrieving a handful of sulfa pills, she wrapped them in waxed paper and hid them in a compartment in the bottom of her purse. She placed her purse, along with her cosmetics case, into her bicycle basket, and then said goodbye to Muriel.

As she lugged her bicycle out of the apartment, a twinge of guilt pierced her belly. *I wish I could trade places with you.* But that was not an option, given the strict duties of their roles. She descended the stairs, wishing that she would have had the foresight to have broken SOE rules by hiding Mabel's photograph in the lining of her suitcase.

CHAPTER 19

PARIS, FRANCE—JUNE 2, 1943

Rose rode her bicycle to Prosper's dead drop, located in a quiet alley in Le Marais. She assumed that Felix's coded message was about the transformer sabotage, or perhaps to coordinate a rendezvous between Felix and Prosper, organizer of the Physician network, whom their subnetwork reported to. Rose disliked not knowing the details of each communication, but she understood the reason why they operated in small, segmented groups. If an agent was captured—and tortured to the point of divulging names and locations of other agents—it prevented the collapse of the entire SOE network in France. As Rose hid the coded message behind a loose brick in the wall, she wondered if she would ever meet Prosper in person, or if he would remain a phantom to her, channeling his spirit through encrypted messages in a dead drop.

Finishing her duty, Rose pedaled to the Montparnasse Cemetery. Rather than placing the sulfa pills into Lazare's dead drop and leaving, she sat at the tomb and pretended to pray. *If I stay long enough, perhaps Lazare will arrive to check his dead drop.* But staying too long, or too short, could create attention. Fortunately, the gravedigger was not working, giving her a few extra minutes of solitude.

There was much that she wanted to know about Lazare. Their time together had abruptly ended, and she felt horrible for not making the effort to inquire more about his parents. *What happened to them?* She knew little about Lazare, other than his childhood injury, and that he'd joined the Resistance after being banned from joining the French army. *I don't even know where you live. Other than hiding a note in a cemetery, I have no other way to reach you.* After waiting far longer than she should have, Rose inserted the sulfa pills into a crevice behind a tomb marker, and then left the cemetery, wishing she had taken time to code a message.

On her bicycle ride home, there were French policemen, accompanied by German soldiers, stopping pedestrians near a large intersection to check papers. She slowed, pretending to look inside a shoe shop window—and recognized that it was permanently closed, given the barren space, save a few cardboard boxes. The word JUDE, as well as the Star of David, was painted like graffiti on the storefront. A dreadful knot twisted in Rose's gut. During her routes as a courier, she'd seen countless anti-Semitic signs and cruel propaganda. And she'd heard whispers from women in ration lines about the French police rounding up Jews for the Germans. *What have they done with them?*

The SOE had schooled her about Nazi anti-Semitism, as well as Hitler's evil plan for the Aryanization of Germany. But neither the SOE, nor the British news reports, had prepared her for the heinous crimes against humanity that were taking place in Paris, and it sickened her to think that the French police were acting as pawns for the Nazis' game of chess. She prayed that the persecution would stop, and that those who were deported would survive. Desperate to know more, she decided she would ask Lazare if, and when, she saw him.

She glanced to the police checkpoint. A man was rummaging through a woman's purse. Deciding to avoid the checkpoint, she pedaled back the way she came. She turned onto a side street, only to witness an elderly couple being harassed by a Wehrmacht soldier. *They've increased their security, likely due to last night's sabotage.*

Rose took a long, detoured route around the city to avoid police and military stops. But along the way, she had to endure seeing her beloved Paris marred by Nazi flags and anti-Semitic posters. Even worse, she witnessed two women who were fighting over their place in a long ration line. One of the women screamed as her combatant attempted to rip a fistful of hair from her head, until the scuffle was broken up by an elderly shopkeeper wielding a broom. Shocked, Rose pedaled away, trying to dispel the horror of Parisians in such a desperate state of survival.

By midafternoon, she found herself in the Place de la Madeleine. Tired, she veered her bicycle to the curb. She dabbed her forehead with a handkerchief from her purse, wondering which street would be the least patrolled route to her apartment. Looking up, she saw a building with a large German sign above the first-floor windows—*Soldatenkaffee*. Rose shivered at the sight of the German coffee shop. *They've created their own bloody cafés.* Through the windows, she saw uniformed soldiers having drinks and eating food. On the corner, a haggard man was picking through scraps in a garbage can. Rose's skin turned hot. As she put away her handkerchief and prepared to leave, a black car with Nazi flags attached to the fenders abruptly pulled to the curb, blocking her path. She squeezed the handles of her bicycle.

"*Bonjour*," a woman's voice said.

Rose turned and saw a young woman with wavy blond hair and bright red lipstick. She wore a floral dress, adorned with a Bakelite cicada brooch with diamanté rubies.

"*Bonjour*," Rose said, trying to contain a quaver in her vocal cords. Through the corner of her eyes, she saw the doors to the Nazi automobile swing open.

"Are you thinking about going inside?" the woman asked, gesturing to the *Soldatenkaffee* sign.

"*Non*," Rose said.

Two German officers wearing shark-gray uniforms stepped out of the vehicle.

"Wise decision," the woman said. "There's a much better place on the next street."

Doors slammed. German jackboots clacked against the pavement.

Goose bumps cropped up on Rose's arms. *Stay calm.*

"That's a lovely attaché case," the woman said, pointing to her bicycle basket. "Are you selling something?"

"Cosmetics," Rose said, watching the officers approach them. Her legs turned weak.

"It's your lucky day," the woman said, smiling. She wrapped her arm around Rose's elbow.

The officers stopped in front of them. Paying little, if any, attention to Rose, the Germans tipped their caps to the woman, and then entered *Soldatenkaffee.*

Rose swallowed. "Do you know them?"

"*Non,* but I think they know me," the woman said, grinning. "I'm Zelie."

"Aline," Rose said, using her cover name.

"May I have a peek at your cosmetics? I'm in desperate need of rouge, cologne, and eyeliner, and anything else you might have for sale. My place is on the next avenue."

Rose was anxious to get home, but she needed a break from the streets seemingly infested with enemy soldiers. And selling a few of her products, Rose thought, could potentially help with validating her cover story, if she were ever stopped and questioned by the enemy. *Are you a socialite or a collaborator?* Rose buried her trepidation and said, "*Oui.*"

Rose, pushing her bicycle, walked with Zelie. The woman's shoes clicked on the sidewalk, turning heads of pedestrians. Within a few minutes, Zelie stopped in front of a grand hotel called Le Cygne. *The Swan,* thought Rose. *She lives in a hotel?* As they prepared to enter, an SS officer stepped through the doors and onto the sidewalk. He removed a silver case from his pocket and pulled out a cigarette.

Rose hesitated, glancing to Zelie.

"It's okay," Zelie said. "Follow me, and bring your bicycle."

Too late to turn around without creating a scene, Rose followed her toward the entrance. The SS officer, upon seeing Zelie, nodded and opened the door for them. *Good God, who is this woman?* Shivers shot down her spine. Entering the building, Rose stared at the back of Zelie's dress, avoiding eye contact with the German officer.

Zelie arranged with a receptionist to place Rose's bicycle behind the front desk for safe keeping. Rose, carrying her purse and cosmetics, followed Zelie into an elevator. The operator, an old man wearing a black cap and sagging suit, manually closed bronze grille doors, and then took them to the seventh floor. With each step down the hallway, angst grew in Rose's gut.

Zelie pulled a key from her purse and opened the door, revealing a hotel suite. The palatial room contained a large four-poster bed with a white duvet and pillows fluffed and tilted against a rosewood headboard. On the opposite side of the room was a navy blue art deco sofa, matching side chairs, and a large liquor cabinet containing an assortment of liqueurs, schnapps, and cognac. A scent of cleaning detergent, mixed with a hint of cheese and burnt cigar tobacco, filled Rose's nose. *Parisians are starving, and there are people living like this?*

"Beautiful room," Rose said, hiding the resentment that roiled in her belly.

"*Merci*," Zelie said. "Cigarette?"

"No, thank you," Rose said.

Zelie went to the liquor cabinet and opened a drawer. She retrieved a cigarette, which she placed into a long, thin ebony holder. She lit the end and puffed on the tip. "Let me see your cosmetics."

Rose took a seat on the sofa and placed her case on a coffee table in front of her. She opened the lid, displaying an assortment of lotions, lipstick, eyeliner, rouge, and cologne. She hoped that she could recall the details of the French products, which the SOE smuggled from France to Britain.

"*Merveilleux*," Zelie said, taking a seat beside her. She picked up a sample-size bottle of cologne, unscrewed the cap, and sniffed. "May I?"

Rose nodded.

Zelie placed a dab to her neck and fanned her skin. "*Charmante*."

Rose glanced to the desk in the corner of the room. On top were neatly stacked manila files. *That's odd—Zelie doesn't look like the bookkeeper type.*

For the next hour, Zelie sampled rouge and eyeliner, taking time to wash her face in the bathroom between applications, as well as puff on her elongated cigarette. Rose learned from Zelie's fondness of speaking about herself that she was a cabaret performer working in a club that catered to German military.

"Before the war, I performed all over Europe," Zelie said, looking at her reflection in a handheld gilt-frame mirror. "Berlin. Brussels. Amsterdam. Prague. Warsaw. Munich. Budapest. And of course, Paris."

Rose grew restless. She contemplated making up an excuse that she had to leave for another appointment. As she was about to speak, the sound of a key being inserted into the door caused her hairs to stand up on the back of her neck.

"Are you expecting someone?" Rose asked, turning to Zelie.

"Josef," Zelie said. She stood and placed her cigarette into an ashtray.

The door opened, and a Nazi officer carrying a leather briefcase stepped inside and shut the door.

Rose gripped the cushion of the sofa to keep her hands from shaking.

Zelie threw her arms around Josef, kissed him on the lips, and then spoke to him in German.

Bloody hell. Rose's breath stalled in her chest.

"Aline," Zelie said, pointing to Rose.

Rose stood and forced a smile. "*Bonjour.*"

The officer nodded, and then wiped his lips with the cuff of his jacket. He placed his briefcase on the desk, and then stepped to the liquor cabinet.

"Josef doesn't speak French," Zelie said, returning to her seat on the sofa. She opened a tube of lipstick.

"Perhaps I should go," Rose said.

"First, give me a moment to make my selections." She applied a bit of lipstick and rubbed her lips together. "Josef?"

The officer looked at her and shrugged.

"I'll try another." Zelie wiped her lips, using a washcloth.

Josef poured a glass of schnapps, and then sat in a chair. Leaning back, he propped jackboots on the coffee table, inches from the cosmetic case.

I've got to get out of here. Rose remained standing, hoping the gesture would expedite Zelie's decision. Discreetly, she glanced to the officer swirling his drink in a crystal glass. The man had short dark hair and bushy eyebrows. His nose appeared rather flat, as if it had once been broken in a boxing match. His mouth was small and pursed, contrary to his muscular, thickset body. His cap had a silver skull and crossbones emblem, and from her SOE training, she recognized him to be the rank of a *Sturmbannführer.*

The man sipped his schnapps.

Josef, Rose thought. *Sturmbannführer.* Her mind raced. The realization of who this man might be turned her blood cold. *Oh, dear God.*

"What do you think about this one?" Zelie asked, showing him another tube of lipstick.

He shook his head.

Rose's heart thumped her ribs. "Zelie," she said, struggling to remain calm. "While you're making your decision, do you mind if use your washroom to freshen up?"

"Not at all," Zelie said.

Rose retrieved her purse, stepped into the washroom, and shut the door. She took in several deep breaths, attempting to gather her composure. She paused, burying her head in her hands. She flushed the toilet, and then turned on the water, pretending to use the facilities. She retrieved her blush and lipstick and, while attempting to steady her quivering hand, she freshened her makeup. She tossed the items into her purse. To gather her courage, she thought of Mum, Dad, and Charlie. *I can do this.*

"Have you decided?" Rose said, opening the door and stepping into the room.

"I'd like these," Zelie said, pointing to a collection of cologne, blush, and eyeliner. "Josef didn't like the shades of the lipsticks."

Rose forced a smile.

"Ihr Lippenstift," Josef said, pointing to Rose.

"He likes *your* lipstick," Zelie said.

Rose swallowed. "I'm afraid that I'm all out of that shade at the moment."

"Then I'll buy yours," Zelie said. "Name your price."

A flash of the suicide pill hidden in the bottom of her lipstick. *Death within seconds.* Rose imagined dropping her L-pill into the Nazi's schnapps. "I'm flattered, Zelie," she said. "But I'd be ashamed to sell you a used tube of lipstick, which is nearly empty. I'll contact my supplier and will deliver you a new one."

Zelie puffed on her cigarette holder. "Will it take long?"

"*Non,*" Rose lied.

"Okay," Zelie said, reluctantly. She pushed her purchases to the center of the coffee table. "How much?"

Rose pretended to add up the items, and then gave Zelie a price in francs, which she hoped was in line with the going rate for hard-to-find cosmetics. And she was relieved when Zelie removed money from her purse and paid her.

Rose picked up her cosmetics case.

"Josef," Zelie said. "*Auf wiedersehen.*"

The officer raised his hand, but made no effort to stand.

"Come back soon with my lipstick," Zelie said.

"I will," Rose said. "*Au revoir.*"

Rose, desperate to leave Le Cygne Hotel, took the stairs, rather than the elevator, to the lobby. She retrieved her bicycle and exited the front doors. Her heart rate soaring, she pedaled toward home, resolute to inform Felix and Muriel of her encounter.

Three streets away from her apartment building, Rose heard the squeal of tires as a black sedan turned onto the street in front of her. The engine roared. She tried to get a good look at the vehicle, but it passed a bus and turned sharply onto another avenue. She hoped that it was an impatient driver, but the continuous grind of the vehicle weaving through the streets caused acid to rise in her stomach.

A moment later, the vehicle raced down a street, perpendicular to her route, giving her a glimpse of a man in the back seat wearing a headset. A comrade, seated next to him, was holding a small antenna out of the window. Her mouth turned dry.

She stood on her bicycle, pushing hard on the pedals. She picked up speed, willing her legs to move faster. Her muscles ached. Her lungs burned. Nearing the apartment building, the vehicle accelerated, circling the perimeter. Braking, she skidded her bicycle to a stop, and then pushed it into the building, banging the handles against the doorframe. She grabbed her purse and scampered up the stairs, toward the growing sound of a piano concerto. She fumbled for her key. Her heartbeat hammered her ribs.

Reaching the door, she heard music emanating from the apartment. She shot the key into the lock. In one swift motion, she opened the door, slammed it shut, and then sprinted toward the kitchen table.

Muriel, wearing her headset, froze. Her hand hovered over her telegraph key.

Felix shot up from his seat near a hand-crank wind-up gramophone.

Rose dashed forward and ripped out a wire jack on the transmitter.

"SD?" Felix asked, his voice drowned by the piano concerto.

Rose, gasping for air, nodded.

Muriel cut the power to her radio.

Felix shot to the window and pulled in the transmitter antenna. Seconds later, a black sedan roared down their street.

Rose lowered the volume on the record player, used to mask the tapping noise of the telegraph key from occupants in the building. But the music had also inhibited Muriel and Felix's ability to hear the vehicle narrowing in on their location.

Felix peeked through an opening in a blackout shade.

The vehicle circled the area several times. Minutes later, the growl of the engine faded, and then disappeared.

"I think they're gone," Felix said, stepping away from the window.

"That was close." Muriel slumped in her chair.

Rose stared at Felix.

"You were right, Rose," Felix said.

It's not about who is right; it's about Muriel's safety, Rose wanted to say but held her tongue. "Shall I inform Lazare to arrange the safe houses?"

Felix nodded, and then turned to Muriel. "No further transmissions until you're someplace safe. From now on, you'll be on the go."

"Aye," Muriel said, her eyes filled with a mixture of relief and uncertainty.

"I'm afraid I have some bad news," Felix said, looking at Rose. "The Germans have requisitioned transformers from other areas of Paris. Power has been restored to the sixteenth arrondissement."

A wave of chagrin swept over Rose. *Lazare and I risked our lives for a few hours of electricity loss to SD headquarters.*

"We were informing London when you came in," Felix said.

Rose took a deep breath and exhaled. She leaned her back against a wall to steady her ravaged legs. "I'm too exhausted to carry my bicycle up the stairs."

"I'll get it for you," Felix said, sounding a bit apologetic.

"I was worried about you," Muriel said, looking at Rose. "What took you so long?"

Rose swallowed. "I was delayed by a woman who wanted to buy my cosmetics; I think she's a mistress to the head of the SD."

Felix's eyes widened.

"She had trouble selecting a shade of lipstick," Rose added, suddenly realizing how ludicrous the story sounded.

Muriel's face turned pale. "You're kidding."

"I wish I was," Rose said.

She told them about her encounter with Zelie, and the man who she thought was Hans "Josef" Kieffer, head of the Sicherheitsdienst—the person leading counterespionage activities against the SOE and French Resistance. If she was right, it would be advantageous for the SOE to know the whereabouts of Kieffer. But the SOE, Rose believed, would likely want her to make more visits to Le Cygne Hotel. And if so, it would place her in more danger than she could ever have imagined.

CHAPTER 20

PARIS, FRANCE—JUNE 9, 1943

Lazare eased his weight on the banister, attempting to silence the creaking on the stairs. With each step toward Rose's apartment, a queasiness grew in his belly. It would be far easier, as well as safer, to thank her for the medicine with a cryptic message placed inside the dead drop for Conjurer, aka Felix. But Rose had been on his mind since the night of the transformer sabotage, and he wanted to extend his gratitude in person. Maybe it was the compassionate manner in which she bandaged his wounds, unaffected by his missing thumb and forefinger. Or perhaps it was the solace and affection he'd felt as they lay together, sharing each other's warmth, in the back of a disabled vehicle while German patrols scoured the arrondissement. Regardless, he yearned to see her again. The opportunity arose when Muriel, whom he'd moved to a safe house outside of the city, made him promise to check in on Rose to make sure she was all right.

Lazare knocked lightly on the door. The sound of footsteps caused his pulse to quicken.

A shadow passed over the peephole. A lock clicked and the door opened, revealing Rose. "*Bonjour*," she whispered, gesturing for him to come in.

Lazare stepped inside.

She bolted the door and turned to him. "Everything all right?"

"*Oui,*" he said.

"Felix is at the garage," Rose said. "He should be returning to his apartment soon. You're welcome to stay here while you wait."

"I came to see you," Lazare said.

"Oh," she said, appearing surprised.

Lazare shifted his weight. "I want to thank you for the sulfa pills."

"You're welcome," she said. "How are your wounds?"

He raised his hands. "*Bien.*"

She touched his hands. "Your fingers have healed splendidly."

Lazare's skin tingled.

"Not much, if any, scars." She released his hands.

"Thanks to your bandages," he said.

"And Felix's apple brandy," she said, grinning.

Lazare smiled. "Muriel asked me to stop by to check on you."

"How is she?"

"Okay, for being stuck in a decayed cottage," Lazare said. "I'll be moving her to another safe house, one with better living conditions, after her next wireless transmission."

"*Merci,*" Rose said. "When you see Muriel, please tell her that I miss her, and that I'll visit as soon as I can. Felix has insisted on temporarily delivering his transmission messages to her, rather than using me as a courier. I think it's his way of apologizing for not moving Muriel sooner, which nearly got us captured by the SD."

"I will," Lazare said. "Muriel misses you, too. And she asked me to tell you not to let your pluckiness get you into further trouble."

Rose chuckled. "That certainly sounds like Muriel."

"Have you gotten yourself into a predicament?"

Rose crossed her arms. "Nothing I can't handle."

Lazare, feeling like he had stumbled into a sensitive matter, placed his hands into his pockets. "I should go. Thank you again for the medicine."

"Would you like to stay for coffee?" she asked. "It's more like barley tea, I'm afraid. But it's quite drinkable."

Lazare nodded.

In the kitchen, Rose placed a dented metal coffeepot on the stove. She struck a match and lit a burner.

His mind raced with ideas on what to say. There was much that he wanted to know about Rose, but he thought he'd start with a question about what might be important to her. He sat at the table and said, "What led you to join the SOE?"

"It's quite a long story," she said.

He pulled a chair next to him and patted the seat.

She sat, placing her palms on the table. "I was a war room typist in London."

Lazare straightened his back.

"Surprised?" she asked.

"Intrigued," he said. "Please continue."

"Let's just say that my French linguistics caught the attention my superiors, and I was contacted by an SOE recruiter." She ran a finger over the edge of the table. "After several interviews, I was offered the position and I accepted. The combat training was grueling. One of the trainers wanted to kick me out because of my scant size and strength, but I managed to convince the SOE that I should stay."

"How?"

"I broke into a major's office and retyped a report."

Lazare's eyes widened.

"The officers quickly determined that I'd forged the document," Rose said. "But it turned out that the ability to burglarize a building is quite an attractive trait for an SOE agent." She grinned. "I didn't feel the need to tell them that I'd simply slipped through an unlocked window."

Lazare chuckled. "Muriel was right."

"About what?"

He looked at her. "You are rather plucky."

Rose tucked strands of hair behind her ear.

"I'm curious," Lazare said. "Why did you give up your life in Britain to fight the Nazis?"

"There's not much left for me back home, I'm afraid." She lowered her eyes. "Except for my friend, Lucy, and the women from the typing room."

"You mentioned to me that you lost your family," Lazare said. "Do you mind me asking what happened?"

She took a deep breath. "My parents were killed in a Luftwaffe bombing raid. My only sibling, Charlie, was shot down while flying his RAF Spitfire over the Channel." She swallowed. "His body was never recovered."

"I'm so sorry." He placed a hand on the table, inches from her fingers. "What were they like?"

"My parents were lovely. Mum was French, and Dad was English. They'd met while Dad was in France during the Great War. They fell in love and, after the war, moved to London, where they opened a small grocery." Rose looked to the ceiling, as if she were sorting through memories. "They were an affectionate couple, always holding hands, kissing, and laughing. Grocery customers often jested that my parents had never left their honeymoon."

"They sound wonderful."

Rose nodded. "Charlie was the outgoing one in the family. He could captivate a crowded room within seconds, and he had the knack of always making the person whom he was speaking with feel as though they were the most important human on the planet. He was sweet, gentle, and always sticking up for his sister, who was the smallest child in class."

"You are fortunate to have had a loving family," Lazare said, feeling his own melancholy swelling in his chest.

"I miss them terribly," Rose said. "When Charlie and I were children, Mum and Dad took us each summer to visit our grandparents in Puteaux. We had lovely vacations, which I never wanted to end."

"Now I understand why your French is perfect," Lazare said. He paused, tucking a strap on his prosthetic inside his sleeve. "Are your grandparents still living in Puteaux?"

"They passed away when I was in secondary school." She stood and poured the coffee-like mixture into cups. "I'm the last of my family tree, I'm afraid."

Me too.

Rose placed the cups on the table. Steam swirled, releasing a faint aroma of barley.

He sipped. "It's good."

"That's sweet," she said. "But I won't be offended if you say it tastes like boiled hay."

An image of having coffee with his parents filled Lazare's head. An ache grew under his sternum. He buried his thought and asked, "Did you join the fight because—" He paused, searching for the right words.

"Because Hitler's Luftwaffe killed my family?"

He nodded.

"*Oui*," she said. "And because I want to see France liberated from German occupation."

He stared into his coffee. *She's lost everything, and she's risking her life to fight.*

"So," Rose said, pushing away her cup. "Did you join the Resistance because of your family?"

"*Non*," he said. "Quite the opposite. They were pacifists, preferring the power of the pen—or in Maman's case, a paintbrush— over armed conflict."

Rose inched forward on her seat. "Tell me about them."

Footsteps in the stairwell caused Lazare to turn. A jostle of keys. The door to an apartment across the hall opened, and then shut.

"Felix," Rose said. "He usually stops by after returning home from the garage."

"What will he think about me joining you for coffee?"

Rose shrugged. "Felix thinks I should be careful around you."

"What do you think?"

She looked at him. "I think I'm safe."

"You are," he said, rising from his chair. "But I should leave."

"Stay," she said.

Lazare hesitated. A deep desire to confide in her about his family stirred in his gut. More than anything, he wanted to carry on their conversation; however, he didn't want to create any trouble for her, especially with the organizer of the Conjurer network. "Another time."

Rose stood and retrieved her purse.

"What are you doing?"

"I'm coming with you," she said.

"I don't think that is a good idea," he said.

"Why?" She stepped to him. "You know my real name. You know the members of our network. You know where I live. You know about my family, both in London and in Paris. And I know virtually nothing about you—not even where you live. Do you think that's fair?"

"We can arrange to meet another time," Lazare said, attempting to dodge her question.

"It might be weeks before I see you again, considering we're still working on the plans for our next sabotage operation, and we haven't yet been notified when the next RAF supply drop will occur. Until then, I'd rather be on equal terms."

"Equal terms?"

"I need to know as much about you as you know about me."

Lazare took a deep breath and exhaled. He deliberated whether to try and convince Rose that it was a bad idea to join him, or to create an excuse that he had other duties to attend to. But he believed, considering Rose's tenacity for joining the SOE, that she wasn't one to be easily deterred. Besides, he wanted to spend more time with her, and it was over four hours until curfew commenced, giving Rose enough time to return to her apartment. "All right, but leave your bicycle. There's no safe place to store it where we are going."

"Okay," she said.

"Follow me to the Montparnasse Cemetery," he said. "Keep a distance, in case I'm stopped to have my papers checked."

She nodded.

He glanced at her wool skirt and heeled shoes. "Put on some old clothing, including the boots you were wearing when you parachuted into France."

"Why?"

"We'll be going underground." He expected that she might change her mind, but without hesitation, Rose went to her room. As Lazare waited for her to change, he hoped that his selfish desire to spend time with her would not result in unforeseen consequences for either Rose or the French Resistance.

CHAPTER 21

THE CATACOMBS—JUNE 9, 1943

Arriving at the entrance of the Montparnasse Cemetery, Lazare kneeled and adjusted his bootlaces. Through the corners of his eyes, he watched Rose cross the street and stop beside him.

"It's on the other side of the cemetery," he whispered.

"Okay," Rose said.

Lazare stood and walked through the iron gate entrance. As he traversed a gravel path, passing rows of ancient crypts and mausoleums, he listened to the faint crunch of Rose's footsteps, and he worried that he might be making a huge blunder. Claudius, as well as his fellow partisans, would be pissed, if not infuriated, to know that he was revealing an entrance to the catacombs to someone who was not a member of the French Resistance. But there were many secret passages to the catacombs—through basement excavations, manhole covers, and sewers. Over a hundred miles of limestone quarry tunnels snaked through the underworld of Paris, and this particular catacomb did *not* connect to Claudius's lair. It led to Lazare's private subterranean sanctuary, where he rested when he could not reach a safe house. Part of him felt like he was betraying Claudius's confidence, and another part of him believed, with great certainty, that Rose was a person he could trust.

At the rear of the cemetery, he stopped near the corner of Rue Émile-Richard and Rue Froidevaux. He scanned the area, the

sidewalks shaded by a row of linden trees. After making certain
that no one was watching, he approached Rose.

"Ahead, there's a manhole cover," he breathed. "I'll open it.
You'll enter first. Descend quickly, but be careful. The iron rungs
might be slippery."

Rose nodded.

He looked into her eyes. "Are you sure you want to do this?"

"*Oui*," she whispered.

"It's not too late to turn back."

"I'm ready," she said.

Lazare retrieved a small metal crowbar—hidden behind a bush
near a stone wall—and slipped it inside his jacket. He waited,
watching an old man pedal a bicycle down the street. Once the
area was clear, he dashed to the manhole cover and pried it open.
He lugged the iron cover to the side, scraping the pavement. Rose
slipped inside, feet first, and descended the metal ladder. He stuck
the crowbar inside his belt and climbed down three steps. Using
an arm and shoulder, he labored the cover back into its place, turning the hole black.

Lazare descended deep into the ground. The chill of the iron
rungs penetrated his hands. "Are you all right?" he asked, reaching the base of the tunnel.

"*Oui*," she said.

Lazare ran his hand along a wall and found a large crevice where
he kept a flashlight. He inserted the crowbar, retrieved the flashlight, and then flipped the switch, shooting a dim beam through
the tunnel. Fortunately, there was no standing water, due to lack
of rain, but the air still smelled stagnant and laced with mildew.

"Your electric torch is almost dead," Rose said, her voice echoing through the tunnel.

"It's okay," he said. "I know the way."

For several minutes he led Rose through the tunnel, until he
reached a chest-height hole, the size of a hubcap, that had been
chiseled through a stone wall. He squeezed through the opening, having to rotate his shoulders, and then helped Rose through
the cavity. They descended deeper, taking stone stairs until they

reached a long tunnel, which looked like the passageway to an Egyptian crypt, its limestone walls decorated with medieval carvings. Farther ahead, Lazare purposely redirected the flashlight beam to the ceiling, but there was little he could do to hide a mosaic bone pile comprised of human skulls and femurs.

"Good Lord," Rose gasped.

"We're nearly there," he said, hoping to alleviate her concern. *It was selfish and foolish of me to bring you here.*

"I read about the catacombs in school," Rose said, her voice regaining poise. "I can see why you chose it. The police or Wehrmacht would have little desire to venture down here. This might be the safest place in all of Paris."

"So far, enemy patrols have not penetrated the catacombs," Lazare said. *I pray that it stays this way.*

They climbed through another, even smaller, hole, reaching an arched chamber. The air was stagnant, but no longer contained the odor of mold. He lit a lantern hanging from a metal spike that had been driven into limestone. A glow filled the room, revealing a fold-up cot, blankets, and a stack of books. Leaning against a wall was his mother's painting, *Arc de Triomphe*, which he'd framed by using broken pieces of lath.

"How often do you stay here?" Rose asked.

"Occasionally," he said, feeling embarrassed about his temporary, but horrid, living conditions. "Many nights, I stay in safe houses, but there are times when it is best for me to stay here."

Rose approached the painting. "It's lovely. Did you make it?"

"*Non,*" Lazare said. "My *maman.*"

"She's quite talented," Rose said. "It should be in a museum so people can enjoy it."

A wave of appreciation washed over him. "Perhaps, after the war, it will find a more suitable home." He took a deep breath. "You're welcome to sit on the cot. Or we can leave, if you've seen enough."

"I'll stay." Rose sat on the cot, and then pointed to the stack of books. "What are you reading?"

"*In Search of Lost Time* by Marcel Proust," Lazare said.

"Is it good?"

"Inspiring," Lazare said. "And quite long, considering the work has seven volumes. You're welcome to read it."

"You do know that by loaning me a book, you'll be required to see me again."

Lazare fidgeted with a button on his coat. "*Oui.*"

"You don't have to stand," Rose said, patting the cot. "There's room for both of us."

He sat beside her, and then leaned his back against the stone wall. "I'm sorry that I couldn't bring you to a more suitable place."

"It's not so bad." Rose nudged him with her elbow. "But maybe next time we could meet at the Ritz."

Lazare smiled. "I'll see what I can do."

Rose leaned her back against the wall, her shoulder touching his arm. "Tell me about your life, before the war."

"I grew up on Rue Cler in the seventh arrondissement," he said. "My parents were immigrants from Warsaw. They came with virtually nothing. Through endless hard work, they created a good life for us. Papa was a journalist and Maman was a painter. They were compassionate parents, filling my life with books and art."

"They sound lovely," Rose said.

Lazare nodded. "I had dreamed of becoming a journalist, like Papa, but things changed when the war erupted. After being rejected from joining the army," Lazare said, raising his prosthetic hand, "I was unable to find work with any of the newspaper publishers, which were under German control after the invasion. The only job I could find was as a janitor, cleaning the floors and toilets at the Gare du Nord train station."

Rose paused, running a finger over a rip in the cot's fabric. "How did you join the Resistance?"

"Initially, I rebelled on my own by posting anti-Nazi propaganda." A lump formed in the back of his throat. "But one day, on my way to work at the train station, I witnessed a German officer shoot a man in the head for reading one of my posters."

"My God," she said, her voice dropping to a whisper.

Lazare swallowed. "I still have visions of the man's face, his wife wailing over his body."

"It wasn't your fault," Rose said.

Lazare nodded, even though he feared that his scars of culpability would likely never fade. "Adamant to fight, I committed lone acts of sabotage. One evening, while setting fire to German vehicles, I was spotted by Wehrmacht officers. If not for Claudius, who had been following me, I would have been killed. Claudius inducted me into the Resistance. He took me in and trained me, even though—" Lazare hesitated, rubbing his chin.

"Your hand?" Rose asked.

My ethnicity. "It's a little more complicated than that," he said. "Claudius accepted me as a partisan. He's more than a Resistance leader to me; he's like an uncle."

"What did your parents think about you joining the Resistance?"

"At first, Maman and Papa did not want me to fight. They didn't condone acts of violence to free France, and they believed that we should wait to be liberated by Allied forces. But eventually, they grew to support my decision." Lazare touched his prosthetic with his fingers. A pang grew in his chest. "Maman painted it. She thought it would help me to look ordinary, keeping me safe."

Rose touched his hand. "What happened to them?"

An ache grew in his chest. "They were arrested by the French police."

"Why?"

His breath turned shallow. "For being Jews."

"Oh, no." Rose squeezed his fingers. "I'm so sorry."

"I had tried to convince them to escape to Vichy France. But they'd refused to leave their home. Last July, the police—acting on orders by the Germans—rounded up thousands of French Jews, including Maman and Papa. They were imprisoned in the Vélodrome d'Hiver, an indoor cycle track, where they suffered unbearable heat and lack of water before being loaded into cattle cars and shipped away."

"To where?" Rose asked, her voice soft.

"I don't know," he said. "There were rumors that the Jews were sent to German work camps. But the roundup included young children and elderly, who were unable to perform labor. I fear that the Germans have far more sinister plans for them. I pray that they're alive, but something, deep in my gut, tells me that I might never see them again."

"They'll make it back," she said, leaning to him. "We must have faith that they'll be all right."

Lazare looked at her and noticed that her eyes were filled with tears. "It's probably not a good idea to be spending time with a Jew, let alone a partisan."

Rose dabbed her eyes with her sleeve. "No less safe than being in the company of a British agent."

He noticed a tear on her cheek. Using his good hand, he gently wiped it away. "It's getting late. You should be getting back to your apartment. Felix will be worried about you."

"Come with me," she said. "There's no reason for you to stay here when I have plenty of space. You can use Muriel's room, while she's away."

"I appreciate your offer, but you and I both know that it is not a good idea."

"I don't care," Rose said.

Lazare looked into her eyes. "I do."

Rose lowered her head.

More than anything, he longed for more time with her. He wished that he'd met her at another time, another place. Rose, Lazare believed, was unlike any woman he had ever met, especially his former girlfriend, Charlotte.

Lazare had dated Charlotte while attending the University of Paris. She had been attractive, gregarious, and her family had a long line of decorated military veterans, including her father, who served as a major in the Great War. She'd been allured, Lazare believed, by his patriotism and passion for journalism. Initially, he thought Charlotte might be the woman he would spend his life with. But things changed when war was declared on Germany, and he was rejected from joining the French army due to his maimed hand. As the able-bodied men left to defend France, Charlotte distanced herself from Lazare, and she eventually refused to communicate with him. He was dispirited. *She's ashamed to be with someone who is deemed unfit for the military.* As time passed, Lazare realized that it was best that they had taken separate paths. More importantly, he realized that he wanted the type of relationship his parents had created—affection without any limitations.

Lazare buried his memories. Willing himself to stand, he extended his hand and helped Rose to her feet.

They spoke little during their trek through the catacomb. As his flashlight faded, he picked up the pace, hoping to get Rose to the entrance before the batteries failed. But soon, the light beam waned, and then abruptly went out.

Lazare shook the flashlight, then slipped it into his pocket. "It's okay," he said, clasping her hand. "I know the way by memory."

Rose squeezed his fingers.

He maneuvered through the catacomb, all the while taking comfort in her touch. A few minutes later, they reached the ladder to the manhole cover. He stopped, but their fingers remained entwined.

"Are you sure you won't come with me?" she asked.

"*Non*," he said, despite his heart prodding him to accept. He released her hand. As he was about to ascend the ladder, he felt Rose lean into him, her arms around his waist. His stomach fluttered.

"Be careful," she whispered.

"You too." Lazare squeezed her, taking in her warmth. He felt her body rise as she stood on her toes. Her lips pressed to his cheek. His heartbeat quickened. And as quickly as the embrace came, she slipped away.

Gathering his composure, he climbed the rungs to the manhole cover. He pried it slightly open, revealing a dark street, absent of movement. He lugged the lid to the side, stepped out, and then helped Rose to the surface. She darted into the cemetery and disappeared. Entering the hole, he lugged the iron cover back into its place. He descended into the catacombs, his skin still tingling from her touch.

CHAPTER 22

PARIS, FRANCE—JUNE 22, 1943

It had been two weeks since Rose had seen Lazare, but thoughts of him, the tragedy of his parents—as well as the thousands of French Jews who'd been rounded up by the police and shipped away in cattle cars—had never left her mind. *What have the Nazis done with them?* Hitler's anti-Semitic pandemic, once believed to have been quarantined to Germany, had ravaged Paris. *If these heinous crimes are taking place in France, what's happening in German-occupied Poland, Czechoslovakia, Norway, Belgium, and the Netherlands?* A wave of abhorrence flooded her body. More than ever, she was resolute to do everything she could to disrupt Nazism and bring the war to an end.

Like Rose, Lazare had endured the loss of family and was secretly fighting the Germans. But unlike Rose, Lazare was forced to hide his ethnicity. She couldn't begin to imagine what it was like to be persecuted because of one's race; to be stripped of human rights, required to wear a yellow star, arrested, sentenced to Nazi work camps, or worse. She wished that there were something that she could do for him, and she toiled over what she could say to convince him to take refuge in her spare room rather than sleep among the ancient dead. To compound matters, she had no idea when she'd see him again, considering they were still waiting for word from London on the next RAF supply drop, for which Lazare and members of the French Resistance would serve as a reception committee. Also, Felix was in the midst of planning, in collaboration with Prosper and his Physician network, a mission to destroy a train trestle between Paris and Arras. Both operations, assuming Rose was chosen to participate, would give her a chance to see him again. But when?

Being alone exacerbated Rose's desire to see him. The loneliness of her apartment allowed her mind to wander, reliving the story of Lazare's *maman* and *papa*, as well as the demise of her own family, all of whom were casualties of Hitler's wrath. And while dwelling upon her own angst, she was reminded that Muriel, who'd moved to another safe house somewhere in the third arrondissement, would no doubt be lamenting over leaving her baby to join the SOE. So, when Felix stopped by her apartment to inform her that he was headed to see Muriel to send a wireless transmission to London, she was determined to join him.

"I want to see Muriel," Rose said. "I'm already going to Le Marais to deliver your message to Prosper. It's close to the third arrondissement."

"No need to have all three of us at the same location during a wireless transmission," Felix said.

"I know that you're trying to protect us," Rose said, recalling how the SD nearly tracked Muriel's transmission to their apartment building. "But Muriel's our friend. She's alone, and she'll be worried sick about her baby."

"*Non*," he said.

"Surely you can relate to the hell she's going through," Rose said. "You're fighting for France's freedom and to bring your son, Mathieu, home."

Felix rubbed his jowl.

"Muriel joined the SOE so Mabel might have a chance to grow up in a world that isn't controlled by a demonic dictator."

"Rose—"

"If you were companionless inside a safe house," Rose said, interrupting, "I can assure you that both Muriel and I would go to extreme measures to check in on you."

Felix sighed. "All right, but I don't want this to become a routine."

"It won't," Rose said, knowing it was a promise she would likely not be able to keep.

Felix gave her the address. Before he changed his mind, Rose retrieved her bicycle. Together, they left the apartment. Felix walked, while Rose pedaled ahead to deliver a coded message, hidden inside a secret compartment of her purse, to Prosper's dead drop in Le Marais. Arriving at the address of Muriel's apartment building, she found Felix, a cigarette in hand, near the entrance. She followed him inside, where they descended a dark stairway and entered a basement apartment.

"It's lovely to see you," Rose said, greeting Muriel.

"I've missed you." Muriel smiled, accentuating the dark circles under her eyes.

"Are you okay?" Rose asked.

"Aye," Muriel said.

The basement flat contained no bed, only a mattress with blankets in the corner of the room. There was a wood table with one stool, a cast-iron stove, and a rusted wash basin, from which water dripped from a corroded faucet. An oval rug, which appeared to be made from leftover burlap bags, covered a masonry floor.

"I was hoping that Lazare would arrange a better place for you," Felix said. "It's nearly as bad as that provincial country cottage you were staying in."

A flash of Lazare's cot in the catacomb. Rose's skin turned warm. "Maybe this is the best that he and the Resistance could arrange. Have you considered that they might be living in far worse conditions?"

Felix raised his brows. "I didn't mean to disparage their efforts to provide us with safe houses. I merely want Muriel to have adequate living quarters, something comparable to our arrangements."

Rose crossed her arms. "I do, too, but—"

"It's fine," Muriel said, stepping between them. "It's a wee dank, but it's perfectly fine. Besides, I'm glad to be back in Paris, close to both of you."

Rose, preferring not to explain to Felix how she'd seen Lazare's living environment, buried her sentiment and said, "I'm sorry."

Felix nodded, and then glanced to his watch. "We should contact headquarters."

Muriel retrieved her suitcase containing her wireless radio and placed it on the table. While she set up the transmitter, Felix placed the antenna outside of a minuscule, ground-level window covered in a layer of dirt from the alley, which was little more than a two-foot, weed-infested walkway between brick buildings.

"I hope we can get reception," Felix said, stepping to the table.

Muriel slipped on her headset, and then flipped a switch on the radio. A hum grew from the transistor tubes.

Felix scribbled a message, requesting headquarters to verify the date of the next RAF supply drop, and slid it to Muriel.

Tension grew in Rose's shoulders, as she realized that this particular shipment would include more than armament and plastic explosives. Hopefully, the drop would contain a unique shade of lipstick, which matched the one that contained her L-pill.

After Rose's encounter with Zelie, who appeared to be a mistress to Hans Josef Kieffer, head of the Sicherheitsdienst, they'd promptly informed London. Felix believed that London might order Conjurer, or perhaps their parent network, Physician, to assassinate Kieffer. But Rose was not surprised that headquarters wanted her to continue delivering cosmetics to Zelie in an effort to gain her trust, potentially allowing her to gain insight into the SD. After all, having knowledge about Nazi counterintelligence could be far more beneficial than exterminating an SD leader. The enemy would simply replace Kieffer with someone as brutal, or perhaps more deadly, and the SOE would be left with no chance of preempting the SD's plans.

Muriel transferred Felix's message into cypher, and then tapped out the transmission, making certain to include both of her security checks.

A moment later, Muriel nodded, letting them know that London was responding, and then wrote out the message, which she quickly deciphered.

```
  No makeup to wear to the party.
Reception postponed.
```

Muscles tightened in Rose's neck.

"Inquire as to how long," Felix said, not taking the time to write out a message.

Muriel transferred his inquiry into cypher and tapped out the transmission. Seconds passed, then she scribbled on a piece of paper. After decoding the message, she handed it to Felix.

```
  Two weeks, assuming the invitations are
available to deliver.
```

"Damn it," Felix said.

"I shouldn't have made the mistake of telling Zelie that it wouldn't take me long to get the lipstick from my supplier," Rose said.

"It's your particular shade that she wants," Felix said. "We might have more delays, so let's give it to her."

"But it's used and contains my L-pill," Rose said.

"Show me," Felix said, holding out his hand.

Rose reached into her purse, and then handed Felix a brass tube.

He unscrewed the bottom, revealing a secret chamber, which held the rubber-coated cyanide tablet. "I'd much rather you dispose of this in Kieffer's brandy. But for now, we'll follow London's orders."

Rose swallowed.

Felix screwed on the bottom, and then slipped off the tube's cover. He twisted the base, raising the lipstick. "Plenty left, and I think I can make it look new by using a little heat to melt the tip."

Rose opened her cosmetics case, which she carried with her as part of her cover story. She gave Felix a new tube of lipstick, providing a model to duplicate.

For the next thirty minutes, Felix worked with precision to switch Rose's lipstick with another tube. Using a knife, heated with a cigarette lighter, he molded the tip to appear as if it had been freshly extracted from a mold. He waved a flame over the balm, turning the edges smooth.

"It looks good," Rose said.

"*Merci*," Felix said. "When I was a Grand Prix racer, I was often faced with improvising repairs. Although cosmetics is far different from mechanics, this reminds me of when I had to fix—in the middle of a race in Monaco—a leaking fuel line with tape and chewing gum."

"Did it work?" Muriel asked.

Felix grinned. "I finished the race, and I beat all of the German drivers."

Rose took the tube and placed it inside her cosmetics case. She slipped her own tube, containing her poison pill and a new shade of lipstick, into her purse. "I guess I should pay a visit to Zelie."

"Good luck," Felix said, stepping to the door. "Stop by later to let me know how things went." He left the apartment, closing the door behind him.

Rose turned to Muriel. A pang of guilt rose in her chest. "I'm sorry that I haven't been able to see you."

"It's okay," Muriel said. "Please, don't worry about me. I signed up to be a wireless operator, knowing full well what the role required. We can catch up, after we win this bloody war. I'll bring you to Edinburgh to meet Mabel."

"That'll be lovely," Rose said.

Muriel paused, running fingers through her hair. "I miss her," she said, a quaver in her voice.

"I'm sure Mabel misses you, too." Rose squeezed Muriel's shoulder. "When you go home, she'll understand."

"You think so?"

Rose smiled. "I know so."

Muriel wiped tears from her eyes, and then walked Rose to the door. "The next time I see you, I don't want to learn that you've done something foolish, like promising shades of cosmetics to SD mistresses."

Rose chuckled. She hesitated, holding the doorknob. "Have you seen Lazare?"

"Yes," Muriel said. "When he gave me the key to this room."

"How is he?" Rose asked.

Muriel smiled. "He asked about you, too."

Rose's stomach fluttered.

"You're a courier," Muriel said. "Perhaps you should find out for yourself."

Rose nodded. She desperately wanted to confide in Muriel about Lazare. Although she didn't think that he would be upset, she also didn't want to risk breaching any lines of confidentiality. *Another time.*

She hugged Muriel and left the safe house. As she made her way to Le Cygne Hotel, her happiness to see Muriel faded. She wondered if Zelie would be at the hotel and, if so, would she be in the company of Kieffer? Shivers ran down her spine. She buried her thoughts, convincing herself that she'd simply deliver the lipstick and leave. But deep down she knew, if given the chance, she'd place herself in peril to probe the desk, which might contain Kieffer's papers.

Rose was relieved to find the lobby of Le Cygne Hotel absent of German officers. Gathering her confidence, she stepped to the front desk attendant.

"I'm here to see Zelie," Rose said, regretting she hadn't obtained the woman's last name.

"Your name?" a gray-haired male receptionist asked.

"Aline." Rose raised her leather case. "I'm delivering her cosmetics."

The man picked up a phone.

Seconds passed. Rose's chest tightened. *Maybe she's gone.*

"*Mademoiselle,*" the man said. "A woman named Aline is here to see you."

Rose squeezed the handle of her case.

"*Oui, Mademoiselle.*" The man lowered the receiver into its cradle. "You can go up. Do you know the room?"

"*Oui,*" Rose said, turning toward the elevator.

At the seventh-floor room, Rose was met by Zelie, who was wearing a cream-colored silk robe and standing in the doorway.

Zelie puffed on the tip of her cigarette holder. "Darling," she said, exhaling smoke, "I hope you have my lipstick."

"I do," Rose said, sporting a fake smile.

As she entered the room, the sound of running water, coming from behind the closed bathroom door, caused goose bumps to crop up on Rose's arms. The unmade bed, the sheets in twisted swirls, prompted carnal visions. Her stomach churned with disgust.

"I can come back at another time," Rose offered.

"Josef is showering," Zelie said, sitting on the sofa. She crossed her legs, exposing her thighs. "I have a few minutes."

Rose joined her on the sofa. Placing her case on her lap, as if to shield herself, she opened the lid and gave the lipstick to Zelie.

"Do you have a mirror?" Zelie asked, removing the cap.

Rose adjusted her case, which contained a small mirror on the interior of the lid.

Zelie leaned in, her robe slightly opening to expose a bare breast. She glided the balm over her lips.

Rose turned her eyes. On the desk was an opened briefcase and a German officer's cap placed on top of a stack of manila files. A curiosity grew in her gut.

"What do you think?" Zelie asked.

Rose looked at Zelie puckering her lips. "Exquisite."

"I'll take it." Zelie, making no effort to cover her body with her robe, went to the opposite side of the room.

The sound of gushing water stopped. Shower curtain hooks scraped over a metal bar. Rose stood, her heart rate accelerating.

"Where did I put my purse?" Zelie mumbled, searching the base of an armoire.

Rose glanced to the desk, a few feet away.

"Maybe I put it in the closet." Zelie opened a door and kneeled, blocking her view of Rose, as well as the desk.

Rose crept to the desk and placed her hand near the papers.

Zelie dug through the closet.

Every fiber in her body craved to flee. But Rose, compelled by her sense of duty, held her ground. She lifted the military cap, bringing with it a medicinal scent of hair tonic. She fought back her fear and, using a finger, she raised the cover of the manila file, revealing the cover page to a report written in German:

Gedeihen/Arzt

She lifted the page, revealing a list of names.

Footsteps grew from the washroom.

A jolt shot through Rose. She closed the folder and covered it with the cap.

"Found it!" Zelie said.

The washroom door opened.

Rose turned, grabbing her cosmetics case.

Standing in the doorway, engulfed in steam, was Kieffer. He adjusted the belt on his trousers. A wad of chest hair sprouted from the neckline of his undershirt, which appeared two sizes too small for his barrel chest. "*Was machst du denn hier?*" he grumbled.

Rose's breath stalled in her lungs.

"*Lippenstift,*" Zelie said, approaching Rose and giving her money.

Kieffer, his brows lowered, stared at Rose. "*Verlassen uns.*"

Zelie wrapped her arm around Rose's elbow and walked her to the door. "In the future," Zelie whispered, "it might be best if you come by a little earlier in the day. Josef is quite fond of our afternoons."

Rose nodded, hoping Zelie couldn't feel her pounding heart.

"Come by in a few weeks," Zelie said, opening the door. "Or sooner if you get your hands on something divine."

"*Oui,*" Rose said.

She took the elevator to the lobby and retrieved her bicycle. Her legs turned weak, and she struggled to pedal away, nearly losing her balance and striking a light pole. She gripped the handlebars to steady herself. As she headed toward her apartment building, her brain labored to piece together the brief flash of the report. *If only I could understand German. With a few more seconds, I could have examined the names on the report and known for sure.* As she speculated on what she'd seen, a looming sense of dread impelled her to change her course to the Montparnasse Cemetery.

Arriving at Lazare's dead drop, she scribbled a message onto a piece of paper:

I need to see you.

She inserted the message into the hidden crevice, and then sped toward her apartment. Her adrenaline surged through her veins. She hoped that Felix would be there. Even more, she prayed that she was wrong.

Chapter 23

Paris, France—June 22, 1943

Rose, out of breath from lugging her bicycle up the stairs, knocked on Felix's apartment. She sucked in air, struggling to slow her heart rate. *Please be home.* Footsteps approached. The door opened, and she darted inside.

"What's wrong?" Felix asked, wrinkles forming across his forehead. He leaned her bicycle against the wall.

Rose's hands trembled. "I'm concerned that the Physician network might be infiltrated."

"*Mon Dieu,*" Felix gasped. "How?"

She told him about her visit with Zelie, and her glimpse of Kieffer's papers. "It was a report, containing a list of people."

"What was the name of the report?"

"It was in German and contained two words. One started with *G*, and the other word began with an *A*."

Felix sighed. "Did you get the names?"

Rose shook her head. "It was a long list and I only had time for a glimpse. The first name was Frank or something similar."

Felix frowned. "And from this, you concluded that the network has been infiltrated?"

Rose's confidence waned. "I think the names might not be German."

"The name, Frank, could be German," Felix said. "Could it have been Friedrich or Franz?"

"Maybe," Rose said.

"But you don't know for sure."

Rose shook her head, her stomach feeling like she'd swallowed a stone.

Felix lit a cigarette and inhaled. "So," he said, blowing smoke, "if I understand correctly, you have an inkling that the SD *might* have a list of non-Germanic names, and from this, you've deduced that the F Section network has been compromised. And your evidence to support the claim is that one of the names *might* be Frank, or something similar."

"When you put it like that," Rose said, crossing her arms, "I sound like a bloody fool."

"*Non*," Felix said. "You simply didn't get the opportunity to thoroughly inspect the papers. The SOE should have provided us a miniature camera."

"It wouldn't have done any good," Rose said. "There wasn't enough time for a photograph."

Felix sighed. "What do you want to do?"

"Have Muriel contact headquarters to make certain that all F Section agents are accounted for," Rose said.

Felix hesitated, rolling his cigarette between his fingers. "We need accurate information."

"There's no time. I may never get a chance to access the papers again." Rose looked at him. "I'll take responsibility. Inform headquarters that Dragonfly has concerns about the security of the network. What can it hurt?"

"Making an unscheduled transmission will give the SD another crack at finding Muriel."

Rose pressed a hand to the ache in her belly. "We have no choice but to make certain the network is safe."

Felix snuffed out his cigarette in an ashtray. "Okay, but I go alone to Muriel's safe house."

"*Merci*," Rose said.

"In the meantime," Felix said, "work on recalling the names on Kieffer's paper."

Rose went to her apartment. She slumped into a chair, her mind deliberating on what she might, or might not, have seen. *Maybe my nerves are causing me to hallucinate.* Unable to eat, she forced herself to drink a cup of hot water flavored with a bit of barley, which did little, if anything, to improve her recall. For three hours, she scribbled letters onto a piece of paper, striving to recreate the names. But it was of no use. After three hours, she was unable to resurrect the images which would, in all likelihood, remain hidden in the vault of her subconscious, as well as Kieffer's briefcase. She abandoned her efforts when Felix arrived at her apartment.

"Headquarters does not believe that the networks have been infiltrated," Felix said.

"Thank God," Rose said, her shoulder muscles tense.

"Get some rest," Felix said. "You've had a hell of a day."

A restlessness stirred within her. "How does headquarters know that they're right?"

He looked at her. "They've been in recent contact with each of the F Section wireless operators. Everyone is accounted for."

"Okay," Rose said. "I appreciate you taking steps to verify with London."

Felix nodded, and then left the apartment.

Rose pondered if she were overreacting, or if there was merit for her disquietude. She thought about Muriel and how the un-scheduled transmission had, yet again, put her friend at risk of be-ing captured by the SD's wireless tracking unit. She felt horrible for Muriel and the other wireless operators, who were continu-ously on the move, like migrating wildebeests. *If a wireless opera-tor was captured, and then tortured to reveal their security checks, could the SD pose as a British agent?* She shuddered, and then buried her thoughts, refusing to imagine that such a vicissitude could betide the SOE. Her mind and body drained, she went to her room and collapsed onto the bed.

A soft knock awakened Rose. Her heart rate accelerating, she sat up in her bed and glanced around the dark room. A sliver of moonlight sprayed through a crack in the blackout shade. She reached under the pillow and clasped her pistol, the cold steel rousing her senses, and then crept into the hallway.

Three light taps on the door. *Felix always knocks once.* Her skin prickled. She flipped off the pistol's safety. Placing her eye to the peephole, she struggled to see, the corridor void of light.

"It's Lazare," a voice whispered.

Rose exhaled, removing her finger from the pistol's trigger. She let him inside and bolted the door. "I'm sorry that you've come so late," she said. "What time is it?"

"Midnight," he said. "I came as soon as I discovered your message."

Memories of the afternoon flooded her head. Rose clasped his hand, wrapping her fingers over his prosthetic, and led him to a sofa. She placed her pistol on a side table, lit a candle, and then adjusted the blackout shade, making certain there were no openings in which light could escape.

"Are you all right?" he asked.

She sat beside him, the candlelight reflecting in his eyes. Anxiety swelled in her chest. She was required to be cautious with intelligence she provided Lazare, or any other partisan. He wasn't SOE, and there were strict protocols on how information was communicated with the Resistance, which was usually dispersed from a network leader. *But wouldn't keeping the Resistance informed of consequential matters in turn protect the SOE?* Also, she wasn't entirely convinced that Felix, or British headquarters for that matter, would give any further consideration to her baseless concerns that the Physician network might be infiltrated by the SD. Deep down, she knew she could trust Lazare. He was risking everything to liberate France. He'd told her about his parents and Jewish heritage, and he'd revealed to her his secret passage to the catacombs. Lazare had held nothing back, she believed, and he'd placed himself in jeopardy by opening up his heart. *Why can't I do the same?* So, she told him everything. About her visits to Zelie, her encounter with Kieffer, and her suspicions—although far-fetched and with no specific evidence to justify her claim—that the SD might have infiltrated the F Section networks.

Lazare rubbed his temples, as if trying to absorb what Rose had said. "Have you informed your superiors?"

"*Oui*," she said. "Felix relayed my concern to headquarters. They believe the network is secure. All wireless operators are accounted for."

"And yet you remain concerned," Lazare said. "Why?"

"Intuition, really," Rose said, feeling a bit irrational. "I find it odd that the head of the SD is carrying a list of English names."

"But you can't recall any of the names, except that one of them might be someone called Frank."

Rose lowered her head into her hand. "I must sound ridiculous."

"*Non*," Lazare said, placing a hand on her shoulder. "I believe in you."

Rose, taking in the comfort of his touch, looked at him.

He gently squeezed her shoulder. "If you're concerned, so am I."

"*Merci*," she said.

Lazare lowered his hand to his lap. "I'll inform Claudius. But for now, I will not mention the possibility of an infiltration to the other partisans. Although I have complete confidence in each of our Resistance fighters, it is feasible that someone could be coerced or bribed to collaborate with the enemy."

Rose nodded.

"For now," he said. "Suspend delivering messages to dead drops."

"How will we contact the Resistance or Prosper?"

"You don't, at least for a few days. If the networks have been infiltrated, the SD will soon determine where the dead drops are located, as well as the safe houses."

Muriel. A knot formed in Rose's stomach. "How will I reach you?"

"Go to the manhole cover we used to enter the catacombs. There's a small gap to fit a prybar. Slip a note through it. Other than you and me, no one is aware of this particular entrance."

"Okay," Rose said.

"I'll work to establish new safe houses," Lazare said. "I'll move you, Felix, and Muriel as soon as possible, but it might take a few days. In the interim, keep on the move as much as possible. Also, I'd prefer that you don't visit Zelie. It's far too dangerous."

"I have no plans of going back there, for at least a couple weeks. But eventually, I need to return." A foreboding lump formed in the pit of her belly. "It's my duty."

Lazare sighed and reluctantly nodded.

"Anything else?" she asked.

"*Oui*," Lazare said. "When was the last time you ate?"

Surprised, Rose straightened her spine. "I don't remember. This morning—yesterday, I think."

He stood and extended his hand. "Come. I'll make you something to eat."

Rose hesitated, feeling a smidge of guilt, even though she knew it was rather irrational not to take time for nourishment.

"There's nothing more we can do tonight," Lazare said, as if he understood what she was feeling. "You can resume your work in the morning, when curfew is over. For now, it'll do you good to eat and sleep."

Rose clasped his hand, feeling his strength lift her from the sofa.

In the kitchen, Rose sat at the table while Lazare scoured the cabinets to gather scraps of food—a withered carrot, an onion, and a nearly eaten tin of tuna. Using oil from the tuna, he sautéed the vegetables in a cast-iron skillet. He toasted a stale endpiece of a baguette after scraping away blotches of green mold.

"Can I help?" Rose asked.

"*Non*," Lazare said, placing the toast onto a plate. "Do you have any tea?"

"I'm all out of leaves, I'm afraid." Rose pointed. "But there's apple brandy under the sink."

"Felix's stash?"

"*Oui*. After today, I could use a drink. Will you join me?"

He nodded, and then retrieved the brandy and two glasses. He dished the sautéed vegetables onto a plate, and then drizzled the roasted bits, left in the bottom of the skillet, over the toast.

"Smells lovely," she said. "Other than my father, you're the first man to make me supper."

"I find that hard to believe," Lazare said. "I'm sure your boyfriend back home has made you many meals."

Rose wiggled her toes inside her shoes, trying to dispel butterflies in her abdomen. "I don't have a boyfriend."

He poured the brandy, and then gave her a glass. "To the end of the war."

"With an Allied victory," Rose added, clinking her glass to his.

He smiled, and then took a drink of his brandy.

Rose sipped, tasting a whisky-like alcohol, which tasted nothing like apples. It reminded her of the evening glasses of scotch that she'd drunk with the SOE candidates at Garramor House. A burn traveled down her throat, causing her to cough.

"Okay?" he asked.

She nodded. "Aren't you going to eat?"

"I've already eaten," he said.

"We'll share," Rose said, patting the chair next to her. "I insist."

Lazare sat.

Rose placed a forkful of carrot into her mouth. She chewed, savoring the sweetness of caramelized onion, and then swallowed. "It's delightful. Did one of your girlfriends teach you to cook?"

Lazare chuckled. "Maman and Papa taught me. They were Polish immigrants who were smitten by French cuisine. They thought it was important for their son to learn how to make his own meals."

She took a bite of toast, the rich drippings from the bottom of the pan awakening her hunger. Her stomach gurgled. "Excuse me."

Lazare smiled.

"Try some."

"I'll get a utensil," he said.

"No need." She forked a bit of carrot and extended it to his mouth. Her heart rate jumped.

Lazare accepted the food, slowly chewed, and then swallowed. "It's good."

"So," she said, her curiosity building in her chest. "You never had a girlfriend?"

"I once dated a woman named Charlotte. We met at the University of Paris." Lazare took a sip of brandy. "But our relationship didn't last long."

"Why?" she asked.

Lazare raised his prosthetic hand. "She was less than impressed when I was rejected by the French army."

"She made a mistake," Rose said, feeling a strange mixture of resentment and indebtedness toward a woman whom she'd never met. "It's a good thing that it didn't work out."

Lazare nodded. "Was there ever anyone special for you?"

"I dated a little," Rose said. "But I never met someone I fancied."

"You will," Lazare said.

"What makes you so sure?" she asked.

"Any man would feel lucky to be with you," Lazare said.

Rose's skin flushed.

"After the war, you'll have loads of suitors," he said. "Eventually, you will meet the right person."

What if I already have? She took a gulp of brandy, trying to quell her thoughts. *Lazare is compassionate, handsome, honest, gentle, and selfless. He's devoted to saving his country and its people. I feel like I can be myself when I'm with him, and he gives me hope of a better tomorrow.* "Haven't given much thought about life after the war, I'm afraid."

"You must have dreams," Lazare said, scooching his chair close. "What do you want your life to be like?"

Rose's mind raced. She ran a finger over the edge of her glass. "I'd love to have a life like my parents."

"Tell me more," Lazare said.

"My parents loved each other, more than any couple I'd ever met. They were always holding hands, hugging, and laughing. They were splendid parents who made every effort to give their children a good life." A subtle grin spread over Rose's face. "My schoolmates often jested that they wanted to have my mum and dad as their parents, which increased in frequency when my brother, Charlie, concocted a tale that we were given free rein to eat as many sweets as we wanted at the Teasdale Grocery."

Lazare laughed. "I would have loved to have met them."

Me too. Her knee brushed his leg, causing her skin to tingle.

"It sounds like you and Charlie were close," he said.

"Inseparable," Rose said.

"I always wanted siblings," he said. "My mother had a difficult childbirth. She was unable to have any more children after she delivered me."

"I'm sorry."

"No need to feel bad for me," Lazare said, swirling his brandy. "They spoiled me rotten."

"I doubt that," she said. She took a swig, feeling a warmth filter toward her stomach.

"Do you want to have children?"

"*Oui*," she said.

"How many?"

"At least two," she said. "How about you?"

"Loads of kids," he said.

She chuckled. "Like twelve?"

"*Non*," he said, smiling. "Two would be nice."

She looked at him, the candlelight shimmering over his face. "Do you plan to become a journalist, like your papa?"

"Absolutely," he said.

"In Paris?"

He nodded. "Unless my heart leads me someplace else."

"Like where?"

He took a sip of brandy. "I've always wanted to visit some of the world's most influential cities. New York. Toronto. London. Hong Kong. Brussels. Melbourne."

Rose tucked strands of hair behind her ear. "You'd love London."

"You really think so?"

She nodded.

"What about you?" Lazare asked. "What will you do after the war?"

"I haven't thought much about it," she said. "I might return to being a typist in the Treasury building." She paused, thinking of Lucy and the women in Room 60, and how far their paths had diverged. She hoped that they were safe, and that she'd someday see them again. "But I won't rule out creating a life someplace else.

With Mum, Dad, and Charlie gone, I have no family to keep me rooted in London."

"Where would you go?" he asked.

She looked into his eyes. "A liberated Paris would be lovely."

Gently, he touched her arm.

Her skin tingled.

"Your food is getting cold," he said, moving his hand to the table.

Reluctantly, she finished eating her meal as the candle burned down to a nub. Lazare, insisting that she enjoy her brandy, washed the dishes.

"I feel doted on," she said.

"Good," Lazare said, wiping a plate with a towel. He put away the dishes, and then turned to her.

Rose placed her glass on the table and stood. "Thank you for the splendid meal."

"You're welcome." He pushed his chair to the table. "You should get some rest."

"Stay," Rose said, her heartbeat accelerating. "You've already broken curfew by coming here this evening. No need to risk going out when there's room here."

Lazare paused, resting his hand on the back of the chair.

"Please." She stepped close. "I'll feel better knowing you're safe."

"Okay," he said.

As Rose reached for the candle, the minuscule flame flickered and then extinguished. The room turned black.

"Do you have another candle?" he asked.

"No need." She found his arm, and then led him toward the extra bedroom. Finding the door, she lowered her hand, her fingers lingering against his palm. "There's a blanket on the bed," she whispered.

"*Merci.*" Lazare touched her hand. Their fingers entwined.

As if by reflex, she leaned into him and felt his arms wrap around her back. Her breath quickened. She looked up, sensing— through the darkness—his lips approach her own.

Lazare gently kissed her. His lips glided from her parted mouth to her cheek, and then rested against her neck.

Rose felt his heartbeat against her chest. "Stay with me," she whispered.

He ran a hand over her hair. "Are you sure?"

"*Oui*," she said, her body molding to his. She relished his kiss, deeper and longer. As their embrace faded, they went to her bedroom, where they undressed each other, gliding their fingers to find buttons. Buckles. Zippers. Delicately, she untied the straps to his prosthetic, the wooden apparatus falling to the floor. With her lips, she caressed his maimed appendages, and then placed his hand against her bare chest.

"I'd never do anything to hurt you," he said, his voice dropping to a whisper.

"Nor I," she breathed. Her heart fluttered, like a bird attempting to free itself from a cage.

They slipped into the bed, where they fell into an embrace, their hands and lips exploring each other. There were no guarantees for a future together, but she wanted nothing more than to be with him—here and now. As their bodies became one, Rose's heartbeat soared, and she wished that the night would never end.

CHAPTER 24

PARIS, FRANCE—JUNE 23, 1943

Lazare slipped out of bed, taking care not to disturb Rose, and put on his trousers. Early-morning sun illuminated a blind, creating a dull glow over the room. He buttoned his shirt, and then paused, his eyes drawn to Rose. A worn bed linen, draping over her body, accentuated the curvature of her hip. Her chest rose and fell, synchronized with the tranquil cadence of her breath. An exposed foot peeked from under the sheet. *Tu es magnifique.*

Rose stirred and opened her eyes. Appearing a bit bashful, she covered her exposed skin with the sheet. "Where are you going?"

"To see Claudius," he said, stepping to her.

She extended her hand. "I wish you could stay a little longer."

He squeezed her fingers, fighting his desire to return to the bed. "Me too."

"We could have breakfast," she said.

"There's no food," he said.

"Precisely," she said, grinning.

He smiled, feeling his body flood with warmth. He pulled her into his arms.

She nuzzled to him.

He lowered his cheek to her hair. A subtle scent of lilac perfume filled his nose, spawning images of their night together.

"When will I see you again?" she asked, her voice turned soft.

"Tonight," he said, regretting that he had to leave.

"Okay." She glided her fingers over his neck.

His skin tingled.

She looked up. Their eyes met.

Lazare drew close, his breath stalling, and gently kissed her lips. He felt her arms wrap around his shoulders and pull him close. Their embrace faded, and she slipped away.

Wrapped in the sheet, Rose walked him to the door.

He left her apartment building, his chest filled with *saudade*. A deep melancholic longing to be with Rose tore at his core. Since losing his parents, he'd felt little more than despair, but Rose had awakened his heart. She'd given him affection, understanding, and—most of all—hope. But what chance of a future did they have? The Nazis were increasing their stronghold on France, and the rumors of an Allied invasion, if true, were months, if not years, away. His parents, who believed that Allied forces would someday liberate France, had chosen to wait out the occupation, while he had chosen to fight. It occurred to Lazare that his parents' love for each other might have contributed to their decision not to flee Paris. Like his parents, his feelings for Rose could complicate matters. While he remained steadfast to sacrifice everything, including his life, to free France from German occupation, he realized that there may come a time when each of them might be forced to choose between duty and desire. He prayed that this predicament would never arise.

Lazare located Claudius in the basement of a café in Montparnasse, which they occasionally used as a safe house. He was glad to find him alone, cleaning a pistol with an oily rag. Smoke rose from the stub of a cigarette balanced over the edge of an oak table.

"I was about to summon you," Claudius said, setting down his weapon. He gestured for Lazare to take a seat.

Lazare sat on a stack of empty wooden crates once used to hold Épernay champagne, given the ink-stamped lettering over the cases. A dampness, laced with the odor of burnt tobacco and waste water, filled the air. Movement caught his eye, and he turned to see a centipede scuttle over the masonry floor. "I have news for you, too."

Claudius removed his beret and placed it on the table. "You first."

Using Rose's code name, Lazare told Claudius about her encounter with Kieffer, her concerns that the F Section networks might be compromised, and the SOE's confidence that all agents were accounted for.

Claudius rubbed his bald head. "Dragonfly is the only one concerned?"

Lazare nodded.

"What do you think?" Claudius asked.

"There isn't a day that I don't fear that the SD will infiltrate the Resistance or the SOE. The number of agents and partisans has grown, which increases the likelihood that someone, if captured, will compromise our network." He placed his prosthetic hand on the table, and then adjusted a strap to his forearm. "It's not a matter of *if* the SD can find their way in, it's a matter of when."

"Do you believe her?"

"*Oui*," he said.

Claudius took a drag from his cigarette. "Why did she come to you?"

"She trusts me."

"I trust you, too," Claudius said, flicking ash onto the floor. "Dragonfly is a courier. She could have easily contacted me."

An uneasiness sank to his gut. He wondered, although briefly, how long it would take Claudius—a man who seemed to know everything that was taking place in Paris—to conclude that he had feelings for Rose. "We've worked together on a sabotage mission." He glanced at the scars on his hand, a result of being mauled by a guard dog. *And she bandaged my wounds and delivered me sulfa pills.*

"*Oui*." Claudius, appearing satisfied with Lazare's response, snubbed out his cigarette on the table, leaving a black scar in the wood. "What do you recommend we do?"

"Suspend dead drop communications," Lazare said. "Until we are certain the locations are not being monitored by the SD. Also, we need to find new safe houses for us and the SOE."

Claudius picked at the edge of the table with a fingernail, stained brown from cigarettes. "That'll take time. And if there is an infiltration, what's to stop the SD from locating the new safe houses?"

"Nothing, except that we'll be harder to find if we are constantly on the move. I'd rather err on the side of caution."

"All right," Claudius said. "If you need to reach me, contact my sister, Marcelline. Do you remember the location of her apartment?"

Lazare nodded. A knot formed in his belly as he recalled his meeting with Marcelline, the nurse who'd gained access to the velodrome and was one of the last people to see his parents before they were shipped away—along with thousands of French Jews—in cattle cars.

"How shall I contact you?" Claudius asked.

Lazare's mind raced with options. Other than his secret hole into the catacombs, he had no other solution, at least for the moment, to provide Claudius with a method to communicate with him. *I told Rose that she was the only other person that knew about my entrance to the catacomb.* Burying his apprehension, he told Claudius about the manhole cover. "It's near the corner of Rue Émile-Richard and Rue Froidevaux. You'll find it."

"All right," Claudius said.

"I'd like to keep this between you and me," Lazare said.

Claudius looked at him. "Agreed."

"*Merci.*" Lazare took a deep breath and exhaled, relieved that he'd gained Claudius's support. "Why did you want to see me?"

"The Physician network has requested us to form a reception committee."

"When?" Lazare asked.

"Tonight."

Lazare straightened his back. "Why such short notice?"

Claudius shrugged. "The SOE decided to fly in a new agent on an RAF Lysander. The plane will land in the field, adjacent to our farmhouse in Ableiges. It'll be quick and less perilous than tracking down air-dropped agents, their parachutes floating over the countryside like dandelion clocks."

"Who should we assign to the committee?"

"I was thinking of you and me," Claudius said. "We'll bring along another partisan."

Angst grew in Lazare's belly. "For the continuity of our Resistance group, it might be wise for us not to participate in missions together."

Claudius rubbed stubble on his chin.

"Simply a precaution," Lazare said. "I'll lead tonight's reception committee, and you can take the next one."

"*Non*," Claudius said, shaking his head. "I'm still the leader of our group, even though I've been transferring much of my duties to you. I'll do it."

A wave of guilt rushed through Lazare. His intent had not been to shirk responsibility for participating in a reception committee. Claudius, a strong-willed and decisive leader, rarely changed his mind through verbal debate. But he also knew how Claudius randomly selected which safe house he would sleep in.

"We're both quite stubborn," Lazare said, pulling a coin from his pocket. "Let's settle this another way."

Claudius eyed the coin.

"*Pile ou face?*" Lazare asked, balancing the coin on the thumb of his good hand.

"You're not going to let this go, are you?" Claudius asked.

"*Non*," Lazare said.

"Very well," Claudius said, shifting in his seat. "*Face.*"

As Lazare flipped the coin into the air, it struck him that the result of the toss would not only determine who would lead the reception committee, it would reveal when he would see Rose again. The coin landed on the table and twirled, determining his destiny.

CHAPTER 25

ABLEIGES, FRANCE—JUNE 23, 1943

Losing the coin toss, Lazare arrived at the farm in Ableiges shortly before sunset. It had taken him the entire day to track down the men and travel for the reception committee. He'd selected two Resistance fighters to join him: Ernest, a rugged lumberman who owned a lorry, which they would use to smuggle the SOE agent to Paris, and Fermin, a man in his mid-fifties who'd lost two sons during the Fall of France. Ernest and Fermin, who'd never turned down an opportunity to fight for France's freedom, had eagerly accepted Lazare's invitation.

Lazare and the men sat in the barn and waited for nightfall. Ernest and Fermin, preparing for an evening without sleep, rested on piles of straw. But Lazare was unable to nap, let alone stop his brain from recounting the day's events. He was pleased to have gained Claudius's support to take Rose's concerns about a potential infiltration seriously, and while he was working to deliver another British agent to Paris, Claudius would be establishing new safe houses and dead drops. But with the demands to arrive in Ableiges ahead of the German-imposed curfew, Lazare was unable to inform Rose that he would be absent tonight. *I wish I'd had time to tell her that I would be gone,* he thought, staring up at the timber-beam ceiling.

He spent the next few hours reliving his time with Rose, over and over, in his head. He'd never met anyone like her before. *She's beautiful, brave, and kind.* For the first time since losing his parents, his heart felt capable of giving and receiving affection. He imagined—although cautiously, considering the casualty rate of Resistance fighters and SOE agents—what it would be like to create a life with her. He visualized waking up each morning nestled in each other's arms. More than ever, he was determined to fight for France's freedom, not solely for his people and country, but so that he and Rose could have a chance of a future together. As twilight gave way to darkness, he grew anxious to complete the mission and return to Paris, where he would apologize to Rose for breaking his promise to see her.

At 1:00 a.m., Lazare roused his comrades, and they made their way into a forest that bordered an untilled field. Once used to grow wheat, the ground was overgrown with stinging nettle and field bindweed. A choir of chirping crickets, cicadas, and katydids decorated the air. Despite the warm temperature, Lazare wore his jacket to hold an electric torch and pistol. The humidity was high, but a near cloudless sky, dotted with stars and a crescent moon, showed no indication of inclement weather possibly delaying or canceling the arrival of the RAF Lysander.

Within the hour, a faint buzz caused Lazare's adrenaline to surge. He ran, along with Ernest and Fermin, into the open field and scanned the sky. The drone of a single-engine monoplane grew. Lazare removed the electric torch from his pocket and flipped the switch, flashing a beam of light. Seconds later, the Lysander came into view. Ernest and Fermin waved their arms, although it was already clear to Lazare that the pilot had seen his signal by the rate of the plane's descent. He stuffed the electric torch into his pocket as the Lysander passed—no more than twelve feet—over Lazare's head. Appearing as if the aircraft had the ability to hover, it landed like a gliding goose onto the field, and then braked to a stop.

Lazare, his pulse pounding inside his ears, sprinted to the Lysander. A strong breeze from the buzzing propeller blasted his face, filling his nostrils with an acrid scent of aviation fuel. A man, seated in a rear cockpit behind the pilot, raised his hand to Lazare, and then jumped to the ground, where he removed an aluminum container that was fastened to the belly of the Lysander. Lazare and the men helped the SOE agent lug the container away from the aircraft. By the time they reached the forest, the Lysander had taken off and disappeared into the night.

"I'm Piper," the agent said, appearing to be using a code name.

"Lazare." He shook the man's hand. "Welcome to France."

The agent paused, appearing surprised to be touching a wooden prosthetic. *"Merci."*

Lazare pointed to Ernest and Fermin, who lifted the container onto their shoulders, like they were carrying a roll of carpet. "Resistance."

Piper nodded.

"Follow me," Lazare said.

Under the cover of the forest, they made their way back to the farmhouse. Near the barn, they left a canopy of pines and stepped into the yard. A metallic click cut through the sound of chirping insects. Lazare froze.

"Halt!" a voice shouted.

Lazare's heart rate soared. He reached for his pistol, but it tangled inside the torn webbing of his jacket.

Ernest and Fermin dropped the container.

Piper reached for his pistol inside a holster that was attached to his flight suit. But a rushing soldier slammed the butt of his rifle into Piper's face, shattering his nose. Piper's head shot back, and his body collapsed.

Fermin attempted to flee, but a bullet pierced his back, tumbling him to the ground.

Non! Lazare freed his pistol from his jacket. As he raised his weapon, a jarring pain pierced Lazare's skull. He crumpled to the grass, and everything turned black.

Dazed, Lazare struggled to lift his head. Guttural voices penetrated his ears. He felt hands rummage through his pockets. Slowly regaining his strength, he cracked open his eyes. More than a dozen Wehrmacht soldiers, moonlight shimmering on their helmets, stood in the clearing. *It was a trap.*

Moaning caused Lazare to turn his eyes to Fermin, who was

feebly crawling on his belly. Lazare attempted to get up, but his body felt broken. Blood dripped from a gash on his head, turning his face wet. Helplessly, he watched a Wehrmacht soldier step to Fermin, pull out a pistol, and then discharge a round into the man's back.

"Bastard," Lazare breathed. Rage roused him to his hands and knees, only to have a German soldier, using a jackboot, kick him in the ribs. A sharp pain pierced his chest. Gasping for air, he expected to hear more gunshots, the soldiers executing them, one by one. *It's over.* Instead, he heard the click of handcuffs placed on Ernest and Piper. Seconds later, he felt a knee press into his spine and his hands yanked behind his back. Pain shot through his arms as the handcuffs were cranked tightly to his wrist bones.

"*Amputierte,*" a soldier laughed, pointing out the prosthetic to his companions.

Indignation flared through Lazare's veins. He tried to wriggle from the German's grasp and received a punch to a kidney. A ravaging burn shot through his guts. Stunned, he curled into a ball.

Soon a Wehrmacht lorry arrived. Lazare, Ernest, and Piper were forced into the back, which was covered by a canvas tarp. As Lazare slowly regained his ability to think, deadened by the concussive blow to his head, he realized that the soldiers had no intention of killing them, at least for the moment. The German soldiers had been waiting to ambush them, and to take them alive, if possible. *They'll torture us to gain intelligence, and then they'll kill us.* And he realized that their kismet might be far worse than Fermin's swift execution.

The vehicle's engine roared, sending a chill through his body. As they pulled away from the farm, all Lazare could think about was Rose. *Please, God, let her be safe.* It was obvious, to Lazare, that their encounter with a Wehrmacht patrol had not been a coincidence. There were too many soldiers, and they knew precisely where to hide. *You were right, Rose. The network has been infiltrated.* His mind and heart ached for a future that would never be. He prayed that she'd somehow be alerted to what had happened, and that she'd find a way to avoid capture.

CHAPTER 26

PARIS, FRANCE—JUNE 24, 1943

Rose sat in the kitchen, staring into a cup of barley tea. The reflection of a wearied woman, who'd stayed up most of the night, peered back at her. With curfew over, the creak of doors and floorboards grew as residents went about their morning routines. She'd slept on the sofa, wanting to make sure that she heard Lazare's knock. But it never came, and with the passing of hours, her restlessness mushroomed. *Something must have come up.*

A fusion of disappointment and apprehension stirred inside her. She forced herself to drink the tea, despite a dull ache in her tummy, and then went to the washroom, where she bathed and freshened her clothes, wrinkled from her night on the sofa. "I've got work to do," she whispered to herself. But her affirmation to focus on her SOE duties only exacerbated her angst for determining why Lazare had failed to arrive.

As she prepared to leave her apartment, she found a note that had been slipped under the door. A lump formed in the back of her throat. She picked up the paper and recognized the handwriting to be from Felix, fueling her discontent.

See me at 2 p.m.

I must have missed him while I was getting dressed. Felix spent mornings at the garage and afternoons in his apartment, so she assumed that they would meet here. It wasn't unusual for Felix, who relied on Muriel to encrypt and decipher communications, not to make the effort to code a vague message. She did, however, feel it was courteous of Felix to leave a message under the door, rather than access her apartment with his spare key.

Rose debated whether to get some rest so her mind would be alert for her meeting with Felix, but she desperately needed food. A memory of the dinner that Lazare had concocted from scraps flashed inside her head. *Where are you?* Burying her thoughts, she lugged her bicycle down the stairs, sending a twinge through her shoulder muscles. She tossed her cosmetics case into the bicycle's basket, and then pedaled in the direction of a ration line.

When she arrived at the Boulay Pâtisserie, the bread line stretched out of the building, down the street, and around the corner. She checked her purse to make sure she had her ration card, and got in line, her bicycle by her side. After waiting for over an hour, the line barely moved. Rumors spread through the crowd that the bakery was running out of bread. People grew agitated. Two women ahead of Rose began to argue over their place on the sidewalk. Within seconds, the women's debate turned physical.

A woman shrieked as she was pushed out of the line. She retaliated by clawing her assailant's face, ripping away skin with her nails.

Unable to stand idle and watch, Rose, along with an old man who was not much bigger than Rose, attempted to push the women apart. But the women fought back, screeching and flailing their arms. People joined in to subdue the women. "She stole my place!" one of the women wailed. Concerned that the police might arrive and question her, Rose decided to forgo her rationed bread. She pedaled away, disheartened, but not surprised, that German occupation had driven Parisians to such hostile acts of survival. *It's getting worse. How long can this continue?*

She traveled to Le Cygne Hotel but didn't go inside. Instead, she glanced up at a seventh-floor window, the shades drawn closed.

Since it was morning, Zelie, a nocturnal woman who performed as a cabaret dancer, would likely be sleeping. Rose shivered, wondering if Kieffer was with her, or if he was at SD headquarters. She had no intention of paying a visit to Zelie, who was well stocked with cosmetics, for at least a week. But she needed to come back to Le Cygne Hotel. Otherwise, she feared that when the time came to do her duty, she might lose her nerve. *I'll come back here tomorrow, and the day after that—or until I'm no longer afraid.* She left the curb, circling the hotel in defiance of her consternation, and then traveled to Le Marais.

She parked her bicycle across from the alley to Prosper's dead drop. She had no intention of leaving a message, or inspecting the cavity hidden behind the loose brick. She'd simply come to scout out the area, and to reassure herself that Prosper's dead drop remained secure. She kneeled beside the stone façade of a closed café, and then pretended to look through her cosmetic case. She scanned the area. The alley was empty, save for a broken wine bottle. On the street, a woman with tufts of gray hair protruding from a scarf walked on the sidewalk. There were no Wehrmacht patrols or police checkpoints.

As she prepared to leave, movement in a second-floor window caused her to pause. A man wearing a fedora peered toward the alley. Her breath turned shallow. She glanced down the street. Over a block away was a parked black sedan. She got on her bicycle, scraping her ankle over a pedal, and traveled in the opposite direction. She took a left onto the next street to gain a view of the opposite side of the alley. When she came around the corner, the sight of another parked black sedan sent a chill through her body. Two men, one reading a paper, the other staring toward the alley, sat in the front seats. *Oh, God.* Rose's heart rate spiked. She pedaled away, hoping the men, whom she believed to be SD, didn't notice her leave the area. She desperately needed to inform Felix, but she also had to warn Muriel. A decision roiled in her gut. Before she changed her mind, she sped toward the third arrondissement.

Everything outside of Muriel's apartment appeared to be normal. No cars. No one peeking from behind window shades. But when she descended the stairs to Muriel's basement flat, the sight of the open door, its frame broken, shot a wave of dread through her body. *No!* She crept inside. Scattered over the floor were Muriel's clothes. Her bedroom was ripped apart, the mattress in shreds, and an armoire was toppled, like a domino, against a wall. Muriel's suitcase containing the wireless transmitter was missing. She struggled to breathe, praying that her friend had somehow managed to escape. Rose turned and froze.

A man holding a wooden rolling pin blocked the apartment door. "Who are you?"

Rose's heart hammered her ribs. "Where is she?"

"They took her," he said.

Rose's heart sank.

Outside, a siren blared. The man raised the rolling pin, like a club.

He called the police! Rose's adrenaline surged. She flipped a small table onto its side, creating a barrier between them. She grabbed a stool and sprang to the sole window in the basement-level unit. Stepping onto the stool, she wobbled, nearly losing her balance. She flipped the lock and threw open the window. Climbing onto the ground, she felt the man's hand grab her ankle. Her heart rate spiked. She kicked, freeing herself from his grasp. As she pulled her foot through the opening, the man swung his rolling pin, missing her leg and shattering the window glass. She scrambled over the ground, scraping her arms and knees, and sprinted to her bicycle.

Using side streets and alleyways, she fled toward her apartment building, where Felix would be waiting to meet her. She prayed—her hands squeezing the handlebars—that she'd arrive in time. Nearing her street, she stopped. Her lungs heaving, she took in gulps of air to catch her breath. She poked her head around the corner of a building. Ahead, three automobiles were blocking the street. A wave of nausea flooded her stomach. Seconds later, Felix—handcuffed, with blood smeared over his nose and mouth—was dragged by two German soldiers down the steps of the building and shoved into the back seat of an unmarked black automobile.

She stepped out of view, her legs feeling like twigs about to snap. Her body trembling, she got on her bicycle and rode away. But where would she hide? The SD had not merely infiltrated the network, they'd discovered locations of SOE apartments, safe houses, and dead drops. She struggled to come to terms with the fact that Muriel and Felix were captured, and she refused to believe that Lazare had met the same fate, despite the likelihood that the French Resistance had also been compromised. With every ounce of her being, she hoped that she was wrong. But deep down, she knew something catastrophic had happened.

Rose found a deserted park, where she stashed her bicycle and hid inside a dense, five-foot-tall barrier of yew shrubs. She lowered her head into her hands and wept. Wiping tears, she vowed to find a way to rescue her friends. But first, she needed to save herself. She hunkered in the underbrush and waited for nightfall, all the while determined to reach the only place left in Paris, she believed, that might be safe. She prayed for a miracle—and that she would somehow find Lazare.

CHAPTER 27

THE CATACOMBS—JUNE 24, 1943

Long after sunset, Rose crawled from her hiding place within the dense yew shrubs. The grind of vehicles had disappeared, leaving the occasional sound of Wehrmacht *Kübelwagens* patrolling the streets. Abandoning her bicycle, she collected her purse and cosmetics case, hoping that her identification and cover story might help her survive long enough to contact SOE headquarters. *And somehow find Lazare.*

The streets of Paris were a maze of murky shadows, given the German-imposed curfew and blackout. She made her way, intermittently hiding in doorways and alleys, to Montparnasse Cemetery. Avoiding the vicinity of Lazare's dead drop, in the event it was being monitored by the SD, she scurried to the far end of the cemetery, near the corner of Rue Émile-Richard and Rue Froidevaux. She pressed her back against a wall, attempting to catch her breath, and then kneeled by a bush, hoping that the crowbar Lazare had hidden was still there. Digging her hands into the root system, she jammed her fingers into a piece of metal, sending a sharp twinge through her knuckles.

She grabbed the crowbar and her belongings, and then dashed into the street. She located the manhole cover and plugged the crowbar into a slot located on the rim of the iron plate. She pried, but it didn't move. Using her body weight as leverage, she fought—

her back and shoulder muscles flaring—to lift the cast-iron cover, but the bar slipped from her hands. She fell, scraping her palms. The crowbar clanged against the pavement, reverberating like a tuning fork. Rose shuddered. *It must weigh over a hundred pounds. What was I thinking?*

As she was about to flee into the cemetery, approaching footsteps caused her adrenaline to surge. She turned, preparing to swing the crowbar.

"Claudius," the man hissed.

She froze, recognizing the bald-headed man wearing a beret.

He extended his hand. "Give it to me."

Rose handed him the crowbar.

Claudius pried up the cover and slid it over the pavement. "Go."

Rose threw her purse over her shoulder. She grabbed her case and descended, using one hand on the rungs. Claudius followed, grunting as he labored to move the manhole cover into place.

Reaching the bottom, Rose blindly searched the area where Lazare stored a flashlight. Before she found it, a flash lit up the tunnel.

"Where do we go?" A small flame flickered from a metal cigarette lighter.

Rose took the crowbar from Claudius and placed it inside a crevice, where she found the flashlight, its batteries dead. Rose pointed. "This way," she said, hoping she could remember the route.

Minutes later, they crawled through a hole in a wall leading to Lazare's compound. She prayed that he'd be inside, despite knowing that she'd find the space empty. A doleful ache twisted inside her gut.

Claudius lit a lantern, casting an amber glow over the limestone chamber. The place was barren, except for a canvas cot, books, RAF food rations, a canteen of water, and the painting of the Arc de Triomphe.

Rose stared at the artwork. Her chest tightened. "Where's Lazare?"

"He and two of our men didn't return from Ableiges," Claudius said, stepping to her. "I assume they're captured."

"*Non*," she whimpered. Tears welled up in her eyes.

"It should have been me," Claudius said, his voice filled with regret. "Lazare insisted on leading a reception committee for an SOE agent who was being flown in on a Lysander." He looked at Rose. "I should have gone in his place."

Rose fought back her sorrow and told him about Felix and Muriel's capture, as well as the dead drops being monitored by the SD.

"*Mon Dieu*," Claudius said. He rubbed his eyes with the heels of his palms. "Some of my men are missing, and the bastards arrested my sister. They'll torture her to get to me."

"I'm so sorry," Rose said.

He removed his beret and used it to wipe his eyes.

"What's happening?" Rose asked.

"I believe that the Physician network and its subcircuits, as well as my Resistance group, have been penetrated by the SD."

Despair surged through her body. "How?"

"Lazare told me about your concern with security, so I contacted a friend who organizes a Resistance network in Tours to determine if he'd noticed anything unusual." He ran a hand over his bald head and looked at her. "Two Canadian SOE agents were recently parachuted into the Loire Valley to establish a new network called Archdeacon. His Resistance group has been unable to establish contact with either of these agents."

"Tours is quite a distance from Paris. What does this have to do with us?"

"Upon arrival in France, Archdeacon was met by two SOE agents with ties to the Physician network. According to one of my men, these agents are also missing."

"But we contacted London headquarters," Rose said. "They informed us that all SOE agents are accounted for."

"Unlike the SOE, much of the French Resistance does not have direct communication with the British."

Rose's mind raced. "If the agents of Archdeacon were captured upon arrival, it would mean that they'd be carrying their wireless transmitter and codes, and it might be possible for the SD to impersonate Archdeacon, transmitting false messages to London

and making the SOE believe that everyone was accounted for."
The thought of Kieffer's list, possibly having something to do with
this, sent a roil of nausea through her stomach.

Claudius lowered his eyes. "It might also mean that the SD
would be able to arrange for the arrival of new agents and supplies
to fall directly into the Germans' hands."

Rose shuddered. A flash of Lazare being captured rushed into
her head. Refusing to believe that all was lost, she buried her mis-
givings.

"What do you plan to do?" Claudius asked.

"I need to get my hands on a wireless transmitter and inform
London."

"Impossible," Claudius said. "The Physician network is collapsing."

"Then I'll contact another network," Rose said.

"How?"

"I don't know," Rose said. "But I must find a way."

Claudius took a seat on the cot and exhaled. Rubbing his knees,
he gazed at the painting. "I didn't know that Lazare was an artist."

"Lazare's mother," Rose said.

Claudius patted the spot beside him.

"How did you know about this place?" she asked, sitting.

"Lazare told me the location, just before he left for Ableiges."

"Me too," Rose said.

Claudius retrieved the canteen and handed it to Rose.

Dehydrated, she gulped water. "*Merci*," she said, handing it
back to him.

"You've grown close to Lazare," he said.

Her chest ached. "*Oui.*"

Without drinking, Claudius placed the cap on the canteen.

"He thinks of you as an uncle," Rose said.

Claudius lowered his eyes. "I think of him as a son."

Rose looked at him, realizing that Lazare had told them about
his secret catacomb chamber, attempting to protect the people he
cared for. She wiped tears from her eyes.

"Have faith," Claudius said, looking at her. "If there is anyone who can evade the SD, it is our Lazare." He stood and handed Rose a blanket. "Get some rest."

Rose curled onto the cot.

Claudius sprawled on the floor and blew out the lantern.

The stygian blackness of the catacomb jolted her nerves. Her breath accelerated, taking in stale air. She wondered how long they would need to stay underground. A day? A week? Horrid visions of Muriel and Felix being tortured by the SD filled her brain. She squeezed her blanket, fighting away the images. She refused to believe that Lazare had been captured. *I'll do everything I can do to find you.* She stayed awake, wondering how she could find a wireless transmitter, warn London, and—most of all—save her friends, and the man who had stolen her heart.

CHAPTER 28

84 AVENUE FOCH, PARIS—JUNE 25, 1943

Lazare, his head throbbing, tugged at his bindings but was unable to free his body, which was tied to a chair with rope. He labored to breathe, the cord constricting his diaphragm. His handcuffed hands were pulled tightly behind his back, and his ankles were fastened to the chair legs with thick leather straps. His holding cell, if one could call it that, was a twelve-by-twelve-foot room with a herringbone-pattern oak floor. The plaster walls, one of which contained a gabled window, were painted a bright white. The cell was absent furniture, save a metal stand containing an assortment of tools reminiscent of a dentist's office. But the instruments were far more macabre than a dental drill or probe. The stand held a hammer, pliers, wire, rope, baton, whip, and—most morbid—a meat hook. Lazare's gut churned with dread.

Lazare, Ernest, and the SOE agent called Piper had been brought to 84 Avenue Foch, a once-palatial residential building now used as the Parisian headquarters of the SD. They were taken to the top floor of the five-story building, Piper's busted nose bleeding over the stairs, and separated from each other. Screams and groans reverberated through the walls, sending chills down Lazare's spine. As he waited his turn, he stared out the window, getting a glimpse of the Paris skyline. It repulsed him to think that if he'd been able to stick his head out of the window, he'd have a clear view of the monument, Arc de Triomphe, that his *maman* had painted many years before.

Approaching footsteps caused Lazare's pulse to accelerate. The door swung open, and two men entered, one of them a German military officer whom Lazare believed to be a *Sturmbannführer*, given the shoulder marks. The officer had dark hair, a broad nose, and an iron cross worn tight to his collar like a bow tie. The other man, who appeared to be a civilian by his tailored suit and tie, had a wiry build and a distinctive laryngeal prominence, as if he had a walnut stuck inside his throat.

The officer adjusted his cap and spoke to his civilian comrade in German, which Lazare didn't understand.

"This is *Sturmbannführer* Josef Kieffer," the civilian said in French, but with a slight German accent. "My name is Eberhard Vogel. I'm the commander's interpreter and assistant."

Hearing the name of the officer whom Rose had encountered caused Lazare's blood pressure to soar. He clenched his hands, which had turned numb from lack of circulation.

"Your papers say your name is Laurent Allard," Vogel said. "What is your real name?"

Lazare stared at the men.

"Your name," Vogel said, stepping forward.

Lazare swallowed, knowing that he needed to stall as long as possible, allowing others time to evade capture. He yearned to know that Rose had fled Paris.

Kieffer frowned. He nodded to Vogel and left the room, shutting the door behind him.

A grin spread over Vogel's face. "The commander allows me latitude with interrogations. Eventually, you'll tell me your name. The names of everyone you know in the French and British networks—and where they hide."

Lazare lowered his eyes to Vogel's polished shoes.

"You'll tell me *everything*." Vogel cocked back his arm and swung his fist.

The punch struck Lazare's jaw, splitting his lower lip. A throb shot through his face. He swallowed, tasting blood.

"Pain," Vogel said, casually walking behind Lazare, "has a way of making one confess their sins."

Lazare took in short gasps, preparing for another punch to the head. Instead, he felt a tug at his hands.

"I see that you're an invalid," Vogel said.

Lazare's skin turned hot.

"Your people must be quite desperate to be relying on broken men." He leaned toward Lazare's ear and whispered, "Perhaps you'll have matching hands when I'm finished."

Lazare wriggled in his bindings. He strained to free his hands, but it was of no use. There was nothing he could do but take everything that Vogel gave him. And for the next few hours, Lazare endured Vogel's fury, the interrogator using all of the tools in his insidious tool box—but one.

CHAPTER 29

84 AVENUE FOCH, PARIS—JUNE 25, 1943

Battered, bruised, and cut, Lazare slumped in his bindings. He felt Vogel grab his hair and yank back his head. Lazare cracked open his eyes, nearly swollen shut from Vogel's punches.

"I already know your associates," Vogel said. "But I want to hear you say the names."

Lazare took in shallow breaths. He turned his head in defiance.

"Foolish Frenchman." Vogel sighed, and then untied Lazare from his bindings.

Lazare, too weak to fight, slumped in his chair.

Vogel removed Lazare's handcuffs, and then unstrapped Lazare's prosthetic. "You'll no longer need this," he said, tossing it into the corner of the room. Vogel reattached the handcuffs with Lazare's arms in front of his body, and then he strung a piece of rope over a hoist that was installed in the ceiling. Picking up the meat hook, he held it for Lazare to see.

Get it over with. Lazare expected to have the hook puncture him, and then be hung like a side of beef. Instead, Vogel tied rope through the eye of the hook. Clasping the hook to Lazare's handcuffs, his arms were hoisted high over his head. Vogel tied the other end of the rope to an anchor in the floor, keeping Lazare's arms suspended.

Struggling to stand on his toes, Lazare's arms throbbed, feeling as if they might pop from his shoulder sockets.

"I'll be back," Vogel said. "Perhaps tomorrow. Or maybe in five minutes. In the meantime, please understand that we've only begun our work together." He adjusted his necktie, as if he were heading off to a business meeting, and left the cell.

There's no hope for me. But the longer I hold out, the higher the likelihood that others will have a chance to hide. To suppress his pain, Lazare turned his thoughts to Rose. And he promised himself that he'd do everything within his limits to save her from the same demise.

CHAPTER 30

THE CATACOMBS—JUNE 27, 1943

Using her fingers, Rose took a bite of tinned mutton, more fat than meat. A bitter, gamy flavor filled her mouth. She slid the can to Claudius, sitting next to her on the stone floor of the tomb.

Claudius took a pinch of meat. "Finish it."

Despite her lack of hunger, stolen by the Sicherheitsdienst, Rose ate the rest of the tinned mutton and washed it down with the water from the canteen.

For the past two days, Rose and Claudius had stayed hidden in the catacomb, surviving on RAF rations that Lazare had squirreled away in his refuge. Rose, desperate to find a way to contact SOE headquarters, wanted to leave after a few hours of rest, but Claudius insisted that they stay longer to increase the odds that the German wave of arrests had subsided. To conserve kerosene, they used the lantern only during meals and to guide oneself to another artery in the tunnel, which they designated as the loo.

Rose and Claudius used their time—most of which was in darkness—to discuss plans for Rose to reach another SOE network, and for Claudius to rebuild his Resistance group. Since the SOE network in Paris—Physician, as well as its subnetworks, Conjurer, Juggler, Inventor, and Farrier—were likely infiltrated by the SD, Rose believed the best chance of locating a wireless transmitter would be outside of northern France. As part of her SOE training, especially for the role of a courier, it was critical that she knew the territories of each of the F Section networks, as well as the code name of their organizers. With few options, she decided to embark on a quest to reach the Pimento network, organized by an agent called Alphonse. Unfortunately, it operated in the southeast quadrant of France, a great distance from Paris.

"The SD will be gaining knowledge from their captives," Claudius said. "The German checkpoints at the train stations might be alerted to an SOE agent posing as a cosmetic saleswoman."

They're torturing them to gain information. Rose took a jagged breath. "Then I'll travel by bicycle."

"Too far," Claudius said.

"I must try," Rose said.

Claudius swirled a bit of water left inside the canteen. "My sister and I had a childhood friend named Simone. She's now a Catholic nun who lives in a convent in Montluçon. She might be able to help you reach Alphonse."

"How far is Montluçon?"

"Over three hundred kilometers," he said.

Bloody hell. She wondered what was the farthest distance she'd traveled on a bicycle in a single day. Twenty miles? Thirty miles? Gathering her confidence, she said, "I can do it."

Claudius smiled. "I can see why Lazare cares for you."

"*Merci,*" Rose said, an ache building in her chest. With each passing hour, her hope had faded. *If Lazare had avoided capture, he would have returned to the catacomb by now.* She shook away her thoughts and asked, "Where will you go?"

"Valmondois," Claudius said. "It's north of Paris, where my sister and I were born. It'll provide me with a safe place to rebuild what remains of my Resistance group, while still being within striking distance of the city."

"Is Marcelline your only sibling?"

"*Oui,*" he said, appearing both sad and grateful to hear his sister's name. "Do you have family?"

"They're gone." She paused, conditioned by her training to never reveal personal information while in the field. But she'd already broken this rule with Lazare, and Claudius was his friend, so she trusted him. *Besides, I might not make it Montluçon.* She took a deep breath and told him—about the Luftwaffe air raid that killed her parents, and how her brother, Charlie, perished when his RAF Spitfire was shot down over the Channel.

"Mon Dieu," Claudius said. "My condolences."

Rose nodded, fighting away images of the bombed Teasdale Grocery. "Do you have a family?"

"Once," Claudius said. "My wife, Georgette, died during childbirth."

"Oh, my," Rose said. "I'm sorry."

"It was a long time ago." Claudius rubbed gray stubble on his chin. "Georgette and I married a week before I had been assigned to the western front. For the past twenty-five years, there isn't a day that goes by that I don't think about her. Georgette was, and will always be, the love of my life."

"She sounds lovely," Rose said. "My parents met during the Great War, too. My mother is French, and my father is British."

Claudius adjusted the lantern's flame, flickering a dull glow over the chamber. "Experiencing war can bond one's heart with another."

"Oui," Rose said, realizing that his comment also applied to her and Lazare.

"You must have faith that he'll be all right," Claudius said, as if he understood what Rose was thinking.

She nodded. "And you'll see your sister, Marcelline, again."

Claudius rubbed his eyes, and then looked at his wristwatch. "Let's get some rest. We'll leave in a few hours."

Rose curled onto Lazare's cot.

Claudius took his sleeping spot on the limestone floor and extinguished the lantern.

Unable to rest, Rose's mind raced. *Will I be able to reach another wireless transmitter? Will I be captured before reaching Montluçon? What will the SD do to Muriel and Felix? Will I be able to contact*

headquarters in time to save other agents? Will I ever see Lazare again?
To calm her brain, she reimagined her time with Lazare, over and
over, until exhaustion compelled her to sleep.

Rose, holding her purse and cosmetics case, stood with
Claudius at the entrance of the catacomb. She'd fixed her hair and
makeup, as well as tidied her clothes—as much as one could in a
catacomb—hoping German soldiers would be less likely to stop
an attractively dressed woman who looked like she was bicycling
through her local village.

Rose looked up, the iron rungs disappearing into a dark void.

Claudius, a flame flickering from his cigarette lighter, glanced at
his watch. "It's 4:35 a.m. I'll go first to remove the manhole cover."

"Okay." Rose took a deep breath, attempting to quell her anxiety.

"Are you sure you won't come with me to Valmondois?"
Claudius asked.

"I have to try to contact London," Rose said. "Agents' lives are
at stake."

"I understand," Claudius said.

She looked at him, his eyes weary. "Goodbye, Claudius."

"*Adieu.*" He closed his lighter, turning the tunnel black.

Rose listened to him climb the iron rungs. She followed, her
angst growing as she ascended the ladder.

Using his shoulder, Claudius lifted the manhole cover and
peeked through a crack, and then labored to move the iron lid,
giving way to a predawn sky.

The scratching of metal against pavement caused the hair to
stand up on the back of Rose's neck. Her breath quickened.

Claudius crawled onto the street and lowered his arms.

Rose handed him her case and purse, and then climbed out of
the hole.

Claudius dragged the cover back into its place. He glanced at
her and darted down the sidewalk.

Rose grabbed her things and fled, her lungs inhaling fresh air
for the first time in days. She hid in Montparnasse Cemetery until
she heard the sounds of vehicles, indicating that curfew was over.

She calmly traveled on a sidewalk, pretending that she was getting an early morning start for work. Instead of heading south, she went to the park. As she searched through the dense five-foot-tall row of yew shrubs, a vile lump formed in her stomach. Her bicycle was nowhere to be found.

CHAPTER 31

THE JOURNEY TO MONTLUÇON—JUNE 27, 1943

Rose crawled from the thick hedgerow, her arms and shins covered in scratches. She dusted green needles from her skirt and jacket, angry with herself that she hadn't made more effort to conceal her bicycle. *Maybe I left a handlebar sticking out of a shrub.* But it didn't matter. Her bicycle was gone, and she'd have to find another means of transportation. The train stations, swarming with German checkpoints, were not an option. Neither was stealing an automobile, given the scarcity of petrol and the enemy roadblocks. Also, purchasing a used bicycle, considering the small amount of change in her purse, was not a possibility. She left the park, knowing exactly what she had to do.

She scoured the fourteenth arrondissement for over an hour. There were few bicycles on the street, and all of them were in the process of being ridden by Parisians getting an early start for the ration lines. As minutes passed, her anxiousness grew. *I'll head south and find one along the route.* As she turned on the sidewalk, she spotted a well-dressed woman riding a bicycle coast to a curb and stop. The woman got off her bicycle, which she chain-locked to a light post, and entered a café.

Rose approached the bicycle. She put down her case, rubbed her arm, and examined the keyed padlock with her eyes. *I can do it.* She glanced to the window. Inside the woman kissed a Wehrmacht officer on both cheeks, and then sat with him at a small table. Rose's heart rate spiked. Pretending to adjust her hair, she removed a hairpin. She leaned against the light post and straightened the wire, recalling her instruction at SOE finishing school. She kneeled and inserted the wire into the padlock, bending the end of the pin slightly.

Laughter drifted from the café.

Her skin prickled. Maneuvering the wire, she tugged, but the lock didn't move. *Focus.* She adjusted the pin and tried two more times, until she felt a metallic click. She opened the lock, releasing a ribbon of chain.

Rose placed her things into the bicycle basket and straddled the seat. Her heartbeat pounded her sternum. She pedaled away, expecting at a moment for the woman and her Wehrmacht companion to dash from the café. But the couple, their eyes on each other, didn't notice Rose loitering near the bicycle. As she fled the fourteenth arrondissement, she recalled how upset she was with Lazare when he'd delivered her a bicycle. "Any French patriot would condone having their bicycle stolen, if it were to aid our liberation," Lazare had said. *It was naïve of me to be upset with him for stealing a bicycle.* She silenced her regret and picked up speed.

Weaving through side streets, Rose reached the outskirts of Paris. The sea of limestone buildings slowly turned to freestanding homes with plots of land. Chirps of sparrows filled the trees towering from both sides of the road. Without a map, she'd memorized the route that Claudius had described, which would take her through small villages and remote countryside. It was a three-day trip by bicycle to Montluçon, but Rose was determined to make it in less than forty-eight hours.

Twenty miles into the journey, Rose's legs burned like molten lead. Her arm muscles ached. She sucked in air, attempting to pacify her oxygen-deprived body. *Muriel and Felix will not get a break from SD interrogators. And neither will I.* She pedaled, cranking the chain wheel, determined to make contact with SOE headquarters.

Behind her, a roar of engines grew. She maneuvered to the edge of the rode, but kept her pace. Within seconds, a convoy of military lorries carrying German soldiers passed her. Wind blasted her bicycle, nearly running her off the road. Shouts and whistles came from the soldiers peering from the back of their lorries. Rose, ire boiling in her veins, forced a smile and waved.

Cresting a hill, near the village of Mondeville, a German roadblock was stationed a few hundred yards away. A jolt shot through her nerves. Her feet slipped from the pedals. *Will they be looking for me?* As she gathered her composure, she spotted an unpaved road. Hoping the soldiers had not noticed her, she veered onto the dirt thoroughfare. Tires bounced on ruts and holes, jarring her body. Her hands, desperately gripping the handlebars, felt like she was wielding a jackhammer. She descended an incline to a barrier of oak trees, taking her out of view of the roadblock.

She labored, her hamstring muscles straining, to pedal on the earthen road. After twenty minutes of her body being rattled and shaken, she turned onto a lane with a narrow swath of grass growing between two tire paths. She veered onto a trail, attempting to find a detour around the roadblock, and soon became lost. Hot afternoon sun blared down on her hair and skin. Sweat dripped down her back. As she was about to retrace her route, she remembered the compass that the SOE tailors had embedded inside a button on the sleeve of her jacket. She braked, skidding to a stop. Fearing that she might be too exhausted to get back on the bicycle, she remained straddled over the seat. Using her thumbnail, she opened the metal button, exposing the Lilliputian-size compass. She guided her arm, spinning the tiny needle, until she located a southern direction. After thirty minutes of trails, including having to push her bike through a barren farm field, she found a paved road well south of Mondeville. Drained, she wondered if squandering her energy was as much risk as traveling through a German checkpoint.

The sweltering heat, compounded by the lack of cloud cover, gradually depleted Rose's hydration. Her head turned dizzy. Her legs weakened, slowing her bicycle to nearly a walking pace. *Why didn't I bring the canteen?* Her mouth dry and unable to produce saliva, she stopped near a farmhouse, the windows boarded shut. She got off her bicycle, her legs stiff and sore, and walked to a stone well only to find that the well was missing its rope and bucket. Driven by thirst, she drank from a stone cattle trough filled with rainwater. She gulped handfuls of water, warm and dirty. Her tummy swelled. Wiping her lips, she felt tiny wriggles on her tongue and noticed that the stagnant water was strewn with mosquito larvae. *Nothing I can do about it now.* She cleaned her mouth, using her sleeve, and then got on her bicycle and rode away. Two miles into her trek, her stomach lurched, and she vomited onto the road.

For the remainder of the day, Rose continued her journey, only stopping to drink from a stream and eat a biscuit that she'd taken from Lazare's stash of RAF rations. She slogged through Orville, Auxy, Nesploy, and Bonnée without incident. But things changed at sunset, when she reached a large bridge spanning the Loire River. Nazi flags were posted near the entrance of the overpass, which was blocked by Wehrmacht soldiers stopping vehicle drivers to inspect their papers. *I don't have the strength to find another crossing. Besides, all the bridges across the Loire River will likely have roadblocks.* She rode ahead and took a spot at the end of a long line of automobiles and lorries.

A soldier checking papers looked at Rose.

Her breath stalled as their eyes met.

The soldier handed papers to a lorry driver and motioned for Rose to approach him.

Oh, no. Rose pedaled around the vehicles, feeling as if her legs were about to give out. "*Bonjour,*" she said, smiling. She slowed, doing her best to hide her fatigue, and reached for her purse.

The soldier shook his head and waved her through the checkpoint.

"*Merci.*" Rose pedaled past the soldier. She crossed the bridge, grateful that there was a long line of vehicles, otherwise the soldier might have taken the time to check a bicyclist's papers.

Well after sunset, Rose reached the village of Coullons. Unable to pedal any farther, she coasted to a stop near a small stone bridge. Her body ravaged, she lugged her bicycle down an embankment to a calm stream leading to a pond filled with croaking frogs. She gathered leaves to use as a blanket and hid beneath the overpass. *I'm halfway there*, she thought, curling into a fetal position. As she drifted toward sleep, her thoughts remained on one thing, and one thing alone—contacting headquarters.

Rose, woken by a dawn chorus of tweets, whistles, and caws, crawled from her makeshift nest under the bridge. She stood, her knees and ankles feeling like rusted hinges. A cramp flared through her calf. Wincing, she fell to her bottom and stretched her leg, attempting to loosen the knots from her muscles. *I need liquids and food.*

She ate her last tin of mutton and a biscuit, and washed it down with handfuls of pond water. As the ruffling of the water's surface subsided, Rose's refection came into view. Her oily hair was a disheveled mess. Dark circles masked her eyes. *I need to look like a local woman merely traveling through her village.*

She removed her clothes and waded into the pond, surrounded by blooming bull rush. The cold water caused goose bumps to crop up on her skin, resurrecting memories of her mum, who had taught her to swim in the icy water of Kenwood Ladies' Pond.

During a winter break in grammar school, Rose had commented, mostly in jest, to her mum that she wanted to learn to swim. But Mum had taken the invitation to teach her daughter to swim quite seriously, and despite the cold climate, she took Rose to Kenwood Ladies' Pond. Armed with singlet bathing suits and rubberized caps, they'd shed their winter coats. Goose bumps cropped up on their arms and legs. Surprisingly, there were nearly a dozen women bathers at the pond, looking like winter nymphs. Mum immediately dove from the dock into the icy water, and then floated to the surface. "It's lovely," her mum said, treading water. Collecting her courage, Rose jumped, feet first and holding her nose, from the dock. The shock of the forty-degree water made her feel like she was sinking in a pool of mercury. She flailed her limbs, unable to reach the surface, and was pulled from the depths by her mum. "I'm going to drown," Rose cried, choking up mineral-laced water. "You'll lose your nerve if you don't keep trying," Mum said, her breath steaming in the frigid air. They returned to the Kenwood Ladies' Pond the following day, and the day after that. By the end of winter break, Rose had not only learned to swim and endure freezing temperatures, she'd learned to face her fears.

Determination bloomed in Rose's chest. She bathed, using a sample-size piece of scented soap from her cosmetic case, dressed, and got on her bicycle before she lost her nerve. But less than thirty minutes into the trip, resurrected pain gnawed at her legs. Her windpipe burned. The quest to obtain a wireless transmitter, Rose believed, was by far the most difficult endeavor she'd ever attempted, including combat training, jumping out of a plane, attempting to scale Lieutenant Clarke's bloody wall, sabotaging a transformer station, and even spying on the head of the SD. Transforming her agony to resolve, Rose pushed on. She prayed that she'd have enough strength to reach Montluçon, and that Lazare, Muriel, and Felix were still alive.

CHAPTER 32

84 AVENUE FOCH, PARIS—JUNE 28, 1943

Lazare, regaining consciousness, felt spasms shoot through his groin and travel down his legs. He clutched his abdomen and coughed, sending a twinge through his ribs. He cracked open an eye, the other swollen shut. The mattress beneath his body was stained with dark-brown splotches. A metal pendant-shaped light fixture hung from the ceiling, and the windows were boarded shut. The room contained several bunk beds—absent blankets or pillows—reminiscent of a dormitory. A few of the beds held men, most of whom appeared to be unable to move due to their injuries. Moans, whimpers, and rasps—mixed with the odor of urine—filled the air.

Lazare had undergone rounds of torture, the worst of which occurred after Vogel entered his cell and said, "So, Lazare Aron, I understand you are a *Jude*." A knot formed in Lazare's stomach. It was only a matter of time, Lazare believed, before a tortured prisoner released his full identity. After all, everyone in his Resistance network knew that he was a Jew. *I'll be dead soon.* Vogel's interrogations were gruesomely intense, both mentally and physically. But despite Vogel's sadistic methods, Lazare had refused to provide any valuable information. However, it was clear that Vogel had already acquired knowledge about the networks when he asked probing questions about Claudius, Prosper, Conjurer, and Sporran. Lazare maintained his silence. But when Vogel said, "Tell me what you know about Dragonfly," a wretched pang pierced Lazare's heart. He hoped that Vogel hadn't noticed his reaction, and that Rose was many miles away from Paris.

Lazare, unable to stand, rolled out of his bed. He crawled over the floor, going from bunk to bunk, checking on the men. None of the detainees was the agent called Piper, as all of the men were French. He found Ernest on a mattress clutching a broken arm to his chest.

Lazare leaned his torso against Ernest's bunk. "What did you tell them?" he whispered.

"Nothing," Ernest groaned.

Lazare's gut ached. "Vogel is going to make you promises in exchange for information. They're lies. In the end, they'll either send us to prison camps or execute us. Our cooperation will have no influence on whether we live or die."

Ernest lowered his eyes.

"We must be strong for France," Lazare said.

"I know."

"When I gain my strength," Lazare said. "I'll set your arm."

Ernest shook his head. "They'll break it again."

Lazare placed a hand on Ernest's shoulder. "Then I'll set it again."

CHAPTER 33

84 AVENUE FOCH, PARIS—JUNE 29, 1943

The door to the holding cell opened, jolting Lazare awake. He lifted his head, his pulse pounding in his ears, and prepared himself for another round of interrogation. But instead of taking him or one of the other prisoners, two German soldiers tossed a man, his face smeared with blood from a gash on his head, into the holding cell. The man crumpled to the ground, and the soldiers left, bolting the door.

The man, facedown on the floor, struggled to get to his knees, and then slumped onto his belly. He labored to crawl to the bunks, but none of the other prisoners, suffering from their own beatings, came to the man's aid.

Lazare forced himself to stand, holding on to the bunk to keep from falling. His joints and muscles flared with pain. Slowly, he made his way across the room, shuffling his feet over the floor. Approaching the prisoner, Lazare recognized him by his bleached hair and mustache. A wave of dread flooded his body.

Lazare lowered himself to his knees, sending a sharp twinge through his thighs. "Felix," he whispered.

Felix raised his head and opened his eyes, one of which had a broken blood vessel. "Lazare." He swallowed, his lips dry and cracked.

Lazare helped Felix into a bunk, having to stop several times while crossing the floor to rest. He sat beside him, tore off a piece of his shirttail, and placed it on Felix's gash.

"*Merci*," Felix said.

"What happened?" Lazare whispered, so the other prisoners could not hear their conversation.

"The SD raided my apartment building," Felix said.

"Was Rose with you?"

Felix shook his head.

Thank God. "Where is she?"

"I don't know. She was out of the building when I was arrested." He adjusted the bandage on his head. "I should have taken her concerns about SD infiltration more seriously. This never should have happened."

"What about Muriel?"

"She's here." Felix took a labored breath. "The bastards interrogated her, and then brought her into my cell. They made her watch my torture, trying to get her to talk. But she maintained a story that she'd never seen me before."

Nausea rose from Lazare's stomach. He hoped that Muriel wasn't being interrogated in the same manner as the prisoners in this room, but doubted that the Nazis, given their medieval interrogation tactics, would differentiate their approach between male and female agents. He prayed that he was wrong.

"How did you get here?" Felix asked.

Lazare told him about the reception committee in Ableiges being a trap by the Germans. "They were waiting for us. A Resistance fighter was killed. They brought Ernest, an SOE agent called Piper, and me here."

Felix cleared his throat. "Piper's dead."

"How do you know?"

"I understand a little German. I overheard the guards talking about an SOE agent with a busted nose and fractured skull. He died before they could interrogate him."

A flash of Piper climbing out of the RAF Lysander filled Lazare's head. *Poor man survived less than a few hours as an SOE agent.* Lazare buried his vision and looked at Felix, his face badly beaten. "Did you tell them anything?"

"Not a damn thing." Felix smiled, exposing a missing tooth. "I got the SD questioning whether I'm SOE or French Resistance. It's probably why I'm in here with you, rather than the holding cell that contains British agents."

"*Bien*," Lazare said. An ember of hope, although faint, filled Lazare's heart, knowing that Rose was not imprisoned at SD headquarters. *Please leave Paris and never come back.*

Felix struggled to sit up, his back leaning against a wall.

"How's the strength in your arms?" Lazare asked.

"They still work," Felix said. "Most of the punishment was to my face and stomach. Why do you ask?"

Lazare pointed. "I need help setting a man's broken arm."

CHAPTER 34

MONTLUÇON, FRANCE—JUNE 29, 1943

Rose, her legs throbbing, bicycled into Montluçon before nightfall. Busted blisters, seeded from hours of gripping the handlebars, marred her hands. Abrasions, which were the diameter of teacups and caused by the seat chafing her inner thighs, stung with each stroke of the pedals. Dehydrated and dizzy, she searched the area for the convent where Claudius's friend resided, only to find the town swarming with Germans. And she understood the reason why when the air turned rank with the odor of heated rubber. Ahead, a large industrial complex—emblazoned with the name Dunlop, as well as swastika flags—spewed black smoke into the air. *Hitler is using France's tire-making capability for his military.* She turned away in search of another route, wondering why Allied bombers had not yet targeted the factory supplying the Wehrmacht and Luftwaffe with tires.

An hour after canvassing Montluçon, she noticed a young woman wearing a black robe and white veil enter a large stone building covered in thick green ivy. A smidge of hope surged through her chest. She slipped from her seat and hobbled, using her bicycle as a crutch. Upon her knocking, the door opened to reveal a blue-eyed nun no more than eighteen or nineteen years of age.

"Can I help you?" the nun asked.

Rose leaned against the doorframe. Her knees quivered. "I'm looking for Sister Simone," she said, her voice raw.

The nun peeked outside the door, glanced in both directions, and said, "Come inside."

"My things," Rose breathed.

"I'll get them."

Rose entered, her feet shuffling over a tile floor.

The nun helped Rose into a chair, and then placed the bicycle in a vestibule. She retrieved a clay pitcher and handed it to Rose.

Rose gulped water, cold and laced with minerals. She wiped her lips, chapped and swollen. "*Merci*."

"I'll let Sister Simone know that you are here. Who shall I say is calling?"

Rose? Dragonfly? Aline? "I'm a friend of Claudius, who grew up with Simone."

The nun disappeared down a long corridor. Minutes later, she returned, accompanied by a nun with pink-hued, wrinkled cheeks.

"I'm Sister Simone," the woman said.

Rose struggled to stand. Her body swayed. "Claudius suggested I see you."

"I haven't heard his name spoken in many years," Simone said. "How do you know him?"

"We work together," Rose said.

Sister Simone placed a hand to a small wooden cross hanging from a cord around her neck. "What type of work?"

"Liberating France," Rose said.

Sister Simone lowered her hand from her pendant. "How can I help you?"

"I need to reach a man called Alphonse," Rose said. "He organizes a network in southeast France."

The nuns glanced to each other.

"Do you know him?" Rose asked.

"*Non*," Simone said. "But we know the areas in which he operates. His network wreaks havoc on the railway lines, infuriating the Germans."

"Can you take me there?" Rose asked.

"Too dangerous," Simone said.

"It's a matter of life and death," Rose said.

The young nun clasped her hands, as if she were about to pray.

"You're in no condition to travel," Simone said.

"I have no choice," Rose said. "If you will not help me, I'll try to find him myself."

"Sister Simone," the young nun said, her voice tentative. "May I have a word with you, alone?"

Simone stepped away with the young nun. Their voices dropped to whispers.

Despite Rose's exhaustion, dire urgency boiled in her stomach.

"All right," Simone said, returning to Rose. "Sister Justine has informed me of where members of Alphonse's group are rumored to be located. You'll stay here with her, while I attempt to make contact."

"*Merci*," Rose said.

"But I can go," Justine said. "I know the area."

"*Non*," Simone said. "It is my history that has led this woman here. I will go."

A lump of guilt formed in Rose's throat. She regretted that her body was spent.

"If I'm able to reach Alphonse," Simone said, looking at Rose, "what should I say?"

The ache in Rose's legs spread to her torso. "Tell him that the British networks in Paris are in desperate need of his help, and that *Dragonfly* needs to see him."

Simone's eyes widened.

"And above all else," Rose said, "make sure he brings a wireless transmitter."

Simone nodded and left.

Rose, her legs frail like dandelion stems about to snap, was helped by Sister Justine to a sleeping chamber, a ten-by-ten-foot room with a small bed and desk. The air smelled of candle wax and ancient timbers. Rose was given a meal of oats and a glass of goat milk, which she hastily consumed. Her clothes, filthy and foul, were taken away by Sister Justine to be washed. She bathed and cleaned her wounds, using a water basin and homemade lye soap, which emitted an ammonia-like odor. She slipped on a robe, provided by Justine, and collapsed onto the bed. As Rose drifted to sleep, she realized that her chances of contacting Alphonse were out of her control. She hoped that Sister Simone, who had a relationship with God, could also create one with an SOE network organizer called Alphonse.

By noon the next day, Rose's stamina improved; however, her calves and hamstrings felt like they'd been beaten with a meat tenderizer. The rest and meals, consisting of porridge and goat milk, had begun to revitalize her body, but not her spirit. Sister Simone had not returned, and with each passing hour, Rose worried that something might have happened to her. At nightfall, nearly a full day since she arrived at the convent, Rose was startled by a knock on her chamber door.

Sister Simone entered, followed by a young man appearing to be in his early twenties, with dark-brown hair and a mustache.

"Thank goodness," Rose said.

The man put down a suitcase and extended his hand. "Dragonfly, I presume."

"*Oui*," Rose said, shaking his hand.

"Alphonse."

The nun turned to leave.

"Sister Simone," Rose said, indebtedness swelling in her chest.

The woman, her eyes weary from her journey, looked at Rose. "*Merci*."

Simone nodded and left, closing the door behind her.

"I understand that you're in desperate need of help," Alphonse said.

"It's far more than that, I'm afraid." Rose took a deep breath, preparing to relive the nightmare of the past several days. She told him about the collapse of Physician and its subnetworks, including her own group, Conjurer. "The French Resistance networks in Paris have also been compromised."

"Bloody hell," Alphonse said. "And headquarters doesn't know what has happened?"

"They believed that all was well at the time of our last transmission," Rose said. "I'm hoping that another agent has gotten through by now. It was too risky for me to attempt to reach another wireless operator in Paris, so I came in search of you."

"Sister Simone told me you arrived on a bicycle. It's three hundred kilometers from here. How did you do it?"

Rose shrugged. "I had no choice but to keep pedaling."

"You were lucky to escape."

Rose nodded, her heart aching to help her fallen companions. She pointed to the suitcase. "I hope that contains your wireless transmitter."

"Indeed," he said. He placed the suitcase on a desk and flipped open the lid. "I came immediately when I heard of your predicament. I have no idea how Sister Simone managed to locate some of my men. Either we are becoming careless with our concealment, or the nuns of this convent are quite resourceful."

"I hope it's the latter," Rose said. Eager to contact London, she helped Alphonse set up the wireless transmitter, which was identical to Muriel's unit, except for the tan hard-shell suitcase with leather trim. She finished by sticking the antenna out of a window, concealed by a curtain.

"Go ahead," Alphonse said, gesturing for Rose to operate the wireless unit.

Rose sat at the desk, put on the headset, and flipped a switch, causing the transistor tubes to hum. A flash of Muriel, tapping away at her wireless unit, sent a pang into Rose's chest. Her brain raced, recalling her code and cypher training, and—most importantly—her first and second security checks: change the first appearing "e" to "u" and misuse the letters "c" and "k" in the initial communication. She scribbled a message, using a piece of paper and pencil inside the suitcase, and then encrypted it. Steadying her finger over the telegraph key, she tapped out the message:

```
Thu wolves have broken into the
physician's farm. Many sheep, inkluding
Conjurer and Sporran, are gone. A sole
Dragonfly circles the pond.
```

A minute passed. Rose chewed on her bottom lip. *Please be listening.*

"Anything?" Alphonse asked.

Rose shook her head.

"I'll check the antenna."

Short and long pulses came through her headset, accelerating Rose's heartbeat. She waved him off and scribbled down the cyphered Morse code message. As she decrypted the message, she grew nauseous, as if her stomach were filled with wriggling worms. She pushed the message to Alphonse.

> *All sheep accounted for. How do you know the wolves have gotten into the field?*

"Bloody hell," Alphonse said, leaning over her shoulder. "They don't realize that the SD has penetrated the network!"

Rose frantically sent another message.

```
Several days ago, I witnessed Conjurer
and Sporran being taken from their pen.
```

Minutes passed before headquarters sent another message.

> *Negative. Sporran and Conjurer remain in contact.*

"Oh, my God," Rose muttered. Her hands trembled.

"Damn it," Alphonse said. "The bloody SD might have forced your wireless operator to tell them her security codes. They're using the wireless transmitter, pretending to be British agents."

"No!" Rose turned to him. "I know her. She'd never give up her security checks." She sent another message to headquarters.

```
Have you confirmed that all security
checks for Sporran are in order?
```

Twenty minutes passed. Rose's anxiety soared. She imagined headquarters sorting through past communications. Pulses through her headset caused her to flinch. She transposed the message and slumped in her chair.

Affirmative. Wolves have broken into the physician's farm. Stand by for further orders.

"Someone at headquarters didn't scrutinize the security checks," Alphonse said.

Rose's hand trembled above her telegraph key. "How could this happen?"

Alphonse rubbed his chin. "My wireless operator was captured last spring, and the SD's counterintelligence communicated with headquarters, nearly luring me into a trap. Maybe your wireless operator, when tortured to give up their security verification, provided the SD with the first check but not the second, which might have confused headquarters. Either way, there was a breakdown in security."

A flash of Muriel being tortured caused Rose's heart to ache.

"It doesn't matter," Alphonse said. "You've accomplished a remarkable feat, Dragonfly. You escaped capture, bicycled three hundred kilometers—evading the enemy—to find a wireless transmitter, and alerted headquarters of the infiltration. Most importantly, you might have saved the lives of many agents."

Rose's eyes pooled with tears. She felt no relief, nor did she feel any self-satisfaction or sense of achievement by convincing London of the infiltration. Deep down, she was grateful that the lives of agents might be saved, but all she could think about was the ones that were lost. She wiped away her tears and waited to receive her orders. But by morning, nothing came.

CHAPTER 35

MONTLUÇON, FRANCE—JULY 5, 1943

In the cloister, an arched stone arcade which ran along the interior walls of the convent, Rose and Alphonse worked to modify Rose's bicycle. The wicker basket, which was adequate for a cosmetics case, was nowhere sturdy enough to handle the thirty-pound weight of a suitcase containing a wireless transmitter. So, they installed a metal carrier running perpendicular to the rear fender. The carrier, a gift from Sister Simone, was repurposed from a broken bicycle rusting away in the cellar of the convent.

Rose tossed a wrench into a toolbox, placed the suitcase onto the carrier—testing its strength—and added the cosmetic case. "I think it will hold," she said, tying down the luggage with cord.

Alphonse examined the load. "Well done."

Rose smoothed her hands over her skirt, grateful for the nuns to have cleaned and pressed her clothes. "Are you certain you will not need the wireless transmitter?"

"*Non*," Alphonse said. "We have an extra one. Besides, I prefer to communicate with London through clandestine courier lines to Switzerland."

It had been five days since Rose informed London of the SD infiltration. SOE headquarters offered to fly Rose, along with Alphonse and members of the Pimento network, back to England on an RAF Hudson that was to land on a field near Angers, France. It turned out that Alphonse's network was also experiencing wrath from the enemy. In addition to the capture of one of his wireless operators, several associates had recently been apprehended. Alphonse, who had a fiancée back home, accepted the offer. But Rose declined.

There's no one back home for me, she'd thought. A chamber of her heart held hope that Lazare had escaped capture, and that her fellow agents were alive. Initially, headquarters refused Rose's proposal to return to Paris and begin the role of an organizer for her own network. But Rose held her ground. After several rather candid wireless transmissions, headquarters agreed for Rose to lead an operation in Valmondois, twenty-five miles north of Paris, with the objective to deliver arms to the French Resistance. Unfortunately, given the collapse of the Paris-based SOE networks, headquarters could not provide a timeline for when new agents would be deployed to join her. Therefore, Rose would not merely be acting as an organizer, she'd also be performing the roles of a courier and wireless operator. She would be, by all accounts, an agent and sole proprietor of her own network called Dragonfly.

"It's not too late to change your mind and come with me," Alphonse said, preparing to leave. "You can always come back later, when the SD arrest waves have subsided. I plan to return in a few months, and I'll stay until France is liberated."

Rose shook her head.

"You wouldn't be quitting. You'd simply be retreating from an unwinnable battle—so you can win the bloody war."

"My heart is telling me that I need to stay," Rose said.

"What about your brain?" Alphonse asked.

"Same," Rose lied.

"Okay," Alphonse said, appearing satisfied. "Good luck."

Rose shook his hand. "You too."

Alphonse left the cloister, the clack of his boots fading on the limestone pathway.

Rose found Sister Simone and Sister Justine tending to a vegetable garden located on a small parcel of land behind the convent. She thanked them for their food, shelter, bicycle carrier, and, most of all, for finding Alphonse.

"You helped me save lives," Rose said. "I wish there was something I could do for you."

"You already have." Simone smiled, soft wrinkles forming on her cheeks. "You're helping France regain its freedom."

Justine clasped a wooden cross worn on a string around her neck. "May God support you in danger."

"*Merci*." Rose got on her bicycle. She left the convent, her gut coiling with gloom. *I'll never see them again.*

She pedaled through Montluçon, getting accustomed to the added weight of the wireless radio, which was a third of Rose's body mass. The bicycle was cumbrous to balance around turns, and even on level terrain it took effort, her sore legs grinding, to pick up speed. The real problem, Rose knew, would come when she encountered hills. She gripped the handlebars, her hands calloused with partially healed blisters, and resolved to worry about inclines later.

On the outskirts of Montluçon, black smoke spewed from the Dunlop tire factory. Rose imagined French citizens, laboring under a Nazi-indentured servitude. And she recalled her request that she'd included in her last wireless transmission to London.

Tire factory in Montluçon under enemy control. Bombing raid required. Dragonfly.

She hoped that headquarters would take her request seriously. Although a mission of this magnitude could potentially result in French casualties, it would be worse to keep Hitler's war machines fitted with tires, prolonging the war and escalating Allied deaths.

Rose's return route would take her through many of the same villages and towns, but with a few significant changes. She would take three days, instead of two, to make the journey, and she would have safe places to hide at night, thanks to Sister Simone and her Catholic network. It turned out that Simone was far more connected than Rose initially thought. While staying with Simone, she'd learned that the sisters of the convent had occasionally harbored downed RAF pilots following escape routes to Spain. Additionally, the nuns often hid Jewish families attempting to escape to Switzerland. She wished that Lazare's parents could have reached refuge with Sister Simone. *Where are you, Lazare?* Her chest tightened. Rose pushed hard on her pedals, sending a burn through her thighs.

For two days, Rose traveled north, taking as many side roads as possible to avoid German roadblocks. She was more prepared for the return trip, considering Sister Simone provided her with bread, plums, a hunk of cheese, and a wineskin filled with water. And in the evenings, she slept in the safety of a convent cellarium, one in Saint-Martin-d'Auxigny and the other in Puiseaux. But despite the food and rest, her legs throbbed. Her spine, from her lower back to the base of her neck, was a tangled mass of knots. The worst sections were on the hills, which required her to dismount and push her loaded bicycle. Summer heat battered her body, evaporating her energy. With each step, her calves flaring with pain, she willed herself up the inclines, all the while trying not to think of her seventy-mile daily trip or, even worse, that the entire journey from Montluçon to Valmondois was over two hundred and twenty miles.

On the third and last day of her trip, she took a midmorning break near a secluded stream in Champcueil. She gulped water and ate her last remaining plum, its sweet nectar bursting on her tongue. With the area heavily wooded and no houses in sight, she removed her clothes and waded into the stream. The cool current soothed her burning feet and massaged her aching legs. A flash of her mother, teaching her to swim in the frigid waters of Kenwood Ladies' Pond, filled her head.

"I won't give up, Mum," Rose whispered, sinking her body into the stream.

She bathed, sat on a sandy bank to allow the sun to dry her skin, and dressed. Preparing to leave, she hesitated as she checked the straps on her luggage. *I need to look like a young woman pedaling through her village.* She removed her cosmetics case and applied blush, lipstick, and dabs of perfume to her neck and wrists. Her body and spirit renewed, at least for the moment, Rose mounted her bicycle and pedaled away.

Two miles into the trek, as she rounded a sharp bend, a

Wehrmacht lorry blocked the road. Rose's heart rate flared. She looked for a place to turn off, but it was too late.

A soldier, standing on the berm with a rifle slung over his shoulder, raised his hand. "*Halt!*"

Rose's mouth turned dry. She tightened her grip on the handlebars to keep her arms from shaking. *Keep calm.*

The soldier, adjusting his helmet, stepped into the road.

Rose coasted to a stop. "*Bonjour,*" she said, pretending to be relieved to take a break from pedaling her bicycle.

The soldier, a blue-eyed young man about nineteen or twenty years of age, given the lack of stubby facial hair, clasped his rifle strap. "*Papiers, mademoiselle.*"

Rose smiled. "You speak French?"

"*Oui,*" he said, abruptly. "*Papiers.*"

Rose removed papers from her purse, stashed in the front basket, and gave them to the soldier.

The soldier examined the papers.

Rose, her legs straddling the bicycle, slid up her skirt and rubbed a knee.

The soldier's eyes wandered.

Clasping a button on her blouse, she puffed the silky material against her breastbone, as if to fan away the summer heat.

The soldier handed Rose her papers. He lifted his helmet and, using his sleeve, wiped perspiration from his forehead. "What's in the luggage?"

Fear flooded Rose's body. She narrowed her sight on the man's Adam's apple. *Slam your bloody fist into his larynx,* Lieutenant Clarke barked inside her head. She buried her combat instructor's voice, knowing that she'd never win a fight with a soldier, especially without a weapon.

"A wireless transmitter," Rose said, calmly.

The soldier raised his eyebrows.

"I was on my way to contact enemy headquarters." She leaned forward, closing the space between them. "I'm a spy."

His eyes softened. A grin spread over his face.

Rose chuckled.

The soldier laughed.

Smiling, she raised her wrist to the soldier's nose. "Smell."

The German hesitated.

"Go on," she said.

The soldier sniffed, his face lingering over her arm. "Nice."

"I sell cosmetics." Rose got off her bicycle, propping the kick-stand, and opened her cosmetics case. She stepped to the soldier. "Where are you from?"

The soldier glanced behind him, as if he were concerned that his commander would appear at any moment. "Hamburg."

"Maybe your wife in Hamburg would like some perfume," she said, displaying the contents of her case.

"I don't have a wife," he said, appearing amused.

Rose's eyes met his. She closed her case and inched close, fighting the revulsion that pricked her stomach. "What's your name?"

"Otto," he said, tentatively. "Yours?"

"You just read my papers," Rose said, touching her hair. "Have you forgotten already?"

The soldier's face flushed.

Rose smiled. "Aline."

"Do you come by here often, Aline?" the soldier asked.

"A few times a week," she said. "Where are you stationed?"

"Mennecy." He adjusted the rifle, slung over his shoulder. "It's twenty minutes north of here on bicycle. I'm usually free in the evening. There's a café in the village. Perhaps you could find time to join me."

"A lovely offer." Rose pondered the German's proposition as she secured her cosmetic case to the carrier. She lifted her skirt, exposing her thigh, and straddled her bicycle.

The soldier placed a hand on the bicycle's handlebar. "How about tonight?"

"I'd love to, but I need to deliver cosmetics to a woman in Paris."

He frowned.

"But I'm free Friday evening," she said.

The soldier grinned. The grind of an approaching vehicle grew. He released his hand from the bicycle.

"*Au revoir*, Otto." Rose pedaled, doing her best to hide the exertion of her legs, driven by the weight of her wireless radio.

"Friday," the soldier called.

Rose waved. *Thank God he didn't want to look foolish by examining my suitcase.* She gained speed, wanting to get as far away from the roadblock as possible. Her heartbeat pounded her chest. Her blood pumped with a slurry of repugnance and confidence. She recalled how her mind had raced, struggling to think of how she could avoid opening her suitcase for the soldier. It wasn't that she had experience flirting with men. Nor did she, a small woman with a less than curvaceous figure, have the attributes—Rose believed—to turn men's heads. It was a childhood memory of her brother, buried deep within her subconscious, that had driven her ploy to deceive the soldier.

One November Saturday before Guy Fawkes Day—when Rose and Charlie were in middle school—Charlie ran downstairs with a shoebox tucked under his arm. "What's in the shoebox?" Mum had asked, stirring a pot of oatmeal. "Fireworks," Charlie exclaimed. "I'm going to make a bonfire!" Mum placed her hands on her hips and said, "Come on, Charlie. What's in there?" Charlie extended the package and asked, "Want to see a mouse?" Mum shrieked and told her son to get rid of the mouse—far from the Teasdale residence. Throwing on her coat, Rose accompanied Charlie to a wooded park. As Charlie placed his package on the ground, Rose prepared to run, in the event the little rodent scurried in her direction. Instead, Charlie grinned and removed packages of firecrackers from his shoebox. Rose's jaw dropped. He handed his sister a book of matches, giving her the honors to light the first string of firecrackers, ensuring her silence regarding his little scheme. Rose, feeling a bit mischievous, lit the fuse. As a barrage of blasts echoed through the park, she marveled how Mum failed to examine the shoebox after Charlie had truthfully told her what was inside. And technically, he hadn't necessarily lied when he'd simply *asked* if Mum wanted to see a mouse.

Sometimes the best deception is no deception at all. Rose pumped her bicycle pedals, attempting to dispel her adrenaline. *Thank you, my dear, sweet Charlie.* She pushed ahead believing, perhaps for the first time since she'd arrived in France, that she was not only capable of being a cunning agent, but that she could also be a competent network organizer.

At sunset, Rose arrived in Valmondois, a rural commune with several hundred inhabitants, given the size of the village center. With her strength depleted, she labored to maneuver through cobblestone streets, which jarred her body like a shaken snow globe. The sound of rippling water led her to an abandoned granary, similar to what Claudius had described before her departure from the catacomb. The three-story stone structure butted up against a river. A broken waterwheel, once used to power the granary, was obstructed with logs and debris. All of the windows, including the front entrance, were boarded shut. Rose dismounted, sending flares of pain through her knees and spine. She agonized to straighten her vertebrae, frozen from hours of being hunched over the handlebars, and she pushed her bicycle to the rear of the building. Locating a locked service door, she knocked and waited. But there was no answer. Getting dark and no place else to go, she picked the lock, using pins from her hair. Stepping inside, which was dark and damp, she felt the cold steel of a pistol pressed against her head.

Rose froze. "I'm looking for Claudius," she said, her heart thumping against her ribcage. The pressure lifted from her temple.

"*Mon Dieu,*" a familiar voice said. "I almost killed you."

Rose exhaled.

A match flared. Claudius lit a lantern, casting a glow over the lower level of the granary, which contained a table, chairs, and several cots, giving it the appearance of being inhabited by squatters. He hugged her and kissed her on both cheeks. He pulled her bicycle inside, lugging it over the doorframe, and bolted the door.

Rose collapsed into a chair.

Claudius sat and removed his beret. Lamplight gleamed over his bald head. "Did you get through to London?"

"*Oui,*" Rose said.

He handed her a half-filled wine bottle.

She drank. The wine contained a bitter, musky flavor reminiscent of diluted vinegar. Despite the offensive taste, she took another swig, and then told him everything—about her journey, Sister Simone, reaching Alphonse, contacting SOE headquarters, and declining to be flown out of the country on an RAF Hudson.

"Why did you come back?" he asked.

"I have a wireless radio," Rose said, pointing to the suitcase on her bicycle. "And I've been promoted."

Claudius scratched a bushy sideburn.

"I'm leading a network, charged with delivering arms to the French Resistance," Rose said. "Which means I'll need your help, assuming you are still in the business of recruiting fighters and receiving armament."

"Of course," Claudius said, smiling. "But it would have been better for you to have chosen to go home."

I can't leave, Rose thought. She took a sip of wine, preparing for what she wanted to ask the moment she reached Claudius. A burn drifted down her esophagus and rested in her belly. She looked at him, praying that he would say the words she so longed to hear. "Any news about Lazare?"

Claudius lowered his eyes.

Rose's breath stalled in her lungs.

"He was captured."

A pang pierced Rose's chest. "Is he alive?"

"I don't know."

"Where was he taken?" she asked, her voice quavering.

Claudius pulled a cigarette from his breast pocket but made no effort to light it. "The Parisian headquarters of the SD."

No! Rose attempted to stand, but her legs gave out. "We must do something," she cried.

"The SD headquarters is well guarded. It would be a suicide mission to attempt to free him." Tears formed in Claudius's eyes. "Lazare is in God's hands. We must have faith that he'll survive."

Rose took in a jagged breath.

"We'll continue our fight, until the day France is free and Lazare comes home." He looked at Rose. "And he *will* return home."

No! This can't be happening! Her dream of reuniting with Lazare came crashing down in a tidal wave of despair. She knew that the chances of surviving a German prison camp, assuming the SD didn't execute him after they tortured him for information, were slim at best. Nausea rose in her throat. Grief-stricken and gutted, she lowered her head into her hands and wept.

Part 3

L'Emprisonnement

CHAPTER 36

AMIENS, FRANCE—DECEMBER 10, 1943

Lazare gripped the iron bars of his prison cell, sending a chill through his fingers. His bad hand felt naked, despite having been stripped of his prosthetic months ago. The hallway of the north wing of the Amiens Prison was dimly lit by caged overhead lights. The cold, damp conditions in the cellblock resembled a meat locker, and the air stank of urine and feces. He angled his head, peering through the iron bars, but saw no sign of the guards.

Felix stood from his bunk, crossed the ten-by-ten-foot cell, and whispered to Lazare. "They'll be coming soon."

A foreboding ache twisted inside Lazare's gut.

Lazare and Felix, as well as several members of the French Resistance, had been taken to Amiens Prison, seventy-five miles north of Paris, after two weeks of sadistic physical and mental torture at Nazi headquarters on Avenue Foch. The skin on his chest and back was marred with scars, caused by repeated beatings with a metal chain, as well as unspeakable things done to him with dental tools. The ability to raise his arms above his head was limited, a result of shoulder dislocations when he'd been bound with rope and strung from a ceiling hoist like a side of beef left to age. The pain and sleep deprivation had nearly broken him, but he'd fought through it all, his mind and heart refusing to give the Nazis any information that could further compromise French networks and, most importantly, lead them to Rose.

Felix, Lazare believed, had also remained silent. In fact, it appeared that Felix had managed to convince the SD that he was not an SOE agent; otherwise, he might not have been sent to Amiens Prison, which the Germans used primarily to detain members of the French Resistance. Lazare admired Felix's loyalty to France, but given that the Germans viewed the French Resistance as terrorists, it might have been safer for Felix to be declared a British agent, giving him a chance, although slim, of being treated as a military prisoner of war.

After their torture at SD headquarters, Lazare, Felix, and a dozen French prisoners were handcuffed and transported by German lorries into the countryside. The prisoners were not told where they were going, generating whispers that they were being taken to be executed. The prisoners, including Lazare, were in too poor of a physical shape to attempt an escape, which would most certainly end with them being mowed down by German gunfire. An image of being riddled with bullets and buried in a ditch filled Lazare's head. *I'm sorry, Rose. I wish there was a chance for us.* He lowered his head into his hands and prayed that she was safe, somewhere far, far away from France.

A few hours after leaving Paris, the German convoy stopped at a rural location that contained a large prison surrounded by a twenty-foot brick wall. Inside were three large prison wings, spanned by two German guardhouses. They were forced to strip and were given brown clothing, identical to the other seven hundred prisoners at Amiens Prison. Lazare was locked inside a cell with Felix and Ernest, where they remained, except for one hour per day to walk the courtyard and irregular latrine breaks at a large wooden outhouse containing a solitary communal bench with thirty holes. Meals—provided twice per day, in the morning and evening—were putrid cabbage broth and sawdust-laced bread.

The clack of German boots turned Lazare's mouth dry. He looked at Felix, his eyes bloodshot, and said, "It's time."

Felix, running a hand through his oily hair, took a deep breath and exhaled.

Lazare turned and kneeled beside Ernest, who had been cap-tured with him in Ableiges and was now sitting on his bunk with his head lowered.

Ernest's body trembled. His arm, broken several times during his torture, had healed with a malunion, creating a bend in the forearm, like a branch of pear tree heavily weighted with fruit. Lazare, with the help of Felix, had set the man's arm as best he could, using cloth wrappings in lieu of splints to hold the bones in place. But, as Ernest had predicted, the SD had broken the arm again and again, turning the hulking Resistance fighter into a shell of his former self.

"Do you need help to stand?" Lazare asked.

"*Non*," Ernest said, his voice gravelly. Using the bunk frame as a brace, he struggled to get to his feet. Tears welled in his eyes.

Lazare placed a hand on Ernest's shoulder.

"I'm sorry," Ernest whimpered. "I said some things during my torture that—"

"You have nothing to be ashamed of," Lazare said. A flash of his own torture caused Lazare's head to throb. *Everyone has a break-ing point. Another few days and the SD might have cracked me, too.* "You've honored France. And I'm proud to have fought by your side."

Felix clasped Ernest's hand.

"*Adieu*," Ernest breathed.

A key clanged inside a lock. Ernest flinched. Three German guards—two with machine guns and one wielding a baton—opened the cell door. The guard with the baton motioned for Lazare and Felix to move to the rear wall.

Lazare and Felix, placing their hands on their heads, backed away.

Handcuffs were placed on Ernest, and he was led out of the cell. The iron-bar door clanged shut, echoing through the stone corridor.

Indignation surged through Lazare's veins. He shot forward and grasped the iron bars. As the soldiers escorted Ernest away, a swell of patriotism burned inside him, inspiring him to shout the verse to a song called *Le Chant des Partisans*. He'd heard it, before his capture, on Radio Londres—operated by the Free French who'd escaped German occupation—which was broadcasted from the BBC in London. The words and melody of the song, which called for the French to rise up, had been seared into Lazare's brain, as well as his heart. Despite the consequences, he raised his voice and sang.

"*Halt!*" The German soldier raised his baton. His comrades stopped and pushed Ernest against a wall.

Lazare continued singing.

Felix pressed his face through the bars and bellowed a verse.

The soldier stepped to the cell door and slammed his baton against the bars. "*Aufhören!*"

Lazare and Felix shot back but continued their chant.

Prisoners locked in a nearby cell belted out the next verse of *Le Chant des Partisans*. Soon, the entire cellblock of prisoners joined in, their voices reverberating through the masonry corridors.

The soldier examined his watch, and then glared at Lazare. "*Ich komme wieder,*" he hissed. He motioned to his comrades to take Ernest away.

Determination flared through Lazare's chest. *You can take our bodies, but you can't take our souls.*

"*Vive la France!*" Ernest cried, being forced from the cellblock.

Lazare and the prisoners continued their chant for several minutes, until a church bell rang in Amiens, signaling noon. The chorus faded. Seconds after the twelfth toll of the church bell, a barrage of gunfire exploded in the courtyard. Tears welled in Lazare's eyes. He resumed his chant, leading the prisoners in two more verses of *Le Chant des Partisans*.

CHAPTER 37

AMIENS, FRANCE—DECEMBER 20, 1943

Lazare, battered and bruised, entered the courtyard of Amiens Prison. Sunlight beating down on his face caused him to squint. Once his eyes adjusted, he mingled through a group of prisoners in search of Felix.

It had been over a week since Ernest's execution, one of nearly a dozen that had taken place since his arrival at the prison. There appeared to be no clear methodology for whom the Germans sentenced to death. If anyone should have been given a reprieve by the Nazis, Lazare believed, it should have been Ernest. After all, the man had been broken under their torture and had given them information. *They want us to live in fear, wondering who will be killed next.*

Following Ernest's execution, the baton-wielding German guard had returned with six comrades. Viewed as troublemakers, Lazare and Felix were separated. Felix was handcuffed and dragged away to a different building, which contained an isolated cellblock. Lazare was held down by German guards, their sweaty hands pinning his wrists and ankles to the concrete floor, and he received a vicious baton beating to his back and legs.

Unable to stand, he remained in his bunk for over a day. When he gained enough strength to crawl, he made his way to a food tin left near the cell door. He forced himself to eat, gagging down

spoiled cabbage. As days passed, the swelling in his knees subsided, allowing him to stand, and then to walk. He spent his week
of recovery reliving his time with Rose. Their conversations about
their families. The eloquent timbre of her voice. How her touch
sent tingles over his skin. He imagined her escaping to Britain and
having a long and joyful life.

Lazare buried thoughts of his lost future and mingled through
the courtyard. He found Felix, his eyes bruised the color of egg-
plant, sitting on the ground near the communal outhouse.

Felix grinned, revealing a missing front tooth. "You're alive."

Lazare sat, sending a spasm through his hamstrings. He winced
and rubbed his legs.

"It looks like they roughed you up a bit," Felix said.

Lazare nodded. "Are you all right?"

"I'll recover." Felix picked a blade of dormant grass and rolled
it between his fingers.

Several German guards carrying machine guns stood lookout
around the perimeter of the twenty-foot wall. A group of Nazi officers were smoking cigarettes near a guardhouse.

Felix nudged Lazare's boot. "There are rumors that Italy has
surrendered to the Allies, and that they've switched sides, declaring war on Germany."

"When?" Lazare asked.

"A few months ago."

A jolt struck Lazare. *We're disconnected from the rest of the world.*

"If the rumors are true," Felix continued, "it's only a matter of
time before an Allied invasion."

An ember of hope smoldered within Lazare. "We must hang
on, until France is liberated."

"It might take months," Felix said.

"Maybe a year or more," Lazare added. A flash of Maman and
Papa, somewhere in a German work camp. *Please stay alive.*

Despite his aches and hunger pangs, the rumors gave Lazare
a resurgence of energy. He invited Felix to join him in a walk
around the courtyard. Lazare, still recovering from his punishment, slowly shuffled over the ground.

"I'm in that building," Felix said, pointing to a wing of the prison.

"How many in your cell?" Lazare asked.

"Two. Both are French Resistance."

"Like you?" Lazare asked.

"Of course," Felix said, a slight smile on his face. "How about you?"

"I'm alone in my cell," Lazare said. "But at the rate of trucks bringing in more prisoners, it is only a matter of time before my cell, as well as the prison's capacity, is full."

"It's your damn singing," Felix said. "Why would anyone want to bunk with someone who sings out of tune."

"I'll try to work on it." Lazare appreciated Felix's attempt to poke fun at him. In a strange way, it made him feel human, something he hadn't felt since his capture.

They took several laps around the courtyard. After nearly an hour, Lazare anticipated that the guards would force them to return to their cellblock. Instead, more prisoners were ordered outside of their cells and to line up in the courtyard. More guards, either carrying rifles or machine guns, emerged from guardhouses and secured positions around the perimeter wall. Soon, prisoners were lined up in tight rows, shoulder to shoulder.

A knot formed in Lazare's stomach. "Something's wrong," he whispered to Felix, standing next to him.

Felix nodded.

A German SS officer, wearing polished jackboots and a cap with a silver skull-and-crossbones insignia, emerged from a guardhouse and stood on a small wooden platform. He gazed over the prisoners, and then raised a tin megaphone to his mouth. The air turned silent.

"By order of the *Drittes Reich*," the officer shouted, speaking in French. "The following prisoners will be executed at 12:00 p.m. on the nineteenth day of February 1944."

"*Mon Dieu*," Felix whispered. "They're going to make the poor bastards suffer by waiting two months for the firing line."

Anger swelled within Lazare.

"Jules Gagneux," the German officer shouted. "Édouard Proulx, Henri Fortier—"

Lazare clenched his hands.

The officer continued reading, his voice echoing through the courtyard. "Pierre Baudin, Fernand Macon—"

A prisoner, two rows ahead of Lazare, fell to his knees. A guard dashed forward, aiming his rifle. Fellow prisoners lifted the man to his feet.

"Étienne Thibault, Francis Neuville, Felix Renaud—"

Lazare's heart sank.

"Bastards," Felix breathed, holding his chin high.

Minutes passed, the German officer continuing to read names, one after the other. *Are they going to shoot us all?* A sickening lump grew in the back of Lazare's throat. He looked to the sky, smeared with gray clouds, and waited for his name to be called.

CHAPTER 38

VALMONDOIS, FRANCE—DECEMBER 27, 1943

Inside the abandoned granary, Rose conducted an inventory of supplies that were stashed inside aluminum RAF dropping containers: cases of plastic explosives, scores of grenades, forty Sten submachine guns, thirty-six pistols, twenty rifles, and boxes of ammunition. *We have enough armament to fight off platoons of Wehrmacht soldiers.* The granary, transformed into a British military supply depository, was used to arm the Resistance in preparation for a future Allied invasion. The British, American, and Canadian forces were pushing back the Nazi tide in Italy. But when and where an invasion of France would occur was uncertain, considering that Hitler's forces had a stronghold on the country and its borders.

Since her arrival in Valmondois, the SOE had declined Rose's requests to deploy agents to join her. So, she served as the organizer, courier, and wireless operator for her own network, Dragonfly. She'd arranged for several RAF airdrops, which she, Claudius, and members of the Resistance smuggled in from landing zones deep in the countryside. And over the past few months, she'd not only brought in vast amounts of British armament, she'd also—with the help of Claudius—recruited over seventy Resistance fighters, most of whom were rural farmers deemed too old or physically unable to fight for the French army when war erupted over Europe.

By all accounts, Rose was the catalyst for rebuilding Claudius's decimated Resistance network, like a phoenix rising from ashes.

Over the past few months, Rose led several French Resistance sabotage missions, destroying railroad lines and a trestle between Paris and Compiègne, delaying the export of French supplies headed to Germany. Her largest mission, she believed, was one in which she had not directly participated in the sabotage. In September, she'd received a coded message from SOE headquarters merely stating:

```
Tires in Montluçon are flat.
```

She was shocked, having forgotten about her recommendation to bomb the German-controlled Dunlop tire factory in Montluçon. She wondered if her request was the reason for the raid, or if the bombing had already been planned and headquarters informed her solely because of her inquiry. *I'll likely never know.* Although she was relieved to know that the German military would no longer be fitting their planes and vehicles with French tires, her heart ached with the thought that innocent civilians, forced by the Nazis to work in the plant, might have been killed. "You did the right thing," Claudius had reassured her. "It'll shorten the war and save lives." She appreciated Claudius's affirmation, but the thought of civilian deaths, like her mum and dad, weighed heavy on her soul.

Rose held little sense of pride for what she'd accomplished. Her parents and brother would no doubt be proud of what she was doing to help Britain and France. But any sense of achievement was drowned by the fact that Lazare was imprisoned. And the only way to free him, she believed, was to help accelerate the Allied invasion. *Someday, the war will be over and we'll be together.*

She'd learned months ago from Claudius that Lazare and Felix had been moved to a nearby prison. Claudius had obtained the intelligence from a man called Dominique Ponchardier, who established the "Sosie" French Resistance network in Amiens. But there was no news on Muriel, and Rose assumed that she'd been tortured and sent to a prison camp. Her heart ached with the loss of her comrades, compelling her to do everything within her power to accelerate the end of the war and bring them home.

Twice, Rose had bicycled to Amiens, a day's round trip from Valmondois. The prison was plotted in a large open field, and it was squared off by four roads, allowing her to circle the perimeter. High prison walls loomed over the encampment, making it impossible to see any prisoners. The only movement was waving swastika flags, posted on the corners of the walls, and occasional German guards, coming in and out of the entrance. She envisioned Lazare, somewhere inside where he was alive and well. She prayed that he was being treated humanely, but deep down she knew that Lazare would be forced to endure torture.

A lock clicked on the granary door. Claudius entered and slipped a key into his pocket.

"*Bonjour*," Rose said, crossing the stone floor. "I'm almost finished with inventorying our supplies. I'll be contacting London this afternoon to schedule another RAF drop."

Claudius, his face pale, slid his beret from his head and pressed it to his sternum.

A knot formed in Rose's belly. "What's wrong?"

"I've received a communication from Dominique Ponchardier." Claudius paused, as if he were searching for the right words. "The Germans plan to execute over one hundred prisoners at Amiens Prison."

A dagger of pain pierced her chest. "Lazare?"

Claudius nodded. "And Felix."

"*Non!*" Her knees wobbled; she clasped a chair to keep from falling. "Could Dominique be mistaken?"

"Unlikely," Claudius said. "A Frenchman who makes supply deliveries to the prison provided Dominique with the names. Lazare and Felix are on the list."

This can't be happening! A wave of nausea flooded Rose's stomach.

"I'm sorry," Claudius said, wiping his eyes.

Rose drew a ragged breath. "When is the execution?"

"The nineteenth day of February."

Rose fought back acid rising into her esophagus. "There must be something that we can do," she cried.

Claudius slumped his shoulders. "Short of an Allied invasion, I'm afraid it's hopeless."

"We'll round up Resistance fighters," Rose said, desperation clouding her judgment. "We'll conduct a siege on the prison."

"It would be futile," Claudius said.

Rose clenched her hands, digging her nails into her palms. "I won't let the Nazis commit a mass execution without a bloody fight!"

Claudius nodded and stuffed his beret into his jacket pocket.

"Can you arrange for us to meet with Dominique?" Rose asked, struggling to suppress her heartbreak.

"*Oui*," Claudius said. "But why?"

"To discuss our options," Rose said, turning to a stairway.

"Where are you going?"

"To inform London."

"I'll set up the meeting." Claudius turned and left the granary, locking the door behind him.

Rose scaled the stairs toward the third-floor attic, where she kept the wireless transmitter. With each step, a cancerous despair spread through her chest. Reaching the attic, she collapsed in a corner covered in dust and cobwebs. She wrapped her arms around her knees and cried.

You can't die! There must be something that I can do! In the sanctuary of the attic, she let down her guard and sobbed, her body trembling like a fragile leaf. And she knew full well that once she returned to her duties as an SOE agent, she'd shed her weak skin. She had no choice, she believed, but to be strong. Irrepressible. Gradually, she gathered her composure. She wiped away her tears and flipped the switch to the wireless transmitter. She put on the headset, steadied her hand over the telegraph key, and tapped out an encrypted message in Morse code, informing headquarters of the impending German execution of over one hundred members of the French Resistance, which would include Conjurer, aka Felix. *And Lazare*, she thought, a pang twisting inside her heart.

Headquarters responded, confirming receipt of the intelligence.

Rose tapped out another message, requesting assistance with a plan to save the prisoners. Minutes passed. She listened, waiting for signals to pulse through her headset but received only silence.

The following day, Rose and Claudius traveled to a remote farmhouse near Abbeville-Saint-Lucien. For transportation, they used a lorry that Claudius kept hidden in a barn. Anticipation stirred in Rose, counteracting her lack of sleep. She'd stayed up all night, deliberating on whether a radical plan to save the prisoners would be embraced by Dominique and Claudius, as well as British Services. *I don't care if they think I've gone mad. We have to try something, otherwise one hundred men, including Lazare and Felix, will be shot.*

As they entered the dwelling, two armed partisans, who looked more like bodyguards than Resistance fighters, led Rose and Claudius to a root cellar. A scent of earth and molded vegetables filled the air. A broad-shouldered man in his mid-twenties, with thin lips and a high, V-shaped hairline, stood near a table and stools.

"Dominique," Claudius said, shaking the man's hand. "This is Dragonfly."

Rose shook Dominique's hand, nearly twice the size of her own. *"Bonjour."*

Dominique gestured for Rose and Claudius to take a seat.

The bodyguards, pistol straps strung across their chests, stood near the stairway.

"Would it be all right if Claudius and I spoke with you alone?" Rose asked.

Dominique, appearing a bit irritated, shifted on his stool.

"I have sensitive information to share with you," Rose added.

Dominique waived off his men, sending them up the stairs. "Claudius tells me that you want to discuss the news of the Amiens Prison executions."

"Oui," Rose said, a knot tightening in her stomach. "And plans to free them."

Dominique removed a cigarette package from his pocket and placed it on the table.

"Are you completely sure of the names of prisoners and the date of the execution?" Rose asked.

"*Oui*," Dominique said. "My source is reliable."

Rose's belly churned, feeling as if she'd drunk a pint of vinegar. "I've been in contact with London. The SOE is in need of the prison blueprints."

Claudius glanced at Rose.

Dominique crossed his arms. "I take orders from General Charles de Gaulle, not the British."

Hairs stood on the back of Rose's neck. *I'll never get his support this way.* Her mind raced. "I once met General de Gaulle in Churchill's war room in London. In fact, I probably have the general to thank for my SOE assignment."

Dominique raised his brows.

"General de Gaulle had said, during my meeting with him and Winston Churchill, that he plans to reclaim France from Germany and return to lead his country. He commented that the French think of him as a rebirth of Joan of Arc," Rose added, leaving out Churchill's banter about the English burning the last one.

Dominique stared at Rose.

"After meeting General de Gaulle," Rose said, "I'm convinced that he'll return to lead a liberated France."

Dominique's lips formed a slight smile.

Claudius lit a cigarette and took a drag. "Can you obtain the blueprints?"

Dominique shook his head. "The Germans are in control of the city and commune records."

"How many of your men are on the list to be executed?" Rose asked.

Dominique dug a thumbnail into a burn mark on the table. "Seventeen."

"Some of Claudius's men, and at least one SOE agent, are on the list," Rose said. "If we do nothing, they'll be shot."

Dominique paused, as if he were recalling the names and faces of his fellow patriots.

"We need the blueprints." Rose leaned forward, her eyes on Dominique. "If need be, have your source draw a sketch of the prison on a cocktail napkin. We need the prison layout to have any chance of conducting a mission to save them."

Dominique took a deep breath and exhaled. "What type of mission are the British considering?"

Rose mustered her mettle to explain a plan that she'd deliberated on all night. The same plan that she hadn't yet communicated to London. The idea had come to her while recalling the Allied bombing of the German-controlled Dunlop tire factory following her wireless transmission to request that the facility be destroyed. When she'd told Claudius about her idea—while enroute to see Dominique—he'd stopped the lorry and nearly returned to Valmondois. But after some convincing by Rose, Claudius agreed to share the plan with Dominique.

"The RAF will perform a bombing raid on the prison," Rose said.

"It's ludicrous," Dominique said, abruptly.

"We have no choice," Rose said. "If we do nothing, they'll all be dead."

"*Non.*" Dominique placed a cigarette to his lips and lit the tip.

"Please, Dominique," Claudius said. "Let her finish."

Dominique puffed, blowing smoke through his nose. "Proceed."

Rose took out a piece of paper from her purse and scribbled a rough diagram of the prison, based on her memory from bicycling around the perimeter. "The RAF will use precision bombing to breach the outer walls of the prison," she said. "Also, they'll destroy the German guardhouses and will spare the buildings which hold the prisoners. But we need to know which building is which."

"It's suicide," Dominique grumbled.

"We must try," Claudius said.

Dominique, his eyes on Claudius, flicked ash from his cigarette. "How do we know that *she* has the influence to arrange an RAF bombing?"

Rose's skin turned warm. A rebuttal percolated inside her brain, but she held her tongue.

"In September," Claudius said, "the Allies bombed the Dunlop tire plant in Montluçon, which was under German control. Rose requested the bombing, and the Allies acted within two months of her wireless transmission."

"This is a prison, not a factory," Dominique said, firmly. "Hundreds of French could be killed."

Rose's heart thudded inside her chest. *We need the architectural plans to have any chance of influencing British Services to commence a mission.* "Dominique, may I ask you a personal question?"

He nodded, reluctantly.

"If you were sentenced to be shot, would you take a chance on freedom, knowing you might die by Allied bombs?" Rose asked.

Dominique's jaw muscles twitched. He tamped out his cigarette on the table, scorching the wood.

A lump formed in the back of Rose's throat. "Or would you choose to remain doomed to death by Nazi bullets?" She clasped her hands and waited for his answer.

CHAPTER 39

VALMONDOIS, FRANCE—DECEMBER 28, 1943

Claudius and Rose, her adrenaline still pumping from her visit with Dominique, entered the granary and bolted the door. After hours of debate, Dominique had agreed to help, but Rose felt no sense of relief. Dominique still needed to successfully steal blueprints and smuggle them to London. And most importantly, she needed to influence SOE headquarters, as well as British Services, to bomb a prison, which, in all likelihood, would result in the loss of innocent lives. *Headquarters might view it as too risky or as a potential political debacle. But I need to try.*

"Do you think you can convince your headquarters into performing the mission?" Claudius asked.

Rose fumbled with a button on her coat. "I don't know. I'll start by telling them that the French Resistance is in the process of smuggling the prison blueprints to London."

Claudius nodded. "Lazare would be so proud of you."

Rose's heart ached. "Thank you for your help."

"It is I who should be thanking you," Claudius said. "You're creating hope, where there was no hope at all."

"I should get to work with informing headquarters," Rose said, fighting back a swell of emotion.

Claudius stepped to the door and paused, his hand resting on the deadbolt. "I have faith that you will see him again."

Rose smiled, his words comforting her like a warm blanket.

"*Au revoir*," Claudius said, leaving the granary.

Despite barely sleeping for the past few days, Rose went to the attic, where she set up the wireless transmitter. She transferred a message into cypher and tapped the telegraph key.

```
Over a hundred French Resistance are
scheduled to be shot on 19 February 1944.
Dragonfly requests RAF to perform an air
raid on Amiens Prison to breach the walls,
otherwise all of the men will perish.
Prison blueprints are forthcoming.
```

Rose's breath quickened. She prayed that Dominique could somehow obtain the architectural diagrams. *But how will the blueprints be smuggled to London? By Lysander? By boat?* Her mouth turned dry. A moment later, short and long pulses flooded her ears. She scribbled the message and deciphered the code.

Message received. Stand by for further orders.

Will they think I've gone mad? Will they reject the request? As she waited for a reply, angst swelled inside her chest. But minutes turned to hours, and hours turned to days. Barely able to eat or sleep, she sent daily wireless transmissions to London, urging headquarters to initiate plans for the mission. After more than a week of communication, she received no confirmation that headquarters was receptive to her requests, or that they had shared the information with British Services. And to make matters worse, Dominique had yet to obtain the prison blueprints. *I won't give up. I'll continue contacting London until the mission is approved. Otherwise, I'll load every last bit of plastic explosive onto a lorry and breach the prison wall myself.*

CHAPTER 40

LONDON, ENGLAND — JANUARY 11, 1944

Deep below the Treasury building in Westminster, Winston Churchill, a smoldering cigar chomped between his molars, sat alone in the Cabinet War Room. Behind a U-shaped table, a map of the world hung on the wall. Colored pins, punched into the map, depicted the Allied invasion of Italy. Combined with Stalin's Red Army advancement in eastern Europe, the Allies were, Churchill believed, squeezing the Axis occupation like a mammoth military vise. Vengeance pumped through his body. *The Führer's defeat is drawing near.* He poured a glass of scotch, added water, and swirled it, releasing peaty vapors.

A knock on the door.

"Enter." Churchill swiveled in his chair.

Maurice Buckmaster, the leader of F Section SOE, stepped into the room and closed the door. "Good day, sir." He removed his cap and smoothed a hand over his thin, wispy hair. "Thank you for arranging to see me on such short notice."

Churchill puffed on his cigar, and then placed it in an ashtray.

Buckmaster took a seat across the table from Churchill. "There's a development in France that I think you should know about."

Churchill took a sip of scotch, a warmth drifting down his throat. "One that requires my privacy, I presume."

"Yes, Prime Minister," Buckmaster said. "We've received intelligence that the Germans plan to execute over one hundred members of the French Resistance imprisoned in Amiens."

"Barbarians," Churchill said, lowering his brows.

"We have reason to believe that there is at least one SOE agent among the condemned," Buckmaster said.

Ire burned in Churchill's stomach. "When is the execution?"

"Nineteenth of February."

Churchill gripped his crystal glass, bulging the veins in his hand. "Far too many of our agents are being captured."

Buckmaster straightened his back, as if he refused to believe that his network in France had been compromised by the SD. "An SOE agent has recommended that the RAF perform a raid on the prison."

"Good God," Churchill grumbled. "What kind of men are you deploying?"

Buckmaster squeezed his cap. "With all due respect, Prime Minister, this particular agent was recruited as a result of your referral."

Churchill drank a bit of scotch. An image of the typist who'd impressed him and General de Gaulle with her French linguistics flooded his brain. "Miss Teasdale?"

"Yes, sir," Buckmaster said. "Her code name is Dragonfly. She's turned out to be quite a resilient agent. After the capture of her network's organizer and wireless operator, she bicycled almost two hundred miles to obtain a wireless transmitter. She has performed dozens of sabotage missions, and she provided the location of a German-controlled tire factory, which was subsequently destroyed by Allied bombs. We've offered, on more than one occasion, for Dragonfly to return to London, but she's chosen to stay in France."

A slight smile formed on Churchill's mouth, and then faded. "She'd kept a photograph of her brother inside her desk. He was an RAF pilot who was killed over the Channel. Her parents, I recall, died in a Luftwaffe raid. Miss Teasdale's fortitude to fight Nazi tyranny was forged from personal tragedy."

"You're quite right, sir," Buckmaster said. "However, Dragonfly has been tenacious with her wireless transmissions, placing her at risk of being detected by the SD. She's adamant that the RAF perform a prison raid."

Churchill rubbed his jowl. "An RAF raid on a French prison will be quite controversial."

"Indeed, sir."

"A mission of this magnitude would require details of the prison's layout," Churchill said.

"Dragonfly has already arranged for the French to smuggle prison blueprints to us. We received them from a Frenchman named Dominique Ponchardier, who leads a Resistance network in Amiens."

"Have the blueprints been examined?"

"Not yet, sir," Buckmaster said. "The Secret Intelligence Service, as well as the RAF, will need to inspect them. Air Vice-Marshal Embry might be well suited to plan such a raid. However, the lives of prisoners will be at great risk."

They'll all be dead anyway. Churchill swirled his scotch.

Buckmaster leaned forward. "If the RAF were to perform such a mission, it might be wise for our records to be ambiguous as to who ordered the raid on the Amiens Prison."

Churchill took a sip of scotch, pondering Buckmaster's comment.

"Perhaps," Buckmaster said, lowering his voice, "the records should reflect that the raid was instigated by the French, feeding the blueprints of the prison to the British."

"Instead of the SOE?" Churchill asked, candidly.

Buckmaster shifted in his chair. "After all, sir, it was Ponchardier who obtained the blueprints and smuggled them to us."

A scapegoat. Churchill poured scotch into his glass, contemplating the ramifications of such a daring mission like a chess master scrutinizing moves against an opponent. *An RAF raid on the Amiens Prison might also keep Hitler guessing as to where we'll commence the Allied invasion of France.*

"Prime Minister," Buckmaster said. "Would you like some time to consider options?"

"No." Churchill plucked his cigar from the ashtray. He puffed, smoke drifting to the ceiling. "You shall have my opinion now."

CHAPTER 41

AMIENS, FRANCE—FEBRUARY 17, 1944

Lazare rolled over in his prison bunk and wrapped a tattered blanket over his body. He shivered, his breath producing a mist in the cold air. The click of a key inserted into the cell door by a German guard prompted him to stir. Lazare and his cellmates, haggard and hungry, slowly climbed from their bunks and made their way to the courtyard. It would be, Lazare believed, one of his last afternoon walks. *In less than forty-eight hours, it'll all be over.*

In the courtyard, coatless prisoners were huddled in groups, attempting to stay warm. The sky was laced with dark clouds carrying a mix of sleet and snow. A frigid, blustering wind caused Lazare's flesh to prickle. Despite the inclement weather, he refused to let one of his last days go to waste by hunkering near the latrines, his nose filled with the odor of excrement. Walking the yard, he found Felix, his arms wrapped around his torso.

"I was hoping that our final days in the yard would have good weather," Felix said, his teeth chattering.

Lazare nodded, blowing warm air into his chilled hands. A gust of wind bit at his cheeks.

Felix glanced toward his prison wing and frowned. "A man in my cellblock hanged himself last night."

Anger burned in Lazare's belly despite his cold and ravaged body.

Since the Germans had announced the names of the prisoners who were to be executed, a few of the condemned had committed suicide, either by hanging themselves with nooses made from clothing, or by cutting their wrists with shanks constructed from soup spoons. And there were rumors that the German guards were placing wagers on how many prisoners would take their own lives before facing the firing lines.

Felix glanced at an armed German guard wearing gloves and a thick wool coat. "The bastards will burn in hell for what they've done."

"We might not get the chance to speak again," Lazare said, lowering his voice.

Felix's eyes filled with sadness.

"When we're gone, others will take our place in the fight for freedom. Someday, the world will be free from Hitler. I wish we could be alive to see the end of the war." Lazare extended his maimed hand. "It was an honor fighting with you."

"The honor was mine." Felix shook his hand. "I guess this is goodbye."

A lump formed in Lazare's throat. "*Adieu.*"

Felix walked away, humming a verse of *Le Chant des Partisans*. He disappeared into a group of prisoners huddling to keep warm.

A mixture of despair and patriotism stirred inside Lazare. *Perhaps we'll stand together on the firing line.* Alone, Lazare took a final lap around the yard. Due to his weak leg muscles, he shuffled his feet over the frozen earth. Snow permeated holes in the bottoms of his shoes, turning his toes numb. But he carried on, step after step, exercising his freedom to walk the ground. As his hour outside came to an end, the snow turned heavy. Icy pellets stung his face. Shivering and wet, Lazare was forced by armed guards to return to his cellblock.

He climbed into his bunk and wrapped himself in a blanket like a cocoon until his shivering subsided. Refusing to allow his last days to be filled with fear, he compelled his mind—one of the few things not stolen by the Nazis—to wander to memories of his parents. A flash of his father typing furiously to draft an article for the newspaper, and Lazare realized—at that very moment—that he wanted to be a journalist, just like his papa. A memory of his *maman* as she meticulously painted a bland canvas, transforming it into an exquisite image of the Arc de Triomphe. Family dinners of lokshen kugel, a sweet egg noodle dish, which was a secret recipe that his parents had brought with them from Poland. A recollection of Maman and Papa laughing and holding hands at a picnic on Champ de Mars. He prayed that they'd somehow survive a German work camp, but he knew the odds were stacked against them.

Lazare rubbed his eyes and turned his daydream to Rose. He imagined what it would be like to survive the war and see her again. He envisioned holding her in his arms and never, ever, letting her go. He wondered what it would be like to get married, have children, and to grow old together. As hours passed, he created an imaginary life deep within the chambers of his heart. But his mind knew that none of this would happen. The chance of being with Rose was gone. And he wished, more than anything, for her to be free. *You'll survive this war, Rose. Your wounds, caused by losing the people you love, will eventually heal. Someday, you'll have a beautiful family of your own.*

"Goodbye, Rose," he whispered. His mind and hope depleted, Lazare drifted into a dark, cavernous sleep.

CHAPTER 42

AMIENS, FRANCE—FEBRUARY 18, 1944

The bells at Amiens Cathedral struck noon, causing Lazare to stir in his prison bunk. Hunger pangs chewed at his stomach, and a chill permeated through his bones. He and the prisoners who were condemned to death in less than twenty-four hours were no longer provided meals. Their German captors, Lazare believed, had no plans to waste food on men who would soon be dead. He expected that the condemned would also be deprived of their last daily walk in the courtyard, but he was proven wrong when a guard entered the prison block and inserted a key into his cell door. Lazare, his breath misting in the cold, climbed out of his bunk and shuffled his feet. *One last view of the sky.*

As the guard twisted the key, a faint hum caused him to pause. He glanced down the hallway to an open door, which led to the courtyard.

Outside, a buzzing rapidly grew, like a giant swarm of bees. Hairs rose on Lazare's arms. With the prison's location near a German airfield, Lazare had become quite astute with recognizing the drone of Luftwaffe aircraft—Focke-Wulf, Messerschmitt, and Heinkel planes—all of which had distinctive grinds to their engines. But the high-pitched roar of these aircraft was quite different. And they weren't headed to the airfield. They were coming in low and fast—directly toward the prison.

An alarm bell sounded.

The guard's eyes widened.

Adrenaline surged through Lazare. He pressed his cheeks between the iron bars, but was unable to see what was happening outside.

"*Luftangriff!*" a guttural voice shouted in the corridor. Germans, their jackboots clacking over the masonry floor, fled the cellblock.

The lone guard fumbled to secure the lock.

Lazare's pulse pounded. With nothing left to lose, except to expedite his execution, he cocked back his arm and lunged a fist between the iron bars, striking the guard in the jaw. But he knew the moment he landed the punch that his weakened state had done little to overpower the German.

The guard, his face filled with a mixture of shock and fury, stumbled into the hallway. He pressed his back against a cell opposite Lazare's and regained his balance.

Shouts erupted. Prisoners shot up from their bunks.

Lazare clasped the key and twisted, but the key jammed.

Airplane engines howled.

"*Halt!*" The guard ripped open the strap on his pistol holster.

Lazare joggled the key. The lock clicked. As he pushed open the cell door—the screech of iron hinges drowned by the roar of aircraft engines—his eyes landed upon the German's scowl. Lazare's hope sank as the guard raised his pistol. *It's over.*

CHAPTER 43

OPERATION JERICHO—AMIENS PRISON—
FEBRUARY 18, 1944

Rose's heart leaped at the sight of an RAF Mosquito bomber squadron, accompanied by Typhoon fighters, soaring—no higher than fifteen feet—across a snow-covered field. She sat behind the steering wheel of a lorry, what she hoped would be an escape vehicle, parked along the side of Albert-Amiens Road, a few hundred yards east of the prison. Farther up the road and west of the prison, Claudius sat inside a black sedan. As the lead bomber veered toward the prison, Rose's breath stalled inside her lungs. Her body trembled. *Please strike the walls and guardhouses—not the prisoner cellblocks.*

Hours earlier—after more than a month of wireless communications urging SOE headquarters to undertake an air raid on Amiens Prison—she received the decision that she'd so desperately prayed for.

    Operation Jericho is a go.

A wave of hope flooded Rose's body. She checked and rechecked her cypher. There was no mistake. Operation Jericho, she believed, was a biblical reference to the battle of Jericho, when Israelites marched around the city blowing their trumpets until the city's walls were destroyed. *Instead of horns, we'll use bombs.*

Hurriedly, she tapped out a wireless transmission, requesting the time of the attack. She doubted that she would receive a reply, but seconds later, headquarters responded.

Midday.

Rose ripped off her wireless headset and sprang from her chair. *No time to prepare Resistance fighters to harbor escaped prisoners.* She fled down the stairs of the granary and retrieved Claudius. Together, they fled Valmondois, each using separate vehicles, which Claudius kept hidden in a barn. They had no time to notify Dominique Ponchardier and the Amiens French Resistance. And given the horrid weather conditions, the roads covered in snow and ice, she worried that they might not make it to Amiens at all. Disregarding her safety, she sped the lorry, its tires spinning and sliding, over rural roads to avoid potential German roadblocks. On two occasions, she encountered snow drifts spanning the road and nearly crashed the lorry into a field. And with the heavy winds carrying more snow, she wondered if the RAF might abort the mission.

Despite the hazardous roads, she and Claudius arrived at Amiens Prison shortly before noon. They parked their respective vehicles on opposite ends of Albert-Amiens Road, placing the prison between them. Normally, vehicles parked on the side of the road would draw attention, but there were several abandoned vehicles along the route, creating a bit of camouflage. She hunkered low in her seat and waited. As minutes passed, the snowfall slowly diminished.

As the first RAF Mosquito closed in on the prison, its belly opened. Rose, her heart rate soaring, shot up in her seat. The Mosquito dropped a large metal cannister, which soared like a javelin, into the base of the twenty-foot prison wall, but it didn't explode.

"No!" Rose shouted.

The Mosquito pulled up sharply, flying a few feet over the prison. German gunfire erupted from the watchtowers. The bomber banked to the left and gained altitude.

Are the RAF using time-delay bombs, allowing low-flying planes to avoid the explosions? If not, she hoped that the next Mosquito would have more success with its payload. But seconds later, the bomb—wedged into the base of the prison wall—exploded, sending a fountain of brick and smoke into the air.

CHAPTER 44

OPERATION JERICHO—AMIENS PRISON— FEBRUARY 18, 1944

A deafening blast shook the prison. The German guard recoiled as he fired his pistol. The bullet whizzed by Lazare's ear and ricocheted off a stone wall. Before the guard could get off another shot, Lazare launched his body, knocking the German into a cell door. But Lazare, his muscles atrophied and weak, was no match for the rugged German, who swung his arm, wielding his pistol like a club, and struck Lazare in the temple.

Pain flared through Lazare's skull, dropping him to his knees. Dazed, he struggled to clear his head.

Gunshots exploded in the courtyard.

The guard, his face filled with scorn, raised his pistol.

Refusing to close his eyes for his execution, Lazare looked up at the guard and noticed movement—two prisoners creeping to their cell door, inches from the guard's back. Resolve roiled through Lazare.

The guard lowered his pistol, the barrel aimed at Lazare's forehead.

An oily-haired prisoner flung an arm through the iron bars, placing the guard in a choke hold.

The guard gasped, firing a shot into the floor. Bits of stone stung Lazare's face.

Shouts from prisoners erupted over the cellblock.

The second prisoner, a short, bearded man, stuck his arms through the iron bars and grabbed the guard's hand that held the weapon. Squeezing his cheeks between the iron bars, the prisoner—like a rabid dog—bit the guard's wrist, while his cell-mate tightened his elbow around the guard's windpipe.

The guard's eyes bulged from their sockets. His legs flailed. He fired his pistol, the bullet striking a cell door.

The prisoners hardened their grip, clamping the guard's neck and wrist to the iron bars.

Gurgles hissed from the guard's gaping mouth. Blood dripped from his hand, and the pistol dropped to the floor.

Lazare, regaining his strength, retrieved the pistol. As he prepared to fire the weapon, he realized that it wasn't necessary—the guard's lifeless body crumpled to the floor.

"Let us out!" the bearded prisoner shouted.

Lazare shoved the pistol into the back of his pants and retrieved the key sticking from the lock of his cell door.

An airplane roared over the prison. Machine guns fired. Seconds later, another explosion—in the vicinity of a guardhouse—reverberated through the prison.

Allied invasion? Lazare unlocked the cell door, releasing the two prisoners who had come to his aid. "Go!"

The prisoners scampered down the corridor.

"Free us!" a hoarse voice shouted from an adjoining cell.

"Unlock the doors!" another prisoner shouted. Arms waved through cell bars.

A choice burned in Lazare's chest. Before he changed his mind, he unlocked a cell door, releasing three prisoners. He went to another cell containing a man who was blinded in one eye, and opened the door. He'd expected German guards to enter the cellblock and open fire, but it became clear, from the machine gun fire in the courtyard, that the guards were occupied with defending against a raid on the prison. So, Lazare unlocked cell after cell, releasing more than forty prisoners, who fled down the hall and into the courtyard, the only exit for escape.

Removing the last two men from their cell, Lazare led them, one of whom was limping badly with a bandage on his foot, down the corridor. As he neared the exit, the courtyard came into view, sending a surge of adrenaline through his battered body. One of two prison guard quarters was destroyed, and along the north wall was a large gaping hole from which prisoners were escaping. But German guards, high in the watchtowers and acting as snipers, were gunning down some of the prisoners who attempted to run away. Bodies littered the courtyard. And to compound matters, there was a group of guards firing machine guns from the building containing the latrines.

The limping prisoner froze. "I'll never make it!"

"We have no choice," Lazare said. "If we stay here, we'll die."

The second prisoner, his eyes filled with fear, clung to the doorway.

Lazare pointed to thick smoke drifting from the burning guard quarters. "Make your way to the wall under the cover of smoke, and then crawl through the hole."

Machine gun fire blasted over the courtyard.

The prisoners inched forward, but didn't leave the protection of the doorway.

A roaring airplane engine compelled Lazare to raise his eyes to the sky. A cannister plummeted from the belly of a plane, marked with a British roundel on the fuselage, as it shot over the prison. A loud clunk, like an oil drum tossed against the side of the cell-block, turned Lazare's skin cold.

"Run!" Lazare pushed the prisoners through the doorway, forcing them to scamper into the smoke-covered courtyard. As Lazare followed, a barrage of gunfire forced him to dive to the ground for cover. He crawled, splinters of charred wood piercing his palms, all the while hoping he could get clear of the blast. A second later, a thunderous explosion jolted his body. He covered his head as a mass of bricks and concrete toppled from the cellblock, battering his torso and legs. Pain ravaged his spine. He struggled to push away bricks, but his limbs were jammed under mounds of rubble. He strained to suck in air filled with smoke and an acrid scent of cordite. The masonry mass pressed down on his ribcage, constricting his breaths to short gasps. His air supply dwindled, stealing his strength. A life, one that would never be, flashed through his brain. Amid his pain and rue, one image remained steadfast. *Rose.* He choked, his mouth filled with soot, and everything went black.

CHAPTER 45

OPERATION JERICHO—AMIENS PRISON—
FEBRUARY 18, 1944

Black plumes spewed from inside the prison. Rose prayed, clasping the steering wheel of the lorry, for Lazare to be safe. Through a drifting ashen cloud, she struggled to see Claudius's car parked at the opposite end of Albert-Amiens Road. She scanned the field surrounding the prison. A dozen prisoners wearing brown dungarees emerged from the smoke and scampered over snow. *The walls are breached!* Rose's heart hammered her chest. Seconds later, more prisoners appeared.

Rose started the lorry's engine and threw the vehicle in gear. As she slammed the accelerator, the tires spun on the icy road. She cranked down her window. "Here!" she shouted, cold air blasting her face.

The prisoners sprinted over the field, their feet sinking in ankle-deep snow. Machine gun fire, erupting from a watchtower, struck one of the prisoners, dropping him to the ground. Attempting to evade bullets, the group dispersed, like scattering mice, except for one prisoner, who helped the fallen man to his feet. The watchtower guard turned and fired his weapon into the prison as if to deter prisoners from crawling through the opening in the wall.

Rose braked, fishtailing the lorry to a stop. She flung open her door and sprinted into the field, her lungs taking in the smell of smoke and expelled gunpowder.

The prisoner aiding the wounded man hobbled toward Rose.

As the prisoners came into view, Rose immediately recognized one of them, despite his severe loss in weight. "Felix!" She dashed forward, clasping his arm, thin and bony.

"Help him," Felix gasped.

Rose placed the injured prisoner's arm around her neck. Together, she and Felix carried the man, dragging his bleeding leg, to the lorry.

Machine gun fire rattled the air and abruptly stopped as an RAF Mosquito buzzed over the prison.

Rose helped the injured prisoner into the back of the lorry and turned to Felix. "Where's Lazare?"

Felix shook his head.

Rose's mouth turned dry. "What happened?"

"His cellblock was hit by a bomb," he said.

"No!" Rose cried. "He might have escaped!"

"I'm sorry," he said, placing a hand on her shoulder. "There's nothing we can do."

A wrenching pang pierced Rose's stomach, producing the urge to vomit. *What have I done?*

"We must save who we can." Felix pointed to prisoners sprinting toward them.

Stunned, Rose's legs remained planted, as if her feet had sprouted roots. She took in gulps of air.

"Rose!" Felix shouted. "Help me!"

Compelled by her duty to save the lives of prisoners, she buried her sorrow and aided three men, one of whom was bleeding from a deep gash on his head. Her legs and arms quivering, she helped the prisoners into the bed of the lorry.

"I'll drive," Felix said, jumping behind the wheel.

Rose got into the passenger seat and slammed the door. "Over there," she said, pointing. Fifty yards away, several prisoners scurried onto the road.

Felix sped the lorry to the men. "Get in!"

As the prisoners dove into the bed of the vehicle, a German guard carrying a machine gun dashed across the field.

Rose, her adrenaline surging, retrieved a pistol from inside the glove box. She fired two quick shots at the guard, but missed.

The guard dropped to his belly and aimed his weapon.

Felix hit the accelerator.

Bullets pelted the lorry, shattering the windshield.

Rose shook glass from her hair, leaned through the open windshield frame, and fired the remaining rounds of her weapon, forcing the guard to hunker in a plow run.

Felix shifted gears and sped away from the prison.

Rose glanced through the rear window. Beyond the group of prisoners hunkered in the bed of the lorry, a cloud of smoke loomed over Amiens Prison. Her chest ached with despair. *I'm so sorry, Lazare.*

"Did you arrange this?" Felix asked, his voice hoarse.

"*Oui.*" Frigid wind penetrating the open windshield frame bit at her skin. "Claudius was driving another vehicle, but I couldn't see him through all the smoke." She prayed that he'd escaped with prisoners.

Felix downshifted the gears, maneuvering a turn.

"I might have killed Lazare," she said, her voice trembling.

"*Non*," Felix said. "You have given many men, who would be shot tomorrow, a chance to live."

Rose's eyes filled with tears. She took in gulps of air.

Felix coughed and pressed a hand to his abdomen. A splotch of blood, the size of a plum, saturated his shirt.

Her eyes widened, "Oh, God. You're hurt." She unwrapped her scarf and pressed it to Felix's stomach.

He winced. Wind whistled through a bullet hole in the driver's door.

"I'll drive," Rose said.

"I'll be all right," Felix said. "Where are we headed?"

"Valmondois." Rose pointed to a side road. "Make a left."

Felix, his former Grand Prix racing skills still intact, spun the lorry—its rear wheels coming around to precisely a forty-five-degree angle—and accelerated down the road.

For the next few miles, Felix maneuvered through backroads. But as each minute passed, his face turned paler and his reflexes more sluggish, until he nearly missed a turn and plowed the lorry into a tree.

"Pull over!" Rose demanded.

Felix, his forehead covered in perspiration, eased off the accelerator and veered to the side of the road.

Rose jumped out of the lorry and sprinted to the driver's door. As she helped Felix into the passenger seat, the prisoners, including the man with the injured leg, crawled out of the bed and disappeared into a forest. *They think their chances are better without us.*

"Hang on." Rose sat behind the wheel and slammed the accelerator.

Felix cupped his belly. "I should have paid more heed to your warnings about an SD infiltration."

"There was nothing any of us could have done," she said.

Felix coughed, expelling phlegm strewn with blood. "I wish I would have been a better organizer for our network. My mulishness has brought you and Muriel nothing but trouble."

Hearing Muriel's name caused her chest to ache. "Do you know where she is being held?"

"*Non.*" Felix's breath turned shallow. "When you make it home, please tell my wife, Harriet, that I love her. And if my son, Mathieu, survives his capture, please relay how proud I am of him."

Rose gently touched Felix's hand, his fingernails stained red. "You will tell them yourself."

Felix's lips formed a faint smile, and he lowered his eyelids.

Rose turned onto a snow-covered dirt road. The deep ruts, bouncing the lorry, caused Felix to moan. After nearly getting the vehicle stuck, she ventured onto a paved road, heading south. Minutes later, her hope of avoiding a roadblock sank.

Thirty yards ahead, two German lorries blocked the road. Six Wehrmacht soldiers wearing trench coats and helmets raised their rifles.

Rose's lungs stalled. She braked, skidding the lorry to a stop. As she attempted to turn the vehicle around, she glanced to the rearview mirror and saw a convoy of Wehrmacht *Kübelwagens*—

unmistakable by their square shape and convertible canvas tops—
closing in on her.

She nudged Felix, but he didn't respond, nor did his chest rise
or fall. *Oh, God. No!*

Rose threw open the glove box, but found no more ammunition
for her pistol. A flash of her L-pill, hidden in her lipstick. Instead
of reaching for her purse, which contained her poison, she revved
the engine. Ravaged with misery, she jammed the shifter into
gear and barreled the lorry toward the roadblock.

The soldiers scattered to the berm and fired their weapons.

Rose ducked behind the wheel as bullets rattled the lorry.
Steam poured from a pierced radiator. A front tire exploded, the
wheel jerked to the right, and her vehicle crashed into a ditch,
slamming Rose's head into the dash. Dazed, she struggled to
crawl out of the driver's window and was grabbed by two soldiers
and thrown to the ground. A knee jammed into her back, sending
a sharp spasm through her vertebrae. Placed in handcuffs, Rose—
her body, mind, and spirit defeated—was dragged by her feet, and
then tossed into the back of a Wehrmacht *Kübelwagen*.

PART 4

CAMP DE CONCENTRATION

CHAPTER 46

RAVENSBRÜCK CONCENTRATION CAMP, FÜRSTENBERG, GERMANY—JUNE 3, 1944

Rose pressed her nose to a small crack in a wooden slat of a train car. She inhaled a smidge of fresh air, a brief reprieve from the stench of sweat, urine, and feces. Inside the crammed compartment were forty-three women, a blend of political prisoners, Jews, Jehovah's Witnesses, and criminals, all of whom were condemned for crimes against the Nazi regime. The days that Rose had been locked in the train car had, for the first time since her capture, given her time to grieve the loss of Felix, Muriel, and Lazare. During her interrogations, Rose was able to piece together that over two hundred and fifty prisoners escaped Amiens Prison, although her German captors had bragged that they recaptured most of them. Her dream of creating a life with Lazare was gone, and the success of the mission did little to dwindle Rose's heartache. *In my resolve to influence a mission to save condemned prisoners, I sacrificed the man I love.*

After Rose's capture, she'd been taken to Fresnes Prison, south of Paris. She was interrogated by the Gestapo ten times, and she endured excruciating torture, including having her back seared with burning cigars. Hardened by the loss of Lazare and her fellow SOE agents, as well as her family, Rose refused to cooperate and stuck to her cover story. "My name is Aline Bonnet, a cosmetics saleswoman," she'd said, refusing to give in to the pain. Her resistance, Rose believed, created a bit of respect with the Gestapo, who already knew bits of her SOE identity, which they appeared to have obtained from interrogations of agents during the collapse of the Physician network.

While at Fresnes Prison, she was transported to 84 Avenue Foch, the Parisian headquarters of the SD. Upon her arrival, Rose was taken to the top floor and placed in an interrogation cell. A moment later, goose bumps cropped up on her arms when Josef Kieffer, head of the SD, entered the cell, his jackboots clacking over the wood floor. Kieffer, his eyes glaring with recognition, slapped Rose's face, splitting her lower lip, and then stormed from the room. For a week, Kieffer's assistant, Eberhard Vogel, interrogated her. But Rose refused to cooperate, inciting Kieffer's anger. And Rose realized that it was far more than her obstinance that had gotten under Kieffer's skin, when Zelie, the young cabaret dancer whom Rose believed to be Kieffer's mistress, arrived at 84 Avenue Foch. Zelie's once-lustrous blonde hair was tangled, her expensive jewelry replaced with handcuffs, and her face was almost unrecognizable, due to a swollen eye and absence of makeup. *He no longer trusts you, and he's trying to determine if you conspired with me.* Although Rose felt pity for Zelie, whose only crime appeared to be sleeping with the enemy, she felt a wave of satisfaction, knowing that she'd infected Kieffer with paranoia. Days later, infuriated by Rose's lack of cooperation, Kieffer ordered Rose to be sent to a prison camp.

The carriage jerked, and the train slowed to a stop. Rose, exhausted from the journey and lack of food, hoped for a German soldier to replenish the empty communal water bucket. Instead, the door to the carriage swung open. Rose squinted, her eyes burning from the abrupt exposure to sunlight. Sucking in fresh air, she tasted salt on the wind. *We might be near the sea. Germany? Poland?*

"*Schnell!*" a German soldier shouted, pointing his rifle.

The women, some of whom carried bags and blankets, climbed out of the carriage. But Rose had nothing. From the railroad station, the women were forced to march along a road that divided quaint villas—some with flower boxes—that appeared to be used for SS housing, given the rows of swastika flags. To the right of the housing was a lake where gaunt-faced women—wearing blue-and-white-striped dresses with white head scarves—were shoveling sand into small rail cars.

"*Schnell!*" the soldiers shouted.

The women quickened their pace.

Passing a large house, which Rose presumed to be the commandant's residence, they reached an iron gate emblazoned with the name Ravensbrück. To the right of the entrance, a masonry building with a tall brick chimney loomed over the camp, conjuring a foreboding cramp in Rose's gut. *Crematorium?*

Inside was a large earthen courtyard, which felt sandy under Rose's shoes. Beyond the courtyard were eighteen long one-story cellblocks. *There are thousands of prisoners here.* Unlike her prison in France, Ravensbrück didn't have towering watchtowers. Instead, it was surrounded by a high wall with electrified barbed wires marked with signs containing a skull-and-crossbones image, underscored by the word, *Halt!* And stuck to the electrified wire was the charred body of a woman, her weathered clothing like a macabre scarecrow. Rose shuddered. *The Nazis left the poor woman to deter prisoners from attempting escape.* Sickened, Rose lowered her eyes, and she wondered how any human being could be conditioned to commit such atrocities.

The women were taken to an administration building, where they were forced to give up their personal belongings. Soon, they were stripped of their clothing and shaved. Naked, they waited for hours for inspection by the SS medical staff. Lined up in rows of five, the women were given brief but invasive medical examinations—checking for disease and objects which could be hidden in a body cavity—and, like cattle, their physical characteristics were discussed among the SS staff. Eventually, the women were given blue-and-white-striped dresses and headscarves, most of which were soiled or stained. *Reused from dead prisoners*, Rose thought, slipping on her dress, which was several sizes too big and hung to the ground. For shoes, the prisoners were given wooden clogs.

Each of the women was provided a felt triangle patch with a

prisoner identification number, and was instructed to sew it onto the left shoulder of their clothing. A green patch was for criminals. Black for those whom the Nazis classified as "asocials," which included Roma, beggars, alcoholics, drug addicts, prostitutes, and pacifists. Purple for Jehovah's Witnesses. Yellow for Jews. Red for political prisoners, which was the color of Rose's patch that identified her as prisoner number 77132.

After sewing on their patches, the women were divided and sent to their assigned cellblock, segregated by the color of patches, but they were not permitted to enter and claim their bunks, nor were they given water or allowed to relieve themselves at a latrine. Instead, the new arrivals were forced—by female guards wielding batons—to stand silently at attention in front of the cellblock. As hours passed, Rose watched more prisoners march into the prison to be processed. *They're all women.* Her legs ached. She shifted her weight to keep her feet from turning numb. The time provided Rose a glimpse of how Ravensbrück operated. While male SS were in charge of the camp, all of the guards were female. The guards, most with their hair neatly done under their caps, wore wool skirts and jackets, along with polished leather boots and belts, and a number of the guards were accompanied by German shepherds tethered with leashes.

By evening, when Rose's knees were about to fail from fatigue, hundreds of prisoners marched into the camp. Soon, more groups of prisoners arrived led by female guards with canines. *They've finished their slave labor for the day*, Rose thought.

"*Achtung!*" German guards, shouted. "Ranks of five!"

Rose lined up, along with thousands of other women standing at attention with their eyes lowered.

For over two hours, guards conducted roll call for their assigned cellblocks. A tall, beautiful blonde-haired guard wearing a black cape appeared on a bicycle. The woman rode from cellblock to cellblock, her cape flying in the wind, to collect tallies from block guards. *Chief guard*, Rose thought.

Rose, her chin lowered, scanned the rows of women. The new prisoners were easy to identify, given their bald or stubbled heads peeking from under their headscarves. The prisoners who had been in the camp longest had regrown their hair, but they were deathly thin, their eyes sunken and the color of lead. *How long can one survive here?* She prayed for an Allied invasion to free the women of this death camp.

An alarm sounded, and the prisoners were released to have their evening meal, a ladle of vegetable stock made from turnips, which was delivered by two prisoners pushing a wooden wagon that contained a large steaming pot. Ravaged and dehydrated, Rose drank her broth, despite the rancid flavor, and followed prisoners into the cellblock.

The barracks were lined with rows of three-tier bunk beds. Although the cellblock had a washroom and toilets, it was densely populated, with women sleeping two to a bunk. The stagnant air contained a stench reminiscent of a stable. Rose walked the rows of bunks, searching for a place to sleep. Bunk after bunk, prisoners, who were reluctant to allow a newcomer to infringe on their space, turned Rose away. *I might have to force my way into a bed.* As she was about to turn around, a woman grabbed her hand and pulled her into a bunk.

Rose's eyes widened. Her heart leaped, recognizing the tall woman, despite the fact that her wavy brown hair had been clipped.

Muriel raised a finger to her lips and whispered, "We must be quiet. Some prisoners serve as spies for the Germans in exchange for extra rations."

Rose hugged Muriel, whose ribs protruded from her dress. "Thank God you're alive," she whispered.

She released Rose and smiled.

"How are you?" Rose asked, her heart flooding with joy.

"Okay," Muriel whispered. "Did they hurt you much?"

"No," Rose said, though the burns on her back had not fully healed.

"I'm so happy to see you," Muriel said. "What happened to Felix?"

A cramp formed in Rose's belly, and she told Muriel about the collapse of the Paris SOE networks, Operation Jericho, and Felix's death during the prison escape. "Lazare's cellblock was hit by a bomb," she said, her voice quavering.

"Oh, dear God. I'm so sorry." Muriel wiped Rose's cheeks. "You had no choice. If you hadn't requested the operation, the prisoners would have been shot. You saved many lives, Rose. Lazare cared for you, and I know he would be proud of what you did to save members of the French Resistance."

Rose appreciated Muriel's attempt to console her, but a deep regret gnawed at her gut. "Where are we?" Rose asked, desperate to rid her mind of Lazare's death.

"Ravensbrück, Germany," Muriel said. "We're fifty miles north of Berlin."

"Oh, no," Rose said. *We'll be the last to be saved by an Allied invasion.*

"Ravensbrück has many subcamps," Muriel said. "All the prisoners are women, except for a small nearby men's camp—they make the bread for us."

"How many prisoners?" Rose asked, not sure if she wanted to know the answer.

"Forty thousand," Muriel said. "Maybe more."

Rose took a jagged breath and exhaled.

"You'll be forced to work as slave labor," Muriel said.

"I'll refuse to work," Rose said. "I'll never serve Hitler."

"Then you'll be sentenced to hard labor," Muriel said. "And if you still refuse to work, you'll be shot. Camp Commandant Suhren cares little about the Geneva Convention rules for prisoners of war. His plans are to exterminate us by working us and starving us to death."

A flash of the ravaged prisoners shoveling sand into railway cars filled Rose's head.

"Did you receive a work assignment?"

"The fabric store," Rose said, recalling the instructions she received during her processing.

"Good. I'm working there, too. It'll keep you warm in the winter, and it's much less arduous than clearing trees or moving sand."

"Okay," Rose said.

Muriel told Rose about the atrocities she'd witnessed in Ravensbrück. Prisoners were often punished by flogging, tied to a post and given twenty-five lashings for minor acts of disobedience, such as collapsing from fatigue during roll calls or failing to make one's bed properly. Transports of prisoners, many of whom were Jews and infirm, were taken away and never returned.

"The selected prisoners are told that they are being relocated to another camp," Muriel said. "But there are rumors that they are being taken away to their deaths."

"Oh, God," Rose said.

A siren sounded. Seconds later, the light went out in the cell-block. Coughs, sneezes, whimpers, and moans filled the air.

Rose shivered. *If there is a hell, I have surely found it.* "We'll get through this, Muriel. And we'll tell the world what the Nazis have done."

"Aye," Muriel said.

Rose, sharing a small, tattered blanket with Muriel, rolled over. Beneath her ear, she listened to the crinkling of straw inside the mattress. With her back pressed to Muriel, she clasped her hands and prayed that they would survive until the Allied troops arrived. But how long? Months? A year? In addition to fighting for survival, she feared that she would also be battling time.

CHAPTER 47

RAVENSBRÜCK CONCENTRATION CAMP— JUNE 4, 1944

At 4:00 a.m. a siren sounded. Rose stirred, wiping sleep dust from her eyes, and climbed down from the bunk with Muriel. Together, they followed prisoners shuffling outside to the court-yard.

"*Schnell! Schnell!*" a female guard shouted, tapping her baton to her palm. "Ranks of five!"

Rose lined up next to Muriel and stood at attention. Despite the thousands of prisoners standing outside their cellblocks, the air was still, except for the chirps of crickets and shouts from guards.

"*Achtung!*" the guard said, swinging her baton to the back of a prisoner's legs, sending the woman to the ground.

Anger burned in Rose's stomach. She leaned forward and then hesitated, contemplating the repercussions of coming to the wom-an's aid.

"Get back in line," Muriel whispered. "You'll be flogged or worse."

Reluctantly, Rose remained standing at attention. Through the corners of her eyes, she watched the injured woman, her head slumped, get to her hands and knees. *Please get up.* Slowly, the woman stood, her legs shaking, and resumed her place in line.

For three hours, the prisoners stood at attention while the guards conducted roll call. After the blonde-haired chief guard collected the tallies by bicycling around the cellblocks, a siren sounded and the food carts arrived. The prisoners were given watery coffee, which appeared to have been brewed from acorns, and a bread ration laced with wood chips. Soon after, the women were marched, led by guards with German shepherds, to their respective work duties.

The SS workshops for tailors, furriers, and shoemakers were located within the Ravensbrück camp, adjacent to the rows of cellblocks. Inside, Rose took a seat beside Muriel at a long wooden table, which formed an assembly line of women tailors. Seated in the cramped room resurrected memories of Lucy and the women of Room 60. Rose's chest ached with melancholy. It had been over three years since she'd worked in Churchill's underground war room, but it felt like a lifetime ago.

A young German guard, wearing a side cap which covered rolled and tucked toffee-colored hair, entered the workshop. At the front of the room, the guard sat at a desk, reminiscent of a schoolmaster. She removed a bamboo stick, which was tucked inside a jackboot, and swatted the desk, producing a loud crack. "*Arbeit!*"

Rose flinched.

The women retrieved needles, thread, and scissors from a basket. In an assembly line, they sewed, and then passed a mouse-gray wool garment down the line. The crate beside Rose's chair contained what looked to be sleeves made of the same material. Her stomach turned nauseous. *Nazi winter coats.*

Without speaking, Muriel taught Rose how to sew an arm onto a German military coat. Tailoring, let alone touching, an enemy coat sent a wave of revulsion through Rose. Not wanting to get Muriel or the other women in trouble for not meeting their production quotas, which the guard tallied on a clipboard, she buried her resentment and stitched. Finishing her sleeve, she passed it to a Jewish prisoner wearing a yellow triangle patch.

Six hours into her shift, without a water or latrine break, Rose's fingers began to bleed, punctured by the repetition of pushing a needle through thick wool without the protection of a thimble. She cleaned her raw fingers, using her dress as a rag, and pressed on. Muriel sewed on the right sleeve, and Rose attached the left sleeve. At the end of the line were piles of finished coats, where the guard conducted random quality checks. Noticing that the guard only examined the start and end of seams—where the thread was tied off with knots—an idea flooded Rose's head.

Finishing her stitching, Rose tied a knot and cut the excess string with scissors. She nudged Muriel with her knee.

Muriel glanced to Rose.

Rose snipped the center of the seam, under the armpit of the coat, and passed it down the assembly line.

Muriel gave a subtle nod. She finished her sleeve and mimicked Rose, cutting the center seam of the right sleeve.

It might take weeks of wear for the sleeves to unravel, Rose believed, but at least it was something. A proud defiance bloomed inside her. *We're still capable of fighting the Nazis, even if we have to resort to sabotaging their bloody coats.* Soon, Rose was vandalizing one in three coats on the assembly line. She spent the afternoon imagining Allied troops defeating a sleeveless Hitler regime.

CHAPTER 48

RAVENSBRÜCK CONCENTRATION CAMP—
SEPTEMBER 10, 1944

Rose, her fingers calloused from months of sewing, stitched the sleeve of a Nazi coat. The female German guard in charge of the SS tailor workshop stepped away for a latrine break, allowing the assembly line of prisoners a brief moment of solace. While rubbing the ache in her hands, Rose peered through a small window. Outside, black exhaust puffed from the crematorium chimney. She shivered. *The final destination for the prisoners of Ravensbrück.*

"Some days," Muriel whispered, sitting next to Rose, "I think that the only way I'll get out of here is through that chimney—as smoke."

"No," Rose said, turning to Muriel, whose cheeks were sunken. "Don't ever think that. You're going to make it home to Mabel."

Muriel nodded, and then wiped her eyes with the back of her hand.

The months of starvation and work had taken a toll on them. Each day, they woke at 4:00 a.m., stood at attention for three hours of morning roll call, drank a cup of acorn coffee and ate a small piece of bread, worked a twelve-hour shift, stood at attention for three hours of evening roll call, drank a ladle of turnip broth, and then collapsed into their bunk. Day after day, they repeated the grueling cycle while the population of the camp swelled with the arrival of new prisoners. With small supplies of food coming into the camp, daily rations diminished, escalating the death counts and fueling the crematorium, which seemed to burn at all hours of the day and night.

A glimmer of hope, however, had occurred in August, when rumors of an Allied invasion of France spread through the camp. And Rose was convinced that the rumors were true when Camp Commandant Suhren received orders from Berlin to withdraw food from political prisoners for a week. "The Allies are coming," Rose had said, trying to raise the spirits of Muriel and the hungry prisoners in her cellblock. "We only need to survive a few more months, and we'll be free."

The German guard, returning from a latrine break, removed a bamboo stick placed inside her leather boot and swatted the work table. *"Arbeit macht frei"*—"Work sets you free"—she said, her voice laced with spite.

The women, their eyes lowered, hastened their sewing pace.

If I were healthy, and if this was another time and place, Rose thought, *I'd break that stick over your backside.* As the guard turned away, Rose clipped a center thread under the armpit of a coat, raising her sabotage rate to four out of five garments.

Rose had grown quite pleased with her sewing skills. She'd become an expert with vandalizing seams that would unravel over time but would remain intact during quality checks. But most of all, she was proud to have included her fellow prisoners in the scheme. In addition to Muriel, Rose had recruited all of the assembly-line women—from various countries and speaking different languages—to perform sabotage on the coats. For Rose and the women, it was a way to resist the Nazis and prove to themselves that they would never give up their fight, even if they had to resort to inconsequential acts of reprisal.

The guard rummaged through a stack of coats. She tugged buttons and lapels, testing their sturdiness. Digging into the middle of the pile, she pulled out a coat and yanked on its sleeves.

The sound of ripping threads caused goose bumps to crop up on Rose's arms.

The guard narrowed her scrutiny of the coat to its right sleeve, which had been sewn by Muriel.

Oh, no. A lump formed in the back of Rose's throat.

Muriel's hands trembled.

The guard stuck her fingers through the unraveled seam, and then tore off the sleeve. "*Wer hat das getan?*" she asked, her face forming a scowl.

Fear filled the faces of the women.

Rose's breath turned shallow. As if by reflex, she stood and faced the guard. "It was me."

The guard glared.

Using two fingers, Rose mimicked a pair of scissors. "Snip. Snip."

In one swift motion, the guard swung back a leg and sank her jackboot into Rose's stomach.

Rose, pain flaring through her abdomen, collapsed to the floor. She struggled to suck in air.

Muriel began to rise from her chair but was stopped by two prisoners.

The guard slid a bamboo stick from her boot and lashed Rose.

Rose curled into a fetal position and covered her face. Stings shot over her back, arms, and legs.

Finished with the beating, the guard slipped her stick into her boot and blew a whistle, alerting guards in an adjacent workshop.

Seconds later, Rose—her arms and back covered in welts—was removed by a team of guards. She expected to undergo a more brutal flogging, which was performed by a cellblock *kapo*, typically a prisoner convict who wore a green triangle patch and acted under the direction of a German guard. Instead, Rose was led past the flogging post and taken to a building—near the camp entrance and next to the crematorium—and locked inside a ground-floor cell. She crawled into the corner, wrapped her arms around her knees, and prayed that Muriel and the other women would not be blamed for the ruined coats, which the guard would surely examine with great scrutiny. *No reason for more than one of us to be punished. But what will be my penalty? Hard labor? Cut rations? Firing line?*

Two hours later, Rose received her answer when an SS officer with a hook-shaped scar below his left eye opened the solid steel cell door.

"*Der Kommandant hat neunzig Tage Einzelhaft angeordnet*"—
"The commandant ordered ninety days of solitary confinement"—
the officer said, his face void of emotion. He left, locking the cell
behind him.

Relieved to not be shot, Rose took in deep breaths. *I can endure this.* She crawled into a wooden bunk missing a mattress and
rubbed the welts covering her skin. But hours later, she learned
that there was more to her punishment when the evening meal
arrived. Through an opening at the base of the door, a prisoner
slipped a tin of turnip broth into the cell. Her shoulders slumped
as she examined the minuscule amount of food. *Half rations. They
plan to starve me to death.*

CHAPTER 49

RAVENSBRÜCK CONCENTRATION CAMP— OCTOBER 7, 1944

The sound of construction caused Rose to stir. She rubbed her ribs, which protruded from her abdomen like a stray dog's, and slowly sat up on her bunk. With unsteady legs, she shuffled to a small barred window placed high on the wall. Too weak to jump, she listened to loud clunks, which sounded like concrete blocks being stacked in the vicinity of the crematorium. *What are they building?*

She'd passed her days of solitary confinement trying to conserve her energy by sleeping. But when she was awake, she forced herself to take laps around her cell, trying to prevent her legs from becoming atrophied. To exercise her mind, she recited childhood poems her mother had taught her, and she daydreamed about the past, most often her brief but salient time with Lazare. *If only things could have been different for us.*

The slat in the door opened for the morning meal. A woman prisoner slipped a half tin of acorn coffee and a bread crust into the cell. With her hand, she motioned for Rose to approach.

Rose kneeled.

"Give me your hand," the woman whispered.

Rose extended her palm.

"From a friend," the woman said, placing a dried sausage in Rose's hand.

Rose stared at the edible treasure.

"Eat it in small increments." The prisoner closed the slat, and the wheels of the ration cart rumbled away.

Muriel. Her eyes welled with tears. She chewed a bit of sausage, its gamy flavor coating her tongue. A surge of gratefulness filled her chest.

The next day, Rose received a hunk of beet hidden in her acorn coffee. Later in the week, she was given another sausage, along with a pat of margarine. Her decline in health tapered off, and her strength slowly began to return. *You're risking your life to smuggle me food. And I promise not to let you down by dying.*

CHAPTER 50

RAVENSBRÜCK CONCENTRATION CAMP—
NOVEMBER 11, 1944

Rose, curled on her wooden bunk with a tattered blanket, listened to the clatter of construction outside. The clack of masonry blocks being stacked filled the air. She wondered if it could be the raising of more cellblocks but ruled it out, considering the noise was coming from the vicinity of the crematorium, which was located a few yards beyond the camp wall. She plugged her fingers in her ears and closed her eyes, hoping she could drift into a deep hibernation and wake when the war was over.

Stirred by a tickling on her cheek, Rose wiped her face. She shivered, feeling a frigid breeze flow through the barred cell window. *Winter is coming. The winds have shifted.* She pulled the blanket, torn and full of holes, around her body like a cocoon. But the clack of hammers and masonry blocks reverberating through her ears compelled her to rise.

Dust covered her bunk. She sat up, soot falling from her blanket. Her breath stalled in her lungs. Wind, carrying what looked like dirty snowflakes, flowed through the barred window. A fine layer of ashes covered the floor. *Cremations—oh, dear God!*

Rose, her stomach heaving, shuffled to the window. Standing on her toes, her calves cramping, she tossed her blanket, again and again, until it wedged into the iron bars. But the makeshift plug did little to block the wind-driven ashes from pervading her cell. Shivering, she curled into a corner and wept. Clasping her hands, she prayed for the souls who perished. She vowed to do everything she could to survive the war, bring the Nazis to justice, and to make certain the women prisoners of Ravensbrück were never forgotten.

CHAPTER 51

RAVENSBRÜCK CONCENTRATION CAMP— DECEMBER 9, 1944

The sound of a key jostling inside the lock of the cell door awakened Rose. She unfurled her limbs, joints stiff from curling into a ball to retain her warmth.

The cell door screeched open. The SS officer who had—ninety days ago—delivered the news of her sentence raised his brows, appearing surprised to see her alive. *"Melden dich bei deinem Zellenblock"*—"Report to your cellblock." He turned and left, leaving the door open.

Rose, shuffling her feet, left the solitary confinement cell. Outside, she crossed a snow-covered ground, the ice seeping into her clogs and turning her sockless feet numb. Still wearing her summer-issued clothing, she clasped her arms around her torso in a feeble effort to fight the cold temperature. Her teeth chattered. Malnourished and fatigued, she stopped several times to rest.

Reaching her cellblock, she found the barracks horribly overcrowded, with three women, sometimes four, to a bunk. She stepped over dozens of women who were curled on the floor. A thick sour stench filled the air. Coming from solitary confinement, the abrupt exposure to the densely packed prisoners was both unnerving and poignant.

Anxious to see Muriel, Rose made her way to her bunk and found three women lying on their bellies and eating bowls of watery soup. "Where's the woman who'd slept here?" Rose asked, her knees turning weak.

One of the women shook her head, mumbled something in Polish, and then slurped her soup.

Rose maneuvered through the masses of prisoners, searching for Muriel or someone she recognized. Near the back of the block, she found a Soviet political prisoner named Yana, a former Red Army medic, who spoke French from having studied in Paris, and who had slept in a bunk near her and Muriel.

"Thank God," Yana said, hugging Rose.

"It's so good to see you," Rose said, squeezing her. "What's happened?"

Yana released her. "While you were gone, trains have brought in thousands more prisoners, some evacuated from Nazi camps in the east, due to the advancing Red Army."

Rose glanced over the crowded barrack, which normally held two hundred women. *How many? Five hundred? Six hundred?* Moans, cries, and coughs filled the air.

"The sanitary conditions are appalling," Yana said. "A typhus epidemic is spreading through the camp."

A foreboding lump twisted in Rose's gut. "Where's Muriel?"

Deep lines covered Yana's forehead. "She's in the back of the cellblock, where I've set up a quarantine area."

Oh, no. Rose leaned on a bunk to steady her legs. "How is she?"

"Your friend is a fighter," Yana said.

Rose drew in a serrated breath. "Why isn't she at the camp hospital?"

"I dare not take her there," Yana said.

"Why?" Rose asked. "Are you no longer working there?"

"I'm still assigned to the hospital." Yana stepped close and lowered her voice. "The doctors have, for quite some time, euthanized patients by giving them an injection of petrol."

"*Mon Dieu,*" Rose whispered.

"They're monsters," Yana said. "I've seen it happen many times with patients, even those who are not terminal, as if the doctors randomly euthanize women when the mood suits them."

"What about the *revier*, the barrack for sick inmates?"

"It's become a death block, where the infirm are left to die." Yana rubbed her forehead, as if she were trying the erase horrid memories etched into her brain. "There's something else you should know."

Rose clasped her hands.

"The Nazis are not satisfied by killing us through work, firing lines, or abhorrent living conditions. Nor are they appeased with transporting groups of women to other camps to be exterminated."

Rose's blood turned cold. A flash of the many transports of women hauled away in lorries and never to return. It had been rumored, since Rose's arrival in Ravensbrück, that the Germans were systematically sending prisoners away to other camps for mass killing.

"I overheard a doctor and an SS officer talking about a gas chamber that is almost finished with construction at Ravensbrück. It's disguised as a washroom."

A jolt struck Rose. "Near the crematorium?" she asked, recalling the construction noise from her isolation cell.

Yana nodded.

"Why are you telling me this?"

"Because they'll soon be murdering women prisoners by the hundreds. And I have no doubt that they will begin with the infirm, and the prisoner classes the Nazis despise most."

Rose dug her nails into the palms of her hands, wishing she could do something to end this hell.

"So," Yana said, placing a hand to Rose's shoulder, "I need to make your friend well."

"I'll help you," Rose said.

"You look like you're in need of medical care, too."

"I look awful," Rose said. "But I can assure you that I have been eating far better"—*thanks to Muriel arranging to smuggle me food*—"than the women in this cellblock."

"Okay," Yana said, appearing grateful for her assistance.

Rose followed Yana, stepping over women who were hunkered on the ground, to the back of the cellblock, where a stained sheet was strung over a line of twine to create a quarantine barrier from women infected with typhus.

"You will begin with your friend," Yana said. She placed a pinch of brown powder, taken from a small cloth pouch, into a tin cup of water. "A Russian remedy; we have no other medicine." She swirled the concoction and gave Rose the cup, along with a handful of bark strips. "Help her sip the tea, and then rub the bark over her skin."

Rose's heart sank when she found Muriel in a bottom bunk, next to two skeletal women who were either sleeping or unconscious. Muriel had lost weight, evident by her protruding cheekbones and clavicles. Her eyes, surrounded by dark circles, were swollen with fever, and a rash covered her skin.

Rose kneeled, tears filling her eyes. "Muriel."

Muriel cracked open her eyelids.

"It's Rose," she said, touching her hand.

"You're alive," Muriel breathed.

"Yes." A tear fell from Rose's cheek, creating a dirty line over her skin. "You saved my life."

"Others helped." She coughed and winced. "You protected us by claiming responsibility for sabotaging the coats."

You gifted me food, when you needed it more than me. "I have tea for you to drink." Rose propped a bundled sheet under Muriel's head, which was hot and covered in sweat, and placed the cup to Muriel's lips.

She sipped, drops dribbling down her chin. "You shouldn't be here. You'll get infected."

"Let's not worry about me," Rose said. "Finish your tea. It contains medicine."

"Later," Muriel said, her voice frail. Her eyes glanced to the ceiling, as if she were searching for something. "I can't remember what she looks like."

Rose swallowed a lump in her throat.

"I've forgotten Mabel's face," she whispered.

"Nonsense," Rose said, fighting back her anguish. "It's merely a symptom of your fever. You'll remember every beautiful feature of Mabel once you've recovered."

Muriel lowered her eyes.

Rose sifted through her memories. A flash of Mabel's picture, placed next to Charlie's photograph during their SOE training at Garramor House. "Mabel is lovely," Rose said. "She has curly brown hair, a button nose—like her mother—and the most adorable chubby cheeks."

A slight smile formed on Muriel's lips, chapped and red.

"And she has a charming checkered dress," Rose added.

Recollection filled Muriel's face. "I made it for her when she was a wee 'un." She paused, clearing phlegm from her throat. "She'll be starting primary school soon."

"Mabel will have outgrown her dress," Rose said. "You'll have to make her another one when you get home. She's going to be a tall, skinny malinky longlegs, like her mother."

Muriel touched Rose's arm. "Aye."

Rose fed the tea to Muriel, but she was only able to consume half of the liquid. She rubbed the bark over Muriel's frail arms, legs, and torso, covered in a light red-colored rash, which faded when pressure was applied. As Muriel drifted to sleep, Rose recalled Yana's story about the gas chamber the Germans had nearly finished building. She shuddered. *I must make you well before the Germans begin rounding up who they deem as useless mouths.*

Chapter 52

Ravensbrück Concentration Camp— December 19, 1944

Rose placed a hand to Muriel's forehead. "You're hot," she said, heat penetrating her fingers. *103 degrees? 104?* Her shoulder muscles tensed.

Muriel's condition had worsened over the past several days. Plagued with a fever and nausea, she was unable to eat the woodchip-laced bread, so Rose fed her bark tea mixed with margarine and mashed turnip smuggled by Yana from the camp hospital. To complicate matters, the textile shipments to the camp had paused, stalling operations at the SS workshops, and Rose was assigned to hard physical labor shoveling sand and unloading barges of coal at the lake. Therefore, she was only able to care for Muriel at night. Despite the grueling labor, Rose felt fortunate that she wasn't transferred to one of the many subcamps, preventing her from caring for Muriel. And as for Muriel, she was—at least for the moment—permitted to remain in the quarantine section of the barrack due to the overflow of typhus-infected prisoners in the hospital ward and death block. Fortunately, the German guards feared contagious diseases, like typhus and tuberculosis, so Muriel and the quarantined women were not required to stand for roll call. Instead, a *blockova*, a woman prisoner whom the SS placed in charge of the barrack, provided the guards with the list of the infirm.

Rose stirred a pad of margarine into lukewarm bark tea. She ladled a spoonful and placed it to Muriel's lips.

"No," Muriel whispered, tilting her head away.

"You must eat," Rose said.

"I can't."

Rose put down the tea. Using a rag, she wiped beads of sweat from Muriel's head.

Muriel, her eyes bloodshot, looked at Rose. "I'd like you to write a letter for me."

A knot formed in Rose's stomach.

"To Mabel."

"There's no need," Rose said, fighting back tears. "You're going to recover. The Allied forces are advancing toward us. We'll soon be saved, and you'll go home."

"Please," Muriel breathed.

Rose pressed a hand to her aching belly. "I have no paper, or pencil."

"You're a brilliant agent." Muriel coughed, too weak to cover her mouth. "I'm sure you'll find something to use."

Reluctantly, Rose scoured the cellblock for writing material. She managed to borrow—in exchange for a slice of bread—a pencil from a Polish woman who sketched drawings of tulips on flat stones, which she hid under her bunk. But Rose was unable to locate paper, which was scarce in the camp. Arranging to bribe a prisoner who worked in the SS administration office to steal writing paper would be risky and would take time, which she might not have. With few options, she quietly left the cellblock.

Outside, a waning crescent moon illuminated the snow-covered courtyard. She scanned the area to make sure no one was looking, and then scurried to the wall of a nearby cellblock, where German guards often congregated to smoke cigarettes. Black dots marred the snow, as if someone had tossed a handful of cinders. She kneeled and picked up a burnt bit of paper. The thought of the remnant touching the lips of a Nazi repulsed Rose. She buried her disgust and collected more cigarette butts.

The next morning, during a three-hour roll call, she observed where several of the guards tossed their cigarette butts. And while the prisoners were receiving their ration of morning coffee and bread, Rose collected the remnants. Her delay of getting in the ration line resulted in receiving only a quarter slice of bread and a splash of coffee. *It's worth it*, Rose thought, dipping a bit of bread-crust into her coffee.

During her day of hard labor, Rose unloaded a barge of coal at the lake. Lifting shovelful after shovelful of black rock, her arm and back muscles flared. It sickened her to think that the coal would be used as fuel to heat the SS offices, commandant's home, and—most of all—the crematorium. *I'll be beaten or shot if I refuse to work. And who will help Muriel if I'm dead?* She shook away her thoughts and tossed a shovelful of coal from the barge.

While working at the lake, she'd found several cigarette butts near a sand pit, which she slipped into her coat. She picked up three more during the march home. And after evening roll call, she scavenged the ground to collect over a dozen bits of paper. In her cellblock, she removed a handful of remnants from her pocket. She unfolded the bits of paper, disregarding any burnt tobacco, and then sharpened her pencil by grinding the tip over a brick. Gathering her writing supplies, she went to the quarantine unit to see Muriel.

Rose sat on Muriel's bunk, which she shared with two ill women, their lungs wheezing as they slept. "Muriel," she whispered, touching her shoulder. "Would you like me to write your letter?"

Muriel cracked open her eyelids. "What's that?"

"Shredded newspaper, I'm afraid." Rose covered the burnt remnants with her hand, hoping Muriel didn't recognize the source of the paper. "It's temporary. I'll place a number on the back of each piece, to keep the proper order, and I'll transpose it once I find some proper stationery."

"Okay," Muriel said, her voice fragile. She gestured for Rose to come close, as if she didn't want to disturb the sleeping women, or she preferred for her words to remain private.

Rose leaned in. For several minutes, Muriel whispered a message to her daughter, Mabel. Rose, her chest aching, struggled to maintain her composure as she scribbled the dictation in shorthand, which she'd learned while studying at Mrs. Hoster's Secretarial Training College in London. Finishing, she numbered the backs of the paper bits.

"Done," Rose said, putting down her pencil.

Muriel slowly shook her head. "Sew it into your dress."

Rose's vision blurred with tears. The reality of what Muriel was asking her to do sent a sharp pang through her sternum. "There's no need."

"Please," Muriel begged.

Rose squeezed Muriel's hand, bony and frail. She bit the inside of her cheek to fight back her tears, and then nodded.

CHAPTER 53

RAVENSBRÜCK CONCENTRATION CAMP— JANUARY 2, 1945

Rose, shivering and exhausted, climbed out of a sandpit and tossed her spade into a wagon. Her muscles ached from a day of shoveling sand at the lake. The hard labor was more about tormenting the prisoners than producing railcars full of sand, Rose believed, considering the ground was frozen.

"*Schnell!*" a blonde-haired guard shouted. She tugged the leash to her dog, who was growling and baring its teeth.

Rose took her place in line, ranks of five, with the other prisoners. The guard blew a whistle, her breath misting in the frigid air, and the prisoners began the march. With each step, the sand inside Rose's clogs scraped at her sockless feet. She was more tired than usual, given that she'd slept only a few hours due to caring for Muriel and the quarantined women. Last night, two ill political prisoners, one Polish and one French, died from typhus complicated by severe malnutrition. By now, the deceased would have been picked up by a corpse squad and taken to the crematorium. Rose's heart wrenched with the guilt of having to choose which women would receive the bits of smuggled food. *If only I could have arranged to steal more bread, they might be alive.*

Muriel's fever had subsided, but she remained weak and unable to walk. Although her progress was slow, she was showing signs of recovery. Her appetite had improved, and last night, for the first time in weeks, she'd eaten something other than pureed turnip soup or medicinal tea when she devoured a half-slice of bread topped with wilted cabbage leaves. "Tomorrow, I'll smuggle you some bangers and mash," Rose had jested, producing a faint but distinguishable smile on Muriel's face.

As the prisoners approached the camp, a stench from the crematorium filled the air. She took in short, shallow breaths, attempting to block out the smell. But the fetor grew worse when the guard ordered the prisoners to take a route that would take them within several yards of the billowing smokestack. Rose glanced at the guard, her polished leather boots crunching over the snow. *You intend to torment us*, Rose thought, a rancor growing inside her.

The crematorium oven roared, causing the hairs to raise on the back of Rose's neck. A wave of heat radiated through the frigid air. She wished she could plug her ears and eradicate the horrid visions swirling in her brain. Marching past the phony washroom, Rose's eyes were drawn to stacks of clothing, most with yellow triangle patches. *Oh, God! The gas chamber is operational!*

Rose's legs turned weak. Her heart wept for the poor women, most of whom were Jews, given the color of the patches. She wondered what had happened to Lazare's parents and prayed that they had not met the same demise. And she pledged, with every ounce of her fiber, that she would do everything she could to survive and tell the world of the Ravensbrück atrocities. Her blood surged with a fusion of misery and vengeance. *Someday, the Nazis will pay for their genocide.*

Inside the camp, Rose entered her cellblock, hoping to find Yana and inform her of the gassing. She weaved her way through the crowded barrack, stepping over women who were curled on the ground. Pulling back the sheet, which partitioned the quarantined women from the rest of the barrack, she stepped inside and froze. The bunks contained new women whom she didn't recognize. And Muriel, as well as the women who'd shared her bed, was missing. A grievous lump swelled in her abdomen.

Yana, feeding a woman a bit of bread, turned to Rose.

"Where are they?" Rose gasped.

"There was nothing we could do," Yana said, her voice shaking. "I returned from my work at the hospital to learn that a group of green-triangle prisoners, acting on orders from an SS officer, loaded them onto a lorry and took them away."

A pang shot through Rose's stomach, as if she'd been punched in the gut. "To a subcamp?"

"No." Yana's eyes watered.

"A death cellblock?" Rose cried, her brain in denial of what her heart already knew.

Yana shook her head. "I'm sorry."

"No!" Rose wailed. "There must be a mistake!" She stumbled to the exit, tripping over prisoners lying on the floor. Propelled by rage, she stormed outside, toward the SS administration building. "Where did you take her!" she cried, her heart ravaged with sorrow. "Bring her back!"

Two female guards sprinted over the courtyard. Within seconds, one of the guards, a tall woman with her hair tied neatly in a bun, slammed a baton into Rose's abdomen.

Pain flared through Rose's organs, and she crumpled to the ground. As she fought to get to her knees, a jackboot smashed into her back, pinning her face into snow. She expected to be dragged away to be flogged or shot. Instead, one of the guards retrieved a bucket and doused her with cold water.

The soaking shocked her body. Her drenched clothing clung to her skin. She gasped, her breath puffing in the frigid air.

A siren sounded.

"In die Reihe, mit den anderen!"—"Get in line with the others!"— a guard growled, pushing her baton into Rose's cheek.

Rose, battered and brokenhearted, struggled to get to her feet. She shuffled toward the cellblock and took her place in line. *I'm so sorry, Muriel.* Tears streamed down her face. As time passed, her sorrow soared and her body temperature plummeted. Three hours later, when roll call finished, she remained standing, despite her inability to feel her hands or feet. Yana and two prisoners helped Rose—her clothes frozen stiff—inside the barrack, where they wrapped her in blankets and held her, sharing their warmth. Slowly, her clothes thawed and her body warmed. With shivering hands, she gripped the hem of her wet dress—containing bits of paper that held Muriel's words—and she curled into a ball and wept.

CHAPTER 54

RAVENSBRÜCK CONCENTRATION CAMP—
MARCH 27, 1945

Rose stood in the roll call square and watched a convoy of lorries filled with prisoners leave the camp. She was relieved to see that the vehicles didn't stop at the gas chamber, where several thousand prisoners—the majority Jews or infirm, as well as asocials (black triangles) and criminals (green triangles)—had been exterminated over the past three months. Instead, the vehicles were rumored to be relocating five thousand female prisoners to the Mauthausen and Bergen-Belsen concentration camps.

The Soviet forces are getting close, Rose thought. Over the winter, thousands of women prisoners—evacuated from camps in Poland, due to Stalin's advancing army—had been brought to Ravensbrück. The frequency of air raid sirens had escalated, and there were stories, from a woman who worked in the administration building, that the SS were moving their records and the workshop machines to safe locations. But women prisoners were still being exterminated en masse at the gas chamber. Each day, the conditions in the camp worsened. Food supplies dwindled. The death cellblock flooded with end-stage prisoners, who were simply left to die. Gassing and cremations escalated, blackening the sky over Ravensbrück. And on a daily basis, women who were desperate to end their suffering threw their bodies onto the electrified fences.

The months of hard physical labor had depleted Rose's strength.

She'd lost weight, her pelvic bones and ribs protruded from her skin, and her regrown, brittle hair had started to fall out. The only things keeping her alive, she believed, were the stolen rations—bits of chocolate, pads of margarine, slices of bread, and spoons of jam—that Yana had smuggled from the camp hospital. But most painful to Rose was the deep-rooted anguish she felt for the loss of her fellow agent and friend, Muriel.

She'd never learned precisely what happened to Muriel and the women in quarantine, although she believed that they were either shot or gassed, and then cremated. Even with the passing of months, her guilt and heartbreak remained raw. *If Muriel hadn't smuggled rations to me in the isolation cell, she might have had the strength to avoid contracting typhus. I should have found a way to hide her while I was working.*

Rose listened to the roar of lorry engines fade away, and she wondered if she would live long enough to see the camp liberated. She entered her cellblock, contemplating whether she should search for a prisoner healthier and stronger than she who might be willing to carry Muriel's message home.

Chapter 55

The Death March—April 27, 1945

Rose stood in the courtyard and listened to the grind of lorry engines outside the wall. A group of SS officers, their heads lowered, stormed inside the administration building. *They know the end is near*, she thought.

Over the past several weeks, the SS had moved thousands of prisoners to other locations. The women, many of whom were Scandinavian, were loaded onto white buses and driven away. However, over twenty thousand women prisoners remained in Ravensbrück, Rose estimated, and rumors swirled inside the cellblocks that Stalin's Red Army was advancing closer to the camp. A hope of liberation swelled inside the prisoners, especially the Soviet women, who began holding their heads high. But today's round of transports appeared unusual due to the increased presence of SS soldiers, and because some of the female guards had not shown up for morning roll call.

As Rose was about to enter her barrack, Yana emerged from the camp hospital and approached her.

"Follow me," Yana said, taking Rose's arm and leading her behind the cellblock. "I overheard an SS officer speaking to a German doctor. Commandant Suhren has been given orders to evacuate the camp."

A surge of hope flowed through Rose's veins.

Yana glanced over her shoulder, as if to make certain no one could hear them. "The Germans plan to leave behind no witnesses who could testify to the atrocities that they've committed. All physically capable women will be forced to march away from Ravensbrück."

A death march. A twinge pierced Rose's stomach. "To where?"

"Northern Mecklenburg, I think." Yana said.

"What about the women who are too weak to walk?"

"They'll be left to die."

Rose's heart sank.

"I'm required to stay and care for the ill," Yana said. "I need to return to the hospital before the doctor notices that I'm missing." She slipped off her coat. "Trade me, mine is warmer."

A siren sounded. Rose's skin prickled. "I'll stay and help you."

"You have no choice," Yana said. "You go, or you'll be shot."

A machine gun fired in the courtyard. "*Schnell!*"

Rose flinched.

"Your coat," Yana pleaded.

Reluctantly, Rose traded coats with Yana. Her eyes widened, feeling lumps inside the pockets.

"Food and bandages," Yana said.

"Thank you," Rose said. "Please, come with me. Maybe you can hide in the crowd and attempt to escape."

"I will tend to the sick until my Soviet comrades liberate us," Yana said, a timbre of uncertainty in her voice.

Rose tried to convince Yana to join her, but she refused. The sound of German guard whistles, followed by gunshots and barking dogs, pierced the air.

Yana hugged Rose. "*Dasvidaniya.*"

"Goodbye," Rose said, squeezing her.

Yana disappeared into a crowd of prisoners filling the courtyard. Rose's chest ached, realizing that she would, in all likelihood, never see her Russian friend again.

Soon, thousands of woman prisoners pressed shoulder to shoulder, congregated at the gate. Hunks of bread were distributed to the prisoners, while scores of SS soldiers carrying weapons climbed out of lorries. The gate opened and the women, like sheep, were herded through the gate, leaving behind the prisoners who were too ill to rise from their bunks.

"*Schnell!*" an SS soldier shouted, pointing a rifle with a bayonet. The prisoners, most wearing wooden shoes and tattered clothing, lumbered forward. They were forced to line up in long columns as the soldiers prodded them from behind. As they marched away, Rose glanced at Lake Schwedtsee, where she'd been forced to perform hard physical labor, and where the SS disposed of human ashes from the crematorium. Her eyes filled with tears as she wondered how many tens of thousands of dead were resting on the lake bed.

Less than a few hundred yards from the camp, the first shot was fired. Prisoners flinched, and through the corner of Rose's eye, she saw a gray-haired woman collapse onto the ground. *Oh, God!*

"*Schnell! Schnell!*" SS soldiers shouted.

The prisoners increased their pace. The sound of coughs, wheezes, and shuffling feet filled the air.

For the afternoon, Rose and thousands of prisoners, many of whom resembled skeletons from severe starvation, marched northwest along muddy roads. Clusters of prisoners were directed by soldiers to travel through fields, only to rejoin the main group a mile away. Like precise, measured tolls of a bell tower, shots exploded every thirty to sixty minutes, killing prisoners who were too weak to keep up the pace. It was clear to Rose that the SS guards were not merely ordered to transport the prisoners to another camp far from the advancing Allied troops. Their plan was also to spread dead prisoners over a vast area in an attempt to hide evidence of their genocide and war crimes.

After a few miles, Rose's leg muscles ached and her lungs burned. *How long before I can no longer walk? Hours? Days?* To distract herself from the pain and death, she turned her thoughts to joyful memories, buried deep inside her mind. Summer picnics with Mum, Dad, and Charlie in Trafalgar Square, where they dined on cheeses, cured meats, fluffy cakes, and cream-filled scones from the Teasdale Grocery. The sense of pride and camaraderie she'd felt when working alongside the women of Room 60 in Churchill's war rooms, and how she'd often jested with her dear friend, Lucy, that one of her typed reports would lead Britain to victory. The elation she'd felt when she, Muriel, and Felix had successfully completed their SOE combat training in Scotland, and how eager and confident they were to join the fight. But most of all, she relived her brief but blissful time with Lazare. His willingness to open his heart and reveal to her how his Jewish parents were rounded up by the French police. How he risked his life to establish safe houses for her and the SOE network. The gentle touch of his hand while guiding her through the blackened maze of the Paris catacombs. The delectable meal he'd prepared for her from scrap vegetables. And the contentment and warmth she'd felt when he held her in his arms. *If only things could have been different for us.*

Long after nightfall, Rose and the prisoners—hundreds fewer than when they began the march—arrived at an unlit train station. Permitted to rest, the women hunkered on the ground. Rose, grateful for Yana's smuggled food, removed a piece of bread and a few small potatoes from her pocket. She took a bite of bread and prayed that her friend, as well as the thousands of feeble prisoners remaining in Ravensbrück, would soon be liberated.

Eyes of a weary woman in her late teens, who wore a red triangle, stared at Rose's food.

Rose broke off a hunk of bread and, along with a potato, gave it to the woman.

"*Dziękuję,*" the woman said in Polish.

"Eat it in small increments," Rose said. "You can survive this. Just keep walking."

The woman nodded and nibbled at her food.

Rose, her legs aching, finished off her food and curled on the ground. Her body and mind depleted, she fell asleep. But a few hours later, given that the sun had not yet risen, they were forced by the guards to march, leaving behind the bodies of women who had died during the night.

Rose and the prisoners slogged over the countryside. Sporadic executions continued throughout the morning, including a Hungarian woman who'd briefly stopped to drink muddy water from a puddle, and a Polish teenager who'd merely tripped over a fallen branch that was blocking the path. Most, if not all, of the prisoners were struggling to keep the pace established by the SS soldiers, and there was little risk that any of the women had the strength to attempt to run away. *They'll shoot anyone fleeing within seconds.* The only option for now, Rose believed, was to continue marching until her legs gave out.

At noon, the women were permitted to rest near a stream, while the guards ate lunch from their backpacks. Rose shared the last of her food with three prisoners who she believed needed the sustenance more than her, given their protruding cheekbones and black, hollow eyes. Taking the bandages from her pocket, she wrapped her blistered feet.

During the afternoon march, scores of women died, either from exhaustion or Nazi bullets. Struggling to raise her head, Rose watched the ground pass beneath her shuffling feet. Her sense of time evaporated, and the bandages covering her blisters slowly turned to shreds from the constant rubbing of her wooden shoes. Burst blisters turned to open sores. With each step, burning pangs shot through her feet. She buried her pain and pushed on, driven by her deep-seated desire to survive this hell, and to fulfill her promise to Muriel.

By evening, Rose had merged into a subgroup of fifty prisoners led by two SS soldiers in their late teens or early twenties, given their smooth faces, who ordered the women to march through a large field. Veering from the road, as well as the main group, sent a sickening lump into Rose's esophagus. She expected at any moment for the soldiers to mow them down, leaving them in the field to rot. Instead, the women were taken to a farm and instructed to enter a barn.

"*Geh rein!*"—"Get inside!"—a soldier shouted, pointing his bayonet.

The prisoners shuffled inside.

As the second soldier lit a cigarette, the flash of the flame illuminated the darkened space, revealing empty horse stalls. A dull scent of manure and earth filled the air. The women, frightened and exhausted, huddled together. Seconds later, the soldiers slammed the barn door closed and bolted it from the outside.

Either they're locking us away for the night, or they intend to burn us alive, Rose thought. Too spent to worry, she wandered through the unlit barn. Finding a small pile of straw already shared by several prisoners, she collapsed onto her belly and slept.

CHAPTER 56

THE DEATH MARCH—APRIL 30, 1945

The third day into the march, their subgroup, which had dwindled from fifty to twenty-two women, did not rejoin the main exodus of prisoners, somewhere to the northwest. A drizzling rain pelted Rose's face and seeped through her clothing. With each labored step, her feet throbbed, and twinges flared through her knees and hips. Her hope of survival had gradually been snubbed out, and her heart ached with the thought of dying with Muriel's message sewn into the hem of her dress. She considered giving the bits of paper to one of the remaining prisoners at the next stop, but it likely didn't matter. *None of us are going to make it to a camp.*

Earlier, the soldiers had changed into civilian clothes, which they'd hidden in their packs. The only things left to identify them as soldiers were their rifles and military coats, temporarily keeping them dry from the rain. *Once our group is small, they'll execute us and desert their post.*

An hour later, the soldiers, prodding the women with their bayonets, forced them to leave a dirt road and travel into the woods. The earth, turned swampy from the rain, caused Rose to lose her left clog. Rather than risk being shot to retrieve it, she walked with a bare, ulcerated foot sinking into the mud. Soon, the prisoners were herded into a small clearing between clusters of birch trees. Rose's chest constricted, turning her breath shallow. The dread in the women's eyes revealed to Rose that they also knew what was about to happen.

"*Halt!*" a soldier shouted.

The prisoners stopped. Broken and unable to flee, Rose looked at the SS soldiers, their eyes void of any human compassion, as if they viewed the women as vermin. Whimpers and the patter of raindrops penetrated the air. The women huddled together, some holding hands in unity, while others prayed.

The soldiers raised their rifles.

Rose, her heart thudding against her sternum, squeezed the trembling fingers of a Polish prisoner. She raised her chin in defiance, closed her eyes, and waited for it to be over.

Gunfire exploded.

Rose recoiled, her heart pounding her ribcage. She buckled over, but remained on her feet. Opening her eyes, she saw the German soldiers, their lifeless limbs splayed over the ground. Seconds later, Soviet soldiers, wearing khaki uniforms and caps emblazoned with a Red Army star, emerged from the forest.

Prisoners clutching one another moaned and cried.

A mustached soldier, who appeared to be the leader of a Soviet scout unit, stepped forward and lowered his machine gun. He stared, his eyes widened with shock, at the cadaverous women.

Rose's eyes welled with tears, and she fell to her knees and wept.

PART 5

LIBERTÉ

CHAPTER 57

LONDON, ENGLAND—JUNE 20, 1945

Rose exited the Aldgate East tube station, which was noticeably absent of Londoners carrying blankets and pillows to sleep underground. As she maneuvered through the crowded sidewalks filled with people coming home from work, butterflies swirled in her stomach. It had been three years since she'd left the key to Lucy's flat on the kitchen counter with a note explaining that she'd accepted a position outside of London, and that she would write when she could. *Will she be upset with me for not telling her the truth? Will things ever be the same between us?* Rose, hoping Lucy was still living in her Spitalfields flat, crossed the street to a four-story brick apartment building.

After Rose and the surviving prisoners had been saved by the Soviet scout unit, they were turned over to the Swedish Red Cross, and then taken, via Denmark, to a hospital in Malmö, Sweden. Three of the death-march survivors, one Hungarian and two Polish, died during the transport, despite efforts of medics to administer food and medicine. They were too emaciated to recover, and Rose was haunted by the thought of the women, who'd fought so desperately to live, dying within days of their liberation.

Rose's health was horrid upon her arrival at the Swedish hospital. She weighed less than seventy pounds, and her ulcerated feet had become infected, impeding her ability to stand. She celebrated Victory Day in Europe, Nazi Germany's unconditional surrender to the Allies, by eating pea soup and pancakes in a hospital bed with her bandaged feet propped on pillows. She spent much of her time in the hospital—between the changing of bandages, rounds of sulfa drugs, and physical therapy—by writing details of the atrocities she'd witnessed in a leather-bound journal. *The Soviets have control of eastern Germany, including Ravensbrück, and British authorities might not receive complete accounts of Nazi crimes.* Despite the pain of reliving her time in captivity, she recorded stories of inhuman conditions, starvation, slave labor, executions, and genocide. Although she was grateful to have survived, her heart ached for the women who suffered in Ravensbrück, and for all of the people who perished in the fight to save Europe from Nazi aggression.

After several weeks of medical care, Rose was well enough to be flown to RAF Tempsford in Bedfordshire, England, where she'd departed—years earlier—to be parachuted into German-occupied France. She was met in a hangar by an officer named Captain Carter, who was acting on behalf of the SOE as a one-person reception committee. Carter, a tall, rugged man with a deep baritone voice, welcomed her home with a firm handshake and thanked her for her service to Britain. He expressed his condolences for her fellow agents, Felix and Muriel, and he provided her with the SOE's protocol for merging oneself back into society.

Carter informed Rose that she was bound to her oath of secrecy, and that the SOE had classified all records of her subnetwork, Conjurer, as top secret. Therefore, even when British authorities decided it was safe to reveal the names and roles of SOE agents who served in Nazi-occupied Europe, the identities of Rose, Muriel, and Felix would most likely remain classified. It would be as if they and their Conjurer network had never existed.

"British authorities have decided it is best to keep the origins of Operation Jericho a secret," Carter had said. "It could be quite controversial, to both Britain and France, if the public knew who instigated the RAF to bomb a French prison—as well as who authorized the mission."

Carter's words resurrected Rose's grief for Lazare, and it saddened her to know that the service of Muriel and Felix might be expunged from history. *Perhaps authorities fear a political quagmire,* she'd thought. Rose considered requesting the names of the decision makers from Carter, but it was clear the decision had been made, and there was nothing she could do about it, at least for now. Setting aside her emotions, she accepted Carter's invitation for a private ceremony, to be scheduled when Rose was fully recovered, to honor the service of her fallen SOE agents. She was given her stored personal belongings, including her photograph of Charlie. She left RAF Tempsford eager to follow through on her promises to Muriel and Felix, but first she needed to see Lucy.

Rose, lugging a small suitcase, climbed the stairs of Lucy's apartment building. Reaching the landing, she took in deep breaths to quell her racing heart. Her feet, conditioned from wearing sockless wooden clogs, ached inside her heeled shoes. She buried her trepidation and knocked.

Seconds later, Lucy opened the door. "Oh, my God!" she gasped.

"Hello," Rose said, her voice wavering.

Lucy threw her arms around her.

Exuberance flooded Rose's body. She squeezed her, not wanting to let her go.

"I'm so happy to see you," Lucy cried.

Rose sobbed, tears of joy dripping down her cheeks.

"Please, come in," Lucy said, pulling her inside. She grabbed Rose's suitcase and placed it in the foyer. She wiped Rose's tears and stared at her sunken eyes and thin frame. "Are you ill?"

"I'm getting better," Rose said, ignoring her fatigue.

"When I didn't hear from you, I feared that something dreadful had occurred," Lucy said. "What happened?"

"I'm so sorry." Rose took a jagged breath. "I feel horrible for leaving without telling you where I was going. I wish I could tell you everything. But for now, I'm not permitted to say."

Lucy paused, as if to process Rose's words. "There's no need to tell me," she said. "None at all."

Sweet, loyal Lucy, Rose thought, sniffing back tears. *Our work in Churchill's war rooms has conditioned us to maintain confidentiality and to not ask questions.* "It's so lovely to see you."

"I have missed you," Lucy said.

"I've really missed you, too." Rose glanced to Lucy's swollen belly and gasped.

"I'm having a baby," Lucy said, rubbing her tummy. "I'm five months pregnant."

"I'm so happy for you," Rose said.

Lucy grinned. "Shall we have some tea? We have lots of catching up to do."

Rose sat at a kitchen table while Lucy served tea and shortbread containing real butter. A flash of the pats of margarine, which Muriel had smuggled to keep her alive, filled Rose's head. A mixture of gratefulness and sorrow stirred in her chest.

For the next hour, Rose caught up on Lucy's life. She and Jonathan, who worked at the London Fire Brigade, were married shortly after Rose's departure. The flat, which Lucy previously shared with two women, was now her and Jonathan's home. Lucy no longer worked in Churchill's underground bunker. After the war, she was transferred to a typist assignment on the fourth floor of the Treasury building.

"It's rather odd to be typing reports near a window," Lucy said, adjusting her glasses on the bridge of her nose. "After working for years in a basement, I feel like I might catch a sunburn."

Rose smiled, nibbling on a crumb of shortbread.

"Will you stay?" Lucy asked.

"I don't want to impose," Rose said, despite having no place else to go.

"Nonsense," Lucy said. "It's decided. You'll live with us, for as long as you need."

"But you're married and expecting a baby."

"Jonathan will be thrilled to see you. You'll take the guest room. If we're lucky enough to have you with us when the baby arrives, I'll put you to work washing nappies."

"That would be lovely," Rose said, blinking tears from her eyes.

Lucy clasped Rose's hand, bony and frail. "And I'll fatten you up with my mum's cottage pie."

For two weeks, Rose slept twelve hours per day, not including naps, as if her mind and body craved hibernation. She woke, often after Lucy and Jonathan had gone to work, and she drank tea and ate slices of cottage pie, which Lucy's mum had delivered on a daily basis. In the afternoon, she dined on fried cod and haddock at a local chip shop, and then exercised by strolling the streets of London.

The East End, which received the worst of the German bombing, still contained piles of rubble, and scores of warehouses, docks, and residences were in various degrees of ruin. In Bethnal Green, a vacant weed-filled lot marked the site of the former Teasdale Grocery, where her parents had once been the source of food and comradeship for the community. *It might take years, or maybe a lifetime, to recover.*

As weeks passed, Rose's health improved. She put on weight, thanks to Lucy and her mum's pies, and her brittle hair slowly grew long and lustrous. But while her body healed, little could be done for her scars, which she inadvertently revealed to Lucy, who assisted her with buttoning the back of an altered dress.

Lucy gasped, staring at dark pockmarks on Rose's back.

A flash of her interrogations—her back seared with burning cigars—turned Rose's blood cold. "I'm sorry you had to see that." She adjusted her dress, covering her skin.

"Bloody bastards," Lucy said. "I can't begin to imagine what hell you endured in that concentration camp."

She knows, Rose thought.

Lucy retrieved a jar of salve. "I'll do my best to erase what they did to you."

"Thank you," Rose said. She opened the back of her dress, and Lucy rubbed salve onto the scars. She buried images of her torture and turned her thoughts to the bits of cigarette paper containing Muriel's message, stashed inside her suitcase. "I'm going to take a trip to Edinburgh to visit the family of a fallen friend."

"When?" Lucy asked.

"In a few days." *After I buy some proper stationery.*

"Would you like me to come with you?" Lucy asked.

"I'd love your company, but I feel that this is something I need to do on my own."

"Okay," Lucy said. "But if you change your mind, I'll join you on a moment's notice."

Rose nodded. The anticipation of delivering Muriel's message caused Rose's chest to tighten. She took a deep breath and exhaled. As Lucy rubbed another round of salve between her shoulder blades, she wished for a miracle medicine, one that could—in addition to healing ugly scars—fade horrid memories and repair splintered hearts.

CHAPTER 58

EDINBURGH, SCOTLAND—JULY 28, 1945

Rose, the odor of diesel and creosote filling her nose, scaled the steps of the Waverley train station and flagged a taxi. Climbing into the back seat, she gave the address to the driver, a bearded man wearing a tweed cap. As the taxi pulled away from the curb, her anxiousness grew. *What will I say when I see them?*

Rose had called Muriel's mum, Glenna, on the telephone earlier in the week. She explained that she was Muriel's friend and in possession of a letter for Mabel. Glenna, her sorrow still raw from the news of her daughter's death, eagerly invited Rose to visit. "The military didn't reveal to my husband, Fergus, and I how Muriel ended up in a German prison camp," Glenna had said. "I'm hoping you might help us with understanding how she died." They agreed on a date and time to visit. Hanging up the receiver, Rose regretted being bound to secrecy by the SOE. *I wish I could tell them everything.*

Using a bit of the money that the SOE had secretly deposited into Rose's bank account, she purchased linen-textured stationery paper, an envelope, and a fine-tip fountain pen from a shop in Spitalfields. While Lucy and Jonathan were at work, Rose retrieved the bits of cigarette paper stored in an empty medical soap tin given to her by a Swedish Red Cross nurse after the liberation of Ravensbrück. She opened the lid and dumped the scorched remnants onto a table, resurrecting visions of Nazi atrocities. Her breath turned shallow.

Gathering her fortitude, she arranged the pieces in numerical order. As she transposed the shorthand onto the stationery, the Scottish timbre of Muriel's voice echoed in her memories. Tears pooled in her eyes. She dabbed her face, using a handkerchief, and finished writing the letter. Eager to rid herself of the Ravensbrück artifacts, she burned the cigarette paper and flushed the ashes down the loo.

The taxi stopped on a narrow street dividing dozens of two-story stone rowhouses.

"That's the address," the driver said, pointing to a red door.

"Thank you." She paid the driver and exited the taxi, which abruptly sped away. With her stomach filled with collywobbles, she climbed three steps to the door. As she prepared to knock, the door swung open.

"Rose?" a woman with wavy gray hair asked.

"Yes," Rose said, clasping her purse.

"I'm Glenna. Please come in."

Rose entered and was greeted with a hug.

"This is my husband, Fergus," Glenna said, turning to a tall man wearing wool trousers with a white button-up shirt.

"Welcome," he said.

Rose hugged Fergus, having to stand on her tiptoes.

They settled into the parlor, a quaint, timber-beamed room that smelled faintly of vinegar, which reminded Rose of the scent of her childhood home after her mum had given it a good cleaning. Rose sat on a sofa, next to Glenna, while Fergus settled down in a leather wingback chair.

"Mabel is in the garden," Glenna said.

Rose glanced to the window. Outside, a young girl, about the age of five, was waving a butterfly net. "She's beautiful."

"Aye," Fergus said. "Spitting image of Muriel when she was a wee child."

Glenna placed her palms together, as if she were about to pray. "You mentioned on the telephone that you worked with Muriel."

"Yes," Rose said. "We worked together on a confidential war assignment. I've sworn an oath of secrecy, but I will tell you everything I can without breaking my pledge to Britain."

"We'd be grateful for anything you can tell us," Fergus said.

For the next hour, Rose shared bits and pieces—avoiding details that would break her oath of secrecy—about a secret European war assignment that led to their capture and imprisonment in Ravensbrück Concentration Camp.

"Oh, my Lord," Glenna said, her voice dropping to a whisper.

Rose touched Glenna's hand, her fingers trembling. "Muriel smuggled me food, and she saved my life."

Glenna nodded, as if she were reflecting on Rose's words.

Fergus scooched onto the sofa and placed his arm around his wife. "How did she die?" he asked, looking at Rose.

Glenna sniffed and wiped her eyes.

"Typhus," Rose said, deciding that it wasn't necessary to include the details of Muriel and the infirm patients, who were stolen from their beds. Her heart ached. "She was the most courageous woman I have ever met."

Fergus, tears forming in his eyes, kissed the top of his wife's head.

"When she was ill, she asked me to write a letter," Rose said, retrieving an envelope from her purse. "She loved you both very much, and she hoped that this letter might someday help Mabel understand why her mum decided to leave her to serve Britain." She handed the letter to Glenna.

Glenna opened the envelope and unfolded the paper. "I need my glasses," she said, a warble in her voice.

Fergus retrieved her eyeglasses from a wooden stand.

Rose, her stomach in knots, sat idle while Glenna and Fergus read the letter.

"Thank you," Glenna said, tears falling down her cheeks. She carefully folded the paper and placed it into the envelope.

Fergus rubbed his eyes, and then turned to Rose. "Would you like to meet Mabel?"

"I would love to," Rose said.

"Would you like to read the letter to her?" Glenna asked.

Rose paused, surprised by the gesture. "Yes, assuming Mabel is okay with me reading it to her. But are you sure?"

"Without you," Fergus said, "Muriel's letter would not have made it home to Mabel. I think my daughter would have wanted you to read it to her."

Rose nodded, hoping she could gather the nerve to read Muriel's words aloud. She stood and followed Glenna and Fergus into the garden. Although the space was small and confined by a head-high stone wall, it was filled with loads of roses, hellebores, dahlias, tulips, and sweet peas. And between the rows of flowers was a winding flagstone path, creating a Lilliputian labyrinth.

"Mabel," Glenna said. "I'd like for you to meet a friend of your mum."

Mabel, who was eyeing a fluttering white butterfly, lowered her net and ran to them.

She looks like Muriel, Rose thought. *Same eyes and wavy brown hair, and she's tall for a five-year-old.*

"This is Rose," Glenna said to Mabel.

Mabel fidgeted with her butterfly net. "Hi."

"Hello," Rose said.

"Mabel is five," Fergus said.

"I'm nearly six," Mabel said, stretching her back.

"Indeed," Fergus said, smiling.

"You knew my mum?" Mabel asked, looking at Rose.

Rose nodded.

Mabel paused, twirling the wooden handle of her net between her hands. "Do you want to help me catch butterflies?"

"That would be splendid," Rose said.

"Your granny and I are going inside to prepare lunch," Fergus said. "We'll call when it's ready."

"Okay," Mabel said, galloping toward a rose bush.

Rose joined Mabel, and for several minutes they spoke little, other than announcing the sight of ladybugs and butterflies. She suspected that Mabel might not be ready to have the letter read to her. And if so, she'd simply leave it with her grandparents, for when the time was right. But Mabel surprised her when she dropped her net and sat on a flagstone.

"What was my mum like?" she asked, looking at Rose.

Rose sat beside her and folded her arms around her knees. "She was lovely. Brave. Honest. Athletic. Smart. Kind. Sweet. And she loved you very much."

"Granny and Granda say that she's in heaven. They cry sometimes." Mabel fiddled with her shoelace. "Sometimes, I cry, too."

Rose swallowed. "It's okay to feel sad."

Mabel nodded, as if she'd been told the same thing by her grandparents. "Granny says I look like my mum."

"I agree," Rose said.

"She's always telling me that I'm going to be a skinny malinky longlegs like my mum."

Rose smiled. "Your mum told me the same thing when she showed me a picture of you as a toddler."

Mabel's eyes widened. "She did?"

Rose nodded. She glanced to her purse, placed on the ground. "Before your mum died, she asked me to deliver a letter to you." She retrieved the envelope. "I can read it to you now, or you can have your grandparents read it to you later."

"Please read it," Mabel said.

She removed the paper, held it so Mabel could see the lettering, and read.

> *Mabel, my dear sweet lamb,*
>
> *I suppose you have many emotions flowing through you, and I can't begin to imagine what you must be feeling by the news that I'm gone. I'm sorry that I had to die when you were a wee child, and I hope that you'll someday forgive me for departing so soon.*
>
> *Leaving you to join the war was the hardest decision I've ever had to make. I did it so you, and generations of children, will have the chance to live in a world free from dictators.*

Mabel tugged on Rose's sleeve. "What's a dictator?"

"It's like an evil king," Rose said, struggling not to cry.

"Aye," Mabel said.

Rose took a deep breath and continued reading.

> *I promise you that I did everything I could to stay alive. I regret not knowing you for longer, my sweet lamb, but it wasn't to*

be. Please know that you've created an indelible mark on my heart that will go with me to heaven. Being your mum has made my life complete, and I'm deeply grateful to you for bestowing on me the gift of motherhood.

Please mind your Granny and Granda. They were lovely parents for me, and I have complete confidence that they will do a splendid job raising you to be a kind and gentle soul. I'm so proud of you, Mabel. Grow up knowing that your mum loves you, more than you will ever know.

Forever and always,
Mum

"I love you, too, Mum," Mabel whimpered.

Rose, her vision blurred by tears, fumbled to fold the paper and place it into the envelope.

Mabel leaned in, resting her head against Rose's shoulder.

Rose drew a deep, shaky breath. She wrapped an arm around Mabel, and together they wept.

Chapter 59

Paris, France—August 14, 1945

Lazare, sitting at the same desk where his papa had once worked as journalist for *La Chronique* newspaper, slid the carriage return lever of his typewriter and tapped the keys. A new prosthetic, used for tasks which required the aid of missing fingers, lay on the side of the desk. His words-per-minute pace, although not fast, was respectable, taking into account a missing thumb and forefinger. The article he was drafting on the Vél' d'Hiv police roundup—which would be viewed by some as controversial, considering his slant on the complicit role that the French police played in the raid—was due in the printing department in less than an hour. Images of Maman and Papa flared inside his brain. He glanced to the clock hanging on his office wall and resumed pecking on the keys, determined to never let the victims of the Vél' d'Hiv roundup—thirteen thousand Parisian Jews, including over four thousand children, who were shipped in cattle cars to Auschwitz concentration camp for their mass murder—ever be forgotten.

Lazare had survived the RAF bombing raid on Amiens Prison due to the heroism of two prisoners, whom Lazare had freed from their cells a moment before the blast. The prisoners, avoiding German bullets and RAF bombs, had pulled Lazare out of the debris and dragged him through a hole in the prison wall. He woke hours later inside the sanctuary of a root cellar owned by an elderly farmer who was sympathetic to the French Resistance. Sharp pain pierced his pelvis and legs. "They're broken," a prisoner had said, kneeling next to Lazare. Concussed and unable to raise his head, Lazare lowered a hand to find his hip shattered. For two days, he hid in the cellar without medical care, other than splints made from sticks and rags, until the farmer located Claudius.

Claudius smuggled Lazare and the prisoners to Valmondois, where they hid in the abandoned granary. The prisoners, preferring to flee farther from Paris, left within days. But Lazare stayed in Claudius's care. Because the hospitals were controlled by the Germans, Claudius arranged for a Parisian doctor and nurse, who set up a makeshift surgical room in the granary, to fix Lazare's broken bones. He underwent two surgeries, one in the granary to stabilize his bones, and another six months later in a hospital—after Paris was liberated—to insert more screws, wire, and plates to his femurs and pelvis. After months of excruciating physical therapy, he regained his ability to stand and walk with the aid of metal leg braces—worn under his trousers—and forearm crutches, which gave him the appearance of someone disabled by polio. Despite his impairment, he was grateful to have survived, especially when he learned from Claudius that Rose was the catalyst for the RAF bombing on the prison. He didn't mind moving as slow as a sloth, a gnawing ache in his bones, or the cumbrous equipment required to enable him to walk. It was Rose's capture that had broken his heart. And the passing of months without knowing if she was dead or alive only exacerbated his sorrow.

It was different with Lazare's parents. When he'd learned—from one of the few survivors of the Vél' d'Hiv roundup—that his parents had been sent to Auschwitz, the Jewish extermination camp, he slowly came to accept that he'd never see them again. But with Rose, he was unable to obtain any leads on where she might have been taken. He'd written, telephoned, and telegrammed numerous consulates and embassies, as well as the British Services, all to no avail. And seven months ago, when he was well enough to work, he joined the newspaper, where he leveraged media sources to inquire into what had happened to Rose. He uncovered a few clues, most of which indicated that many of the captured female SOE agents were sent to either Dachau, Natzweiler-Struthof, or Ravensbrück concentration camps. Many of the female SOE agents in Dachau and Natzweiler-Struthof, both liberated by US Army forces, were rumored to have been killed. But gaining details on any prisoner who had been sent to Ravensbrück was nearly impossible, considering the camp was liberated by the Red Army, and its territory was now in the hands of the Soviets. It might be months or even years, Lazare believed, before he learned what might have happened to Rose. Undeterred, he continued his inquiries, enlisting the help of his well-connected friend, Claudius. And each day, he prayed that she was alive.

Lazare finished typing his article and slid the paper from the roller. As he scanned over the piece, a knock came at the door.

"Come in," Lazare said.

Claudius entered and closed the door.

"*Bonjour*," Lazare said, picking up a telephone receiver. "It's good to see you. I was about to call the printing department to pick up a piece. If you give me a moment, it'll give us time to visit."

"It can wait," Claudius said.

Lazare lowered the telephone back to its cradle.

"I've come from seeing my sister, Marcelline."

A flash of the nurse, who'd gained access to the Vélodrome d'Hiver and delivered his parents' last message, filled Lazare's head. Marcelline, clever like her brother, had talked her way out of her arrest during the collapse of the Parisian SOE and French Resistance networks. "How is she?" Lazare asked.

"She's well." Claudius took a seat across the desk from Lazare, slid his beret from his head, and grinned. "Rose is alive."

Lazare's heart leaped. "*Dieu merci!*" He struggled to stand, forgetting his crutches, and fell back into his seat. "Where is she?"

"London," Claudius said.

Tears of joy flooded Lazare's eyes. "How did you find her?"

"Marcelline helped me contact European Red Cross units," Claudius said. "Rose was in a Swedish Red Cross hospital. And now she's home." He pulled a piece of paper from his pocket and slid it to Lazare. "Before Rose left the hospital, she provided them with her contact information in London. It's an address for a woman named Lucy."

Lazare stared at the paper. His chest swelled with happiness.

"Perhaps I should leave and allow you to make arrangements to contact her," Claudius said.

Lazare's elation faded. He lowered the paper to his desk and glanced at his crutches. "I'm not going to see her."

Claudius raised his brows. "What do you mean?"

"There are no words that can express my gratitude for your help in finding Rose. But I do not plan to see her."

"Because of your disability?"

His question stung Lazare. "The doctor believes it's only a matter of time before I'm confined to a wheelchair." *I will not do that to her.*

Claudius rubbed his head, as if he were trying to absorb what he'd heard. "Have you considered that she might believe that you were killed in the Amiens Prison air raid? Do you want her to live a life of guilt, believing that a mission she masterminded led to your death?"

"*Non,*" Lazare said, a pang piercing his stomach. "But I also don't want her to blame herself for my condition. She saved my life, and many others who were condemned to be executed."

"Then go to London and tell her." Claudius stood and placed his beret on his head. "The next time I see you, I hope that she is with you." He turned and left.

Lazare's heart and mind were torn. He wanted to find Rose, hold her in his arms, and never let her go. Equally, he wanted what he believed to be the best for her, even if it meant that he would not be part of her life. For hours, he deliberated over what to do. Long after the employees of the newspaper had gone home, he took out a piece of paper and began to write.

CHAPTER 60

WESTERHAM, ENGLAND—AUGUST 16, 1945

Rose, wearing a navy dress borrowed from Lucy, left the apartment building and waited on the sidewalk. Anticipation buzzed in her belly. She checked her watch, and then retrieved a telegram from her purse.

Rose Teasdale is hereby summoned to attend a private assemblage for recognition of duty. At 2:00 p.m. on 16th August 1945, a chauffeur will arrive to transport you to the reception.

No address and no names, Rose thought. *It must be the discreet ceremony to honor the Conjurer network that Captain Carter had mentioned when I arrived at RAF Tempsford.*

As she placed the telegram into her purse, a sedan pulled to the curb and stopped.

The driver, wearing a striped gray suit, got out of the vehicle. "Miss Teasdale?"

"Yes," Rose said.

"Good afternoon," he said, tipping his cap. "I'm Archibald, your chauffeur." He helped her into the back seat, and then took his place behind the wheel.

"Where are we going?" Rose asked.

"Westerham." He pressed the accelerator and pulled away.

"In Kent?"

He nodded. "We'll arrive in an hour."

Rose, preparing for a long drive to the English countryside, rolled down her window and leaned back in her seat. A warm breeze ruffled her hair. *Who will attend? Captain Carter? SOE leaders?* Soon, her mind drifted to her recent visit to Edinburgh.

She'd felt immense relief and honor by delivering Muriel's message to Mabel. *Muriel would be so proud of her sweet, bonnie child*, Rose had thought while meeting with her in the garden. If she were fortunate to someday have a daughter, Rose wished that she'd be precisely like Mabel. But her Lazare was gone, and she couldn't begin to imagine creating a life without him. Not yet. Perhaps, not ever. She'd left Muriel's family, promising to return to visit them soon. But delivering Muriel's message had fulfilled merely half of the promises that she'd made to her fallen SOE agents. *When I return to Lucy's flat, I'll contact Felix's wife, Harriet.*

An hour later, the chauffeur veered the vehicle into a gated driveway of a palatial brick manor. The house, which was partially wrapped in lush hillside gardens, was situated on a large parcel of land.

"What is this place?" she asked.

"Chartwell."

Chartwell? Where have I heard that name?

The chauffer exited the vehicle and opened Rose's door. "I'll remain here and will take you home after you're finished."

Rose nodded. As she approached the entrance, a slender thin-haired man, who appeared to be a servant, given his black tie and tailed jacket, appeared in the doorway.

"Welcome to Chartwell, Miss Teasdale," he said.

"Thank you," she said.

"Follow me, please." He left the doorway and walked along a stone path. "It's a lovely day. You'll be seated outside."

Rose followed him around the house until they reached the entrance to a garden.

The man stopped and gestured for Rose to proceed. "Good day, Miss Teasdale." He turned and left.

Rose gazed over the rolling property. *Fifty acres? One hundred acres?* Several lakes were covered with brushwood, as if the owner had attempted to camouflage the estate from Luftwaffe air raids. She entered a narrow garden path, which was bordered by overgrown rosebushes and shrubs. *Even grand places like this have endured a bit of neglect from the war,* she thought, stepping over sprawling vines.

At the center of the garden was a small table. Seated in a chair was a man wearing a blue coverall and a felt hat. *A gardener? Where is Captain Carter?* A unique scent of burning cigar tobacco pervaded her nose, resurrecting visions of the underground war rooms. Her pulse quickened.

"Good afternoon, Miss Teasdale," a staunch voice said.

Rose froze. "Prime Minister?"

Winston Churchill stood from his chair and greeted her with a handshake. "I am no longer prime minister."

A flash of last month's shocking election results—in which the Labour Party won a landslide victory and appointed Clement Attlee to be prime minister—filled Rose's head. Her face flushed. "I'm deeply sorry, sir."

"No need for an apology," he said.

"I guess I was expecting—" She swallowed, attempting to hide her bewilderment.

"Someone else?"

"Yes, sir."

A smile formed on Churchill's face. He gestured to the table, which contained a pot of tea, crumpets, assorted small sandwiches, and a bottle of Pol Roger champagne. "Would you like to join me?"

"With pleasure, sir."

"Do you prefer tea or champagne?" he asked.

She sat, clasping her purse to her tummy. *I could really use a drink.* "Champagne."

Churchill poured two glasses and handed one to Rose.

She squeezed the stem, attempting to steady her hand.

"To victory," he said, clinking her glass.

Rose sipped, tasting the dry, grapefruit-like flavor of the champagne.

"How do you like it?" he asked.

"It's splendid, sir." Her mind raced with what to say. She glanced over the estate, which provided a vast view over the Weald of Kent. "Your home is lovely."

"Thank you," he said. "The war has taken a toll on its upkeep. It will take toil and sweat to return Chartwell to its original grandeur."

Rose nodded.

Churchill slid a tray of food to her.

Feeling obligated to eat, she selected a crumpet and nibbled.

Churchill took a gulp of champagne. "I assume you are wondering why I've summoned you."

"I am, sir."

Churchill's eyes met with hers. "On behalf of the British Empire, French Republic, Special Operations Executive, and Allied forces, I extend our immense gratitude to you for your gallant service. In spite of all terror, fury, and might of the enemy, you endured and surmounted them all."

Images of her torture flooded her brain. Her breath turned shallow.

"You displayed heroic resistance," Churchill said. "Despite the cost and agony of your journey, you have conducted your duties admirably, and with the highest moral conviction."

"Thank you, sir."

Churchill paused, clasping his hands. "Please accept my deepest sympathy in your most sorrowful loss of Conjurer and Sporran."

Felix and Muriel. She nodded, fighting back tears.

"As you may already be aware, the leadership of British Services and SOE are undergoing swift change. Records of confidential missions, as well as the brave souls who conducted them, are categorized by sensitivity." He retrieved his cigar from an ashtray and took a drag. "I regret that the story of your valor is classified as top secret, the highest level of classification."

Rose, attempting to quell her nerves, took a swig of champagne. "How long, sir?"

"The identity of Dragonfly and the Conjurer network will remain classified for one hundred years, perhaps indefinitely."

She slumped her shoulders.

Churchill, his eyes filled with determination, leaned forward. "The request and the true purpose of Operation Jericho will remain a secret; however, your courageous acts will forever burn in the hearts of our people."

"I wish things could be different," Rose said. "Not for me, but for my fellow SOE agents who sacrificed their lives."

"So do I," Churchill said, his voice sincere.

"May I ask you a question?" she asked.

"By all means," he said.

"Why did you choose to meet with me?"

"You suffered severely, Miss Teasdale, and I am forever indebted to you for your service." Churchill took a sip from his glass. "Furthermore, I am the one to thank, or to blame, for your SOE recruitment."

Rose straightened her spine. "Joining the SOE was voluntary. Hitler threatened our country's survival, and I chose to fight."

"Your parents and your brother would have been proud of you," Churchill said.

You remember them. Thankfulness swelled inside her.

He tapped ash from his cigar. "May I ask you a question?"

"Of course."

"Did you really pedal a bicycle two hundred miles through German-occupied France to obtain a wireless transmitter?"

"Yes," Rose said. "However, that was the journey to Montluçon. Including the return trip, it was almost four hundred miles."

Churchill smiled. "Well done, Miss Teasdale."

Rose nodded, and then picked at her crumpet.

He finished his drink. "Do you like goldfish?"

"Sir?" Rose asked, surprised.

"Goldfish," he repeated.

"Indeed, sir."

"Follow me," Churchill said, retrieving a walking stick. He led her from the garden to a small pond, which was free from brushwood, unlike the lakes on the property. From under a wooden bench, he retrieved a tin can and handed it to Rose.

Rose glanced inside the tin, which contained a tarnished spoon and wriggling larvae. Her eyes widened.

"Aristocratic maggots from Yorkshire," Churchill said.

"Oh," Rose said, attempting to hide her aversion to writhing grubs.

"They are for my darlings." Churchill tapped his stick on the paved path and pointed. "See?"

Rose gazed at the pond. Water rippled.

"They can hear me." Churchill rapped his stick on the ground.

Several Golden Orfe, pale yellow in color, with streaks of orange and gold, came to the surface. Some of the goldfish, Rose estimated, were over a foot in length.

"They're magnificent," she said.

"There were many more fish before the war," Churchill said. "They were decimated by otters, and I'm working to restock the pond."

"They're quite beautiful," she said, carefully making her way to the water's edge.

Churchill motioned to the can.

Using the spoon, Rose tossed maggot larvae into the water.

The goldfish, their mouths wide, raised their heads and swallowed the food.

Rose smiled.

"Feeding goldfish is quite meditative," Churchill said. "It is here where I reflect on the past and contemplate the future."

Rose, feeling honored to be invited to Churchill's privy pond, tossed another scoop of food.

Goldfish gobbled.

Churchill grinned.

For the next hour, they sat on the bench, taking turns feeding Golden Orfe. They spoke nothing further of the war, nor did they discuss what tomorrow might bring. When their time came to an end, Churchill walked her to the automobile, where they said their goodbyes. As the chauffeur drove away, Rose peered through the rear window and watched Churchill disappear from sight. A mixture of gratefulness and melancholy filled her body. *We will never see each other again.*

CHAPTER 61

LONDON, ENGLAND—AUGUST 21, 1945

Rose, sitting on the spare bed of Lucy's apartment, folded a stack of clothing and placed it into a suitcase. Anxious to return to France, she closed the lid and fumbled to secure the latches. *One more promise to fulfill.*

She'd spent the past few days reflecting on her meeting with Churchill. She was enormously grateful for his time, recognition, and words of comfort. Although she understood the reasons why the government classified the Conjurer network as top secret, she was saddened to know that Muriel and Felix's stories, as well as her own, would remain unrevealed for at least a century. *For the rest of my life, the Conjurer network will be a phantom.* Rather than dwell upon decisions that were out of her control, she resolved to expend her energy toward emotional healing and creating a new life. She suspected that Churchill, who was no longer prime minister, was also planning his future but on a much grander scale. Therefore, immediately upon her return from Chartwell, she telegrammed Felix's wife, Harriet, and scheduled a date to visit her in Saintes, France.

As Rose carried her suitcase to the foyer, the door to the apartment opened and Lucy entered holding an envelope decorated with ink and postage stamps. "You received a letter in the post. It's from France."

Rose sighed, wondering if Felix's wife had written to cancel her visit, and why she'd chosen to use the post rather than a telegram on such short notice. She took the envelope, which had no return address, feeling grateful that it had arrived before she embarked on her trip. But the Paris postage caused her to freeze, and the unique handwriting, identical to the numerous dead drop communications she'd received as a courier, turned her legs weak. Her hands trembled. She shuffled to the kitchen table and slumped into a chair.

"What's wrong?" Lucy sat beside Rose and placed a hand on her shoulder. "You're shaking."

Rose stared at the handwriting. "I think it's from someone I thought was—" She swallowed her words, struggling to come to terms with the realization that it was Lazare's handwriting and not her imagination.

"Do you need some privacy?"

"No," Rose said. "Please stay."

Lucy, as if she could read Rose's mind, retrieved a butter knife from a kitchen drawer and gave it to her.

Rose, her heart pounding, carefully cut open the flap. She slid out the letter, unfolded the paper, and glanced at the signature. Her eyes flooded with tears. "He's alive!"

"Who?" Lucy asked, her eyebrows raised.

"Lazare, a man that I'd met in France," Rose said, blinking away tears. "I'd thought he'd died in the war."

"Oh, my!" Lucy gasped.

Rose took a deep breath and wiped her eyes.

> *My Dearest Rose,*
> *I pray that this letter finds you well. I am overwhelmed with bliss from the news of your survival, delivered from our dear friend, Claudius.*

Rose's chest fluttered with delight. *Claudius is alive, too!*

> *Words cannot express my gratitude to you for saving my life. Claudius informed me of your courage to free the prisoners in Amiens. If it wasn't for your valiant efforts, over one hundred members of the Resistance, including myself, would have been shot.*

I'm deeply sorry that you were captured. I wish there was something that I could have done to prevent the network collapse. I cannot begin to imagine what you must have gone through during your interrogations and imprisonment. It saddens me to think that they might have hurt you. I pray that any wounds you might have incurred will vanish as you begin a new life.

Regrettably, I have no news on Muriel and Felix. Perhaps you already know what has happened to them. I hope that someday I'll learn of their survival. There isn't a day that goes by that I do not think about you, and the heroism of your compatriots to liberate France. I will forever be indebted to your selfless acts of gallantry to free our homeland from Nazi oppression.

Flashes of Muriel and Felix filled her brain. She took in a deep breath and continued reading.

After my escape, Claudius and I hid in Valmondois, where we continued our resistance until the Libération de Paris. *Last year, I returned home and began working as a journalist. I hope that my words can honor the stories of the brave liberators and innocent victims, so that their noble sacrifices will always be remembered.*

You're a journalist, just like your papa, Rose thought. *Your parents would be so proud of you.*

Much has changed since Victory Day. There is no easy way for me to tell you this, but I feel that you must know that the course of my life has changed over the past eighteen months. The comfort we shared during the war was sublime. Please know that I have no regrets, and I will forever cherish our time together. But with the liberation, and the passing of time, I've come to believe that we are not right for each other.

Rose's shoulders slumped. Her mouth turned dry.

Perhaps this is of little importance to you, as I assume you are well on your way to rebuilding a new life in London. You are a

remarkable woman, Rose. I'll remember you always, and I wish
you a long and happy life.
  With all my friendship,
  Lazare

Tears streamed down Rose's cheeks. "It doesn't matter. He's alive, and that's all that's important."

"Are you okay?" Lucy asked.

Rose, despite feeling both elated and gutted, nodded and slid the letter to Lucy.

"Are you sure you want me to read this?"

"Yes," Rose said. "I'm tired of keeping secrets. Besides, it's more personal in nature than of confidential military intelligence, and I don't think I can endure this on my own."

"All right." Lucy read the letter, and then placed it on the table. "Bollocks," she said, her voice dropping to a whisper.

Rose swallowed her apprehension. And for the next hour, she told Lucy—without disclosing any confidential SOE information—about her time in German-occupied Paris, and how she met a member of the French Resistance named Lazare.

"My God," Lucy said, pushing up her eyeglasses on the bridge of her nose.

Rose expected Lucy to be upset. Bemused. Perhaps even slighted by the fact that she'd hidden so much information from her. But Lucy surprised her.

"Were you fond of him?" Lucy asked.

Rose nodded. "I thought he felt the same way about me. But maybe we were merely two people seeking comfort from the duress of the war."

Lucy ran a finger over the edge of the table. "Did you love him?"

She paused, surprised by Lucy's unvarnished truth, and then nodded.

"Will you write Lazare?"

Hearing his name caused Rose's stomach to ache. "No." *He's chosen a new life without me.*

Lucy squeezed Rose's hand. "Your secret is safe with me. I'll never tell a soul."

"I know," Rose said. "I trust you."

"I must say," Lucy said, grinning, "you are by far the pluckiest woman I've ever met."

Rose forced a smile and placed the letter into the envelope.

"Maybe you could delay your trip," Lucy said, glancing at Rose's suitcase. "I'll call off ill from work, and we'll have few days of fun."

"Thank you," Rose said. "But despite my weepy appearance, I could not have received more splendid news. My friends, Lazare and Claudius, are alive."

"Very well," Lucy said.

Rose stood, her knees a bit dodgy, and placed the letter in her purse. She hugged Lucy. "I'll be back—well before your baby is delivered. I promise."

"I hope so," Lucy said, squeezing her. "I'm counting on you to wash the nappies."

Rose chuckled, briefly lifting the flurry of emotions that was ravaging her heart. She picked up her suitcase and left, her mind reeling from Lazare's letter. As she began her journey to visit Felix's wife, she hoped that she'd be able to fight her internal compass, the one that pointed to her true north—Paris. Her train trip would take her through Gare du Nord train station, and she prayed that she'd have the resolve to not disembark from her carriage.

CHAPTER 62

SAINTES, FRANCE—AUGUST 23, 1945

On Rose's train journey from Calais to Saintes, France, she read Lazare's letter over and over. More than anything, she was thankful that Lazare was alive. But with each viewing of his words, her jubilation slowly turned to heartache. *He doesn't want to see me. Our time together meant little to him.*

The most distressing part of the trip was when the train stopped briefly in Paris. Passengers shuffled in and out of the carriage. Flashes of her torture by the SD on Avenue Foch filled her head, turning her blood cold. She slumped in her seat, attempting to block out the memories of Wehrmacht patrols, starving Parisians, and the collapse of the SOE network. And now, somewhere in Paris, Lazare was creating a new life without her. She fought the urge to flee the train and see him. *But what would I say? He's already made his intentions perfectly clear.*

Arriving in Gare de Saintes train station, Rose was met by Felix's wife, Harriet, a willowy British woman in her late forties with a raspy timbre in her voice. Harriet greeted Rose with a huge hug, thanked her profusely for coming to see her, and then drove her to Felix's family vineyard. They sat in a courtyard, where they ate assorted cheeses, cured meats, fruit, and drank glasses of cognac.

"I was with Felix when he died," Rose said, the alcohol doing little to loosen the knot in her stomach. "He wanted me to tell you that he loves you, and how proud he is of Mathieu for joining the French army."

"Thank you." Harriet stared into her glass of cognac. "Mathieu did not survive his German capture."

"I'm sorry," Rose said.

Harriet nodded.

As they carried on their conversation, it soon became clear to Rose that Harriet speculated that her husband had been a spy for the British. But Harriet didn't press Rose for details. Instead, Harriet preferred to tell Rose stories about how she, a British woman, fell in love with Felix, a French Grand Prix race car driver. And how they chose to live on Felix's family estate to raise their only son, Mathieu, who dreamed of someday running the family vineyard.

Rose enjoyed hearing Harriet's stories, which she told by flamboyantly waving her hands like an orchestra conductor. Harriet came from a humble background, a family of sheep farmers in England, while Felix's family, which owned a vineyard and cognac distillery, had significant wealth. But much of the family money was gone, and the vineyard, which had been billeted by German officers during the occupation, was in shambles.

"The bloody Germans drank all the wine and nearly all the cognac, and they set fire to many of the grapevines when they fled," Harriet said.

Rose shook her head in disgust. "Will you go back to England?"

"No," Harriet said. "I'll rebuild. Years from now, this vineyard will once again flourish."

"Felix and Mathieu would be proud of you," Rose said.

Harriet smiled and poured more cognac. "To freedom," she said, raising her glass.

Rose, her head buzzing from the liquor, tapped her glass to Harriet's. She admired the woman's dedication to restore the family vineyard on her own. As the afternoon progressed, Harriet insisted that Rose stay for several days.

"Think of it as a holiday, except that I'll be putting you to work in the vineyard, and I'll be paying you with food and cognac," Harriet said.

Rose had planned on staying a day or two. But Lucy was still several weeks away from delivery, and most of all, she dreaded the train ride that would take her through Paris. *A few extra days might allow me to make plans for an alternate route home, perhaps a long boat ride from Bordeaux to England.*

Rose sipped her cognac, a burn flowing down her throat and into her belly. "Yes, a holiday working on your vineyard would be lovely."

CHAPTER 63

PARIS, FRANCE—SEPTEMBER 2, 1945

Rose's breath quickened as the train chugged into the Gare du Nord train station. She opened her purse and touched Lazare's letter. She wiggled her toes inside her shoes, attempting to dispel her unease. *I'll simply say goodbye, and I'll leave on the evening train.*

Her time with Harriet had done wonders to clear her head. Tending to the ravaged grapevines—a variety of Ugni Blanc, Folle Blanche, Colombard, and Sémillon—was both meditative and therapeutic. But when she wasn't working the land or washing old bottles in the distillery, her mind was on Lazare. *He views our affair as merely an act of seeking comfort in the war. Perhaps he's found someone else. Regardless, he doesn't feel the same way I do.* And as her time in Saintes came to a close, she hadn't made plans to take an alternative route home, bypassing Paris. Instead, she decided to see him one last time, if only to create closure from the past.

Rose left the train station and made her way through the tenth arrondissement. The roasted scent of coffee and fresh baked pastries, drifting from a nearby café, filled Rose's nose. She walked along crowded sidewalks, absent Wehrmacht patrols and swastika flags. Although many of the storefronts were closed, with a few still containing ugly anti-Semitic graffiti, it appeared to Rose that Parisians were on their way to restoring their once-beautiful city.

Lazare's letter did not have a return address, nor could she recall the name of the newspaper where Lazare's papa had once worked, so she located a newsstand. She rummaged through the papers until she found a publication called *La Chronique*, which contained a headline article written by a journalist named Lazare Aron. Her pulse rate accelerating, she obtained directions to *La Chronique* from the newsstand attendant and left.

Twenty minutes later, she arrived at *La Chronique*, housed in a Lutetian limestone building. Her tummy fluttered with nervousness. *What will I say?* She took a deep breath and stepped inside to a frenzy of ringing telephones and tapping typewriters.

"May I help you?" a young female receptionist asked.

"*Bonjour*," Rose said, squeezing the handle of her suitcase. "I'm here to see Lazare Aron."

The receptionist's telephone rang. She picked up the receiver and cupped her hand over it. "Down the hall and on the left."

"*Merci*." Rose turned and walked down the hallway, overhearing two men discuss news of a Japanese surrender. She picked up her pace, anxious to reach Lazare's office before she lost her grit.

The door to his office was open. The sound of Lazare's voice triggered Rose's heart to thump against her ribcage. Her legs turned weak. She peeked inside and saw him sitting behind a massive double pedestal mahogany desk and speaking on the telephone. Except for full cheeks, no doubt due to better food, and neatly trimmed hair, he looked the same.

"Emperor Hirohito formally signed the agreement on Japan's surrender," Lazare said, holding the telephone receiver. "The hostilities in the Pacific are over. We'll have the details in tomorrow's newspaper."

The hair stood up on the back of Rose's neck. She mustered her nerve and knocked on the doorframe.

Lazare swiveled in his chair. His eyes widened, and then softened. He smiled and motioned with a hand to come in.

Rose, her breath stalling in her chest, approached the desk and lowered her suitcase.

"I need to go," Lazare said to the person on the telephone. "In the morning—" He extended a hand to Rose.

Rose clasped his fingers. Her skin tingled. She blinked her eyes, fighting back tears.

Lazare hung up the phone. Squeezing her hand, he stared at her.

"*Bonjour*," Rose said.

Remaining seated, he leaned forward and pulled her toward him.

Bending over the desk, she greeted him with a kiss on both cheeks.

"*S'il vous plaît*," he said, releasing her hand. "Have a seat."

Rose sat, the desk between them feeling like a wall. "I was traveling through Paris and couldn't resist seeing you."

"You look good," he said.

"You too," she said, a thorny awkwardness pricking at her stomach.

His smile faded as he rested his hands on a stack of papers. "You received my letter?"

"I did."

"I wish I had a better way of explaining why I—"

"There's no need to explain," she interrupted, desperately wanting to avoid rehashing the letter.

He paused, running a hand through his hair. "How are you?"

"Okay," she lied.

"I'm so sorry, about everything."

She nodded, suddenly feeling distant, despite sitting only a few feet away from him. She took a breath and blurted, "Muriel was killed by the SS in Ravensbrück Concentration Camp. Felix died from a gunshot wound as we fled the RAF raid on Amiens Prison. I thought you would want to know."

"Oh, *mon Dieu*." Lazare slumped his shoulders.

A gray-haired man carrying a manila folder rushed into the office. "This is the material you requested for your article. The printing department needs your finished piece within ninety minutes, if you want it to make the next print run."

Lazare nodded and took the folder, and the man abruptly left.

"My condolences," Lazare said. "Muriel and Felix were brave agents and friends. Neither I nor France will ever forget them." He took a deep breath and exhaled. "My apologies for the interruption. The office is in a frenzy. Japan officially signed the agreement of their surrender, and everyone is working to release details in the next newspaper edition."

"I understand." Rose, feeling as if she was impinging on his time, crossed her arms. *The war is over, and so are we.*

Lazare placed the folder on his desk. "Thank you for the Amiens Prison raid."

"Your gratitude should go to the RAF," Rose said.

"*Non*, Claudius told me what you did to facilitate the mission. If it wasn't for you—" The telephone rang.

Rose flinched.

"*S'il vous plaît, excusez-moi*," he said, picking up the receiver.

While Lazare carried on a conversation with someone about the details of the Japanese peace agreement, Rose tapped her foot against the floor, attempting to dispel her restlessness. She glanced to her suitcase. An urgency to leave rushed through her veins.

"Forgive me," Lazare said, hanging up the phone.

Rose looked into Lazare's dark-brown eyes. A flash of their night together. An image of his embrace. She buried her memories and said, "When you see Claudius, will you say hello for me?"

"I will," he said.

Rose looked at her watch, making no effort to read the time. "I should leave if I'm going to make my train."

Lazare's phone rang. He frowned, and then looked at Rose.

"You need to answer that," she said. "The world needs to know that the war in the Pacific is officially over."

Lazare placed a hand on the ringing phone, but didn't pick up the receiver. "It was wonderful to see you."

"You too," she said, struggling to hide her heartache.

"*Au revoir*, Rose." He lowered his eyes and picked up the receiver. "*Bonjour*. I was calling to verify a few things on Japan's agreement . . ."

"*Adieu*," Rose whispered. Dazed and gutted, she picked up her suitcase and left. Two streets away and unable to suppress her emotions any longer, she sat on a curb and cried.

CHAPTER 64

PARIS, FRANCE—SEPTEMBER 2, 1945

Lazare, his hands trembling, hung up the phone. He retrieved his crutches, slipped his forearms through the braces, and labored to stand. Shuffling to the window, a twinge shot through his femurs and pelvis. He stared through the glass, marred with dust and water stains, struggling to catch one last glimpse of her. Outside, pedestrians mingled over the sidewalk. He scanned the crowd until he found her, as she crossed the street and disappeared from view. Regret ravaged his soul. *I let her walk out of my life. What have I done?*

His vision blurred with tears. "It's for the best," he whispered, struggling to quell his remorse.

On seeing Rose, the woman who saved his life, it had taken every ounce of his will not to hold her in his arms and profess his true feelings. It was, and always would be, one of the hardest decisions he'd ever had to make. Above all else, he wanted what was best for her, even if it meant that he would endure a life of solitude. *I have to let her go. I'm broken. She deserves to be with someone who will not be a burden to her.*

As he adjusted his crutches, a pain flared through his legs. He took a deep breath and exhaled, attempting to dispel a tide of anguish flooding his chest.

His cherished memories of his time with Rose had enabled him to withstand his torture and imprisonment. *Without the hope of seeing her again, I would have died at the hands of my captors.* For the past two years, which had been the most dreaded days of his life, he didn't know whether she was dead or alive. Now, he was elated that Rose had survived the war, and that she would have a chance for a long and beautiful life, one in which she could build a family of her own. Yet, he was grief-stricken. He was no longer the able-bodied man he once was, and his dream of a future with her was gone.

Memories of their time together surged through his head. On the night of their transformer sabotage mission, she had bandaged his mauled hands with compassion and tenderness. The touch of her fingers sent butterflies through his stomach as he guided her through the secret passage of the catacombs. She showed boundless bravery when she pedaled her bicycle through German-occupied streets to deliver dead drop communications. She fought courageously to liberate France, and her tenacity to mastermind the Amiens Prison raid saved scores of French Resistance prisoners who were scheduled to be executed. He could still smell the scent of her hair as she nuzzled next to him, her breath flowing in gentle waves over his chest. How joyful he'd felt to wake next to her and realize, at that very moment, that he wanted to be with her forever.

Lazare gripped his crutches, struggling to bury the past. He was torn. His heart urged him to go after her. *It's not too late. She's headed to the train station.* But his brain prodded him to let her go. *She's better off without me.* He stared at his legs, crooked and held together with screws and wire. *You'll soon be in a wheelchair,* his doctor's voice resounded in his head. The war had stolen everything—his parents, thousands of Parisian Jews, many of his friends, French Resistance comrades, his vitality, and, most of all, a life with the woman who had captured his heart.

A gray-haired man holding a stack of files poked his head into the office. "We're going to open champagne to celebrate the official end of the war. Want to join us?"

"*Non,*" Lazare said, staring out the window.

The man glanced at his watch. "Would you like me to deliver your piece on the Japanese surrender to the printing department?"

Lazare, fighting back tears, turned to him. "Please, give it to another journalist to finish."

The man raised his brows. "Are you okay?"

Lazare shook his head.

A champagne cork exploded. Cheers erupted in the hallway.

We won our freedom, Lazare thought, *but I lost the love of my life.* Heartbroken and devastated, he lumbered out of the building, his metal leg braces squeaking under his trousers.

CHAPTER 65

PARIS, FRANCE—SEPTEMBER 2, 1945

At the Gare du Nord train station, Rose, her spirit shaken and her eyes drained of tears, joined a crowd of people gathering for the train. Once in Calais, she'd need to take a ferry to Dover, England, and then travel by rail to London. But it was late, and she would no doubt miss the last ferry to cross the Channel. And for the moment, she cared little about her itinerary. All she could think about was Lazare. *Was your affection for me a manifestation of the war? Did you meet someone else? Were my treasured memories, created under the stress of working as an SOE courier, merely misshapen dreams?*

A whistle blew, wheels screeched over rails, and the train chugged to a stop. The engine hissed, the carriage doors opened, and the crowd entered, emptying the landing. Except for Rose. Despite being buried in an avalanche of despair, her heart was firmly planted in Paris. *I need to know precisely what happened between us, no matter how much the truth will sting.*

Rose reached *La Chronique* well after business hours. The building was dark except for an amber glow of a desk lamp in a second-story window. She rapped on the locked entrance door. *Please be here.* She pressed her ear to the door and heard nothing, except her thudding pulse. She pounded on the door until her knuckles turned raw. As she was about to give up, a deadbolt clicked. The door opened, revealing a man who appeared to be in the process of working on a printing press, given that his shirt sleeves were rolled up to his elbows, and his hands were stained with ink.

"*Bonsoir*," Rose said.

The man wiped his hands with a rag and frowned. "*Mademoiselle*, the office is closed."

"I'm sorry to disturb you." Rose peeked into the building. "Is Lazare Aron here?"

"*Non*," he said. "The journalists have left for the evening."

"Do you know where he is?"

The man shook his head and began to close the door.

Rose shot out her foot, blocking the door from closing. "I have an urgent package for him."

"I'll put it in his office," he said.

"*Non*," Rose said. "He needs it tonight."

"Either give it to me or come back tomorrow," he said, his voice impatient.

Rose's mind raced. "The package contains newly released documents on the Japanese peace agreement," she said, recalling Lazare's phone interruptions earlier in the afternoon.

The man tucked his rag into his pocket.

"*S'il vous plaît*," Rose said. "Lazare needs these documents this evening. I'd be happy to deliver them to his residence if you can provide me the address."

The man hesitated, rubbing stubble on his chin.

"The information is crucial," Rose said, raising her suitcase. "*La Chronique* will be the first to report the news, assuming you'll permit me to deliver the information to Lazare tonight."

The man eyed the luggage. "Wait here." He turned and disappeared down the hallway.

Is he going to ring Lazare? What if he doesn't want to see me? Rose's shoulder muscles tightened.

A moment later, the man returned. "He lives in Le Marais," he said, giving her a slip of paper.

Under the dull glow of a streetlamp, Rose glanced at the paper, which contained an address written in pencil. "*Merci*."

The man nodded and closed the door.

It would have been faster to take a taxi, but a thirty-minute walk would give her time to prepare for what she wanted to say. Her pace was slow, despite her drive to bring closure to her torment. Traveling along Rue d'Hauteville, she rehearsed her words over and over again. *Did you ever have feelings for me? Did our time together mean nothing to you? Have you created a new life? Did you meet someone else? What happened?*

As she neared the alley to Prosper's dead drop in Le Marais, her skin prickled with goose bumps. Visions of SD scouring the area in search of wireless transmissions swirled inside her head. A flash of Muriel's ransacked apartment. An image of Felix, handcuffed with blood smeared over his face, being dragged away by German soldiers. A cold chill shot through her body. She shuddered and quickened her pace, attempting to flee the past.

Minutes later, she found his ground-floor apartment located inside a narrow building on a cobblestone street. Her stomach churned with angst as she approached the door. The muted sound of tapping typewriter keys emanated from the apartment. *I can do this.* She gathered her courage and knocked.

"Come in!" Lazare shouted, still typing. "The door is open!"

Rose took a jagged breath and exhaled. She entered and gently closed the door behind her.

"Paulette, place the groceries in the kitchen," Lazare called. "I'll put them away."

Who is Paulette? Rose's chest ached, imagining him living with another woman. *Is he married? Engaged? I'm such a fool! If I leave now, he'll never know I was here.* She turned and clasped the doorknob. *But if I go, I'll never know for sure.*

Her limbs trembling, she put down her suitcase. She inched across a hallway and entered the living room, void of furniture, except a large oak desk, a few chairs, and a gilt-framed painting that she immediately recognized. *Arc de Triomphe.*

Lazare, seated at the desk with his head down and facing toward her, tapped the keys of a typewriter.

"It's me," Rose said, her voice faint.

The tapping ceased. Lazare, his eyes wide, looked up from his typewriter. "I thought you had a train to catch."

"I did." Rose stepped forward and noticed that Lazare's eyelids appeared a bit swollen and red. She paused, observing his subdued, fragile demeanor.

Lazare wiped his eyes. "Is everything all right?"

No, Rose thought. "We didn't get much of a chance to speak this afternoon."

"I'm sorry," he said. "The office was a bit hectic."

"Now that the war is officially over," Rose said, "maybe things will settle down."

"Perhaps." He gestured to a leather chair across from his desk. "Please, sit."

Rose folded her arms. "*Non, merci.* I can't stay."

He nodded.

She glanced at the picture on the wall. "Your *maman*'s painting is beautiful."

"I added a new frame." His lips formed a slight smile. "It looks far better in my apartment than the catacomb."

An image of sitting with him on a cot, deep within a secret subterranean chamber, flashed in her head. "I know how much her painting meant to you. I'm glad you were able to save it."

"*Merci.*"

"It was insensitive of me not to inquire about your parents this afternoon," Rose said. "Did you ever find out what happened to them?"

"They were sent to Auschwitz, the Jewish extermination camp," Lazare said, a doleful resonance in his voice. "They didn't make it out."

An ache twisted inside Rose's stomach. "I'm so sorry."

He fidgeted with a pen on his desk. "Is that why you came?"

"*Non*," she said. "I wanted to ask you if—" She swallowed a lump in the back of her throat. "Did our time together mean anything to you?"

"It did," he said, his eyes lowered.

"But it didn't matter enough," she said. "Your letter hurt me. After everything we've been through, you made no effort to see me."

"I'm sorry. Things have—" Lazare ran a hand through his hair.

"Tell me," Rose said.

He looked at her. "Things have changed."

He's found someone else. Rose felt like she was punched in the gut. She straightened her back, struggling to maintain her composure.

"I wish things could have been different," he said.

Me too. "I understand," she said, doing her best to hide her sorrow. "Much has happened over the past few years—for both of us."

"Far too much." Lazare clasped his hands together. "Are you all right?"

"Of course," she lied.

"I'm glad that it happened," Lazare said. "I have no regrets."

"Neither do I." Rose's chest tightened. "But I thought we had something more than two people merely seeking comfort from the war."

Lazare shifted in his seat.

"I thought we were friends."

"We are," Lazare said.

"It doesn't feel like it," she said. "I accept that you have a new life. I'm happy for you, but friends talk to each other. Friends care for each other. Friends take time for each other."

Lazare's shoulders slumped.

"We've endured so much. A war. Imprisonment. Torture. The death of our families." Her hands shot to her hips. Her pulse accelerated. "I'm disappointed that our time together didn't mean more to you."

"It does—"

"Then why were you so eager for me to leave this afternoon? You didn't even have the courtesy to walk me to the—" She froze. Her mouth turned dry.

He lowered his head.

As if by reflex, she maneuvered around the desk, and her eyes were drawn to metal crutches on the floor. Her heart sank.

Lazare swiveled his chair and faced her.

"Your legs," Rose said, her voice quavering.

Lazare retrieved his crutches.

"How were you hurt?" she cried.

Lazare labored to stand.

Her body trembled. "Was it the RAF raid?"

He shuffled to her, metal braces clinking on his legs.

Tears flooded her eyes. "I did this to you."

"*Non*." Lazare leaned forward on his crutches and clasped her hand. "You saved my life."

"I need to know what happened," she pleaded.

"All right," he said, his voice dropping to a whisper. He released her fingers, and then led her to the kitchen.

A moment later, they sat at a small wooden table with a freshly brewed pot of coffee. Her hand wavered as she stirred a spoonful of sugar into her cup.

"It's made with real coffee beans," Lazare said, as if to lighten the emotional weight of what he was about to reveal. "I hope you like it."

Rose nodded and glanced at his crutches propped against the wall. A wave of hopelessness washed over her. "Please, tell me everything."

Lazare took a deep breath and exhaled. After a long pause, he spoke. "In late December of 1943, while being held captive at Amiens Prison, all of the prisoners were forced to line up in the courtyard. Instead of roll call, a German officer stood on a podium and announced the names of over one hundred prisoners who were sentenced to be shot on February 19, 1944. Felix and I were on the list."

"Oh, *mon Dieu*," she whispered. "I cannot begin to imagine the distress you and the prisoners must have endured."

"No more than you suffered in Ravensbrück Concentration Camp," Lazare said. "I'm so sorry. I wish that there was something I could have done to prevent your capture."

An image of the crematorium chimney filled her head. A flash of human ashes, covering the ground like snow. Her stomach ached. "Please continue."

"On the day before the executions, a German guard was on the cellblock to permit prisoners one last walk in the courtyard. As he unlocked my cell door, the first RAF bomb struck the prison. The guard was stunned. I attempted to steal his key for the cellblock, but I was too weak to fight. Fortunately, two prisoners in an adjacent cell were able to kill the guard, otherwise I would have been shot."

Rose clenched her hands, digging her nails into her palms.

Lazare closed his eyes, sifting through his memories. "I tried to flee the cellblock, but a barrage of German gunfire prevented me from leaving the building." He cleared his throat. "That's when an RAF bomb struck the building. I lunged forward, attempting to avoid the blast, but I was buried in rubble."

Rose's vision blurred with tears.

He rubbed the rim of his cup with a finger. "Two prisoners pulled me out of the debris and dragged me through a hole in the prison wall. I woke up hours later inside a root cellar owned by a farmer who was sympathetic to the French Resistance. My hip and legs were crushed."

She wiped her eyes.

"We hid in the cellar for two days, until the farmer located Claudius, who smuggled me to an abandoned granary in Valmondois and arranged for a doctor and nurse to fix my broken bones. I underwent a second surgery after Paris was liberated."

"I did this to you," Rose said, her voice trembling.

"*Non.*" He gently clasped her hands. "You saved my life. If it wasn't for you, over one hundred men would have been executed."

Rose sniffed. A tear dropped onto his hand. He made no effort to wipe it away.

"I will be forever grateful for what you did," he said. "It must have taken immense courage and perseverance to influence British Services to conduct an RAF raid on a French prison." Tears formed in his eyes. He gently entwined his fingers with hers. "I'm alive because of you."

Rose's breath stalled in her chest.

He leaned close. "I—"

A knock came from the door.

Lazare exhaled. "That will be Paulette."

Girlfriend? Fiancée? Rose unlaced her fingers and slipped her hands away.

"I can ask her to come back later."

"*Non*," Rose said, wiping her cheeks. "I'd like to meet her."

He rubbed his eyes and called, "Come in."

The door opened and closed. Heels clicked against the hardwood floor. Rose squeezed her seat, bracing herself to meet the woman in Lazare's life.

An old woman, wearing a black scarf and carrying a bag with a baguette sprouting from the package, entered the kitchen. "*Bonsoir, Monsieur* Aron."

Rose's eyes widened.

"*Bonsoir*, Paulette," Lazare said. "May I pay you tomorrow for the groceries?"

"Of course," Paulette said, placing the bag on a counter.

"*Merci*," Lazare said. "Paulette, I'd like for you to meet my dear friend, Rose. We met during the war."

Rose stood. "It's nice to meet you," she said, attempting to conceal her surprise.

Paulette greeted Rose, exchanging a kiss on both cheeks.

"Rose and I haven't seen each other for quite some time," Lazare said. "My apologies for our tearful appearance."

"No need to be sorry," Paulette said. She turned to Rose. "I'm delighted to see him have a visitor. I tell him he works too much. Even when he's home, he's typing on his typewriter, all hours of the day and night."

"We have much to report in the newspaper," Lazare said.

"Our occupiers are gone," Paulette said. "It's time to savor our freedom."

"I couldn't agree more," Rose said.

Paulette smiled. "It's best that I leave, so you can catch up on lost time." She gave Lazare a motherly pat on the shoulder, and then left the apartment.

"I was expecting Paulette to be your—" Rose paused, feeling relieved, as well as a bit ashamed by her envy.

"Oh," Lazare said. "There's no one like that." He clasped his cup but made no effort to drink. "Paulette lives upstairs. With my long hours as a journalist, she's kind enough to pick up my food."

"She's sweet."

He nodded.

Rose pondered, although briefly, whether to sit or remain standing. Tension, which had been eased by Paulette's visit, flooded the room. Her eyes locked on the metal braces protruding from the cuffs of his pants. A pang pierced her sternum. "Does it hurt?"

Lazare ran his hands over his knees. "Not much."

"Truthfully?"

"It's not as bad as it looks," he said, his voice tentative.

Tears welled up in her eyes. "You said nothing in your letter about being injured. Why didn't you tell me?"

Lazare retrieved his crutches and hobbled to her. "I didn't want you to feel responsible for what happened to me."

"But I do."

He gently touched her arm. "I'm thankful to be alive. I wouldn't be here if it wasn't for you."

"You should have told me," she said. "I would have been here for you."

"I want what is best for you."

"What about my feelings?" She touched his maimed hand. "Don't I have a say in the matter?"

"I'm not the man I used to be," he said.

"You're still the same to me." She leaned against him, resting her head on his chest. "You gave me the strength to endure a concentration camp. My memories of you kept my dreams alive."

Tears filled Lazare's eyes. "I hoped and prayed that I'd see you again." His jaw quivered. "But I don't know how long I'll be able to walk."

"It doesn't matter to me," she cried. "You are what is best for me. Maybe I'm right for you."

Leaning on Rose, he dropped his crutches and wrapped her in his arms. He squeezed her tight. "I never stopped thinking of you."

"Nor I," she breathed. Tears streamed down her face. Waves of emotion flooded her body.

Together, they wept. The years between them melted away. He kissed her tears.

"There must be a reason we both survived." Rose tenderly touched his face and looked into his eyes. "Don't you believe in fate?"

EPILOGUE

PARIS, FRANCE—MAY 8, 1969

A soft patter of keys striking the inked-cloth ribbon emanated from Rose's antique Remington Noiseless typewriter. Beams of morning sunlight streamed through the balcony windows of her apartment in Saint-Germain-des-Prés, located in the sixth arrondissement. She finished the last line, pressed the carriage return lever, and slipped the paper from the roller.

"Finished," Rose whispered, placing the last page of her manuscript on the desk.

A blend of fulfillment and nostalgia stirred within her. It was fitting, she believed, to finish her book—telling of her role as an SOE courier, as well as documenting the atrocities she suffered in Ravensbrück Concentration Camp—on *La Fête de la Victoire*, a national holiday in France to mark the anniversary of the end of World War II in Europe. After years of laborious and heartrending work, the book was done.

She began work on the manuscript four years ago, upon returning from the state funeral of Sir Winston Churchill. With the exception of visits to see her dear friends Lucy and Jonathan, and their three children, Malcolm, Bridget, and Lynda, she seldom visited London. On a frigid day in January 1965, she waited in a line, which was over a mile long, for over three hours to enter Westminster Hall. Four somber guardsmen wearing full ceremonial uniforms stood vigil with their heads bowed. As she approached Churchill's coffin, which was draped in a Union Flag and surrounded by six tall amber candles, a memory of feeding his beloved goldfish flashed through her mind. She began to weep. *The identity of Dragonfly and the Conjurer network will remain classified for one hundred years, perhaps indefinitely,* Churchill's staunch yet compassionate voice chimed in her head. *The request and the true purpose of Operation Jericho will remain a secret; however, your courageous act will forever burn in the hearts of our people.*

The following day, Rose stood along the crowded funeral procession route, which traveled through Whitehall, Trafalgar Square, the Strand, Fleet Street, and up Ludgate Hill. Over a million people lined the streets of London, and the entire nation mourned the man who led them through the darkest of days. Rose prayed in silence as the gun carriage with Churchill's casket inched by. Sniffles and whimpers filled the air. *He's not merely the leader who saved Britain and, perhaps, the free world, he's the man who changed my life, forever.*

Returning home to Paris, Rose became determined to document the story of Conjurer, a subcircuit of the Physician network, which was classified by the British government as top secret. *When I'm gone,* Rose thought, *or when I'm no longer bound by an oath of secrecy, the world will know about the courageous sacrifices of Felix and Muriel, the atrocities that occurred in Ravensbrück Concentration Camp, and who instigated Operation Jericho.* She worked on the book in the early hours of the morning, before she went to work as an administrative assistant at the British embassy in Paris. On weekends, she hunkered away at her desk, revisiting the ghosts of the past and tapping away on her typewriter. And now, four years after she started, the book was finished.

Floorboards creaked in the hallway.

Rose stood.

"*Bonjour, ma chérie,*" Lazare said, peeking his head into the room.

Rose smiled. "I'm finally done."

Lazare grinned. He walked with his crutches to Rose. "I'm so proud of you," he said, hugging her.

She released him and looked into his eyes. "I couldn't have done it without you."

"That's sweet." He leaned in and kissed her. "But I believe you can accomplish anything you set your mind to."

She ran her fingers through Lazare's salt-and-pepper hair. *You always have a way of making me feel good about myself.*

"Have you decided what you want to do with the book?" he asked.

"I want to publish it, but my heart still feels a sense of duty. And it's difficult to disregard the potential ramifications of breaking my oath of secrecy." An image of Churchill, a cigar chomped between his molars, filled her head. "I believe that Churchill played a role in authorizing Operation Jericho, whether he wanted to prevent the execution of over one hundred French prisoners, or he thought the RAF raid on Amiens Prison would keep Hitler guessing as to where the invasion of France would take place. Either way, the mission saved my future husband."

Lazare smiled. "And our future children."

A swell of indebtedness filled Rose's chest.

Lazare had proposed to Rose less than a week after they re-united in Paris. A month later, they were married, and she moved into his apartment. Soon after, she was contacted by the British embassy in Paris to fill an administrative position. The ambassador claimed that Rose was highly recommended, but was unwilling to provide the source of the referral. Desperate for a job, she accepted, suspecting that the position was arranged by either Churchill or the SOE.

While Rose began what would be a long and rewarding career at the embassy, Lazare worked as a journalist at *La Chronique*. Although his primary assignment was to cover world events, he made it a personal pursuit to influence the French government to denounce its role in the Holocaust and the historical revisionism that denied France's culpability for the 1942 roundup of thirteen thousand Parisian Jews. For over two decades, the French government declined to apologize for the role of French policemen in the Vél' d'Hiv roundup, but Lazare never gave up his quest. "Someday," Lazare often said to Rose, "our president will acknowledge that the roundup was a crime committed by France."

It was Lazare's endless resolve, Rose believed, that also enabled him to walk. Over the past twelve years, he endured two more surgeries, one on his pelvis and another to his femur. At times, his pain was unbearable, especially during the winter. But he never complained. For twenty years, he proved his doctors wrong by delaying their prediction that he'd be confined to a wheelchair. Regardless of Lazare's affliction, it never slowed him down with helping raise their son, Charlie, and their daughter, Magda.

Charlie, named after Rose's fallen brother, was the oldest. A sensitive and clever boy, he adored visiting Lazare at the newspaper. Now in his final year of studies at the University of Paris, Charlie dreamed of becoming a journalist, just like his papa.

Magda, named in honor of Lazare's *maman*, was born two years after Charlie. A sweet, artistic child, Magda loved to paint and sculpt, often decorating the family apartment with watercolor paintings and clay sculptures of cats. Magda, who had grown into a beautiful young woman, was now studying at the École Nationale Supérieure des Beaux-Arts.

Although the children's grandparents perished in the war, Rose and Lazare's dear friend and former French Resistance comrade, Claudius, filled the void splendidly. After France's liberation, Claudius opened a café in Montparnasse, where he kept a private, small table in the kitchen for Magda and Charlie, where they congregated after school and on weekends. Magda and Charlie thought the world of Claudius. And Claudius treasured his time with the children, spoiling them with decadent pastries, hot chocolate, and gifts, much like a real grandparent would do.

"I have something for you," Lazare said.

Rose's eyes widened.

He reached into his pocket and placed a gold art nouveau dragonfly brooch in her hand.

"It's lovely," Rose said, running a finger over a pearl embedded in the piece.

He pinned it on her jacket. "I was waiting for you to finish the book so I could give it to you."

"*Merci*." Rose hugged him and gave him a peck on the cheek.

"I'll support you with whatever you decide to do with the manuscript."

She looked into his eyes. "I will never take you for granted."

"Neither will I, *ma chérie*." He pressed her hand to his lips.

A key jostled inside a lock. The apartment door opened, and Charlie and Magda entered, followed by Claudius, who was carrying a wreath of gladiolas, carnations, and chrysanthemums.

"Oh, my," Rose said. "It's beautiful."

Claudius removed his beret and smiled, crow's feet forming in the outer corners of his eyes. "The florist did an incredible job with the arrangement."

"Thank you for picking up the flowers," Lazare said.

"It's an honor," Claudius said. "I made sure that all of their names were included on the ribbon."

Charlie and Magda greeted Rose with a kiss on each cheek.

"How are you, Maman?" Charlie asked.

He knows it will be a rough day for me. "I'm all right," Rose said. "I have everyone I love by my side."

Magda glanced at the manuscript on Rose's desk. "I'd like to know more about what you did during the war."

Rose's hand wandered to her brooch. *I was an SOE agent, and my code name was Dragonfly.* "Someday, I want you and Charlie to read it."

Magda smiled.

As children, Magda and Charlie sometimes inquired about what their parents did during the war. After all, it was impossible to hide Lazare's injuries, as well as the scars on Rose's back. Playing the role of protective parents, Rose and Lazare did not provide details. However, they went to great lengths to teach their children about the values of liberty, equality, and justice, as well as to always remember the people who sacrificed their lives for France's liberation. But Magda and Charlie were becoming adults, and their questions about their parents' actions in the war occurred more frequently. *Eventually*, Rose thought, *they will know everything.*

An hour later, Rose, Lazare, Charlie, Magda, and Claudius arrived at Avenue des Champs-Élysées. As they made their way to a crowd gathered at the Arc de Triomphe, a knot formed in Rose's stomach. *So many lives were lost. My mum, dad, and brother. Lazare's parents. Muriel. Felix. A million French and British. Millions of innocent Jews.*

Lazare, adjusting a crutch, drew Rose close to him.

She leaned into him, and for the next forty minutes, they listened to the Victory in Europe Day ceremony commemorating the millions of men, women, and children who sacrificed their lives to liberate France and Europe from Nazi tyranny. After the service, and as the crowd of Parisians and veterans began to disperse, Lazare led them to the base of the Arc de Triomphe.

Claudius handed Rose the wreath.

Rose kneeled, placed the flowers at the base of the monument, and then clasped her hands. She said a silent prayer that a world war would never happen again, and that people who gave their lives so future generations could have a chance to live in freedom would never be forgotten.

AUTHOR'S NOTE

While conducting research for *Churchill's Secret Messenger*, I became fascinated by Operation Jericho, an RAF bombing raid on Nazi-held Amiens Prison in France. The objective of the mission—which took place on February 18, 1944, one day before over one hundred French Resistance prisoners were to be shot—was to breach the walls of the prison and free the captives. The daring RAF Mosquito attack, which was filmed by a camera in one of the planes, was successful in breaching the perimeter prison wall and destroying a guardhouse, but it came at a cost. Out of the 717 prisoners, 102 were killed, 74 were injured, and 258 escaped, although 182 were recaptured. I was surprised to learn of the controversy as to who requested the raid and whether it was needed. Some speculate that the Special Operations Executive (SOE) or French Resistance instigated the operation, while others believe that the raid was designed by the British to sidetrack German military intelligence away from where the Normandy landings would take place a few months later. The mystery surrounding Operation Jericho—its true purpose and the person who authorized the mission—served as inspiration for writing this story.

During my research, I became increasingly captivated by the SOE, also known as "Churchill's Secret Army." During World War II, 39 of the 470 SOE agents in German-occupied France were women, most of whom performed the role of a courier or wireless operator. I was moved by their courage and willingness to risk their lives to free Europe from Nazi occupation. Many of these brave women were captured, tortured, and killed, and several of the agents provided inspiration for creating Rose Teasdale's character. For example, Rose's leadership, firearm skills, and cover story as a traveling cosmetics saleswoman were inspired by Pearl Witherington. Rose's perilous bicycle journey of almost two hundred miles (over three hundred kilometers) in two days was influenced by a similar act of valor by Nancy Wake. Also, the experiences of Odette Sansom were instrumental in creating Rose's interrogation and torture by the Gestapo, and her solitary confinement in Ravensbrück Concentration Camp. It is my hope that this story will commemorate the brave women who served in the SOE.

In addition to the SOE, I was intrigued to learn about Room 60 of Churchill's underground Cabinet War Rooms. The room contained typists and switchboard operators who were all civilians. Many of them stayed underground day and night, sleeping between shifts in a sub-basement known as the "dock." During my fact-finding, I stumbled upon an extraordinary video interview of Joy Hunter, who was a typist in Churchill's War Rooms. I was captivated by her story of Winston Churchill's cordial, sympathetic, and sometimes humorous interaction with the civilian staff. The interview sparked my curiosity, and I wondered what might happen if Churchill had arranged for one of the War Room typists to be recruited for his secret army. It was then that I imagined Rose to be a typist turned SOE agent.

Rose's F Section SOE assignment is inspired by the true story of the Physician network, also known as Prosper, the code name of its organizer. The Physician network was infiltrated in 1943 by the Sicherheitsdienst (SD), a Nazi intelligence agency. The collapse of Physician and its subcircuits resulted in the capture of nearly thirty SOE agents, as well as hundreds of French patriots working with the SOE. In *Churchill's Secret Messenger*, Rose's network called Conjurer is a fictional subcircuit to Physician. I created her subcircuit with the hope to provide readers a view of events taking place during the fall of the Physician network, as well as create a story line on Operation Jericho, which remains an enigma to this day.

It was an absolute honor and pleasure to research the life of Sir Winston Churchill. I spent many enjoyable hours reading and listening to his speeches, as well as scouring over reports of his personal life, such as his home, Chartwell, and his passion for his Golden Orfe. I strove to display Churchill as a confident wartime leader who inspired hope in the darkest of times, as well as to reveal little-known aspects of his personality, such as his friendly and caring demeanor with civilian workers in the underground bunker. Also, it was my endeavor to reflect Churchill's complex relationship with Free French leader Charles de Gaulle.

During my research, I discovered many intriguing historical events, which I labored to accurately weave into the timeline of the book. For example, the spring of 1942 was when the SOE began recruiting women to be secret agents. Rose was parachuted into the outskirts of Paris several months after the first women SOE agents, Lise de Baissac and Andrée Borrel, were parachuted into occupied France on September 24, 1942. The arrest of Lazare's parents is set during the Vél' d'Hiv roundup (July 16 and 17, 1942), when French police arrested over thirteen thousand Parisian Jews, including over four thousand children, who were shipped in cattle cars to Auschwitz concentration camp. Also, the meeting between Churchill and de Gaulle—discussing the controversial Free French invasion of two small islands under Vichy control near the Canadian coast of Newfoundland in December of 1941—was used to highlight Rose's linguistic skills and gain Churchill's interest in having her recruited for the SOE. I attempted to accurately reflect the timeline of events at Ravensbrück Concentration Camp, including the death march and liberation by the Soviet Red Army. Additionally, I strove to precisely depict various types of RAF aircraft, as well as the training and equipment provided to SOE agents. Any historical inaccuracies in this book are mine and mine alone.

Numerous historical figures make appearances in this book, most notably Winston Churchill. It is important to emphasize that *Churchill's Secret Messenger* is a story of fiction, and that I took creative liberties in writing this tale. In addition to Churchill, Charles de Gaulle, Captain Selwyn Jepson, Major Gavin Maxwell, Hugh Dalton, Maurice Buckmaster, Dominique Ponchardier, Josef Kieffer, and Alphonse (code name for SOE agent Tony Brooks) appear in the story. I believe it is important to recognize Captain Selwyn Jepson, a British mystery author who served as the SOE's senior recruiting officer. He was a strong proponent of female agents, and he viewed women to have more ability for isolated bravery than men. Although Captain Jepson's recruitment interview with Rose is fictional, I believe including him in the tale captures the spirit of the book. Also, I invented Churchill's call to Hugh Dalton, the minister of Economic Warfare, whom Churchill appointed to take responsibility for his secret army. My research found no records of Churchill personally recommending individuals to be recruited for the SOE. Also, the Paris catacombs were used as a hideout for Lazare and his French Resistance group. My research revealed claims that the French Resistance utilized the catacombs during the German occupation. Although I was unable to locate specific names of Resistance fighters, I simply couldn't resist including the subterranean underworld of Paris as a setting in the story.

Numerous books, documentaries, and historical archives were crucial for my research. *SOE in France 1941–1945* by Major Robert Bourne-Paterson and *Shadow Warriors of World War II, the Daring Women of the OSS and SOE* by Gordon Thomas and Greg Lewis were incredibly helpful with gaining an understanding of the British circuits in France, as well as the motivation and experiences of SOE agents who risked their lives to free Europe. *Ravensbrück: Life and Death in Hitler's Concentration Camp for Women* by Sarah Helm was an exceptional resource for gaining insight into the atrocities that occurred at the German concentration camp exclusively for women. Also, the 1947 film *School for Danger*, produced for the Central Office of Information by the RAF Film Unit, provided a terrific view of the training and deployment of SOE agents. Additionally, the 1944 newsreel *The Jail Breakers*, by British Pathé, included the actual film footage of the RAF raid on Amiens Prison, which was a tremendous resource for writing the scene of Operation Jericho.

It was a privilege to write this book. I will forever be inspired by the valiant service of British SOE agents and French Resistance during World War II, and I will never forget the 13,000 Parisian Jews who were rounded up by the French police. I'll always remember the atrocities of Ravensbrück Concentration Camp, which imprisoned some 130,000 women, of which an estimated 30,000 to 90,000 died or were killed. It is my hope that this book will pay tribute to the men, women, and children who perished in the war.

Churchill's Secret Messenger would not have been possible without the support of many people. I'm eternally thankful to the following gifted individuals:

I am deeply grateful to my brilliant editor, John Scognamiglio. John's guidance, encouragement, and enthusiasm were immensely helpful with the writing of this book.

Many thanks to my fabulous agent, Mark Gottlieb, for his support and counsel with my journey as an author. I feel extremely fortunate to have Mark as my agent.

My deepest appreciation to my publicist, Vida Engstrand. I am profoundly grateful for Vida's tireless efforts to promote my stories to readers.

I am thankful to have Kim Taylor Blakemore as my accountability partner. Our weekly progress reports helped us to finish our manuscripts on time.

My sincere thanks to Akron Writers' Group: Betty Woodlee, Dave Rais, John Stein, Kat McMullen, Gus Yanez, Carisa Taylor, Sharon Jurist, Rachel Freggiaro, Tim Carroll, and Devin Fairchild. And a special heartfelt thanks to Betty Woodlee, who critiqued an early draft of the manuscript.

This story would not have been possible without the love and support of my wife, Laurie, and our children, Catherine, Philip, Lizzy, Lauren, and Rachel. Laurie, you are—and always will be—*mi cielo.*

CHURCHILL'S SECRET MESSENGER

ABOUT THIS GUIDE

The suggested questions are included to enhance your group's reading of Alan Hlad's *Churchill's Secret Messenger.*

Discussion Questions

1. Before reading *Churchill's Secret Messenger*, what did you know about the British Special Operations Executive (SOE) in World War II? What did you know about the French Resistance?

2. What are Rose's fears while working as a typist in Churchill's War Rooms? How does the death of Rose's parents and brother motivate her to join the SOE?

3. What are Lazare's motivations to join the French Resistance? If he had not endured a childhood hand injury, what do you think his life would have been like?

4. Describe Rose. What kind of woman is she? When Rose is called upon to fill in for a French interpreter, she is surprised to find herself in a meeting with Winston Churchill and General Charles de Gaulle. Describe how Rose handles the meeting. What did Churchill see in Rose that influenced him to have her recruited for the SOE? How does Rose overcome her lack of stature and strength to pass SOE training?

5. While working in German-occupied France, Rose and Lazare fall in love. What brings them together? Why does their relationship develop so quickly? At what point do you think Rose realized she loved Lazare? How is the war, particularly the risk of being captured by the SD, a catalyst for their affection? What are Rose and Lazare's hopes and dreams?

6. Describe Muriel. What causes Rose and Muriel to quickly form a friendship? Is there anything Rose could have done to save Muriel? Why is Rose determined to survive Ravensbrück Concentration Camp and deliver a message to Muriel's daughter, Mabel?

7. Describe Felix. What makes him a competent SOE network organizer? What are his weaknesses as a leader? Why was he

reluctant to move Muriel, a wireless operator, to alternative safe houses to avoid detection by the SD?

8. Prior to reading the book, what did you know about the Vél' d'Hiv roundup? What could Lazare have done to save his parents?

9. Prior to reading this story, what did you know about Operation Jericho? If you were Rose, would you have arranged an RAF bombing raid on Amiens Prison, knowing that it might kill the person you loved? What are the consequences of Operation Jericho?

10. What are the major themes of *Churchill's Secret Messenger*?

11. Why do many readers enjoy historical fiction, in particular novels set in World War II? To what degree do you think Hlad took creative liberties with this story?

12. How do you envision what happens after the end of the book? Do you think Rose will remain bound to her oath of secrecy? Will the classified records of Rose and her network, Conjurer, ever be released to the public? What do you think Rose and Lazare's lives will be like?

Connect with Us

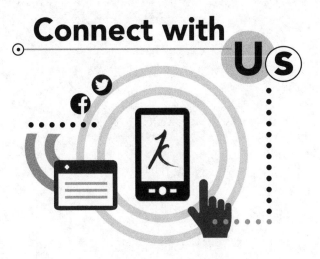

Visit us online at
KensingtonBooks.com
to read more from your favorite authors, see books
by series, view reading group guides, and more.

Join us on social media

for sneak peeks, chances to win books and prize packs,
and to share your thoughts with other readers.

facebook.com/kensingtonpublishing
twitter.com/kensingtonbooks

Tell us what you think!

To share your thoughts, submit a review,
or sign up for our eNewsletters, please visit:
KensingtonBooks.com/TellUs.